"I MUST HAVE BEEN CRAZY TO STAY AWAY FROM YOU."

Raf peppered Holly's face with tiny fiery kisses that sent her blood leaping.

Her hands came up to hold his face; her palms against his lean jawbones demanded that his mouth find hers. She gave herself to the ecstasy of his kiss. It began to make up for all the time they had been separated, as if that time hadn't really existed.

No time existed now, only Raf, his lips warm and masculine. The musky scent that was peculiarly his had her mind reeling. Her lips opened; his kiss deepened, pulsing a thrill to her nerve ends.

When at last he lifted his head, she clutched him and moaned softly.

"Easy, honey," he said. "We've got all night...."

LUCY LEE
Is also the author of
SUPERROMANCE #10
HEART'S FURY

Gregory Godwin's jaw jutted out like the rocks of his isolated northern island when he told Polly she couldn't leave. And his voice was firm.

Polly confronted him coldly. She'd brought his nephew here; her responsibility was ended. She had to get on with her own life. And that didn't include days spent peering at a cliff full of birds—even with someone as rugged and vital as this wealthy businessman turned ecologist!

Besides, though Gregory was formidable, overbearing—Polly knew she was attracted to him. Seeing him daily in this fairy-tale situation would be asking for trouble....

LUCY LEE
THE RITE OF LOVE

A SUPERROMANCE FROM
W🌐RLDWIDE

TORONTO · NEW YORK · LOS ANGELES · LONDON

Published December 1982

First printing October 1982

ISBN 0-373-70044-X

Printed in Canada

CHAPTER ONE

To GET TO PIERRE, South Dakota, they had to change planes in Chicago and again at Minneapolis. With a minimum of complaining, Holly Cameron and three other fashion models carried their heavy tote bags through the gate and across the tarmac to the smaller prop plane.

"We should have got a porter," one of the girls grumbled.

"There weren't any," came the resigned reply.

The third, older model said, "I never let my makeup out of my hands—not when I'm going on location, not since the time my bag got lost in the Virgin Islands...and no place to shop! Nothing but thatched huts."

Despite the brisk pace, Holly found breath enough to gasp, "What did you do?"

Marian shrugged. "It turned up next day. Still, I lost a day's work. Luckily I wasn't the only model."

"Imagine if you had been!" The model called Naomi shuddered.

"The agency was rather unhappy as it was," Marian noted wryly.

Their photographer, his assistant and the stylist had already boarded, and other passengers, mostly businessmen, were settling into their seats, opening papers, putting briefcases and jackets into overhead racks, but when the four tall striking young women began moving down the aisle, all action stopped. Heads were raised; men turned to look after them. The pretty airline hostesses receded into the background.

Naomi's thick shoulder-length hair was the color of wheat straw; Marian was a brunette, and Claire's brown hair matched her warm brown eyes. Holly's thick curly mop was a strawberry blond that glowed like a candle flame, even when, as now, she wore it caught back into a simple out-of-the-way ponytail. Several men's eyes were drawn irresistibly to the escaping tendrils curling at neck and temple. Her dark blue eyes, framed by naturally dark lashes, gazed frankly from left to right, looking for an empty seat.

The photographer and his assistant were sitting together. Marian was with the stylist, who had once been a model herself, and Claire was paired with Naomi.

Two rows back Holly spotted an empty aisle seat and slid into it, for some reason extremely aware of her seatmate, a man in a dark suit. Accommodating herself to the space allotted her, she made an unnecessary to-do of settling her tote bag under the seat in front and fastening the seat belt, postponing the time when she would have to look at him, acknowledge him in some way, since they would be sitting in narrow intimacy for the next couple of hours. At length she relaxed and glanced casually toward the window.

The man's tawny eyes met hers, sparkling like chips of topaz. For a wild moment Holly felt his glance darting right into her mind. Not that she had any thoughts to hide, but to receive such an intense look from a complete stranger was a mite upsetting. She was used to admiring glances and knew how to fend off would-be pursuers without causing hurt feelings, but this man's look was hardly admiring. Piercing was the word for it.

She made herself smile tentatively. He nodded solemnly. The eyes between dark fringed slits glinted with what might be a twinkle. The rest of the lean brown face remained impassive, yet alert. His wide mouth was strongly molded, the nose almost hawk-like. High cheekbones in the lean face gave him an austere look. His chin tilted in a way that made Holly think of someone used to gazing into far distances. His hair must be the kind, she thought, that people spoke of as being black as a raven's wing. She had never seen a raven, but when she searched her mind for a better description, she could come up with nothing, actually too flurried to think. His hair was fashionably cut but straight as an Oriental's, which made her wonder if he might be an American Indian. After all, she and the rest of the photographer's crew were headed for a Sioux Indian reservation.

When he spoke, however, it was with the flat western twang Holly had begun to notice in Chicago.

"Surely four such beautiful girls together can't be accidental," he said.

Holly smiled her beautiful smile, taking his compliment in stride. "No, we're on a job."

The plane began taxiing toward the runway, and the passengers' attention was claimed by the captain giving information over the loudspeaker that the plane would arrive in Pierre—he pronounced it "Peer"—at five twenty-six.

After takeoff the passengers settled back to read or doze. Holly had been hoping to catch a catnap, as she and the others had left New York early that morning, but the man beside her generated such a vibrant quality that she could no more think of sleeping than if she'd been alone with him in a boat.

The hostess proceeded down the aisle with offers of coffee or alcoholic beverages. Holly requested coffee. The man beside her ordered bourbon on the rocks.

Beneath them the Minnesota farming country was a grid of green splashed with lakes and ponds.

When their drinks came, Holly sipped her black coffee nervously and burned her tongue. She sat back in her seat with a quick indrawing of breath. Inadvertently she glanced toward the window. Beside her the man raised his glass in a silent toast. She gave him her most minimal smile, but as he sipped his drink, she took the opportunity to observe him under the pretext of studying the cloud-patched sky.

The outfit he was wearing was no businessman's suit. The jacket, of smooth-woven broadcloth with a faint stripe, had a dark suede yoke, and his necktie— if you could call it that—looked like a braided leather cord, although actually all Holly could see of it were the dangling ends tipped with silver and held in place by a triangular silver ring where the knot should have been.

Was he wearing boots? Impossible to know—his feet were stretched under the seat in front. He looked to be tall and rangy and perhaps in his mid-thirties.

The hand holding the plastic glass on the tray suspended before him was no businessman's hand, either. It was sun-browned and calloused. The nails were manicured, but the fingers looked capable of crushing the plastic glass like a paper cup.

He chomped an ice cube between his teeth and swallowed. She found herself fascinated by his jawbone, his brown masculine neck.

"Did you say you're all going to a job in Pierre? Are you entertainers?" He, too, pronounced it "Peer," and she thought he looked a little skeptical, as though they might be up to something shady.

Holly flushed. Did he think they were strippers? Hoping to discourage further questions, she said shortly, "No, we're going to Fox Butte."

"Fox Butte? On the reservation?" He was plainly taken aback.

"That's right."

"Oh." He raised his chin in acknowledgment, his eyes speculative.

Bemused, Holly guessed at the emotions now warring in his breast—innate reserve was fighting against the friendly curiosity of the Westerner. Curiosity won. "Oh, going up to the powwow," he suggested. A smile gleamed in his dark eyes, and the corners squinted into wrinkles. "You don't call that work, do you?"

With an inward sigh Holly gave up and overcame her own reserve.

"We're fashion models. We're going there to be photographed against the background of the powwow." Even as the words left her lips, she regretted saying them. The tawny eyes moving over every detail of her appearance turned cold, and Holly realized how silly her purpose sounded. An Indian powwow was probably a serious event. It might be semireligious, for all she knew. Again she was struck by the thought that the man might be Indian, except for those golden eyes.

All her carefully acquired poise and New York sophistication deserted her. "It's f-for a Western-wear catalog," she stammered. "Western wear's going to be very f-fashionable this year."

"Fashionable, eh?" The man's strong mouth twisted into a scornful smile.

Holly shrugged and pushed back into her seat. "It's a living," she muttered.

"A good one, I gather." He ran his eyes over her, taking in her pure-silk blouse and the designer suit she had been able to buy at a huge discount. The color of blueberries, it matched her dark blue eyes.

"How old are you?" he asked. "Twenty-five, twenty-six?"

Holly had been about to try another sip of coffee. At his question she gasped and set her cup on the tray in front of her with a clunk. "I'm twenty-two!"

"Oh! Pardon me." He had the gracelessness to grin.

Clod! Holly thought. *Twenty-six, indeed!*

It occurred to her to stop his questions by asking some of her own. "Do you live in Pierre?" she queried, not because she wanted to know, but in the hope that she might annoy him in return by taking him for a city person.

"God forbid!" His tone merely held amusement. "I'm flying on to Rapid City. My ranch is near there."

"Then you're a cowboy?" She knew the difference between a ranch hand and a rancher, but she felt a fierce desire to pay him back.

She experienced a spurt of temper when he said, "That's right. A far different world from the glamour of yours, I imagine."

"There's nothing glamorous about posing in winter fashions at some resort where everyone else is wearing bikinis," she countered angrily.

His eyes assessed her figure, and she felt herself begin to blush. What had made her say that?

"I'll bet you've spent your share of time in a bikini," he suggested.

Holly shrugged one shoulder. She faced forward and closed her eyes to calm her chaotic thoughts. She could feel his gaze still upon her.

"How long will you stay in Fox Butte?" he asked abruptly.

Holly was slow to open her eyes and answer. He already knew too much about her. It was time to let him know she didn't want to begin a lifelong friendship. "Three days," she answered coldly.

She closed her eyes again. *I could tell him something about Rapid City if I wanted to,* she thought, *something that might interest him if he lived near there.* But she was darned if she'd tell him anything.

Did she really look twenty-six? She glanced at her watch. How much longer was she going to have to share a seat with this boor? She forgot his eyes upon her, and her bosom swelled and her nostrils flared. Then the frightening thought came. Maybe she did look twenty-six! She bit her lip. It was a good thing she'd arranged to take a vacation. She'd known she'd needed a break from the exhausting pace at which she'd been working. Modeling jobs had come her way steadily for the past year, but she'd been afraid to turn any down because there was no way to be sure when the next booking would occur. And Bill had needed the money....

The expedition she had agreed to help with didn't exactly sound restful, but it would be a change of pace. Cooking for six people—seven, including herself—would be work, but it wouldn't be a strain— merely monotonous. She was looking forward to the monotony.

Her thoughts wandered back to the day her brother, Bill, had come home to the apartment they shared, pleased with the news he had to tell her.

"Professor Gray invited me to go on his expedition!"

Holly, home from an exhausting all-day photographic session under hot lights, had showered and was relaxing on her slant board. She gazed at her brother upside down, and he dropped onto their worn couch to come closer to her eye level.

"The one I've been telling you about," he continued, "to South Dakota, to actually retrieve some fossils. Professor Gray's got a secret spot out there where he thinks he's going to find some complete skeletons—a place on some ranch way off the beaten track." The light in Bill's eyes faded. "Of course I told him I couldn't go, but it was a big honor to be invited. He asked only four graduate students."

Holly sat up and studied her brother fondly. A year older than she, he had the family good looks and red gold hair, but his was straight, and his fair skin was peppered with freckles.

"You told him you couldn't go?" she repeated.

He nodded. Behind his glasses his blue eyes were serious. "Heck, I can't afford anything like that. Besides the fare out and back, the members are supposed to pay their share toward camp expenses."

"How much?"

Bill shrugged. "I don't know. Plenty. Besides which, I can't afford to take off for ten weeks without working. I was planning to get a summer job."

Holly set her jaw. "I think you should go."

"Na-a-ah." Bill hunched a shoulder. "Besides, I wouldn't feel right about leaving you all on your own." Before Holly could open her mouth to protest that she didn't need a big brother supervising her, he grinned. "I know, you think you have everything under control."

"You want to go, don't you?" Her words were a statement.

"Sure, but it's out of the question."

"No, it's not!" Holly's voice was sharp with sisterly exasperation. "What do you think I've been working so hard for?"

Bill shook his head. "You're all but supporting me now—paying all the apartment expenses."

"And still I've got money ahead," Holly said cheerfully. "Find out how much it would cost," she begged. "You haven't had a vacation since mother and daddy died, and look at all the places I went last winter—Puerto Rico, Mexico, Jamaica."

"Yeah, working."

"Nevertheless," she insisted, "I think it's your turn to get away. You'd be working, too."

Bill grinned. "Yeah, I suppose I would—out in the hot sun with my delicate complexion."

She shook her head at him. "Call up Dr. Gray now," she urged, "before he chooses someone else. At least ask how much it would cost."

She stood at her brother's elbow while he made the call. Holly had met Professor Gray at a tea for the paleontology department; he hadn't hesitated to tell her that her brother was an outstanding student.

"Dr. Gray?" she heard Bill say, and then continue lightheartedly, "I've got my sister here twisting my arm. She thinks I shouldn't have turned down the expedition without finding out how much it would cost.... Oh, that much? Besides the air fare?... Yeah, I realize all that outdoor work makes people hungry.... My sister? You're joking!" He eyed Holly over the receiver, shaking his head. "All right, sir. Very well, I'll tell her." Nodding, he scribbled numbers on the phone pad. "Okay...yes, I'd certainly like to.... Oh, I'd get credit for a lab course if I went? Yes, that would make some difference. I need more lab credits in order to graduate.... Okay, sir, we'll get back to you."

He hung up and stared at Holly, a glint in his eyes.

"What did he say?" she demanded, jumping with impatience.

Her brother drew a deep breath. "He said that if you wanted to come along as cook, they wouldn't have to hire one. The saving would probably more than cover the cost of our food and the rental of our equipment."

"Hmm!" Smiling, Holly shook her head. "If that's what you'd have to pay...." She pointed to the amount scribbled on the pad. "In ten weeks of modeling I could earn a lot more than that."

"Yeah, but you need a vacation, too," Bill argued. "A really long break. You look tense all the time." He studied her face critically. "You're getting little lines around the eyes."

Holly moved to the mirror and inspected her face—not because she was vain, but because her looks were her livelihood, hers and Bill's till he got his master's degree in paleontology and could teach.

"I suppose we could sublet the apartment," she ventured. "That would save two or three months' rent."

"You mean you'll do it" Bill's sudden enthusiasm made it obvious how much he wanted to go.

Holly hedged. "Don't you think I'd better talk to Dr. Gray and ask exactly what I'm supposed to do? And we'll have to find out the dates so I'll be able to tell the modeling agency. I don't know what they'll say about my going off for the whole summer."

But the agency had said to go ahead; it wouldn't hurt for a popular model to be unavailable for a month or two. And then the marvelous coincidence had happened. Holly had been chosen for the catalog of high-fashion Western wear, to be photographed in Fox Butte one week before the expedition was due to assemble in Rapid City.

Dr. Gray had immediately taken advantage of that lucky development. The powwow and the photo-shooting session were taking place this weekend; the fossil hunters were scheduled to arrive the next

weekend. Holly, therefore, could go on to Rapid Cit
as soon as her modeling job ended and use the inter
vening week to contact the expedition's supplier an
work with him. If she would take charge in this way
Dr. Gray could see no reason why she and the sup
plier couldn't have the camp all set up by the time th
others arrived.

Holly had protested that she hadn't the least ide
of how to set up a camp, but she had been overrule
by her brother and the professor, who said, "I'v
written the supplier specific instructions. I've tol
him the general location in which I want the camp
within a radius of a couple of miles. I'll leave you t
choose the spot—a stream bank with cottonwoods, i
you can find such a place. The main thing is to get th
supplier started. He'll have to round up a lot of gea
and haul it out there. I know these people. They wai
till the last minute because they think we're a frivo
lous lot who may never show up." Dr. Gray ha
grinned. He was a tall gangling man with hair suspi
ciously black for his age, which Holly guessed to b
in the late sixties. His expression was sardonic—th
eternal doubting Thomas—but something about hi
personality and his method of teaching drew fierc
loyalty from his students.

Loyalty enough, Holly thought drowsily as th
plane droned on, to cause Bill to rope her into the ex
pedition, even though she still suspected she woul
have been better off to take two weeks' real vacatio
and then carry on with her job. Still, if she reall
looked older than her age. . . . Maybe Bill was right
She needed to spend the whole summer in wide-ope
spaces, doing relaxing physical work.

She had almost succeeded in putting her fellow passenger out of her mind, for she reached the suspended state between sleeping and waking, the one she'd found to be the best in which to pass time on a flight. But suddenly his voice intruded.

"Does your group come from Chicago?"

Slowly Holly raised her dark-lashed lids and brought her lovely blue eyes into focus on his face.

"No." She blinked and straightened in her seat. "New York."

"I'm sorry," he apologized quickly. "I didn't think you were asleep."

I'll bet you didn't care, she thought with annoyance.

He was looking at his watch. "You've had a long trip, then. It's almost five o'clock. How about a cocktail?"

"I don't think the hostesses are serving anymore," Holly murmured, not wanting to see him embarrassed by being refused.

"I'll get one," he affirmed. With assurance he motioned to the hostess and said to Holly, "What would you like?"

She didn't want anything at all, but with his tawny eyes upon her, she heard herself saying helplessly, "Vodka and tonic would taste good."

He raised his face to the waiting hostess. "Vodka and tonic for the lady, please, and I'll have another bourbon on the rocks."

No smile accompanied his request, yet the trim hostess appeared delighted to wait on him. Holly's chin went up in just the slightest tilt. She didn't like arrogant men, but she had to admit to herself that

this man wasn't aware of his arrogance. It wa
more—she sought for words with which to phrase th
impression he gave—it was as though he were th
natural heir to immense lands.

Then a thought of an entirely different nature oc
curred to her. Had her drink merely been an excus
for him to buy another for himself? No, one stole
glance at his lean jaw and wide firm mouth made he
dismiss such a suspicion as ridiculous. This man, sh
knew instinctively, would need no excuse to do any
thing he wanted.

She moved nervously in her seat. It was absurd
but every time she looked at him, she felt breathless.

While they waited for their drinks, Holly pretend
ed to stare out of the window and tried to keep he
eyes from straying to his face. Could it be this ver
masculine man who was making her breathless an
giving her weird little twinges in her stomach? Per
haps she ought to have eaten something more tha
plain yogurt at the Chicago airport.

The propeller-driven plane was not flying at th
high altitude of the big jets. The clouds were a
above them, white and puffy, making Holly thin
picturesquely of smoke signals. Between blue sky an
green earth lay a narrow belt of blurred horizon
Underneath the plane stretched the prairie, no longe
lake-dotted like the eastern counties of the state. A
the squares now were solid green or gold, intersecte
by ruler-straight roads.

The man beside her wasn't inclined to chitchat
and Holly's poise had totally deserted her. Sh
couldn't think of one simple sentence that didn'
sound either impertinent or idiotic.

At last their drinks arrived. Holly smiled her thanks at the stewardess. Clutching her glass, she swirled the ice, stirring it around and around with the red swizzle stick etched with the airline's name. The dead sound of ice against plastic did nothing to relieve the tense silence hammering in Holly's ears beneath the drone of the plane, but at least the drink gave her something to do with her hands.

It took effort to raise her eyes to meet the man's frankly interested glance. When she did, lightning seemed to flash across the space between them. His tawny gaze held hers for the time it took to draw a breath. Then she lowered her dark lashes, hiding from his look like a shy schoolgirl.

Had he felt that flash? It was impossible to guess. His face had remained impassive.

Holly's attention skittered from her drink to the back of the seat before her to the tray on which his glass rested to the silver triangle holding his Western tie. She saw his hand lift his drink. She knew she must thank him and join him in taking a first sip.

Bravely she again met his eyes, pinning on the kind of smile a model knew how to manage, no matter how uncomfortable or exhausted she felt. He bent his head in a grave nod and drank.

The sight of his tilted jaw and closed lids, his black hair and the brown hand holding the fragile plastic made her senses reel. He was more than good-looking. It seemed to her he was more alive than any man she had ever met, like a mountain lion lolling on a ledge, able to shift in an instant into cold springing power.

But she was being crazy! She didn't even like terribly macho men. She preferred, she reminded herself,

intellectual sensitive men such as her brother, Bill
Charles, the fashion photographer—men who un[d]
stood a woman's feelings, men you could be frie[n]
with. This man would never settle for friendship [w]
a woman. Holly's breath caught at the though[t]
what he would want—passion and compliance. [?]
in the Black Hills where he was going, no doub[t]
had a woman—or two or three—ready to give [him]
what he wanted. Holly rejoiced that her path and [his]
would soon separate, because she hated the way
sitting beside him turned her mind around.

Hastily she gulped her drink. As the cold t[o]
touched her tongue, she realized a drink had been [ex]
actly what she needed to steady her nerves. No,
to steady her nerves. Nothing was wrong with [her]
nerves! She needed a boost to revive her flagg[ing]
spirits—that was all. She dreaded to think of the l[ong]
trip still ahead for her group, the rented cars t[o be]
picked up at the airport, the drive to Fox Butte.

When Holly had first been considered for [the]
modeling job, she had looked up Fox Butte in [the]
atlas to see how far it was from the Badlan[ds.]
Boasting a population of five hundred and th[irty]
people, it lay north of Pierre in the huge Cheyen[ne]
River Indian Reservation that covered two vast co[un]
ties. Lake Oahe formed its eastern border, look[ing]
on the map like a river in flood, which in a wa[y]
was—the mighty Missouri, dammed and tamed. [To]
the north lay another big reservation, Standing R[ock,]
appearing every bit as bleak and roadless.

Holly stared in concentration at her drink, rem[em]
bering that Fox Butte was nearly ninety miles f[rom]
Pierre—another two hours' travel. It would be e[asy]

o'clock before her group reached the motel. Not bad. Early enough to allow them all a good night's sleep.

She found herself wishing idly that this flight could go on much longer, like a flight to Europe—the idea rose unbidden—so that she and the man next to her could fall asleep together, his hand perhaps touching hers.

Nonsensical thought! Holly took another swallow, hoping the potion would do something magic—take away her mental discomfort or return her to reality.

Still the man beside her remained silent. Perhaps he was waiting for her to speak. Was it her turn?

Frantically she sought something sensible to say. "Are you returning from Chicago?" she queried at last in a tight little voice that sounded like a stranger's to her own ears.

"Yes, a quick business trip." Once more he lifted his glass to her with a nod. "I make my trips there as short as possible. Fortunately the cattle business is mostly on the range where the cattle are, not in any Chicago office."

"How many cows do you have?" Holly thought her question logical, but for the first time a real expression crossed her companion's face. His eyes crinkled. He was laughing at her. "I haven't counted them lately," he drawled. "Several thousand, I guess."

Her poise gone again, Holly murmured, "Really?"

The next moment the plane banked sharply, showing a town below them, streets, blocks of houses. Pierre, at last. Holly drew a deep breath. As her bosom rose, she felt the rancher's eye upon her and

turned quickly, ready to intercept his stare. Her co[n]
fidence was coming back, now that she would so[on]
escape his proximity.

However, he gave her a wide-eyed look. "They[']
never believe me when I get home and say I've met [a]
glamorous model."

Holly smiled graciously, but she was asking herse[lf]
harshly, who wouldn't believe him? Probably h[is]
wife. Holly felt a stab of regret. What would it be li[ke]
to be his wife? She knew sudden stinging envy. T[he]
plane bounced on the ground, sending the sti[ng]
through her every fiber. While it was still taxiing [to]
its stop, the passengers getting off at Pierre began ri[s]
ing from their seats and retrieving jackets and brie[f]
cases from the overhead racks.

Holly unfastened her seat belt and pulled her to[te]
bag from under the seat in front of her. Almost relu[c]
tantly she stood up to go. Her farewell smile for h[er]
fellow traveler was brave and a little wistful.

A quotation came to mind as she threaded her wa[y]
down the aisle: "We will not see his like again." S[he]
longed to glance back for one last look, but it was be[t]
ter not to. He was no more than a passing shadow, [so]
why prolong the sadness, which was all in her imagin[a]
tion? He probably didn't have a wife. More likely he['d]
had one and made her so miserable that she'd left hi[m.]
Holly tried to smile at her nonsensical thoughts, b[ut]
her lips refused to obey. They only twisted sadly.

The passengers leaving the plane straggled acro[ss]
the tarmac to the terminal building. Holly was stron[g]
ly aware that the rancher's window permitted him [a]
view of her retreating figure—if he bothered to loo[k.]
Not that it mattered.

She caught up with Marian and the stylist, Augustina.

"I suppose Charles is driving," Marian was saying. "Who'll drive the other car?"

"Buddy, of course," Augustina answered. "What are assistants for?"

There was the usual delay while they waited for the wardrobe boxes to be unloaded. Charles and Buddy went off to sign up for the cars.

When the camera gear and the boxes of clothing to be modeled had been loaded into the two station wagons, Charles called their group together and asked, "Dinner in Pierre or after we get to the motel?"

Everyone voted for the motel. Like Holly, they wanted to get to the end of their journey.

CHAPTER TWO

EVENING WAS SETTLING over the plains as they dro[ve]
out of Pierre into the setting sun, Charles, Augusti[ne]
and Marian in the first car, Buddy and the oth[er]
three models in the second one. Holly shared t[he]
back seat with much of the camera equipment.

Up front, Buddy and the girls chattered. Holly w[as]
glad to have a period of quiet and reflection. Stari[ng]
from the car window, she found the vast emptine[ss]
soothing. The road ran straight and level betwe[en]
stretches of grassland reaching to either horizon, a[nd]
they met almost no traffic. Endless pastures we[re]
fenced with endless strands of barbed wire. Occ[a]-
sionally small herds of black cattle were to be see[n.]
Were *his* thousands of cattle black? She had thoug[ht]
all beef cattle were red.

She stretched her shapely long legs with a sigh a[nd]
let her thoughts dwell on the rancher. That seem[ed]
safe enough, no more than daydreaming, really. [He]
would have arrived in Rapid City by now and be [on]
his way to his ranch. Holly pictured him driving [a]
shiny black car of vast power.

They made the turn north toward the reservatio[n]
while the sun still lingered at the edge of the va[st]
empty sky. Naomi was studying the road map. ''[I]
bet we should have eaten in Pierre,'' Holly heard h[er]

say. "People don't eat dinner at nine o'clock at night outside of New York. They go to bed at nine o'clock, for Pete's sake. Look, this town is tiny!" She stabbed a red-polished nail at the spot on the map marked Fox Butte in the midst of the lavender rectangle that represented the Cheyenne River Reservation.

Looking over the back of the seat, Holly silently agreed. The whole area of the map showed nothing but the red line of the highway and some blue wavery lines marking rivers or creeks flowing toward Lake Oahe.

"In another hour you'll know," Buddy said laconically, his tone and his Brooklyn accent making it clear he disdained this part of the country. Certainly they had no other choice but to keep driving. The map showed not one town on the whole straight fifty-mile stretch.

It was after dark when they finally reached the turnoff to Fox Butte, and there they caught their first sight of Indians. A pickup came bouncing out of a dirt side road with three people inside and four gangling girls perched on the edge of the truck bed. The pickup swept in front of the station wagon Charles was driving and headed toward the grove of trees and buildings that marked the town.

Buddy followed Charles, who followed the pickup down the town's single street, where all three cars fell in behind two more dusty automobiles filled with people. At the end of the three-block street the procession turned right onto a tarmac road. More trees were outlined against the sky, and a lopsided one-way sign indicated the campground.

"I see tepees!" Naomi exclaimed. "There—above
the trees! See the tops?"

Craning to look out over the stack of camera
equipment, Holly caught a silhouette of cone-shaped
tips against the evening sky. The ends of bare sticks
protruded from the cones, just as in all the pictures
she'd ever seen. The station wagon rounded a bend
and they found themselves driving through the camp.
The headlights of the cars showed glimpses of a curving line of white tepees neatly pitched in a double row
following the line of the circular drive.

"There they are!" Claire squealed. "How exciting!"

"Look how many there are!" Naomi cried.

Holly, too, felt a rising excitement. She thrilled
suddenly at being privileged to attend this gathering.
On seeing the old dusty cars full of dark-skinned people, she had quickly sensed that this powwow, or
fair, or whatever they chose to call it, had not been
arranged for the pleasure of white tourists. Indeed,
she felt a faint gnawing worry. Would they be welcome?

Up front, Buddy was complaining. "What's
Charles doing? This can't be the way to the motel."

In the car headlights Holly caught only frustrating
flashes of tepees, some with light glowing through
their canvas sides, and men and children crossing the
road between the slow-moving vehicles.

"Why is he taking us through here?" Charles demanded. "I'm starving!"

Suddenly they came to the end. The circling drive
made a sharp bend, and they were drawing away
from the camp, turning back onto the road leading

townward. Charles pulled up beside a man trudging along the dark roadway, apparently to ask directions. After that, instead of turning into the town's main street, he kept on going straight.

"There it is," Buddy said. A flickering neon sign against the night-blue sky proclaimed MOTEL.

After a brief wait while Charles and Augustina checked them in, they were at last entering their rooms. The four girls were sharing two rooms; Charles and Buddy were bunking together, and Augustina had reserved a suite for herself and the wardrobe boxes, with space to lay out in sequence the dozens of garments they had come to model.

Tiredly Holly dropped her tote bag on one of the twin beds and then straightened. "Listen!" she commanded Naomi, who was to be her roommate.

The other girl had gone directly to the sink and was washing dust and makeup from her face. There was no need for her to turn off the tap in order to hear the sound coming through the open window. It gathered volume—the steady thudding of a drum and then, borne on the night wind, men's voices, high-pitched, chanting.

"The natives are restless," Naomi remarked flippantly, and went on with her face washing.

"It really is the powwow!" Holly exclaimed, fascinated. "Are they already dancing? I thought it was to begin tomorrow."

"Maybe they're practicing," Naomi suggested. "Sounds as if they need it."

Holly ignored the other girl's sarcasm. She was finding the strange sounds in the midst of this huge empty country too intriguing for her to take notice of anyone's grumpiness. A spurt of enthusiasm erased her fatigue. Opening her suitcase, she took out a shirt and a pair of soft jeans and slid her feet out of the high-heeled shoes she had been wearing all day into leather thong sandals. She started to knot her shirttails at her waist and then thought better of it. She was only a guest at this celebration, and good taste seemed to dictate that she not dress conspicuously, so she tucked her shirttails into her pants. Combing her thick red gold locks, she tied them back with a red bandanna. When Naomi had finished repairing her makeup, Holly cleansed her face and put on a minimum of cosmetics.

Meanwhile, excitement continued to give urgency to her preparations. Perhaps after they'd all eaten dinner, Charles or Buddy would go back to the campground just to watch. Holly did so want to be a spectator for a little while before she had to start working tomorrow, concentrating on her own appearance and on following Charles's directions.

The café connected with the motel was still open, but it was a place of plastic booths and bare plastic-topped tables. Holly and Naomi discovered their party already established in the largest booth. The menu offered barbecued beef, steak, halibut and a large salad bar, of which the models happily availed themselves.

"How do you plan to work this?" Naomi demanded of Charles while they waited to be served. "You don't expect us to run back and forth to the motel every time we have to change costumes, do you?"

"My dear girl," Charles said shortly, "I can see you've only worked with cheap outfits."

Naomi flushed. "I have not!"

Augustina, part of whose job it was to keep peace and mother inexperienced models, reached across the table to pat Naomi's hand.

"Don't you worry, honey, that's all taken care of. At least we hope it is. We're getting a big rented house trailer tomorrow."

"Motor home," Charles corrected.

"Motor home, whatever you call it, for a dressing room. They're going to park it right in next to the tepees. Besides dressing there, you girls can use it to relax between shots, take showers, keep cold drinks in the refrigerator...."

"Will we be coming back here at noon?" Claire queried.

"Probably," Augustina said. "We planned for Buddy to drive the whole motor home back here whenever we're ready for a new set of clothing. Whether it's at noon depends on how early our dear Charlie gets started." She was the only person who dared call him anything but Charles.

While they ate, the sounds of the drumming came faintly through the night air, with intermittent pauses between dances, perhaps, because during that time the voice of an announcer could be heard, though too far away to be understood.

"I wonder if they're going to beat those tom-toms all night," Buddy worried.

Charles shrugged. "I could sleep through anything after all this fresh air."

"So could I," Marian agreed.

Holly wasn't so sure she could. Something about the steady thumping and the faint shrill voices struck a responsive chord in her, making her wonder with a glint of amusement if she could possibly have Indian blood in her own veins. If so, it would have to be Long Island Indian, for neither side of her family came from farther west than New Jersey. Three of her great-grandfathers had landed together from a foundering Finnish ship and had married into a Finnish community.

"Anybody want to go back to the powwow for a while?" Charles inquired casually while Augustina was taking care of the bill.

"I do!" Holly responded.

"Anybody else?"

The others shook tired heads. "Not when I have to get up at the crack of dawn," Marian said.

"Take the key," Naomi told Holly. "I'm going straight to bed."

"We won't stay more than half an hour," Charles offered. "I know you girls have to wash your hair." But still he had no other takers.

"Oh, Charles, I'm so glad you want to go," Holly bubbled, sliding into the station wagon. "I don't think I can get to sleep until I see what they're doing over there."

Charles smiled at her as he turned to back the car. He was a lean intense man in his early forties, his hair already thin, his dark eyes bright and quick. Holly wondered if he ever relaxed, but of course she had seen him only during working hours. He lived alone at the back of his huge photography studio, and perhaps all he ever did was work. His one-room living quarters, which she had visited on one occasion when he had asked her to make coffee, contained just the essentials and a huge stereo set.

He wasn't much of a talker, either. He made no reply when Holly said, "I can't wait to inspect this place in daylight!"

After a pause she asked, "Did you bring your camera?"

"Sure thing," was all he replied, but it occurred to Holly that she'd never seen him without a camera, either in his hands or hung about his neck.

"I wish I had one," she said longingly, although she had but that moment thought of it. "It would be fun to take the pictures instead of always being the subject."

Charles took his eyes from the road to shoot her a glance. "Do you mean that?"

"Yes, I do. I want to *take* pictures instead of just pose for them. When I think of all the places I've been and all the interesting people I've seen—in the Caribbean, for instance—I feel really sorry I don't have a record of those trips."

"I've got a spare you can borrow."

"Have you? I'd love to use it!" Holly enthused, "but I must tell you, I don't know the first thing about operating one."

"The camera I have in mind is simple enough. The rest is all practice, a little talent helps. I figure that people with no talent don't stick to photography very long."

"Well," she said with a laugh, "I'm not planning to put you out of a job."

"Here we are," Charles announced. He pulled the car off the road into a field of broken weed stalks and parked it alongside some others.

Walking toward the lights and the loudspeaker, they found themselves at the back of white wooden bleachers that circled a grassy arena. The bleachers were no more than four tiers high with a roof overhead. Lights shone on the trodden grass in the center, which at the moment was empty. A dance had just ended.

Charles and Holly found seats among the spectators and sat soaking up the atmosphere. A white couple was seated next to Charles. The man, in straw hat and boots, looked like a rancher. Beside Holly were three teenage Indian boys wearing jeans and T-shirts. Sitting below her on the bottom tier were two Indian women with braids down their backs.

In front of a small reviewing stand a circle of six men sat around what appeared to be an ordinary bass drum. Holly was bemused and somewhat disappointed that it wasn't a tom-tom made from a hollow log.

Thud, thud, thud, thud went the drum. One man began to chant in a high falsetto the Indian words that the other singers took up in unison. At first to Holly's ears the song sounded like nothing more than rhythmic howling. Nevertheless her fatigue had gone. She was keenly aware of everything around her. Her whole body felt alert, ready to respond to the primitive rhythm, to the blood pulsing in her veins. Listening intently, she decided that one singer began the phrases in a high carrying voice, to be picked up by the others in deeper male tones. Learning to appreciate another culture's music must be the most difficult feat of all, she thought. One could learn language and customs and probably get used to any food. She wasn't particularly musical, but she rather thought one would have to learn from infancy to appreciate these alien sounds.

From one of the entrances the line of waiting dancers began to enter the field, proceeding two by two with stately steps that became more and more impressive as the line lengthened.

The dancers came on slowly with the same kind of double stamp Holly remembered from grade school or from the movies, but never had she seen real Indians close at hand in breathtaking costumes.

The two men in the lead were wearing marvelous headdresses of dark feathers, dark clothing and wide anklets of steel bells the size of Ping-Pong balls. The bells jingled rhythmically as the men led the dancers in a circle around the field. Behind them came more male dancers, wearing bells and feathers, moccasins and headdresses and breastplates of bones made into beads. Each dancer's costume was different, so that Holly felt she couldn't possibly see everything, no matter how long she watched. Behind the pairs of male dancers with their stamping and bells came the women, the older ones dignified and thickset, wearing shawls and ornaments over shapeless dresses encircled by wide beaded belts. They were not quite as enthusiastic in their stamping, often missing some steps while they caught their breath. After them came the young girls, more simply costumed in straight-hanging elkskin dresses and high moccasins, not dancing flat-footedly, like the men, but on tiptoe, as became supple maidens. Following them came children of all sizes. One, dressed in a miniature version of his father's costume, trailed tirelessly at the man's heels like a well-trained mascot.

Beside Holly, Charles's flash went off as he sought to capture the entire scene. She heard him mutter,

"I'll have to get closer than this to get any details of the costumes."

"Go ahead," Holly told him, "I'll be all right here." But he hardly heard. His feet crunched on the sandy gravel as he jumped down from their seats on the top row.

"I'll be back. Boy, what an opportunity!"

Holly felt she could go on watching forever. The steady drumming had a hypnotic effect.

The six singers continued to thump out a rhythm, using drumsticks tipped with sheepskin. Gradually the tempo increased, and a few young dancers, without losing the stamping rhythm, began spinning rapidly in time to the beat.

As suddenly as it began, the dance ended.

"Thank you very much," the announcer said clearly.

Just then a touch on Holly's arm made her start so violently that the rancher beside her turned to stare. It was Charles. He was below her at the back of the grandstand.

"I've got to get some of these people to pose for me," he stated urgently, and left her again.

The dancers were walking unselfconsciously about the area, talking to friends while they waited for the next dance, much as at any social event. Holly saw Charles approach one of the men, who graciously consented to allow Charles to explode the flash in his face.

Over her shoulder Holly spotted a motley collection of stands set up to sell Indian jewelry, woven baskets, food of some sort and soft drinks.

Suddenly she felt terribly tired. She wished that

another dance would begin or Charles would decide to leave. But now that he'd started taking pictures, Charles probably wouldn't stop till he ran out of film. She thought she'd take him up on his offer to lend her a camera, and when she got to Rapid City, she would buy one. It would be fun to have pictures of Bill unearthing his first fossils.

The moments sped by while she followed her own thoughts, at the same time letting her eyes rove over the scene. How much more colorful it must be in daylight, she thought. Like a child, she wanted to hurry to bed so she could wake up and find that morning had arrived.

Over the loudspeaker came the announcement that a guest singing group would perform next. Holly was amused but at the same time a little ashamed that in her ignorance they sounded exactly like the first group. A moment later Charles turned up.

"All right, let's go." He put up a hand to help her down.

"Hope you enjoyed your preview," he remarked as they made their way back to the car through patches of light and darkness.

"I did," she affirmed. "When can I have the camera?"

"At breakfast. But I won't have you off taking pictures when you're supposed to be modeling," he added belligerently.

True to her word, Naomi was in bed when Holly returned. "Well, did you see some Indians?" she asked sleepily.

"It was marvelous!" Holly sighed, undressing for her shower. "You should have come."

"No need. I can hear the racket from here, eve over the air conditioner," Naomi grumbled.

"It was impressive," Holly said. Put off by N omi's narrow-minded attitude, she closed her pret lips, determined to say nothing more, and began t chore of bringing her strawberry-blond locks to clea and shining perfection.

WHEN THE WAKE-UP CALL came at six o'clock ne morning, Holly swung her long shapely legs out bed with an eagerness that surprised her and seem to annoy Naomi.

"Must you be so darned enthusiastic?" Naor complained.

Benevolently Holly pardoned her. *Perhaps she always grouchy in the mornings,* she thought. S herself was feeling too excited and alive to let anyo else's mood spoil her enjoyment.

At seven o'clock the group assembled in the ca for coffee, juice and the day's directive. The mot home was due to pull into the motel parking lot any moment, and Buddy would load into it the war robe boxes containing the clothes to be modeled th day. Augustina had stayed up half the night pressi the outfits. The girls, perfectly groomed but attir in their own jeans and slacks, would ride to t campground with Charles in the station wago From then on they would be entirely at his beck a call. Augustina had worked out on paper to the la detail the combinations of skirts, blouses and swea ers, the accessories and shoes or boots to be wo with each outfit and the girl to model the outfit, a cording to her type and her color of hair.

As Charles finished with one model, the next was to be dressed and waiting. Often the script called for doubles and triples—two and three girls posing together.

It promised, Holly knew, to be a long grueling day, especially if things didn't go right. She herself felt a little dubious. The powwow was certainly exciting and colorful, but as a setting for fashions, she wasn't sure of its suitability. All her jobs on location had been in quiet places, with nonmoving backgrounds such as old arches and crumbling ivy-covered walls. Of course, Charles was an excellent photographer; undoubtedly he had worked with locations like this previously, or he wouldn't have been chosen for the assignment. Nevertheless she felt a little jumpy. And so, it appeared, did Augustina, judging by the shrillness of her voice and the way she rapidly downed two cups of black coffee....

The motor home arrived. At seven-thirty the station wagon followed it to the campground.

"The light's perfect!" Charles exulted.

Holly could feel the tension ease among his subjects-to-be, though Naomi was heard to whisper, "Look at the dust!"

Seen by daylight, the canvas-covered tepees stood in a double circle around the perimeter of the campground, the tops of their poles bare against the early-morning sky. Among the tepees Holly noted a sprinkling of tents and pickup campers. Few people were stirring. The dance, she recalled, had gone on until a late hour. She was enthralled to see numerous horses tied about the campground.

Buddy parked the motor home, and Charles pulled

in beside it. "All right, you girls, get to it. I want somebody out here, ready, in exactly five minutes. Meanwhile, I'll be prowling around."

"Remember you're a paleface," Marian cautioned in a lowered voice.

"No peeping in tepees," Claire added.

"Get dressed!" Charles ordered, and stalked off.

Holly's first outfit was adorable. It consisted of a white cotton shirt with eyelet ruffled yoke, collar and cuffs, worn with a gathered wool skirt of earth-tone stripes, layered over a show-offy embroidered cotton petticoat. Brown boots, suspenders and a narrow blue bandanna tied under the collar gave the outfit a totally country look. She pulled her glorious hair up from the temples, letting it hang curling to her shoulders in the back, further enhancing the look of an old-fashioned heroine.

"Perfect," Augustina commented when Holly finished making up her face and presented herself for approval.

Holly sat carefully on the edge of a seat until Charles called for her. Going out to him, she passed Naomi coming in.

"Coffee," Naomi groaned. "All I could think of was how much I wanted another cup of coffee."

Holly smiled. She had worked with Naomi previously on location, and she knew how ethereal Naomi's pale beauty appeared in photographs. No one would ever guess that her thoughts were on anything so down-to-earth as morning coffee.

"Over here," Charles said. He led Holly and Buddy to one of the rustic arbors set up beside more of the tepees. It was a frame of upright poles set in the ground, the roof made of freshly cut leafy boughs laid close enough to provide shade. Two sleek brown horses stood tied to one of the posts. Whether the occupants of the tepees were asleep inside or had gone off visiting, Holly had no way of knowing.

"This is somebody's living space," she whispered to Buddy when Charles indicated he wanted her to pose in the light shade with the horses looking on.

Charles overheard. "Then shut up and give me the shots I want so we can get out of here," he callously ordered. "Dust off your boots. Buddy, give her something to dust them with."

Doing her best to appear pleasant instead of angry, Holly turned this way and that, looked at the camera, looked away, spread her skirt, flung her hair about, posed every way she could think of. One of the horses snorted when Buddy set the flash off in its face, but nobody came to chase them away.

Nevertheless Holly was strongly relieved when Charles decided he'd taken enough shots there and led her over to the bleachers from which they had witnessed the dancing. He began to photograph her against a setting of whitewashed poles and rough wooden planks.

"And now against a cottonwood," he said finally.

"Is that what these are—cottonwoods?" Holly asked, indicating the huge old trees that formed the grove.

"They're the only trees that will grow out here," Charles sneered.

"They're beautiful," she insisted. "So big and old, they might have been here when the buffalo were."

"Quit talking and smile!" Charles growled. "Turn your head."

From this start the day proceeded, with changes of clothes and changes of background. But the same wearying poses had to be held again and again with the models trying to keep from squinting in the bright light and, above all, trying to keep fresh-looking despite dust and fatigue.

After some mild curiosity at first, the Indians ignored them, going on with their visiting as though fashion models and flash cameras didn't exist.

At ten-thirty the Sioux and their guests held a parade. They rode through the campground on horseback and on the hoods and tops of cars, displaying their costumes and saddles, beadwork and other finery. The participants in the parade were announced by loudspeaker from a spindly grandstand, but when Charles decided to pose three models together against the moving background of costumed Indians, Holly, Naomi and Marian saw nothing but parked cars and spectators emerging from the tepees.

Holly experienced only the sounds—the neighing and clip-clopping of horses, the shrill cries of children, some chanting and drumming and bells from floats on the back of trucks. Over all crackled only partially intelligible introductions from the loudspeaker.

When Marian complained about not seeing any of the action, Charles said, "Maybe I'll let you watch the parade tomorrow. But we're not here on vacation. White man here to exploit Indian," he added with a phony accent that sounded more Oriental than anything else. He didn't bother to keep his voice

down, and Holly noticed that a slim dark girl lounging against one of the cars clearly overheard. Holly
wanted to blush for Charles's brassy big-city ways.
When he wasn't working, he could be pleasant or
quiet and withdrawn. As soon as he put a camera to
his eye, he became autocratic, overbearing and totally insensitive to everything but the scene he was cap-
turing. Apparently he had forgotten he'd promised
to lend her a camera, but if she and the other girls
weren't going to have any free time, she'd have no
chance to take pictures. Perhaps he'd remember
when the day's work was over, she thought hopeful-
ly. When he worked, he worked.

The parade went twice around the circular drive.
After it passed by the second time, Charles dismissed
the three girls. "Tell Claire I'm ready for her," he
shouted as they started back to the big van, bent on
relaxing with cold drinks before getting into the next
outfit.

"My hair feels dusty already," Naomi said. "I
wonder if I'll have time to wash it and blow it dry
before Charles calls me again."

"There's no electricity!" Marian reminded her.

"Your hair looks okay," Holly said honestly.
"You could try brushing it. That's what I'm going...." She broke off as she caught sight of the
dark girl waiting in front of the dressing van.

"Who's that?" Naomi whispered. "She's been
hanging around all morning."

"She's waiting for us," Marian muttered. "Another one who wants to be a model."

The girl had the figure for it, though perhaps she
wasn't tall enough. She was wearing tight-legged

jeans, a dark blue silk shirt and cowboy boots. Her hair was black and thick and straight. She was wearing it in two braids, but she didn't have Indian features. In fact, she had a tilted little nose and blue eyes.

Holly smiled encouragingly.

The girl did not smile in return, though she wasn't shy, either. "Hello," she greeted them. "I gather you're three of the models?"

"Yes, we are," Naomi replied aggressively.

"I'm a reporter from the *Pierre Chronicle*," the girl stated. "I'm doing a story on the powwow, and I'd like to talk to you a little bit about your part in it, if you don't mind."

"We're not part of it!" Naomi sounded offended.

Marian said, "We don't really have time to talk right now. We have to change clothes."

"Just a couple of questions," the girl persisted. "Are you having a good time?"

"No." Naomi's reply was to the point.

"We're not here to have a good time," Marian said.

Holly tried to soften their bluntness. "We haven't had a chance to have a good time so far, but I got to see the dancing last night. It was marvelous," she added lamely. She had the girl's unsmiling attention, but she felt the girl had preferred Naomi's opinion, because she immediately turned back to Naomi and Marian.

"Do you find the powwow interesting?"

Naomi rolled her eyes heavenward.

"We haven't seen the powwow," Marian said. "All we've seen is dust and horse manure. Excuse me, miss, we really must change and relax for what little time we have." She pulled open the door to the trailer, and she and Naomi disappeared inside.

Scribbling in her notebook, the reporter turned away.

"*I* think the powwow is interesting," Holly put in hastily. "I don't know much about American Indians, but now I've been here, I'd like to know more."

The girl paused. She raised one eyebrow. "What will you do to find out more?"

"I don't know. I haven't thought that far." Holly smiled and shrugged. "I bought a tape of traditional songs of the Sioux."

She had found a booth selling recordings of Indian singers and had had the vague thought of listening to the tape over and over to see if she could begin to distinguish one song from another. At any rate, it would be a unique souvenir to take back to New York.

"Indeed?" The girl's eyes gleamed.

Holly felt a wave of insecurity. "I hope you're not going to quote any of our nonsense," she said. "It's pretty hard work, posing in the hot sun, and we're all a little on edge."

"But that's when a person's true feelings tend to come out," the girl replied sweetly. "Thank you very much." She swung on her booted heel and strode away.

"I have a feeling we said the wrong things to that reporter," Holly announced when she was inside.

Augustina was standing beside the small refrigerator. "Tab or Mountain Dew, Holly?"

"Tab."

"So what?" Naomi was saying. "She can quote me, for all I care."

"Yes, who cares what they say in 'Peer'?" Marian seconded, and the incident was forgotten.

At noon the group drove back to the motel for a brief break over lunch. Charles decided the hazy clouds were diffusing the sun's glare enough so he could go on shooting, so they returned to the campground and to work.

At midafternoon a long line of Sioux began dancing their way through the campground, displaying traditional finery. Charles followed them like a madman, posing his models as close as he dared and shrieking, "Turn! Turn! Turn!" as he clicked away, pausing only to change models and film.

"I've had some tough assignments, but this takes the prize," Marian groaned, dragging herself back to the motor home and collapsing in a chair. "I've got South Dakota grit in my teeth and South Dakota dust in my hair and the smell of South Dakota horses in my nostrils. How much longer is he going to go on? I wish these darned Indians would all go home!"

"That's what Charlie's afraid of," Augustina soothed. "We're hoping the gathering will get bigger tomorrow because it's Saturday, but we've had conflicting statements about Sunday. We heard before we came out here that Sunday is the big day. Now the motel manager says that last year they started taking down the tepees on Sunday morning. We were told they hold the ceremonial dance of Sioux warriors on Sunday, but Charles hasn't been able to find out the time or anything. These people aren't very cooperative, so you can see why he's upset."

The four girls nodded tiredly.

Charles called it quits at four o'clock, and everyone returned thankfully to the motel to shower and collapse. There was no question of going to watch any dancing that night. All Holly wanted to do was bathe and rest.

Or so she thought, until she lay stretched on her bed in the darkened room. Above the gentle hum of the air conditioner came the amplified sounds of the celebration.

"How does Charles expect us to sleep?" Naomi groaned.

Holly still found the sound exhilarating, but unfortunately it wasn't conducive to sleep. Before she knew it, she was thinking about the man on the plane, going over all the moments of the trip that she could recall: how he looked, what he had said—which, when one thought about it, had been nothing at all. Yes, one thing. He had called her a glamorous model. He had said, "They'll never believe me when I get home and say I've met a glamorous model." Who were "they"? Cowboys? The men he worked with? Lying there thinking about him, she decided "they" couldn't have meant his wife. Men didn't come home from business trips and brag about having met glamorous women. Or did they? Maybe his wife was so secure in his love she wouldn't feel threatened by glamorous women from the outside world. Not that Holly wanted to be a threat to anyone's wife.

She tossed and turned. The more she tried to relax, the more her mind replayed the looks and the words spoken by the man on the plane.

Darn it, she thought, punching her pillow, *he's probably sound asleep in his bunkhouse or whatever.* That thought was a mistake. Her tired mind began making a whole new set of pictures for her. What did he wear to sleep in? What would it be like to sleep next to him? She was drowsily shocked by the direction of her musings. *Forget him,* she told herself sternly. *You know you'll never see him again.*

In Rapid City I might, the imp in her brain replied.

Oddly enough, lulled by that thought, she fell asleep.

CHAPTER THREE

CHARLES PRESENTED HOLLY with the promised camera the next morning at breakfast. "It's set on automatic," he told her. "All you have to do is focus and snap the shutter. It's loaded now. When you've used up the roll, I'll show you how to reload."

"Turning into a camera buff?" Buddy asked.

"An Indian buff, I think," Holly replied, referring to the tape she had bought. The thought that back in the city this exciting celebration would become a fading memory depressed her.

"We're right on schedule," Charles announced over the coffee cups. "If you girls work as well today as you did yesterday and if everything goes right, we should finish up tomorrow morning."

So the models spent another hardworking day being photographed in front of the booths of turquoise jewelry—which they had no chance to examine; beside rickety oilcloth-covered tables where menus on hand-lettered signs all listed the same offerings: Indian tacos, fry bread, hamburgers, Pepsi, coffee; beside tepees; beside Indian children playing in the dust; and in the pastures beside shining brown horses and spotted Indian ponies.

They had been told that June in South Dakota would be cool enough so that they wouldn't be uncomfortable posing in fall and winter clothing. Whoever said that had been quoting temperatures in the shade. Wrapped in a sweeping fringed shawl of oatmeal-colored cashmere and posed in the sun beside a canvas tepee, Holly felt perspiration spring from her forehead and roll down her cheeks. Augustina, hovering nearby in the shade, hurried forward to mop Holly's brow.

"Smile, honey, you're earning a hundred dollars an hour," Charles drawled. Fashion photographers were forever using that line to remind their models to look pleasant. Holly hardly heard him; her smile of gratitude was for Augustina.

At last she was shedding the final garment she was assigned to model that day. Gratefully she climbed into her jeans. Some aluminum folding chairs had come with the motor home. Augustina and Marian had carried two outside and were sitting in the trailer's shade. Holly toted out a chair and joined them.

She wondered if the Sioux women were as miserably overheated in their buckskin dresses as she had been in the fall and winter woolens. Perhaps so. Two of the women that afternoon had shaded themselves with umbrellas while they danced.

A group of five men, two wearing headdresses, came strolling along the road, deep in a discussion in their own tongue. Idly Holly watched them.

Suddenly her eyes widened. The man on the far side looked like—he looked like the man on the plane! She craned her neck, but his face was half hidden by the feathered headdress of his companion. It couldn't be! He'd been going to Rapid City, which was at the western edge of the state.

Holly slumped back in her chair.

"Where's Naomi?" Augustina asked.

"Lying down," Holly said.

"That's what we'd all better do as soon as we go back to the motel," Augustina recommended.

I could stroll after those men, Holly was thinking, *and prove to myself that it wasn't he. I wouldn't be conspicuous. Everyone's walking around. But what's the point? I'm so tired I'm seeing things. Why does that man haunt me? I guess because I'm still in South Dakota and I found him attractive. I wonder if I'll ever meet a man like that again. Not in New York certainly.*

To change her thoughts, she made herself get up and fetch the camera Charles had loaned her. She sat in her chair and began snapping shots of passersby.

Rounding the corner of the motor home, Buddy exclaimed, "That's the laziest way of taking pictures I ever saw!" He was wearing a straw cowboy hat, as were half the males in the campground. His face and shirt were sweat streaked. He eased a heavy camera bag from his shoulder with a sigh. "Anything cold to drink inside?"

"Mountain Dew," Augustina said. "Everything else is gone. Where's Charles?"

"Coming."

Charles and Claire appeared a moment later. With a sigh of relief Holly slid into the station wagon to ride back to the motel. However, she stared at the groups of Indian men in the hope of catching another glimpse of the one who looked like the man on the plane, but the motor home soon raised such a dust that the station wagon, following behind, was enveloped in a cloud.

"Shut the windows!" Clair coughed. "Aren't we dusty enough?"

Sunday morning, Holly's final costume was a luxurious version of the Western prairie look. It consisted of a suede skirt with ruffled white petticoat and a ruffled blouse of work-shirt blue topped by a thick cowl-collared sweater whose knit design had been copied from Indian rugs. A big silver-and-leather concha belt hugged the sweater to her waist. Turquoise earrings, a turquoise-and-coral necklace and laced boots completed the outfit.

Charles had discovered a pasture uncropped by the horses and was making the most of it. Holly stood in the grass, sat in the grass with skirt spread and petticoat showing and lay full length in the grass, propped on one elbow, supposedly at ease. Singing crickets made an unbelievable racket and threatened to spoil Charles's shots by making Holly start when they jumped onto her clothing. The dusty grass made her want to sneeze, and the heat made her skin prickle until she longed almost irresistibly to scratch. But part of the job was to resist, to make no movement that wouldn't photograph beautifully, so she took the poses Charles wanted and tried to keep her mind on what she was doing and not think about possible meetings on the streets of Rapid City.

When Charles finished with her, she returned thankfully to the comparative coolness of the motor home. She stripped and eased herself into the tiny shower, grateful that Buddy had managed—somehow—to obtain a water hookup.

She emerged feeling like a new person. The clothes she'd been assigned to model had all been photographed, and Charles was apparently satisfied.

Buddy came into the motor home and dropped into a seat, glancing at his watch. "I heard the big war dance is going to start at eleven-thirty. Think Charles will be done by then?" He turned to Augustina.

"Looks like it," she answered cheerfully. "I'm planning to go back to the motel and have the world's biggest Bloody Mary by way of celebration."

"Don't you want to see the dance?"

"Not really," Augustina said. "I want to see the lights of Manhattan."

"Me, too," Marian agreed.

"I want to see the war dance," Holly said quickly.

"You'd all better stay," Buddy urged. "It's the highlight of the fair."

"You're probably right," Augustina allowed reluctantly, "since we're here."

Buddy glanced at his watch again. "Then let's head out toward the arena and find seats."

In the short time Holly had been inside, a bank of dark clouds had risen ominously in the west. Augustina noticed the clouds, too.

"Thank heavens that held off till now," she commented.

Holly hoped rain wouldn't spoil this day's festivities, either.

Spectators had begun to gather on the bleachers, but the announcer's booth was still empty.

"I'm dying to try some of that fry bread," Holly announced. "I've been watching people eating it for two days."

"Let's go," Marian said. "I want to look at the turquoise jewelry."

Leaving Augustina and Buddy to hold their seats, the girls went outside to the ring of booths surrounding the arena.

The fry bread came in rounds the size of the paper plates they were served on. The Indian woman selling it said it was made with baking soda and skillet fried. However, it was bread, and Holly realized she could easily eat too much of it.

They nibbled on the bread while brooding over the turquoise and silver jewelry. Eventually Marian bought a showy many-stranded turquoise necklace. Holly decided on a ring in the classic flower-petal design.

The next booth sold items made by Sioux craftsmen. Holly fell in love with a pair of dangling earrings of white porcupine quills and red beads. "Made by Red Bear" was written in pencil on the card they came on. She also bought a skinning knife of buffalo bone, typical of the kind used before the white man brought steel. She laughed as she paid for it. "I don't know whether I got this for my brother or me," she told Marian. "Isn't it a marvelous primitive tool? Feel how sharp the edge is. It's for skinning buffalo."

"Just what you need," Marian quipped.

"Eating!" a familiar voice exclaimed.

They turned to find Charles, Claire and Naomi behind them. Holly was giving them pieces of the fry bread when the loudspeaker crackled, making them decide it was time to return to the bleachers.

Six singers strolled out into the arena to sit on

folding chairs surrounding the drum. They took up drumsticks; the announcer spoke the invocation, and the singers began to perform. The music carried a wilder tone and a faster beat than any Holly had heard heretofore. It was immediately evident that this dance wasn't for the displaying of finery. According to the brief write-up about the powwow that Holly had found in her motel room, it was the dance of all able-bodied men of the Sioux tribe—in other words, a demonstration of strength, of the number of braves the tribe could summon, should the need arise.

"Of course, it's all ceremonial now," the woman sitting behind Holly was explaining to the man with her. "But it still means something. It represents the number of adult males who have survived the ravages of modern civilization—fast cars and liquor and disease."

Holly bit her lip. She wished she hadn't overheard the words about unromantic realities. Maybe that's why the girl reporter had sneered, she thought. *Perhaps my romantic view of Indians is more annoying than the view of people like Naomi, who are totally uninterested and admit it.*

She had no further philosophical thoughts. The circling braves were passing in front of her no more than six feet away, bare to the waist, brown skins glistening with oil. Stripped for battle, they were wearing buckskin pants or jeans and moccasins. Black hair, braided or unbraided, flew about their heads with the fervor of their movements. As a head-dress, each man wore only a single eagle feather, tipped with a touch of red. Silver armbands threw back the light like glittering weapons. Thunder rumbled away to the west, as if on cue.

Almost without surprise, Holly saw the man from the plane. It was as though a subconscious message had been clear all the time: this is the place for him.

He passed right in front of her, wearing buckskin trousers and moccasins like that of all the other men. Silver armbands emphasized bulging biceps. His hair looked longer than she remembered—perhaps because it was flying about with the movement of the dance.

Holly sat turned to stone, unable to take her eyes from him, deafened by the drumming, the chanting and her own blood singing in her ears.

Then I did see him yesterday, she thought dazedly. *I wonder if he's seen me.* He could hardly have helped doing so if he had been around the camp at all. The activities of Charles and the models had been highly conspicuous, though largely ignored by the Indians.

The excitement rising in Holly's breast made her feel ready to burst with delight, with pride. She wanted to point him out to her companions, but they would never believe her. All she could do was sit watching, filling her eyes with the sight of him.

The line circled the field, and other dancers blocked her view. She craned this way and that, afraid of losing sight of him altogether. Enough men had entered the field to make the double row of dancers almost a complete circle.

At last she saw him coming around again. His head was up and he was...he was looking straight at her! Or so it seemed, but he made no gesture of recognition. His eyes didn't widen in surprise. The momentum of the dance carried him past her. His gaze remained fixed on something before him, something only he could see.

Holly's heart was thudding as hard as the drum. As her eyes sought to follow him, her mind seethed with questions. Why hadn't he told her on the plane he was coming here? Why hadn't he sought her out, now that he was here?

The answer that came to mind was crushing: he hadn't wanted to. The excitement in her breast subsided a little but rose again as she caught glimpses of him on the far side of the circle.

The tempo of the drum quickened: the men moved faster. A few dancing alone in the center were leaping and twirling and uttering yipping cries, inciting the others to more fervor.

Should she—dared she—call attention to herself by standing up when he came by next time? It didn't seem like a good idea. Indian women didn't behave in that brash way. They acted quiet and unassuming. Besides, what if he didn't see her then, either? No, this was no time for attracting attention. He must know she was here. She had told him this was where she was going.

The question was, how could she get to talk to him? She didn't ask why she must talk to him or what she would say. She knew only that she longed to meet him face to face, say hello, perhaps even learn how far his ranch was from Rapid City. Oh, why had she been so stupid and smug as not to tell him she was going to the Badlands? Again she fought the desire to stand up so she could see better. Standing up wouldn't allow her to see through the dozen Indians dancing between her and him and would only make her conspicuous. She contented herself with straining her eyes to distinguish his bobbing head from all the others.

Buddy nudged her, and she started. "Holly? Are you in a trance? Didn't you want to take some pictures?"

She gulped and glanced at the camera in her lap. "Yes. I did." *I can take* his *picture when he comes by again,* she exulted. Oh, if only she were closer—down there on the bottom tier! She considered moving down—there was a space.... Charles would move.

She glanced around. No Charles. He had already gone off to find a better vantage point.

Holly slipped down to the bottom row and focused her camera on the dancer presently at the spot where the man on the plane would soon appear as the dancers came around again.

Now I hope he doesn't notice me, she thought. But the idea of getting a picture of him—maybe several— made her bold.

He was coming! Lithe, broad-shouldered and so handsome! She caught the blaze of tawny eyes in his bronze face. She snapped his picture and realized with satisfaction that he had been looking straight into the lens.

In her excitement her fingers fumbled with the tiny lever that advanced the film. By the time she was ready to take another picture of him, his back was to her, half hidden by another Indian. How many more times would they come around? Their faces were gleaming with sweat, despite the fact that clouds had covered the sun.

They circled the field once more, and Holly snapped two more photos, though this time the man on the plane was staring straight ahead as though nothing filled his mind but the rhythmical stamping of his moccasined feet to the beat of the music.

No doubt a real photographer would have followed him on around the circle, squatting near the ring of dancers and taking pictures unselfconsciously. But Holly wasn't up to that. Probably she never would be. If only one of these turned out to be good!

What was his name? Was it Indian, like some she had read in the local paper: Joe Pretty Paint, Kenneth Flatlip? He had looked so sophisticated on the plane. That was what fascinated her now. He had looked real there; he looked even more real here, dressed as a native. She felt both attracted and alienated. He probably had an Indian wife and a bunch of kids. Nevertheless, ignoring convention, her senses continued to say to her: here is a man.

"Some of those guys look better than anything I've seen in a long time," Naomi declared.

"I can't tear my eyes away from them," Claire agreed.

Had they, too, been looking at the man from the plane? Holly was taken aback at the sharp jealousy that filled her heart.

The chant ended as abruptly as it had begun, and the dancers filed off the field on the far side through an opening in the bleachers.

Too late Holly thought, *why didn't I go over*

there? She could have stood where he'd have had to see her as he passed by. No, she could never have done such a thing. Her world and his were as many miles apart as they would have been had they spoken different languages. Only by the merest accident had they spent two hours together. It was just that in him she suspected she had met a real man—tough, gentle, loyal, proud. A man without hang-ups, who admired women and probably never felt threatened by anything less than blizzards and rattlesnakes. Clearly he was loyal to and proud of his heritage, or he wouldn't have troubled to come all this way. Loyalty had become an old-fashioned word, but Holly respected it.

She stirred from her trance to hear Augustina calling the crew together. "Lunchtime!" They piled into the station wagon to return to the motel. The wind struck in huge gusts as they were driving, hurling dirt and twigs across the road, but no rain fell, and presently the wind blew itself out.

They were sitting in the restaurant when Charles joined them, carrying a newspaper.

"Look at this! We made it big in the *Pierre Chronicle*."

With an effort he kept the paper from being snatched from his hands by Augustina.

The *Pierre Chronicle*! Holly remembered the girl reporter who had questioned them and her feeling that they'd said all the wrong things.

" 'Fashion Models Exploit Indians' Ceremony,' " Charles read aloud. " 'A group of New York fashion models and their *cameraperson*—' get that '—are attending the Sioux Fair at Fox Butte this weekend in order for the models, tall, strikingly healthy pampered young women who have made a career of being beautiful, to be photographed against the realistic background of an Indian powwow.

" 'Unfortunately the reality behind the pictures of the new fall Western fashions will never be seen. The reality of dignified ceremonial and religious dances will be hidden by long-stemmed females wearing the latest whims of the clothing industry; for example, an antique concha belt over a designer sweater, the price of which would buy a family cow. The concha belt was once a family heirloom. How it came into the hands of New York promoters, we who live among the day-to-day problems of native Americans know only too well. . . .' "

"What?" Augustina interrupted.

"She—the writer's a Leona Selby—says she knows only too well how you came by that marvelous concha belt. Dishonestly, she's implying."

"I did not!" Augustina exclaimed.

"The article gets better," Charles said with irony. "If you can call it an article. I thought newspaper reporting was supposed to be unbiased. She quotes you girls. Listen.

"When questioned whether they found the powwow interesting, the ladies said, 'No, and we're not having a good time. All we've seen is dust and horse manure.' Someone should explain to these Easterners who came here for realistic chic that with horses comes manure.

"However, these are minor carpings. This reporter's main criticism is the vast arrogance with which the fashion industry has appropriated a centuries-old celebration and utilized the Sioux Fair as background for its advertising, paying its models one hundred dollars an hour while making free use of the color provided by Sioux culture and religion.

"As of this writing, the tribal council has received no financial compensation from these people, although they have made use of every one of the fair's facilities and activities."

"Whew!" Claire breathed as Charles finished.

He lowered the paper and looked around the table "What on earth did you girls say to her?"

"She asked us if we were having a good time! Naomi explained in an injured tone. "I said no, an Marian said we weren't here to have a good tim didn't you?" She turned to the other model.

"*I* said the powwow was interesting," Holly i serted. "I felt at the time she didn't want to hea that."

Charles was shaking his head. "Two days. Yo ladies have got us into trouble in two days."

"Oh, we have, have we?" Naomi cried shrill "Who goes around saying, 'Smile, honey, you'i earning a hundred dollars an hour'?" She made grinning exaggerated face.

Charles was silenced.

"This dame must have an ax to grind," Bud commented. He had picked up the paper and wi reading the article for himself. "Sounds like she's s her sights on being an investigative reporter."

"With nothing to investigate until we can

along." Charles gave an annoyed nod of agreement and then shrugged. "Well, we're finished now. They can kick us out anytime, for all I care."

Augustina nodded, but she added thoughtfully, "When I get back, I could suggest to the ad manager that a contribution to the—what is it—the tribal council might be in order."

Buddy finished eating and stood up, grinning. "I think I'd better fetch the motor home over here before the locals attack and burn it. Somebody want to drive me over in the station wagon?"

"I will," Holly offered.

"Wear sunglasses, and try not to look conspicuous," Buddy said with a laugh.

Even before seeing the man from the plane, Holly had planned to spend the whole afternoon at the campground, taking photographs and people watching. This new development gave her second thoughts. If she tied her hair in a bandanna and put on the faded jeans she had brought for the fossil camp, she wouldn't stand out as a model. But would he recognize her? Of course he would! She had the whole afternoon in which to accidentally run into him. She didn't intend to spend it hiding in her motel room.

Naturally they found the mobile home exactly as they had left it. Holly waited while Buddy got the vehicle ready to roll. "See you back at the motel," he said.

"If you don't need the station wagon, I'm going to hang around awhile and use the camera," she told him.

"Be my guest. I have plenty to do getting the wardrobe boxes ready to ship back to the exploiters."

Holly laughed. Buddy's refusal to take the article seriously made her heart lighter, too. The Indians had ignored the models for two days. There was no reason to think they would pay more attention because of a newspaper article.

For a while she sat in the bleachers. The afternoon was still cloudy. Holly watched Sioux women in traditional dresses and shawls circle the field. She felt she could go on watching the color and pageantry forever. She treated herself to an Indian taco and had eaten perhaps half when Charles suddenly plumped down beside her and removed the paper plate from her hand.

"You shouldn't eat this stuff!" he remonstrated. "Calories, calories!" And he proceeded to devour the rest himself, folding the beans, tomato and lettuce inside the fry bread. "I was so busy reading the paper out loud I forgot to grab lunch. Anyway, no one's stoned me."

"Me, either," Holly laughed. A blue-shirted blue-jeaned young man had arrived with Charles and was peering over his shoulder, waiting to be introduced. Now he nudged Charles's arm.

"Holly," Charles said through a mouthful of taco, "this is Gary Cannon, TV photographer from Pierre."

Holly gave the young man a look that was half fearful, half merry, as if to say, "What kind of publicity do you have in store for us?" But she stated simply, "We're not popular in Pierre."

"Sure you are! Don't pay any attention to Leona Selby." The young man was thin, sandy-haired and sported a wispy mustache. His eyes were friendly and admiring.

"Are you working today?" she asked. The festivities seemed to be winding down. Fewer dancers were circling the field, and behind the stands more and more carloads of people were pulling out.

"No," he assured her. "I'm on my own. I came up to tape one of the singing groups."

"Oh?" Holly said, aware that she didn't even know enough about the singing to ask intelligent questions.

Charles finished the taco and wiped his hands on his handkerchief. "Gary knows Leona Selby," he told Holly. "She's trying to build herself a reputation so she can move on to Denver or Minneapolis."

Holly's gaze traveled to Gary, and he nodded.

"Her article had a point," Holly allowed, "but it isn't our fault. I mean, we're just earning a living. All cameramen—pardon me, camerapersons—say, 'Smile, honey, you're earning X dollars an hour.' That's their way of reminding us to look pleasant, no matter how hot the lights are."

"I'm sure you couldn't look unpleasant," Gary quickly replied.

"Hah!" Charles said and Holly sighed. She hated being treated to fulsome compliments. She decided it was time to leave. Anyhow, she hadn't caught one glimpse of the man from the plane. If he'd had any desire to see her at this fair, he'd had ample time to find her. She'd been hanging about all afternoon.

Admitting disappointment, she drove back to the motel, showered and dressed for dinner. Since this

would be their last evening together, the whole cre
would be dressed a bit formally. Augustina had
vited them to her room for predinner drinks.

Holly had tossed into her bag before leavi
New York a slinky black one-piece dress from
department-store sale rack—the kind of little dr
whose look depended on the figure underneath. We
ing no other jewelry but the dangling porcupine-qu
earrings she had bought that morning, she brushed I
beautiful red gold hair into a glowing mane and we
along to knock on Augustina's door.

The others had already assembled. "You're late
someone called out.

Charles had brought the TV cameraman. Holly w
amused to see that the presence of more than o
model made him tongue-tied. His ears turned red. I
was quaffing his drink and sticking close to Charles

The models seldom allowed themselves more th
one glass of white wine, so it wasn't long befc
everyone, Gary included, headed for the café.

They settled into their usual big circular boot
Holly slid into the seat, hardly noticing that Gary h
lost his shyness enough to slide in beside her. She
the talk flow around her. She wasn't exactly
pressed, but she was thinking wistfully that the m
from the plane could have come and said hello. Th
was all.

She was facing the door. Suddenly it opened, a
Leona Selby entered. Her white skin appeared
striking contrast to her dark braids, red lipstick a
navy blue silk shirt and jeans.

Naomi gasped. "It's her! She's the one who wr
the article!"

"She looks like a bitch," Claire said nastily.

"She wouldn't have the nerve to come back here!" Marian gritted. "Holly, is it really her?" Marian was woefully nearsighted.

But Holly couldn't answer. Her heart had stopped in her throat. Behind Leona Selby, holding the door for her, was the man from the plane, still wearing Indian garb. He had added a fringed buckskin shirt. Around his neck and dangling on his chest was a tremendous necklace of blue stones alternating with something white, like animal teeth, and huge dark curved things that Holly knew instinctively were claws—bear claws.

Before she had time for a longer look, his tawny eyes made contact with hers. She thought she might faint, but he looked away after giving her a brief sardonic bow. Her lips felt stiff; yet somehow she managed to smile in return. Blood began to sing in her ears. Her hands were icy. She used them to cool her burning cheeks. He was with that Leona! Then he must have read the article. What bad luck! Good heavens, could the woman be his wife?

They moved to a table on the far side of the room, where Holly couldn't see them without craning her neck.

The crew around Holly's table buzzed angrily.

Before Holly could hope that no one had noticed Leona's escort, Claire remarked, "Did you see that gorgeous Indian? It looked as if he bowed to us!"

Gary laughed. "He's not an Indian. He's one of the biggest ranchers in western South Dakota. Oh, he may have Sioux blood, but he's not a reservation Indian."

"Look, Holly's blushing!" Augustina pointed out. "Was he bowing to you, Holly?"

With several pairs of eyes staring at her, Holly again put her hands to her cheeks. "I sat with him on the plane," she explained, laughing at the truthful simplicity of the explanation, well aware that no one wanted to believe her.

Her cheeks were still pink, her eyes sparkling with laughter, when the man with Leona looked her way again. He was sitting so that he faced her party. He could see the top of her red gold head, and when, as now, the person across the table from her shifted slightly, he could glimpse her face.

Holly turned to question Gary and found that young man studying her. "You *are* blushing," he said.

"No, I'm not!" she told him furiously. "I'm just excited. If that man is a rancher, what's he doing at a powwow?"

Gary shrugged. "As I said, he may have some Indian blood. They like to get as many men to show up as possible for the dance of the warriors. It looks good, you know. They're proud of the fact that American Indians aren't a dying race anymore."

"Do you know his name?" Charles leaned forward to ask.

"Valcour. Raf Valcour."

Holly breathed a little easier. Then he wasn't Leona Selby's husband—unless she used her own name. Bravely she put the question. "He's not married to that reporter, then?"

"Him? No!" Gary laughed. "I'd say he's one of the state's most eligible bachelors. She's from his hometown. He probably ran into her here. Or she ran after him. That's more likely."

Men were as catty as women, Holly reflected. In this case she was glad.

"He's gorgeous," Marian noted, staring frankly in his direction. "So that's what kept you so quiet during the last part of the trip!" she teased Holly. "What did you say his name is?" She turned to Gary.

"Raf Valcour. He owns thousands of acres in the Badlands."

"Isn't that where you're going, Holly?" Charles asked.

"Maybe you'll run into him," Marian suggested. "I hope you do."

"The Badlands?" Gary was asking in Holly's ear.

Their food arrived. While the others ate, Holly explained to Gary about going to cook for fossil hunters.

"If they discover anything good, let me know, will you?" he begged. "I'll put it on TV. You, too."

A bachelor, Holly's heart was singing. Raf Valcour—short for Rafael, no doubt, Raf Valcour. She could only pick at her food. Luckily no one noticed. They were too busy talking.

The meal over, Holly got up to leave with the others. She had no choice. She could hardly remain alone at the big table, drinking coffee and waiting to watch Raf Valcour and Leona Selby leave the café and get into his car—or hers.

"What are we going to do this evening?" Naomi asked as the women strolled back toward their rooms. Charles, Buddy and Gary had driven away in

one of the station wagons, probably to find a bar
somewhere off the reservation and talk about
photography.

Holly put her hand in her purse. She still had the
keys to the other car. She knew she would like nothing better than to drive about the countryside for a
while, fast, letting her hair blow—fast enough to
escape her envious thoughts. For Raf Valcour to be a
friend of that reporter's was almost as bad as for him
to be married.

"I'm going for a drive," she told Augustina.
"Buddy left me his keys." Not quite true, but he
hadn't asked for them back.

"All right," Augustina replied. "Get back by
dark, or I'll worry."

"Anyone else want to come?" Holly asked lightly.
She wouldn't mind having company, someone to
keep her from thinking.

"I'm counting on the rest of you for bridge!"
Augustina shepherded the three other models before
her.

Holly got into the car and discovered she had no
desire to drive out onto the lonely empty road that
ran east and west past the town. There was nothing to
be seen in either direction but miles and miles of rolling grassland, all the way to the flat horizon. Instead
she decided to return to the campground and maybe
photograph trunks of the huge cottonwood trees
before dark. Growing in clumps throughout the little
valley below the butte, they made a pleasant grove.
Judging by the size of their trunks, they might have
been shading Sioux gatherings for a century. It was
almost sunset. She wouldn't have time to drive far.

At the campground a good many tepees still remained. From one came the sound of a radio or a tape recorder; in another someone was playing a guitar. She paused to listen. Then she locked the car and went to photograph the cottonwoods.

Dusk had fallen by the time she returned. She looked toward the bleachers, silent now and empty, except for a handful of children playing about the supporting posts. Holly turned her steps in that direction, intending to sit once again in the place where she had watched him dance by. She hadn't changed out of her dress and high heels after dinner, and her heels sank alarmingly into the well-trodden dirt and pebbles underfoot. She would do better, she told herself, to try to banish him from her thoughts instead of recalling him.

Nevertheless she sat on the rough board seat and closed her eyes. She could hear the drum; she could hear the singing, and for an instant she was able to see him, the way she had first glimpsed him today, standing out among all the other dancers, the picture complete in every detail yet without substance.

With a sigh, blinking her long lashes, she opened her eyes. The next instant she smothered a scream. A shadow loomed beside her. The board trembled as a man lowered his body upon it. Raf Valcour!

"I wanted to speak to you in the restaurant," he said, "but you were surrounded."

Raf Valcour—and no figment of her imagination. Her throat was tight, her mind a blank except for the thought that he was here beside her.

"You do remember me, don't you?" he asked humorously.

"Oh, yes," she breathed, unable to respond to his light approach. He had found her at last, but so silently, without warning. So easily, too! As though he knew right where she was and could have spoken to her any time throughout the afternoon—if he hadn't been with Leona.

"You creep about like an Indian," she said resentfully.

He was instantly apologetic. "I'm sorry. It's these moccasins. In boots I make as much noise as anybody else."

She didn't quite believe him, but she had to laugh.

He said, "That's better. You're too beautiful to look angry."

Coming from him, she didn't mind the trite compliment. He uttered it as though he meant it. But with the next breath he was saying things she didn't want to hear, as if he had memorized the words and was laying them in front of her.

"I couldn't leave without seeing you once more. I suppose you already know how beautiful you are or you wouldn't be a model." He was studying her face, his eyes devouring her features.

"I don't spend a lot of time thinking about it," Holly retorted sharply.

He continued to stare down his hawk nose at her, making her extremely uncomfortable. "On the plane I thought you were a beautiful woman, but out here you look like a creature from another planet."

The idea struck Holly coldly. It paralleled too closely her own thought that they were people from different worlds. She wasn't from another planet. She was just as real as he was...as real as his girl friend Leona. Miffed, she cried, "Why? How am I different from that reporter?"

Raf Valcour didn't answer immediately. Perhaps he was surprised that Holly knew his companion. "Are you asking to be told that you're prettier than she is?" he drawled. "You are, but that's not what makes you different. You lead a life of ease and glamour and—I'd guess—what folks out here consider artificiality." He sounded amused. "Leona *works* for a living."

Without thinking—because if she'd thought, she'd never have dared—Holly swung her arm and slapped his handsome face. "I work, too, you oaf!" she spat, stung by his condescension.

She leaped to her feet, intending to rush to her car. At the first step her heels sank into the gravel, and she swayed. Strong arms encircled her. Before she could scream, his tawny eyes, ablaze like yellow flames, made her lose her breath. The lips that covered her mouth were so masterful, so unbelievably thrilling, that she was caught. The rest of her breath escaped in a sigh that left her leaning against his chest. The bear-claw necklace made a rigid barrier between them—a painful barrier.

The way he was holding her made it impossible for her to raise her arms. She struggled and twisted without result. Besides, his lips on hers were giving her a caressing message she wanted to continue receiving. He'd said he had come to find her. His reaction to her was the same as hers toward him: desire. In the motel, in bed and half asleep, she had let herself imagine what his kisses would be like, and now. . . . His kiss was better than anything she had imagined.

Nevertheless she had to make some effort to bring this scene to an end. She wasn't a sophisticated wanton. She didn't want him to think she was.

She attempted another feeble struggle, not putting her heart into it. To her disappointment, he took his lips from hers and would have removed his arms, but she swayed, still unbalanced on the rough gravel. He gripped her shoulders, holding her steady till she found her footing.

"Okay?" he asked.

Over his shoulder she saw Charles, Buddy and Gary. They were strolling along the almost empty drive. At the sight of them Holly remembered her anger.

"I *do* work for a living," she gritted. "I work harder than any reporter! I earn more money, too!" She stalked off, out from under the roofed stands, and called to the cameramen. Raf Valcour made no move to detain her.

The men stood waiting. Gary offered his arm. Holly took it, throwing an angry glance over her shoulder in the hope that Raf Valcour was watching. If he was, he would only be amused.

The tangled emotions in Holly's heart made her thankful the men kept on discussing cameras. Gary squeezed her arm against his side, and she felt sincerely grateful. How could she have been so audacious and foolish as to slap that man? She should have shrugged off his comments. But then he wouldn't have kissed her. God knew what he was thinking now!

She tried to tune in on the discussion. Cameras! What had she done with Charles's? She had left it lying on the bleachers.

"Oh, my gosh!" she said under her breath, coming to a halt.

Gary peered inquiringly at her.

"I left Charles's camera over there, where I was sitting."

"All right, let's go get it." Still holding her arm, he turned her toward the stands.

It was deeply dusk now. Holly had to watch where she was treading until she reached the stands. She looked up then to see Raf Valcour lounging on the shadowed bleachers. He was holding the camera.

"This what you're looking for?" he asked pleasantly.

"Oh, thank you." Holly sighed with relief, in part for the camera, in part because she wasn't facing Raf alone.

"I was going to take it over to the motel," he said, and Holly found herself forced to meet his tawny-eyed gaze.

"It's—it's not mine; it's borrowed," she stammered.

Suddenly she was sorry Gary was there, sorry she had run away. Her heart felt wrenched. Raf Valcour might have invited her for coffee at the motel. Or they might have stayed there on the bleachers, just talking. She wasn't from another planet. For some reason it seemed important for Raf Valcour to know that.

Instead she said, "Thank you again," and walked away, her arm linked in Gary's as though she were his prisoner.

CHAPTER FOUR

MONDAY MORNING AT BREAKFAST the modeling crew made no secret of the fact they couldn't wait to get back to New York. Holly felt no similar longing. Telling herself again and again that she was crazy to think she might meet Raf Valcour on the street in Rapid City, she nevertheless continued to think about the possibility. Imagining the surprise in those tawny eyes if they came face to face made her want to giggle. He wouldn't be able to keep his face impassive then!

Breakfast over, they finished packing and carried their bags to the cars.

"Is that all you're taking?" Marian asked in surprise when she saw Holly's single suitcase. "Look at this!" she called to the other two girls. "Holly's so sick of clothes she doesn't intend to wear any all summer."

"What does one wear on a fossil dig, Holly?" Naomi inquired.

"I'm not *digging*," Holly explained once more. "I'm cooking."

"Ho, so all you need is aprons," Naomi quipped.

"Are you going to wear an apron?" Augustina demanded in shocked tones. "Can you girls imagine our beautiful Holly done up in a big white apron?"

"Can you really cook, Holly?" Charles asked in a voice of respect.

Laughing, Holly shook her head. "I don't know. Bill's professor insists I won't have any trouble."

"He probably figures he can eat anything if he's got Holly to look at," Buddy chaffed. Buddy was beginning to make it obvious he had a crush on Holly. She wished he wouldn't be so blatant about it. She'd heard he had a nice little girl friend in Brooklyn, and he himself was inches shorter than Holly or any of the other models.

Smiling, she said, "I hope you're right, Buddy. I hope I can charm him till I get my act together. But seriously, my brother and I take turns cooking at home, so it shouldn't be too different. He's the one who recommended me."

Augustina patted Holly's shoulder in a motherly way. "My dear, with your competence I'm sure you can make a good job of anything."

Holly's face grew faintly pink at the compliment. Coming from Augustina after they had worked closely together for three days, it had real meaning.

"Holly, I'm serious," Marian persisted. "Aren't you going to need more clothes? What's in there?"

Holly shrugged. "Blue jeans and shorts and tops."

"What if you're invited out to dinner or something?"

Holly smiled her lovely smile and shook her head. "I don't expect to be. But I'll have a couple of spare days in Rapid City. I might shop around there for some authentic Western things."

"Don't you think ours are authentic?" Claire

cried, meaning the clothes the girls had been modeling.

"Holly doesn't want winter clothes!" Marian rejoined. "If I were you, I'd buy some cute little plaid shirts and some real Western riding pants...maybe some fancy Western boots." Marian's eyes twinkled. "I'd show those cowgirls a thing or two!"

"Holly had better look out some cowboy doesn't show her a thing or two," Charles advised. "One of them might rope and hog-tie you, sweetie, and we'll never see you in New York again."

"Yes, you will," Holly replied flatly. "You'll see me in the fall, after we've dug up all the fossils."

At last everything was packed into the station wagons, and they set off.

"Well, it's been an enlightening three days," Buddy remarked as the scattered buildings of Fox Butte fell behind and the rolling grassy hills surrounded them.

Claire and Naomi agreed with him. Holly said nothing, but her agreement was heartfelt. They had all been enlightened regarding Indian powwows, and she herself had discovered that a man's kiss could be devastating even when one disliked the man. He thought her lazy and stupid. He hadn't said that in so many words, but he'd made it clear enough. The last person she wanted to meet in Rapid City—or anywhere else—was Raf Valcour.

The eastbound plane left before Holly's. She bade her friends goodbye and found a paperback cookbook for sale at the newsstand. Then she sat in the lounge reading recipes until her flight was called.

She arrived in Rapid City at noon and took a taxi

from the airport. Checking into a motel near the center of town, she spent the afternoon alternately swimming and lounging beside the motel pool, letting herself unwind. She had spent an exhausting three days—no matter what some people thought! Did Raf Valcour have any idea what it was like to get up at dawn, work hard all day and then try to sleep to the drumming of tom-toms, knowing you had to be up at dawn again to do another day's hard work?

She ate a light supper in a modest restaurant across from the motel, feeling self-conscious under the stares of the other diners. She was glad to return to the seclusion of her room and shower and wash her hair.

She awoke at the crack of dawn as though it were a workday, but thanks perhaps to the swimming and lounging all afternoon or the quiet night's sleep, she felt wonderfully refreshed. Anyway, she reflected as she applied a minimum of makeup, cooks as well as models had to rise early, so it was probably just as well to keep up the habit.

Feeling brisk and businesslike, she called the supplier, whose name was Judson, only to be told he was out of town and wouldn't be back till Thursday. No wonder Dr. Gray had wanted someone on the scene making sure the supplier took their expedition seriously! Agitation crept into Holly's voice as she explained the purpose of her call to the woman, who said she was John Judson's wife.

Mrs. Judson's calm replies and slow friendly speech soon made Holly understand that Mr. Judson simply hadn't expected anyone from the group to arrive early. She assured Holly that "Jud" could begin moving things as soon as he returned on Thursday.

Holly hung up, realizing she had two whole days without a single commitment. What a godsend! She couldn't remember how long it had been since she'd had a similar two days. In New York, if nothing else, there was always housework or grocery shopping that needed doing.

The other paleontologist with the expedition, Dr. Young, had suggested that while Holly was in Rapid City, she might like to visit the museum at the School of Mines. She could learn there, he said, about the animals that had roamed the area when the sediments that formed the Badlands were laid down—a time midway between the age of the dinosaurs and today.

Holly wanted to see the exhibits. Even if she was only the cook, she wanted to understand the purpose of the work.

The thought of cooking made her wonder if food buying would be her responsibility, too. She made a note to ask Dr. Gray when she telephoned.

The sunny day was distinctly cool when she opened the door to assess the weather, and she was reminded that this was the high prairie. Rapid City lay at the foot of the Black Hills, near the edge of the Rockies. Not that she had much choice of wearing apparel. No matter, tomorrow she could spend the whole day shopping if she liked. Meanwhile, today she would wear her newest blue jeans and a lacy summer sweater of sand color, with a V neck and short sleeves. Pulling back strands of golden hair from her temples, she fastened them atop her head with a silver clasp and let the rest hang curling to her shoulders.

In the lobby the desk clerk called a taxi for her. A

short while later she was duly delivered to the parking lot at the School of Mines.

"Follow the dinosaur tracks," the cabbie said as he drove off.

At her feet Holly saw three-toed tracks in yellow paint. A line of them led along the sidewalk to one of the older buildings.

Must have been a very small dinosaur, she muttered to herself. Maybe there were small dinosaurs, for all she knew.

She crossed the campus slowly, savoring her feeling of relaxation. Birds were singing. From between the buildings came the sound of a lawn mower. Someone was working on the beautiful lawn. Three girls passed in front of the building to which the tracks led. What would it be like to go to a college like this? Holly felt a moment's envy of those South Dakota coeds wearing blue jeans and no makeup. Sheltered, probably financed by well-to-do parents, they had only to get good grades and marry mining engineers... or ranchers. The thought of ranchers... *a rancher...* brought such a bitter sensation of envy of the girls that she trod up the stone steps with a clatter of her low-heeled sandals. Raf Valcour was not to be thought of again, she admonished herself.

The museum was on the second floor. On the left were the exhibits Dr. Gray had urged her to see.

Moving slowly from one window to the next, Holly found buttons to press giving recorded explanations of the scenes. In one diorama were oreodonts—extinct relatives of pigs, camels and sheep. Their fossilized remains, Holly learned, were common in the Badlands. The display showed three skeletons, one carrying unborn twins. In the foreground lay a cluster of fossilized bones, indicating the disorder in which fossils are discovered. Also in the foreground were fossilized turtle shells, looking exactly like any turtle shells she'd ever seen. The background was painted to show typical Badlands formations. Above the diorama a painting showed what browsing oreodonts and the countryside might have looked like thirty-five million years ago.

The next view held the reconstructed skeleton of a titanothere the size of a rhinoceros.

"Titanotheres are extinct relatives of horses, tapirs and rhinos," the tape announced. "Superficially they resemble rhinos more than horses or tapirs. Titanothere remains are fairly common in the lower rock layer of the Badlands, although good specimens are rare. Titanotheres became extinct in North America shortly after this animal died. Theirs are the largest animal remains found in the Badlands."

In the third panorama Holly was intrigued by the skeletal remains of two ancestors of camels—light graceful animals the size of sheep—that ranged South Dakota forty million years ago.

She turned away from the dioramas to gaze at the other exhibits. A few more people had come in and were wandering about. She went down the row of cases, looking at fossilized shells and at stones gathered from around the world. She was amused to discover some objects called coprolites. The accompanying card explained that they were fossil excrement. Astonishing! Some scientist, or several together, had decided which prehistoric animals had excreted them. Holly could only marvel.

The most impressive display, she thought, was a block of stone showing the way fossil bones usually appear when discovered. Half embedded in stone, they were so scattered she marveled that anyone could put them together into the semblance of a skeleton. To compare them to bits of a jigsaw puzzle made the job sound too easy. Pieces of a puzzle would interlock, and presumably they would all be there. Bones didn't fit together; they were held together by muscle and sinew. According to the card, the block of sandstone held two skulls and assorted limb elements.

Holly shook her head. No wonder Bill needed so much training!

Mischievously she bought postcards of the displays to send to friends back in New York, then left the building and strolled toward the center of town, looking for a place to have lunch.

For a while as she walked, her eyes flew to every passing car, but as the blocks of residences stretched on and on, she became less self-conscious. After all, Rapid City was the second largest town in South Dakota, and the chance that Raf Valcour would be driving about town on a Tuesday morning was highly unlikely. She would never see him again, and she might as well put his face and figure out of her thoughts.

She ate lunch, wrote her postcards and decided to do what Marian had suggested—indulge in a really well-made pair of cowboy boots.

She found a store featuring Western clothes. Assessing them against the kind she had been modeling, she felt sure the ones for sale in Rapid City were

more authentic. Here they were sold not only
tourists, but to authentic cowboys and rodeo rider
male and female.

She chose slant-heeled boots of tan leather, t
tops decorated with five-petaled flowers of crear
colored leather and stitched to represent stems a
leaves. There was more fancy stitching over the i
steps. To wear with the boots, she bought straigh
legged jeans designed for riding. The jeans needed
tooled leather belt with a silver buckle, which s
added as a birthday present to herself—her birthda
had been in February, and she hadn't given herself
thing at that time. Next it seemed pointless not to g
a blue cowboy shirt with dark blue yoke and cuf
and studs instead of buttons, and it was easy to co
vince herself that a straw cowboy hat was a necessi
if one was going to be out in the sun a lot. Finally s
purchased a sleeping bag, which was a requirement.

She left the store feeling light-headed but please
If she ever found occasion to wear these clothes, i
one would guess she was from New York.

And how pleasant it was to shop here! The stor
were uncrowded, the dressing rooms spacious, a
the clerks took time to be helpful. Tomorrow, s
decided, she would visit some dress shops and b
herself a party dress. One should always be prepare
for a party, or what was the point of being young?

Rapid City, which was surrounded by the begin
ning of the Black Hills, plainly was a tourist tow
but its cleanliness and air of prosperity made Ho
feel kindly toward it, as though it were a wel
behaved youngster. Still, she found it hard to reali:
that the Indians with thick black braids walking t

streets were real people, not props brought in by the Chamber of Commerce.

Back at the motel Holly again took advantage of the pool. Floating on her back, the only person in the water, she felt again that lack of pressure to do, go, hurry. She thought about what she'd seen at the museum, then about her new boots waiting to be tried on again with her stiff new jeans. And the shirt and belt! She laughed to herself at the thought of meeting Bill wearing her new outfit.

RAPID CITY HADN'T ALWAYS BEEN so well behaved, she learned from the taxi driver next morning.

"We call it Damn Eyesore Park," the driver grumbled when she told him she wanted to go to Dinosaur Park, but Holly's big blue eyes, glimpsed in the rearview mirror, soon improved his outlook on life. Never had he had a lovelier fare, and somehow she made him feel like a great guy.

"This town looks pretty stuffy now," he volunteered, "but it was rowdy in the old days."

Before taking the Skyline Drive to the park, he drove her through town along Rapid Creek.

"This used to be the Rapid River," he explained with a jerk of his head. "There used to be an island over there...before they filled in part of the creek. And there was a house on the island called Black Nell's—a whorehouse, if you'll pardon the word." Again his eyes met Holly's in the rearview mirror.

Holly gave a little shrug and an encouraging smile.

"Well, one Saturday night there was a storm, and the river rose up and washed out the bridge. The men that were there were marooned for the rest of the night. Next morning all the women in town were waiting on the bank to see whose husbands had been marooned. They weren't just waiting, either. They had rolling pins and umbrellas! And you know, the other women felt so sorry for the unlucky ones that when the husbands came wading across, they all pitched in and beat them up. According to the old-timers, it was a regular ruckus.''

Holly couldn't help laughing. Women might not have been liberated in those days, but they stood up for one another.

At Dinosaur Park she found the life-size reproductions of dinosaurs amusing. Watching two children delightedly climbing on the tail of one of the monsters, Holly wished she hadn't had to give Charles back his camera. *I'll buy one,* she thought. *I'll take that film to be developed and buy a little Instamatic.* Suddenly she couldn't wait to see if the pictures of Raf had come out. How disappointing if they hadn't!

She spent the afternoon shopping. It was wonderful to have all the time in the world to try on clothes. The saleswoman at the final shop enjoyed the session as much as Holly. "You look marvelous in everything you put on," she exclaimed truthfully. "If I had hair and a figure like yours, I'd spend all my money on clothes."

Holly smiled to herself, thinking how surprised the saleslady would be if Holly told her she spent most of her money on her brother's education. Then she sighed. She looked like a butterfly, so everybody expected her to be frivolous. Nobody wanted to believe she was as hardworking as an ant.

At last she found a dress she couldn't resist and

returned to the motel, rather relieved that the two days of total leisure were coming to an end. She was beginning to grow bored—and also lonely.

Again she took advantage of the motel pool. She understood that in the area where the expedition would be working, water was scarce. She should swim while she had the chance.

Later, lounging by the pool, Holly tried planning the first week's menus. During a phone call the previous night, Dr. Gray had suggested a budget. Today Holly worried that it might not be realistic. Well, potatoes and spaghetti were cheap—and bread. She decided optimistically that she could make the money stretch if she had to.

However, when she went to bed that night, she had trouble sleeping. Dozens of hungry people seemed to be holding up empty plates, and no matter how much food she dished up, it was never enough. First she was running out of spaghetti then stew. At last a cowboy—looking vaguely like Raf Valcour—appeared with an armload of bread and a large jar of peanut butter. She slept soundly the rest of the night.

She awoke early with a pleasant feeling toward that man Valcour—which was ridiculous. No sooner had she dressed and breakfasted than she was summoned to the phone.

"Jud here," came the unmistakably Western tones. "My wife said you called while I was away. You ready to go out and pick a campsite this morning? I've got a pretty good idea where the prof wants to be, so if you're ready, we'll just load up a truckful of gear and get on out there. Can you drive a jeep?"

"No!" Holly gasped.

"Well, you'll have time to learn. Two days before the others come, eh? I'll get my boy to drive it out. You'll have plenty of space to practice in," he added cheerfully. "I figured we'd pick the spot today and set up the tents, and tomorrow morning I'll bring out the house trailer, if that's all right with you."

"It sounds all right." Holly was cautious.

"You ready to buy your food? I understand you're in charge of keeping those brainy types from starving to death."

Holly laughed. "Yes, I am."

"Why don't you come over to the store? While I'm loading the truck, my boy can take you shopping for groceries." He began giving her detailed instructions on how to find his store. At last she managed to interrupt.

"The taxi driver will know, won't he?"

"That's right, you don't have a car!" A deep chuckle came over the wire. "Tell you what, you wait right there, and I'll pick you up. I'm at the house, and it's no trouble to come by. If you'd had a car, the prof wouldn't have had to hire a jeep, would he? You can check out of the motel while you're waiting. You'll be staying out to the camp tonight."

"I will?" Holly asked faintly.

"Sure thing. You'll have everything you need there. See you in ten minutes," came the hearty voice.

Holly packed her suitcase and put most of her new purchases back into the paper bags that said OLD-WEST OUTFITTERS—SADDLES & TACK. She wished fleetingly for a New York shopping bag. Out there, where everyone owned cars, shopping bags didn't seem to exist.

Just for fun she twisted her hair into a thick braid down her back. Wearing much washed jeans, a white shirt and her new cowboy hat, Holly was waiting outside the motel office when a shiny pickup truck, the biggest she had ever seen, pulled into the driveway. The driver got out, removing his cap as he came around to Holly, his hand outstretched.

"Miss Cameron?" He was a wiry cheerful-looking man, whose blue eyes in a tan leather face were on a level with her own. They opened wide as he frankly looked her up and down. "I'm Judson."

Shaking his outstretched hand, Holly judged him to be in his forties, maybe older.

"These your things?" he asked, picking them up. "There'll be room in front for you and them both."

The pickup's seat was wide enough to accommodate the driver and three passengers, Holly discovered when she climbed in.

Mr. Judson was silent while he turned the truck around and maneuvered it into the traffic. At the first stoplight he gave Holly a sidewise glance.

"So you're a cook?"

"I hope so." Holly's smile quirked.

"Ever done it previously?"

"Not for seven people," Holly admitted.

Mr. Judson gave her another glance that was at once appraising and benevolent. "A pretty girl like you shouldn't have to do that kind of hard work."

There it was again! This man, too, thought she was a butterfly. She was silent, unable to think how to reply. Bill hadn't considered her too fragile to be a cook. He'd seen it as a change of pace. This guy didn't know what he was talking about!

Mr. Judson shook his head. "I guess that team of brains won't notice too much what they eat." He grinned.

"My brother is one of the team," Holly said proudly. "That's how I got roped in."

"You're a good sister, are you?"

"Yes, I think I am."

Judson pulled around behind his store. "There's the jeep," he said, waving a hand at the basic-looking vehicle parked in the corner of the yard. "It's been checked over and greased. You folks shouldn't have any trouble with it."

Holly eyed it warily. It did look as though it could put up with any number of people learning to drive it.

Judson's son turned out to be a gangling seventeen-year-old, more interested in exploring the Black Hills than in girls. No time waster, he said Holly might as well begin by driving them to the supermarket.

It was a morning of new experiences—struggling to learn how to shift, buying what looked like enough groceries for twenty ravenous ditchdiggers.

"That amount of food won't last long," Judson said when they returned to his store. "You won't want to be coming all the way into Rapid City to do your shopping, either. I'll introduce you to the storekeeper in Vista. He's not very good for fresh stuff, but he can get all the frozen meat and canned goods you need."

They left Rapid City about midmorning, the oversize pickup loaded with three tents, a chemical toilet, cots, camp tables, picks, shovels, sledges and crowbars. Holly and Jeff Judson followed in the jeep. Once Holly got the vehicle into the right gear, driving it down the highway presented no problem.

"We'll get a sandwich in Vista," Judson told Holly and his son.

East of the foothills surrounding Rapid City, the land was flat and grassy. The bared earth on banks and road cuts was pale, almost white.

Holly had driven some miles when it occurred to her that she might have been premature in moving out of the motel. Well, she could check back in.

The road led straight ahead as far as the eye could see. Now and then they passed a few head of browsing cattle and once a cowboy "riding fence," as the term was. Otherwise the scenery consisted of flat green pasture and puffy white clouds filling the sky.

Ahead and on the left the horizon changed, became jagged. Beyond the rolling green pastures a pale broken barrier had risen.

"Is that it?" Holly had to shout to hear herself over the noise of the engine and the rushing wind.

"What?" Jeff pulled himself out of his teenage trance.

"The Badlands?"

"Oh, yeah." Jeff slumped back against the seat.

The broken land remained on the horizon. The road continued straight and sunny. Holly was glad she'd elected to wear her straw hat.

After almost an hour trees appeared, indicating a town, and they came to a white frame building that had been converted into a stable, judging from the horse-filled corral beside it. Across the road, which had widened, was a gas station and a scattering of decrepit abandoned-looking buildings. A dirt road led off to other buildings among the trees. More sleek horses were penned behind a barbed-wire fence alongside two mobile homes.

"This is Vista," Jeff announced.

Mr. Judson was parking the pickup parallel to a barnlike building of blue corrugated metal.

Holly parked beside Mr. Judson and leaped nimbly down. The lack of doors, once you got used to it, might become quite a convenience.

Judson was getting out of his truck when a battered red pickup with high slatted sides for hauling stock rolled up beside him. Holly looked at the driver, and her knees went weak. She grasped the jeep's windshield for support.

CHAPTER FIVE

HOLLY WATCHED THE DRIVER get out of the truck and step onto the sidewalk.

He said, "Jud!"

Mr. Judson replied, "Valcour!" and they shook hands.

Raf Valcour was wearing tight blue jeans, dusty boots and a work shirt. By contrast, his straw hat appeared new. He didn't look like a rich rancher or an eligible bachelor. He looked like a cowboy taking time to run into town. Hanging in the back window of his old pickup was a gun rack bearing a rifle. On each end of the gun rack hung a coiled rope.

"What are you doing out this way, Jud? Camping?" Raf was peering at the gear in the back of the truck.

"Not me," Judson said. "I'm setting up for some fossil hunters from back East. Down your direction. You're just the man I want to see. We stopped here to introduce the young lady to Henry Brightwing."

For the first time Raf gazed beyond Mr. Judson to Holly and Jeff.

Holly met the look of total shock in Raf Valcour's tawny eyes with a mischievous grin, forgetting how angry she'd been last time she'd seen him. With a sensation of triumph she watched his lean jaw drop.

He recovered in the blink of an eye while Judson was turning to introduce her and his son.

"Holly, this is Raf Valcour. I think his ranch will be the nearest place to your camp. Raf—Miss Cameron. She's the expedition's cook. They sent her out early to set up camp."

"Glad to meet you, Miss Cameron." Raf removed his hat. The eyes that met her challenging look were veiled, exactly like those of hawks she'd seen in the zoo.

"We were going into the Shorthorn for a sandwich," Judson told him. "Care to join us?"

"I'll do that," Raf said. "I came in to see Henry Brightwing myself about some supplies. I'll join you in a few minutes. Glad to meet you, Miss Cameron, Jeff."

"Tell Henry I'm bringing him a new customer after we get something to eat," Judson called.

"I'll do that." Raf replaced his hat and strode into the store.

"This way." Judson took them through a weedy lot to the back door of the saloon. "They keep the front door padlocked during the day," he explained. "I guess they open it at night. I don't know; I never was here then."

He led the way to a booth. Jeff and Holly followed, kicking through sawdust several inches deep.

"You never told me about this place, dad!" Jeff sounded aggrieved.

"I don't tell you everything, son." Judson winked at Holly. She twinkled back, but his words had nothing to do with her glow of excitement. While she cast her gaze about the much decorated room, her heart was beating so wildly she thought everyone must hear its heavy thumping. He lived nearby!

The ceiling of the long room was decorated with dozens of heavy black marks like cattle brands burned into the acoustical tiles. There were also holes in them that might be bullet holes. A vacant space beside their booth was filled with used truck and tractor tires. The bar stools were steel drums topped by the metal seats of old farm machines.

Mr. Judson ordered four beers and four hamburgers. Holly opened her mouth to protest, then thought better. This was not the place to order white wine! She also had a pretty strong feeling it was not the place for a woman to be, except maybe at noon, as now, in the company of men.

The decorations were so lavish as to be almost theatrical: a cow's skull with red lights in the eye sockets, polished steer horns on the wall above their heads, old framed photographs and drawings, rodeo posters. Was the place decorated for tourists? Or was it really the hangout of cowboys and Indians, the mementos accumulated as in a family parlor? She couldn't keep her eyes from roving about. There was so much to see!

Mr. Judson was sitting beside his son, leaving the seat beside Holly vacant. Her back was to the door through which Raf would come. While her eyes roamed over the saloon's decor, her ears listened for the sound of boots scuffing through the sawdust. Or would he come silently again?

Judson went to the bar and picked up the four brimming glasses. Holly took a sip of beer to dispel the dryness in her mouth. Excitement was like a lump in her stomach. She would never be able to eat more than a bite of the hamburger. Raf would notice and think her wasteful of food—or worse yet, would see with those hawk's eyes that his presence was stealing her appetite.

She did hear the scuff of his boots when he crossed the floor, and when he appeared beside the booth, she looked up with a smile. He slid in beside her, and the moment felt complete. She was with three strangers in a totally alien atmosphere, and yet she felt—she knew—that with this man beside her, she'd feel at home anywhere. She basked in his nearness while he and Judson carried the conversation, talking about people, places, events she had never expected to hear of again.

Raf turned to her so suddenly she choked on a swallow of beer. "So you're cooking for this outfit! How many?"

"Seven, including me."

"Think you can do it?" He raised one black eyebrow.

Meeting his eyes, Holly felt short of breath. Nevertheless she managed to say pointedly, "I'm quite used to hard work."

The glint in his tawny eyes told her she'd merely amused him. "Whose group is it?" He was looking across the table, so Holly let Judson answer.

"Professor Gray, from that college in New York City."

"Ah, I thought he'd be back. When's he coming?"

"Saturday," Holly supplied.

"I'm surprised I didn't get a letter from him," Raf said. "He's an old friend."

Judson looked faintly embarrassed. "I was supposed to phone you, but I've been out of town, and then this young lady arrived sooner than expected.... Let me get you another beer. Holly?"

"No, thanks."

The boy, Jeff, mouth full of hamburger, shook his head.

Raf turned a look of amused interest on Holly. "Something of a change, eh, from model to cook? Now cooking I do call work."

Holly's blue eyes blazed, but with Jeff's curious gaze upon her, she was unable to produce a devastating reply. She attacked her hamburger in angry silence.

When Judson returned, Raf asked him if the professor had said anything about wanting horses. Judson shook his head.

"I did him a favor last time," Raf said, "my contribution to science." To Holly he added, "Tell the professor I've got four or five riding horses, if you folks want them. I'll contribute a wrangler, too. He can peel potatoes in his spare time, carry water, that sort of thing."

Holly ground her teeth but decided she must thank him. She saw that her forced thanks amused him. She wished she hadn't let him see he'd made her mad, hadn't let him know he could affect her emotions in any way. But when she remembered the way he had kissed her at the campground in Fox Butte and the way she had responded, she thought it was definitely too late to make him think she was emotionless.

She was still angry when the beer had been downed

and the hamburgers—all but hers—consumed and they rose to go.

Raf clapped his hat on his head and left them at the door, his boot heels crunching on the gravel of the vacant lot.

Judson led Holly and his son through a side entrance into the general store.

It was full of merchandise under the immense open space of the high barnlike ceiling. Everything was covered with fine white powder—the local dust too light-colored to look dirty. Henry Brightwing and his wife stood behind a counter. A car had driven up, and three Indians were in the store; a woman covered with a shawl, a man wearing a green T-shirt and matching green headband and a boy with a red T-shirt and red headband. Conversation stopped when Judson's party entered.

Except for their black hair, Henry Brightwing and his wife might have been any midwestern farm couple. He was wearing overalls and had no noticeable accent.

"Sure she can shop here," he told Judson. "I'll get her anything she wants if I know ahead of time."

"Okay, Holly?" Judson asked.

Holly smiled her agreement but left the store feeling very much an Easterner.

Her last responsibility—that of choosing a campsite—was simplified by the limited choice. Only one grove of cottonwoods grew in the area where Dr. Gray wanted to be. Everywhere else was sparse grassland or low, bare, eroding hillsides—the outer limits of the Badlands, which loomed to the northeast. The trees were a couple of hundred yards off the rough dirt track. Judson turned the loaded pickup toward the grove and bounced over the grassy flat. Holly swung the jeep and followed.

Beneath the cottonwoods the ground was smooth and level. The light dirt made Holly think of sand. Judson left the truck and walked over to the jeep.

"What do you think about this place?"

"I think it will be nice," Holly affirmed. It reminded her of scenes from old Western movies. She walked over to the creek on the far side of the grove. Judson and Jeff followed.

"The water's white!" she exclaimed, revolted.

Judson laughed. "It ain't pretty, that's for sure. It ain't good for much, either." He shook his head. "About all it does is grow cottonwoods."

"Our chemistry teacher told us this dirt here has a little electricity," Jeff said, as though ashamed of the knowledge. "That's what keeps it from settling like ordinary mud. The grains repel each other and stay suspended." He flushed with embarrassment.

"A lot of the ranchers have problems with the water," Judson added.

Out on the prairie a meadowlark was singing a welcome.

Across the creek the land rose in a bare bank too steep or too quickly eroding to support grass or weeds. The ground atop the bank was flat—another level of prairie.

"You're at the edge of the Badlands here," Judson explained. "Erosion's just beginning, or maybe it'll never come this far—I'm not sure how they explain it. Jeff could probably tell you if he wasn't tongue-tied just driving around with a pretty girl." Doubling

his fist, he punched his son playfully on the shoulder.
"Holly, before we unload, you better tell us what
kind of layout you want."

"Layout?" Holly's arched brows arched higher.
"Oh, you mean where to put the tents? You'd have a
better idea than I would."

Judson nodded. "Maybe so." He picked up a stick
and drew a plan in the dirt. "What they did last time
was to put the tents and the trailer in a circle and put
the worktables in the middle. The toilet can be out of
sight over there behind those trees." He indicated a
pair of cottonwoods. Together their trunks were wide
enough to conceal a car.

Looking at the grove, Holly suddenly wondered
whose property they were on. "Who owns this?" she
inquired, suspicion nagging at the back of her mind.
If Raf Valcour's ranch was the nearest one. . . .

"The government," Judson said.

The grove suddenly felt different, and a weight
rolled from Holly's spirit. But she had rejoiced too
soon.

"It's national grassland," Judson explained. "The
government leases it to local ranchers."

"Cattle?" Despite an effort to prevent it, her voice
squeaked. "You mean there'll be cows coming
around here?"

"Not with you folks here. They're wild; this is free
range stuff. They don't want to see you any more
than you want to see them."

"Then won't the rancher who's leasing this grass
object to our camping here and driving his cattle
away?"

"I assume the professor's been in contact with

him, as he was with me. Leasing federal grassland doesn't give the rancher rights to anything but grass and water. No fossil rights, for instance.''

Holly breathed a sigh of relief. Raf Valcour had said he hadn't heard from Dr. Gray; therefore this land must not have anything to do with him.

She stood around feeling useless while Judson and his son, with a minimum of effort, set up three green tents that, as soon as they were up, appeared to belong amid the trees. They set two cots in each tent, and Holly picked the tent she would share with the female student. She deposited her sleeping bag on one of the cots, feeling out of her element. Where did one put things? There wasn't even a box for a night table. She heard Jeff calling her and went outside.

"I'm putting the groceries in this tent for now," he said, fastening back the door flap.

"Fine," Holly replied. Tomorrow when Judson delivered the big old Airstream trailer that was to be her kitchen and Dr. Gray's office and bedroom, she would put the food away properly.

Judson handed down an armload of shovels and picks, which Jeff dumped under one of the battered tables.

"You going to eat inside or out?" Judson asked, adding before Holly could answer, "Outside, I expect, so I'll need to hunt you up some benches and chairs. You can crowd seven people into the trailer if it rains, but not if the professor's using the table for a desk.''

Holly hadn't visualized eating meals outside. In fact, she hadn't quite visualized any of this, never having been involved in anything more rugged than girl-scout camp. This would indeed be camping. What if she discovered she hated it? *Don't think like that,* she cautioned herself. If the other people wer pleasant, it would be casual and fun.

"Here's your dishes." Judson thumped three card board cartons onto one of the tables he had set up "Jeff's got the cooking equipment. I think you' find everything you need."

Holly said distractedly, "I don't know where I'm going to keep it all!"

"If I were you, I'd put the extra supplies under th beds. For now, anyway."

"Good idea," Holly said, hoping to sound a though she knew how to take charge.

"Holly!" Jeff called. "I'm putting your suitcase i your tent."

"No! I'll be needing it tonight."

She saw Judson regarding her blankly. "You' going to stay here tonight, aren't you?"

"Here?" Holly's big blue eyes widened. "Alone?

"That was the idea," he said gruffly. "You'd b here to look after all this. Not that the country's fu of thieves, but to leave this stuff here with nobod looking after it would be asking for trouble."

Holly was too appalled to answer. Her eyes swep the grove, the wide prairie beyond. "I—I—there no stove. I didn't plan on cooking just for m self."

Judson nodded understandingly. "I guess I shou have made it clear you'd have to stay. I kind of too it for granted. Tell you what, while Jeff and I fini up here, drive yourself back to Vista and pick some bread and cold cuts to tide you over. When bring out the trailer tomorrow, you'll have a regular-size stove."

There was nothing Holly could do but agree. *After they leave, I'll get in the jeep and drive to a hotel,* she thought. Judson would never know the difference. Unless somebody stole the tents! Or the toilet. Why hadn't she thought of this in New York? She should have guessed that once the camp was set up, she'd have to stay in it!

She drove to Vista alone, rather proud of the fact she was able to do it, shifting from one gear to the next—if not smoothly, then at least without killing the engine more than once. *A horse,* she thought, eyeing the countryside and the pale jagged hills to the northeast. It would be fun to explore on horseback with Bill if he had any time off from his academic work.

She had bought bread in Rapid City. At the Vista general store she purchased sliced turkey, orange juice and a small can of spinach for something green. She had already stocked up on cereal and powdered milk for breakfast.

She had no trouble finding her way back to the campsite. In this country of few roads, it was impossible to lose one's way, she reflected. In daylight anyhow.

The first thing she saw was that the grove now looked like a camp. Also, the pickup truck was empty. The portable toilet had disappeared discreetly behind the tree trunks. Her hands tightened on the steering wheel. The Judsons were ready to leave. They were sitting in two of the folding chairs, waiting for her.

"Does the jeep handle pretty good?" Judson asked.

"It seems to." Holly tried to speak brightly, but something in her voice or face gave her away.

"Now there's no reason to be scared," Judson said soothingly. "I wouldn't dream of leaving a young girl out here alone if there was."

"I could stay, dad," Jeff offered, "and go back with you tomorrow."

Hope rose in Holly's heart, but Judson's next words quenched it.

"You think Holly would feel safe with you around, eh?" he teased. "Trouble is, I need you to help hitch that doggoned trailer."

So that was that. "I'll be all right," she said firmly. "As you say, you wouldn't leave me here if there were any danger."

"Exactly," Judson said.

Only her secret thought that she could leave in the jeep if she wished to enable her to keep her shoulders straight and wave gaily to Jeff when the truck turned onto the road and gathered speed.

Holly looked at her watch. Five o'clock. What was she supposed to do, now that she was here? She hadn't thought to bring a book, and she didn't have a radio. Oh, yes, there was the cookbook! At least they had provided her with lanterns—bright ones, Judson had assured her.

Beyond the cottonwoods the grassland shimmered in the sunlight. It didn't look as though it would ever be dark. When it was—well, she could light the lamp and go to bed. In the morning the Judsons would return with the trailer. She could sleep in that tomorrow night and lock the door. But a tent.... She looked at it and shivered. Even if she zipped up the door flap, what was to keep some invader from cutting a hole right through the side? Or a cow, for that matter? A cow could probably put its horns through canvas without half trying. She looked at the jeep and thought longingly of the interstate highway running along the north side of the Badlands. In her imagination she saw it lined with the fluorescent signs of motels. She went into her tent and got out one of the folders she had bought at the museum. A map showed the interstate at least thirty miles away over back roads. No, she'd better stick it out here. After all, Judson had assured her....

She stepped outside the tent and took stock. She was going to be here for two months, not just tomorrow. She might as well make herself at home.

A checked red-and-white plastic tablecloth was packed with the dishes. Holly chose for the dining area a bare spot under one of the huge trees. She discovered a broom and began sweeping the ground clear of twigs.

It's like playing house, she thought cheerfully.

She placed one of the lightweight folding tables in the center of the area and covered it with the plastic cloth. Immediately the camp achieved an expectant air, as though someone were coming for dinner. If only they were!

"Well, I'm having dinner," she said aloud, and began rummaging through the boxes to find a knife, fork, plate and tumbler.

She was pouring orange juice when she remembered she'd packed a bottle of sherry before leaving

New York. Where was it? Still wrapped in a pair of jeans!

She bounced into her tent and rifled through her suitcase. There! Just what she needed—courage. She carried it out to the table and looked at her watch. Too early—a long evening stretched ahead.

I'll take a stroll around the grove, she decided, and noted that she felt like a castaway on an island whose shores ended where the grass began.

Dead limbs lay everywhere. A campfire! *I have paper,* she thought. *And matches.* Jeff had reminded her to buy matches to light the camp lanterns.

Carrying the wood back to camp and selecting a place to build the fire seemed to take a lot of time, but when she consulted her watch, only half an hour had passed. All right, she'd have the sherry now. After dinner (dinner!) she'd read the cookbook until time for bed. Reading recipes was guaranteed to put her to sleep.

She drank a glass of sherry, then ate her turkey sandwich and canned spinach. The sunlight faded slowly into a haze. There was still light to read by, but the air grew cooler. She had packed a sweater; she found it in her suitcase and put it on. The tweedy blue color repeated the blue of her eyes. Her golden hair shimmered in the fading light. She unbraided it and brushed it to hang in a cloud about her shoulders. Something to do.

When she left the tent this time, there was no doubt—dusk had fallen. She was both glad and frightened. Glad that time was passing...the night had to be got through before morning would bring the Judsons. But when night did come, it was going

to be so dark! She probably wouldn't see a light anywhere. Unless a car passed on the road. And what if
it stopped, turned in? She felt the hair rise on her
scalp. It might be better not to light either a fire or a
lamp. But it was so early to go to bed—eight o'clock!
She didn't feel she could ever fall asleep. How did
Mr. Judson *know* it was safe here? Had he ever
camped alone? She bet he hadn't. Or if so, he'd had a
gun. Her mind jumped to the memory of the rifle in
Raf's truck. Why was he carrying a rifle if the country was so safe? He had a rack for it, as though it
were standard equipment, like a spare tire.

She returned to her seat at the table and poured
another glass of sherry. She sat sipping it and staring
around the now shadowy grove, listening, hearing
rustlings and snappings she hadn't noticed earlier.

The idea of a blazing fire pushing back the darkness became more and more appealing. Which was
better: to attract the attention of human beings or to
have half-wild cattle stumbling over her tent? Did
cows walk around at night or sleep?

She picked up the matches and knelt beside the
stack of wood she had built. She was about to push
some crumpled sheets of the *Rapid City Gazette*
under the wood when she felt the ground tremble.
Something was walking in the grove! She raised her
head, listening. A steady clip-clop. A cow! She remained crouched, frozen into immobility, her eyes
probing the gray light under the trees.

"Anybody here?" a voice called.

She released her breath. At least it was a human
being, not a wild animal.

The man came riding into the half circle formed by

the tents, and she recognized him—Raf Valcour.

He saw her crouching by the unlit pile of sticks. Evidently he read the fear in her pose, because he said without preamble, "Jud leave you here all alone?"

"Yes." She stood up, throwing a quick glance at the jeep. It offered no escape. But this man hadn't come to harm her, she felt almost sure.

"How do you like camping by yourself in strange country?" he asked.

"Uh—okay," she lied.

He dismounted. She stepped back as he approached, unconsciously wiping her dusty sweaty hands on her jeans.

The golden eyes flicked over her. His impassive face relaxed as he saw the paper crumpled and tucked under the hit-or-miss heap. "Is this the fire or the woodpile?" He sounded amused.

"The fire." She tried for dignity, but she was suddenly overwhelmed by his lighthearted comment—by relief, really. She felt a sob rising in her throat and choked.

"Now watch," he directed. "This is the way to build a campfire." He squatted easily, balancing on the balls of his feet. The pointed toes of his black boots were squared off across the tip. She recognized with a little thrill that they had rows of stitching on the instep, just like hers. New boots—the stitching was still white. His narrow jeans stretched tight across his muscular thighs. He had changed his shirt since she'd seen him this afternoon. He now wore a clean white one under a black leather vest. He'd changed his hat, too, to a black felt trimmed with a band of silver conchas. He was so handsome, but in a scary way, because she'd never met anybody like him. A quiver of excitement ran down her back. Had he changed his clothes to come visiting her?

"This is the way, see? First paper, if you have any, and then small stuff, laid very carefully on top of the paper, and then some twigs a little bigger and so on, till you get it going. And then you add the logs, or whatever you have." Still squatting he struck a match.

Together they watched the miracle of fire, the flames eating away the paper and then the weed stalks and twigs. By contrast the surrounding grove was almost in darkness.

Holly looked at the horse, standing patiently where Raf had dropped the reins. For a moment she felt resentful. He was behaving so normally, while she was on the verge of hysteria, or, if that was exaggerated, at the very least her knees were trembling. Should she offer him sherry? Would he take it amiss?

He stood up, so much taller than she, tall though she was. She turned hastily toward the table. "I can offer you a glass of sherry, Mr. Valcour."

"And I can offer you some lemon pudding, Miss—uh—Cameron."

"Pudding?" Her blue eyes gazed unbelievingly into his tawny ones. She was betrayed into a laugh.

He went to his horse and took something from a pouch behind the saddle. He brought it to the table—a white plastic dish like a margarine container. The ordinariness of it banished her remaining distrust. Ravishers didn't bring puddings.

She met his eyes with such a laughing face that he looked stunned.

"My housekeeper makes a first-class lemon pudding," he stated defensively. "Or perhaps it's called a pudding cake."

Whatever it was called, she thought as she unpacked bowls and spoons, he was here to keep her company, to drive away the loneliness for an hour or two. Then he'd ride off home to his bunkhouse... wouldn't he?

At that thought she threw him a quick look and found him watching her.

"What made you agree to stay?" he asked. "You don't seem to be much of a camper."

"I didn't have any choice!" Dividing the cake onto two plates, she explained. "Mr. Judson said someone had to be here to look after the gear."

"Nonsense! If he thought that, why didn't he leave his son?"

She looked at Raf with respect. "I thought of that, too. But he said he needed Jeff to help hitch the trailer or something. Jeff did offer to stay with me."

"Judson's right, of course. You're safe enough out here."

She thrust her lip out. "There are dangerous people everywhere," she reminded him.

He had removed the black hat and placed it on one of the worktables. Now he unfolded the other chair and sat across the table from her, his face expressionless. "Here we are again. I seem fated to run into you."

"You can't call it fate," she said spiritedly. "I told

you I was going to Fox Butte, so you shouldn't have been surprised to see me there.''

"And you knew you were coming here, so you weren't surprised to see me today.''

"Yes, I was," she contradicted him. What would he think if he knew she had hoped to see him every day that she had been in Rapid City?

"Can you really cook?''

"Why does everyone act so surprised?'' she asked, nettled. "There's not so much to cooking plain food. Not half such hard work as modeling.''

"So I understand," he said, putting one hand to his lean brown jaw.

His meaning came as such a surprise that she burst into laughter. Then, embarrassed to see that his face was perfectly straight, she covered her unruly mouth with her hands. But above her fingers her blue eyes danced. She was relieved to read an answering twinkle in the tawny depths of his and found herself blushing.

"I'm sorry I slapped you," she said forthrightly. "You had no way of knowing, but that article in the Pierre paper had us all on edge.''

Would he acknowledge his friendship with the writer of the piece?

He shrugged. "I deserved it. Besides—" his eyes crinkled "—I got the best of the exchange.''

Holly froze, a forkful of cake halfway to her mouth.

"Tell me about this group that's coming," Raf said quickly, before she could think of an answer. "How did you get roped into doing the cooking?''

The pudding cake, helped by sherry and the fire,

had begun to soothe Holly's nerves. The once ominous surroundings now seemed friendly and relaxed.

"I keep thinking it's raining," she said, listening to the stirrings in the leaves overhead.

"That rustling? That's the cottonwood leaves themselves. The flat stems let them blow against each other in the slightest breeze." He rose to put more wood on the fire.

Her portion of cake finished, she told him all she knew about the expedition and how she had become involved. She tried to make the story entertaining, afraid that at any moment he might get up and leave.

"So you're supporting your brother?" he said when she had ended.

"Not supporting him. Just helping out."

"Do you know these other people?"

"I met them briefly at a tea before I left."

"This job may turn out to be harder than you expect."

Holly's lower lip jutted determinedly until she saw Raf's eyes upon her mouth. Quickly she changed her expression.

"What makes you say that?"

"My housekeeper, partly. She thinks cooking for six men is a hard job. I also remember the last group the professor brought here. The first cook they had quit after two weeks."

"Is that what you think I'll do?" Something about his cool assurance awoke belligerence.

"I hope not," he said with meaning, and the flush of temper drained from her cheeks, leaving her eyes sparkling in the firelight.

Before she could reply, he stood up. "Bedtime, I think."

Holly gasped, disappointment her foremost emotion. She had trusted him as she would a friend. What was he going to do?

He was watching her, his eyes nothing but black holes, his high cheekbones turned to burnished copper by the fire, his thin-lipped mouth an imperious gash across his strong-jawed face. With a shiver she fought against remembering how that mouth had covered hers, demanding and seductive at the same time.

"I brought a bedroll," he said at last. Was that a trace of laughter in his voice? "If it'll make you feel more comfortable, I'll stay. I'll stretch out in one of the other tents."

"Would you?" she cried. She heard her voice dripping with gratitude, but she didn't care. Her relief was heartfelt. "Western men really are gentlemen," she said happily. "I always thought it was a myth."

He gave her a look over his shoulder as he piled more wood on the fire. "Well, we're not such monsters that we would leave little tenderfeet to camp out alone—speaking for myself, not Judson." He turned from the fire and came toward her. "I'll be leaving at first light, so...."

He took her face in his hands. Her eyes closed, she felt his lips brush her forehead, and then, his fingertips no longer caressed her cheeks. Her flash of hope that he was going to kiss her the way he had at Fox Butte was dispelled. She opened her eyes in dismay. He was walking toward the fire.

"If you hear something crashing about in the

night," he called, "it's only Buckskin. All right, fella, you've worn this long enough."

Holly stood where he left her and watched him unsaddle the horse.

"I'll hobble him out on the grass, but he may come looking for me about morning," Raf said, seeming to know she was still watching.

She turned on her heel and entered her tent, suddenly furious to find herself in the dark. Why hadn't she lit one of the lanterns? Why hadn't he? He was such an experienced camper! She hadn't thought about washing her face or brushing her teeth, and now she couldn't even see to find her pajamas!

She thought she heard him come back while she was undressing, but how did she know? He might have resaddled his horse and ridden off to the comfort of mattress and box spring. As soon as she could slip into pajamas, she peered through the tent's mosquito-netting window and was ridiculously relieved to see him pass the fire carrying his bedroll and saddle toward the nearest tent.

She lay listening to the vast unfamiliar silence and thought about this man who had come to keep her company.

Each time she had seen him the circumstances had been different...he had been different. On the airplane he had been a businessman; at Fox Butte, a native...no...well, yes. Almost. But he had kissed her like a sophisticate. It had been, upon consideration, a very practiced kiss. And then, her thoughts hurried on, this afternoon in Vista he had been a dusty cowboy in a battered truck. Tonight he had been almost a friend.

Tonight, too, he had found out all about her, and she hadn't found out anything about him. She knew no more than what she had learned from Gary: one of the state's richest ranchers, one of the state's most eligible bachelors...oh, yes, with a housekeeper who made lemon pudding cake.

She was almost asleep when something very close began a wild yipping that sent shivers along every nerve. She was out of bed and on her feet in a second. From farther away she heard answering yips. Unzipping the tent flap, she was surprised to see the grove dappled with moonlight. Through the leaves she caught a glimpse of a huge cheese-yellow ball rising above the high bank.

Again the nerve-tingling series of yips.

"Raf!" her voice shrilled. "What's that?"

"Coyote." His voice came muffled from the nearest tent.

She crept back into her sleeping bag, feeling foolish.

CHAPTER SIX

SHE AWOKE TO BROAD DAYLIGHT and sat up instantly, knowing she was too late. He would have gone. She dressed and went out. There was no sign that he had ever been there. He had even taken the plastic dish. But she was going to be here two months. Surely she'd see him again. The thought of seeing him reminded her of the pictures she'd taken. They must be ready by now... and here she was, miles away from Rapid City. But tomorrow, when she went to the airport to meet Bill and the others, she'd be able to get the pictures then, she thought with a rush of joy.

By the time Holly had washed her face in cold water and drunk her orange juice, the Judsons arrived in the pickup, smoothly pulling a silver trailer. Judson parked the trailer expertly, stationing it to complete the circle. He then took Holly inside to show her the kitchen's conveniences. He explained how to turn on the connections for the bottled gas and how to switch bottles when the time came.

"The refrigerator runs on gas, too, so you're all set. I don't know what the professor has in mind about water. The best thing he can do is get some rancher to haul in a barrel every day or two. Seven people use a lot."

When they wished her good luck and drove away, she turned happily to the task of setting up her kitchen. The amount of space was remarkable. She hummed as she began carrying in the sacks of food and the boxes of dishes and utensils. She brought her sleeping bag in, also. Tonight she would have a door to lock!

She inspected the trailer's bedroom and living room, fascinated by the clever conveniences and well-thought-out storage. Dr. Gray should be very comfortable here.

I'll be comfortable in the kitchen, too, she thought. *If it gets too warm, I'll prepare things outside under the trees.*

By late afternoon she had time on her hands. She wondered if the general store in Vista sold paperbacks. Or transistor radios. Somehow she didn't think so. She realized she was eagerly looking forward to going to town in the morning.

You'd think I'd been here a week, she said to herself, *instead of twenty-four hours.*

She strolled about the grove and built up a stack of fallen branches so the new arrivals could build a campfire if they wished. Tonight she intended to light a lamp and sit inside the trailer. She had found a battered deck of playing cards in a drawer. Instead of biting her fingers, she could play solitaire.

She stood at the edge of the grove and stared wistfully at the road, wanting to see a car or a truck drive past. Oh, well, tomorrow everything would change.

Tomorrow I'll be too busy to think, she told herself.

She was turning back when she spotted a man riding a horse where the creek wound along the foot of the high white bank. No, two horses! But only one rider. She held her breath, hoping.

They came on at a steady jog, and she recognized the black hat with the silver conchas and the set of the broad shoulders. Raf! She stood admiring the way he sat in the saddle, relaxed, at one with the animal. The extra horse was saddled, too.

She waved; he must have noticed her by now. She turned and ran to her tent. Habit was strong. She wanted to be sure she looked her best, but it was hard to tell when one had only a makeup mirror. The trailer! One closet door sported a full-length looking glass. Holly ran to stand in front of it. She saw a tall slim girl in jeans and leather thong sandals, with pretty suntanned ankles. Her shirt was clean and her makeup fresh.

When she stepped out of the trailer, Raf thought her welcoming smile would have made a ride of twice the length worthwhile.

He dismounted and removed his hat. She noted he was wearing a blue shirt today under the leather vest. His expression, as nearly as she could guess, was benevolent.

"So you're all set?" He nodded toward the trailer.

"As far as my part is concerned."

"Did you sleep well?" he inquired.

"Yes, after I found out what was making that noise."

"I should have warned you. I forgot you Easterners never hear coyotes." He smiled.

The unexpectedness of his smile was stunning because Holly had come to believe he never allowed himself to be human. And because his smile was so rare, Holly felt she'd won a prize. She warmed to the approval in his eyes.

"This lady is Brown Betty," he said, taking the spare horse by the bridle and bringing her forward. "She's for you to ride. I'm assuming that girls who model Western clothing must know how to ride."

"You're assuming far too much," she said, laughing. "Girls who model Western clothing only have to look as if they know how to ride. But I do ride, and Brown Betty is a beauty." Holly stroked the white-blazed forehead. "Thank you so much!" She hesitated, looking up into his face. "Could—could we go for a ride now?"

"I had in mind more than that," he told her. "I had in mind taking you back to the ranch for dinner. Are you ready for a little civilization?"

He was laughing at her, but he was so right. Civilization. . . .

"A—a shower?" she asked boldly.

"If you like. Or a swim."

"You have a swimming pool?" Her face mingled disbelief and delight.

"Heap big pool. Heap clean water."

"Oh! Oh, how heavenly!" Her laugh responded to the satisfied amusement in Raf's tawny gaze. "I'll get my suit." She paused, looking down at her sandals. "I'll have to wear something else to ride in."

"Weren't you wearing boots yesterday?"

"Of course! I'll be ready in a minute." She rushed distractedly to her tent, happily aware he had noticed and remembered what she had worn yesterday. And now real cowboy boots to ride a real horse! How clever she had been to buy them!

She mounted Brown Betty with some trepidation. Were Western horses wilder? No, Brown Betty was a lady, east or west.

Raf lit a lantern and set it on the checked table-cloth. "Just so the place won't look deserted," he said. "And so we won't lose the camp."

"You couldn't get lost here, could you?"

"Not really. The camp's right beside the road. I could have driven over to get you, but I thought you might enjoy this. I'll drive you back if you aren't ready for quite so much riding in one day."

"All right," Holly bubbled. "I'll let you know." She rode away from camp with him without a backward glance.

The ride was long, and there was nothing to see but undulating land covered with grass, except for occasional outbreaks of white eroding earth.

"I never believed such country existed," Holly exclaimed. "Even when I saw it in movies, I always thought that right on the other side of the camera was probably a town or a highway full of cars or a railroad. But it's really real!"

Raf made the ride doubly enjoyable by pointing out things Holly would never have seen for herself or, if she had seen them, wouldn't have known what they were. As they rode through a scattered patch of arresting white flowers on slender wiry stems, he said, "Sego lilies. The Indians and the pioneers ate the bulbs when they had nothing better. The Mormons were grateful enough to make it the state flower of Utah."

He pointed out a trio of pronghorn antelope. Once Holly spotted them, the shining white and light brown of their coats stood out clearly against the green hillside.

They talked easily, with long silences between. Holly was busy trying to absorb everything—the thrill of riding with Raf, of being taken to his ranch; the simple pleasure of riding a horse, listening to the creaking leather, the steady clip-clop; living in the sheer perfection of the moment.

"The ranch house is in a cottonwood grove, too," Raf told her. "My French ancestor chose the spot years ago. It's a nuisance. Cottonwoods are forever getting struck by lightning. The house even burned down some years ago, but do you think my father would rebuild anywhere else? No. The new house went back on the old foundation. Now it's a so-called ranch-house style, which the old one wasn't."

"What was it?"

"A two-story frame house. Like the banker's in Rapid City."

"Do your parents like the new one?"

"Dad didn't live to see it finished."

"I'm sorry," Holly said quickly.

Raf said, "It's been ten years. My mother didn't want to stay after dad died. She lives with my sister in California."

Ten years! Had he lived alone in his new ranch house for ten years? She glanced sideways at him. His tawny eyes were fixed on a point in the distance."

"Yes, I live in the house alone," he said moodily.

"You don't sound very happy about it." She

spoke lightly to break the solemnity—and because she felt obscurely pleased.

He snorted. "I was thinking about something else. See those birds circling up there?"

"Yes. Are they eagles?"

"Turkey vultures."

"Ugh!" Holly shivered without meaning to.

"They have a purpose in the world. What bothers me is that their purpose right now is one of my cows. I found her this morning. Can't figure out what killed her." His frowning eyes were directed between his horse's ears.

"What will you do?"

"My foreman's supposed to have a look. He knows more than most vets I've met."

He had adroitly switched the subject, whether because he didn't want to talk about personal things or because he preferred living in the present, Holly had no way of knowing.

The ranch, to Holly's startled view, might have come straight off the TV screen or out of *Better Homes and Gardens*. The natural wood of the house was stained dark brown. It was shaded by a few tremendous old cottonwoods, interspersed by smaller ornamental trees that curtained part of the sprawling dwelling from sight. The lawn was green and smooth, the surrounding rail fence newly painted white. The horses, knowing their way, turned into the drive, and Holly was treated to an unexpected view of a riot of hollyhocks—pink, white, red, wine red—lining both sides of the drive.

"How beautiful!" she exclaimed as the horses

moved briskly between the two rows. "Who planted them?"

"My mother. She thought small flowers were a waste of time."

Holly caught a reminiscent gleam in his eyes and for an instant was able to imagine him as a small boy, dark, golden-eyed, his movements probably as controlled then as now, his face as solemn and expressionless. Had his mother known what emotions were locked behind that blank exterior? Perhaps not. She hadn't managed to help him unlock himself to the point of his being able to share his life with someone else; that was obvious.

The ranch house was separated from the rest of the buildings by a double row of bushes and small trees. On the working side of the hedge everything was equally neat. The drive ended in a circle at the dooryards of three frame cottages painted red with white trim. The corral beside the biggest barn held two horses. One whickered, and Brown Betty gave an answering neigh. Both mounts halted at the corral gate.

"Wait and I'll help you down," Raf said. "You may find you're stiff if you haven't ridden lately."

Holly had no intention of dismounting by herself. For the last half of the ride she had been thinking longingly of the swim Raf had promised.

"Take your foot out of the stirrup and put your hands on my shoulders," he directed.

She did so, thrilling at the contact of her palms with the hard muscles of his shoulders. His strong long-fingered hands clasped her waist. In one fluid motion he swung her free of the saddle. He released her as she felt the ground under her feet.

A black-haired youth appeared from the barn. He stared at Holly from under the slouched brim of his hat. Raf handed him the reins. "Thanks, Junior," he said, and to Holly, "Ready for that swim?"

"Very much," she admitted, removing her hat to let the breeze blow through her damp curls.

The pool was in the ell formed by the house, its blue-tiled depths looking infinitely inviting.

Raf showed her into a luxurious cabana at one end. He paused before leaving her. "I'll ask Mrs. Jones to put our clothes through the washer and dryer while we swim. That way we won't smell of horses at dinner." He disappeared—presumably to change into trunks and inform the housekeeper of their arrival.

Holly stripped and changed with the speed learned from modeling, with the result that she had swum the length of the pool and back before Raf appeared, bearing tall drinks.

"You were in a hurry," he remarked, setting the glasses on a poolside table.

"Yes." Holly clung to the edge of the pool, furtively assessing the man before her while pretending to wring the water out of her hair. White trunks emphasized the coppery brown of his skin. His lean appearance on horseback was deceptive. She had forgotten how broad-chested he was when seen at the powwow. The muscles of his bared torso rippled in the sun, his chest lightly powdered with black hair growing toward a center line, a little black path leading down into his trunks. His long legs looked hard and masculinely beautiful.

"Come out and drink this before the ice melts," he called.

Climbing the ladder at the end of the pool, Holly knew a moment of doubt, despite the fact she had every reason to be self-confident about her figure. How pale her skin looked! Those two afternoons by the pool in Rapid City hadn't tanned her a bit. Why had she ever chosen a pale green bikini?

"Towel?" he asked when she came dripping up to him. He handed her a thick brown square the size of a small rug.

She resisted the urge to wrap it about herself. Instead she dropped into the lounge chair and threw him a quick shy glance. "It's a perfect pool!" she enthused.

A spark in his tawny eyes made her feel he liked what he saw, even if her skin was too white.

"Feel free to use it anytime. I'll invite the others, too, when I meet them."

The others! Holly was horrified at her reaction. She felt miffed, possessive. She wanted him all to herself. How foolish of her! Foolish and selfish.

They swam and lounged, talking lazily about nothing. The exercise in the cool water, the gentle warming of the sun's last rays, were the perfect treatment for overworked muscles.

By the time Holly had stripped off her bikini and climbed back into magically fresh clothes, she felt marvelous—relaxed yet strong and supple. She smiled into the mirror. Brother Bill hadn't envisioned this when he'd insisted she needed a change of scenery. The dressing room was even furnished with a hair dryer. Using it, Holly wondered whom it had been provided for. Did Raf often invite girls to swim? When did he run his ranch? Or was that the foreman's job? Raf didn't give the impression of being a playboy. Maybe the foreman's wife swam here, or neighbors and friends. It wouldn't be hard to find willing visitors. Look how eagerly she'd accepted the invitation.

Deftly she coaxed her hair into flyaway curls that made her look ultrafeminine, despite jeans and plaid shirt. Raf's eyes, when she met him on the patio, told her she'd succeeded, though all he said was, "Sherry?" and turned to the portable bar.

They had barely settled down, when a dark heavyset man in dusty jeans appeared.

"Miss Cameron," Raf said, "this is my foreman, Joe Old Elk. Joe, Miss Cameron. She's with the team of fossil hunters the professor's bringing out this year."

The man nodded, as unsmiling as Raf.

"Beer, Joe? Excuse me a minute, Holly, while I talk ranch business."

From their detailed discussion Holly gathered that Raf was indeed a working rancher who had taken an afternoon off—a rare afternoon, she wanted to believe.

The men covered a surprising variety of topics: calves in the south corral, a bunch going to market; hay ready to be cut on the west forty; the probable reason for the death of the cow Raf had mentioned; the condition of some horses; the breakdown of a tractor; gossip about a neighbor. Holly had finished her sherry by the time Joe Old Elk left.

"Day-to-day problems of a ranch," Raf said. He was about to refill her glass when Mrs. Jones appeared to announce dinner was ready.

They entered the house by a sliding glass door that opened onto a breakfast room. The round table was set for two with an elegance that contrasted strangely with blue jeans and cowboy boots, until Holly remembered that Gary, the TV man, had said, "One of the biggest ranchers," and the room fell into place around Raf. He had, she realized, the ability to make his surroundings drop into the background, no matter where he was.

Dinner consisted of steak, baked potato and a salad. It was exactly what she'd been invited for—a home-cooked meal at a ranch house. Wine was the exception. Raf filled crystal glasses with a superior vintage.

"Did you say a French ancestor chose this place?" she inquired, beginning on her salad. "Do you mean your family has always lived here?"

"My French ancestor was a comparative latecomer." Raf cut his steak with swift strokes. "His wife's family had been here for generations." His tawny eyes watched her from under black eyebrows like wings.

"You mean...." A smile radiated across her face as she understood. "She was an Indian...a Sioux! That's why you were at that dance."

"That's right." His eyes studied her over his wineglass.

"You must be very proud."

He shrugged, but she read a flicker of pleasure in his eyes. *I'm beginning to know what he's feeling,* she thought. He's not expressionless; he's just unusually subtle.

"My mother is part Dakota, too," he said. "And my grandmother."

For an instant Holly regretted her pale skin. Shoving the thought aside, she asked, "What brought the Frenchman here?"

"Beaver. Trappers were the first white men to come. They used the Missouri River and its tributaries as a highway. A lot of them settled down with Indian wives. My ancestor's son homesteaded this place—my great-grandfather Jacques. Something about the Badlands fascinated him. There were still fossils lying about. The firstcomers gathered them in wagonloads. Jacques worked as a guide for some of the early scientific expeditions. He spent more time gathering fossils than he did farming. They couldn't farm much in those days without wells, but there were homesteaders all over the place after the railroad was built. It was my grandfather and my father who made this place into a ranch. My grandfather realized before a lot of other people that this land is no good for farming."

"I can't wait to see the Badlands," Holly said.

"You haven't seen them?" He sounded as though she'd been remiss.

She shook her head. "I'm waiting till the others arrive. I thought we were camping in them, but I guess not."

Raf's eyes squinted in what might be a smile.

"You're camped closer than you think. You're on the up side of the Badlands wall. The plains have eroded into mountains in reverse. On this side of the wall you can be riding along on what appears to be a long stretch of rising plain and suddenly come onto a world of pyramids and ridges and steep-walled canyons right below your feet. Some people find this country grotesque, but for me—and Professor Gray, I suspect—it's a fascinating place."

Holly was a little surprised to hear him talk so imaginatively. Was it his Indian blood that gave him a love for this strange cream-colored land?

As though he regretted speaking of his feelings, he changed the subject.

"Have you always lived in New York City?"

Holly told him about the small community on Long Island. "Almost everybody was of Finnish or Swedish descent. My father was the high-school principal. He and my mother were killed when the new stadium collapsed. My brother had just started college. I was beginning to get some modeling jobs, so we sold the house and moved to an apartment near the school."

"Why not near your modeling jobs?"

She smiled and shrugged. "They might be anywhere."

"Even South Dakota," he agreed.

For some reason his words made her feel she didn't belong anywhere. "Tell me more about the Badlands," she said resolutely. "What made them?"

"Rivers rushing down from the Black Hills, they say. They spread mud and gravel and sand across the flatlands and built up a floodplain. Then the climate changed, and erosion began. The torrential rains we have are followed by weeks of hot weather. The eroded shapes dry and bake.

"While the marshy plain was still being deposited by rivers that no longer exist—millions of years ago, you understand—" Holly nodded eagerly "—the grass was plentiful. The animals that evolved were grazing animals, except for the saber-toothed cats and a kind of wolf. Over millions of years their bones sank into the mud and became fossils. When the climate changed, the land began eroding instead of continuing to build up. The Badlands are essentially a belt of erosion about fifty miles wide. The pinnacles are bare, but there are acres of flat tableland, too. The grass forms thick roots that resist erosion, except for the bare sides. Of course, eventually the tablelands erode into bare peaks or mounds. There's a road up Buffalo Table and others in Pine Ridge."

"The reservation?"

Raf nodded. "There are back roads in the park, too, but the rangers don't encourage tourists to explore there."

"Why not?"

Raf shrugged. "An incident a few years ago—nothing serious."

Clearly he wasn't going to elaborate.

"Did your great-grandfather keep any fossils for himself?" Holly asked over dessert—again Mrs. Jones's pudding cake.

"I'll show you when we've finished."

By the time she had laid down her fork and swallowed the last of the coffee, darkness had gathered in the room. Raf led her into a carpeted hallway and through another door into a big comfortable living room that overlooked an expanse of lawn and the hollyhocks lining the drive.

"Nobody wants privacy out here," he commented. "We want to see who's coming." He flipped a switch. On either side of the big fireplace concealed lighting lit up a wall of glass shelves. On the shelves was a collection of what was unmistakably turtle shells, ranging from specimens three feet long to others the size of an English walnut.

"He had a passion to collect," Raf said.

Holly went to stand in front of the shelves. Raf followed her; she could feel his breath on her hair.

"What's the difference between fossils and plain turtle shells?" she asked, striving to speak naturally.

"Your brother could tell you better than I can about the various ways fossils are formed. These, I've been told, are replacements. The chemicals that originally made up the shells have been replaced by other chemicals—those that make up stone."

He opened a sliding glass door and took out a turtle shell the size of her fist and let her feel the weight of it.

"Great-grandpa also collected ancient animal skulls. He was a shrewd man. He kept records of where he found every skull. Perhaps he learned that from the scientific parties he guided. The Badlands weren't made a park until 1939. When my grandfather took over this place, he sold the skulls through the years and added land to the ranch."

"What a wonderful story!" Holly enthused.

Raf was looking at her in a way that made her heart thump. His eyes were in shadow, but the firm line of his lips was caught like well-lighted sculpture. Nervously she crossed the room to stand before the window. The hollyhocks had faded to a uniform gray. From the direction of the stables came a long whinny.

"It's getting dark," she said foolishly.

"Yes, I'd better get you back to camp. Shall I drive you, or do you feel like riding?"

"Alone?" Against her intention her voice quavered.

"Not alone! Do you think you could find your way alone?" He laughed down at her—actually laughed!

"I—I'd like to ride." It would mean spending more time with him. "If you don't mind riding back again. . . ." She gulped, feeling the color rise in her cheeks, and despised herself for not handling the conversation better. That wasn't the right thing to say! But surely he didn't plan to spend another night in the tent, now that she had the trailer and could lock herself in.

"Then we'll ride," he said briskly. "Come with me while I saddle up."

"I'd like to learn how," she said, happy that he hadn't seemed to notice any innuendos in her clumsy remark about his riding back.

The horse he was riding and Brown Betty had been put in the barn. While Raf was saddling Holly's mount, the youth appeared and wordlessly began saddling Raf's bay.

"This is Junior, my foreman's son," Raf said. "Junior, this is Miss Cameron. She's going to be cooking for the professor's team over by Buffalo Table."

Under Holly's smiling hello the boy's eyes shifted. Was he shy or down on females?

To the music of creaking leather and jangling bits they trotted down the drive and turned south. The sun had disappeared behind the straight line of the horizon, but a wisp of pink cloud still reflected light.

Riding across the prairie at night was eerie. It never really grew dark. The world was a huge flat saucer, and she and Raf were at the center of it. A glow emanated from the edges. Overhead innumerable stars were a silent reminder of infinity. The thought of the millions of years it had taken to change a little dog-sized creature into a horse, of the myriad days and nights this prairie had lain under rain and snow, was too awesome to put into words.

The night breeze fanning Holly's cheeks brought a scent of green growing things. How unimportant was one human being twenty-two years old! And yet.... She *was* important. She sighed.

Raf said, "Vast, isn't it?"

"It certainly is," she agreed. "People can't say this part of the United States is overpopulated. I haven't even seen cows. I thought this was grazing land."

"It takes a lot of land to support one cow out here. You'll see them."

"How can you tell where we're going?" she asked, suddenly worried. It would be easy to get lost out here at night.

"I'm keeping an eye on the North Star."

Holly's curved lips flew open. "You're joking!" she exclaimed.

"No, I'm not. See the Big Dipper there? See that

star above it—the North Star? I'm keeping that behind us."

For some reason Raf's explanation made her spirits rise. It made her feel less insignificant, as though the North Star had been put there purposely in the midst of this vast nothingness to guide the generations of mankind.

They had been riding for perhaps half an hour when she noticed a glow beyond the straight line of the eastern horizon. She called it to Raf's attention.

"What do you think it is?" he asked. His amused tone put her on her mettle.

"A town?" she suggested after discarding other possibilities such as a baseball field or a prairie fire.

"You'll see in a minute."

A gleam of orange crept above the horizon, then more.

"The moon!" she laughed. "Of course!"

As it climbed, it bathed the prairie in unearthly light. Holly wished she were a coyote, wished she could run through the grass and howl at the round orange disk. She would have liked to urge Brown Betty to a run, but Raf didn't suggest it. Probably it wasn't safe to gallop across the prairie at night.

Not another light was to be seen. They might have been in the mid-Atlantic.

Unexpectedly Holly yawned.

"The hour or the company?" Raf inquired.

"Neither. I'm sorry."

"We're about there."

"How can you tell?"

"I see fence posts. That's the road."

No wonder he was fearless riding across the prairie

at night. He had landmarks, as well as the North Star. Encouraged by his fearlessness, Holly saw no reason she couldn't handle this cooking-camping job.

The lantern beckoned them for the last half mile. When they rode in, it was sitting on the table as Raf had left it. The camp was unchanged.

Raf dismounted. Coming around to Holly, he raised his arms. Strong hands encompassed her waist, and she felt featherlight as he swung her down. But this time her booted toes barely touched the ground before he pulled her against his hard warm chest. His hands, still at her waist, gripped her ribs in a viselike hold that sent the air whooshing from her lungs. She could scarcely draw her breath before his lips came down on her mouth. The quick smoothness of his motions took her by surprise. She wasn't sure whether she welcomed this behavior. Her hat slipped from her head and plopped in the dust.

How silent he was—and how intense! Before she could protest, he had locked her in his arms and she was being kissed hungrily, her lips pressed back gainst her teeth. He hadn't kissed that way at Fox Butte. He'd been sensual and persuasive.

Exerting all her strength, she pushed him away and glared up into his face, well aware that, despite three tents and a trailer, they were still the only two human beings within miles. Her mind fought against a tangle of emotions to find something to say. A little niggling whisper in her brain said, *maybe he's more man than you know how to handle.*

Stumblingly she muttered, "They—they kiss different in South Dakota, I guess."

"Perhaps I'm a little rusty," Raf offered, stooping to pick up her hat.

"You weren't rusty at Fox Butte!" Holly shot back, then wished she hadn't.

He said, "Let's start again, shall we? You can't expect a lonely cowboy to get his hands on you and then let go."

Brown Betty stamped an impatient hoof.

"Easy, girl," Raf soothed her. He led Holly out from between the two animals to the door of the trailer.

"Let's get something straight," he began. "I *am* a little rusty. Ranch work in the spring doesn't allow time for gallivanting. What do you want me to do, say, 'Please, Miss Cameron, may I kiss you?'"

"I—I don't want you to do anything," Holly stammered, digging her boot toe into the dust.

"Too late for that," he answered humorously. "You've already made me realize I'm out of practice, and since you're the only handy object...."

She felt strong fingers clasp her jaw as he tilted her face to his. His mouth met hers gently this time, teasingly, nibbling her lips, tickling and then his lips pressed firmly, coolly. That very coolness sent warmth zinging through her veins. His arms, though they were holding her gently, were like steel bands. She had never been embraced by a man with such hard muscles. He could easily be rough without meaning to be.

It was heady; it was what she wanted. Yet it was scary. Her blood raced. How far would he want to go? She might already have overstepped the bounds of safety in encouraging this man.

He held her in the circle of one arm, his fingers easily cupping the soft rise of her breast. His other hand began a slow exploration of the curve of her hip, then moved. She next felt work-roughened fingers against the silken skin of her neck. His touch sent little electric shocks to her brain, numbing it, so that all her awareness was centered on the pressure of his lips and the touch of his fingers moving downward from neck to collarbone to the flesh beneath her blouse.

She tried to control her breathing. He mustn't know how she adored his touch. He was sure enough, practiced enough, now. His lips strayed over her face as he whispered, "Pretty woman...pretty woman."

Her teeth locked to keep from moaning, she ground out, "I have a name!"

"Pretty Holly Cameron," he breathed into her ear. "Pretty little city girl."

It was seldom anyone called her "little," and for some reason being called a city girl reassured her. He wasn't going to overpower her and drag her into the trailer. Suddenly she trusted him again. Her arms had lain lightly on his shoulders. Now she responded, pulling herself against his broad chest. How big he was—and he looked so deceptively slim!

Pulling herself against him left no room for those stroking fingers to glide inside her blouse—not for the first moment. But then his tongue slipped into her parted mouth, and he turned her body a little away from him. His right hand stroked her neck once more, and then the fingers were deftly undoing the top button and then the next. Her senses reeled under the excitement of his mouth. His fingers bared her breast, lifted it free of her bra. She gloried in the thought of warm living flesh—her breast, his fingers. Her nipple hardened under the teasing touch of his forefinger. A shiver beginning at the nipple sped down and down, across her belly, down the insides of her legs to her knees, weakening them.

Somewhere in a corner of her brain she knew it was time to tell him to stop. Long past time! She had never let a man arouse her to the point where she didn't want to say no. She had been careful about whom she went out with. Models who let themselves be pawed soon lost the fresh and dewy look photographers wanted. Or so she'd been told.

She broke away from his kiss, panting. "No, please!" she cried.

"Sure?"

"Yes!" she answered fervently. She had always avoided macho men. Now she knew why. They were as dangerous as she had feared.

Reluctantly he took his hand from her breast, cupping instead her soft jaw, his thumb exploring her full lower lip. He bent his head to put his ear to the skin above her bared breast.

"What a thudding heart! Fright or passion?"

"Fright," she whispered, telling only half the truth.

"All right. Time for good little girls to be in bed." He patted her on the fanny and turned away. "Wait a minute, I'll bring you the lantern.

"Don't forget to lock your door," he said when he handed her the light. "Tell the professor I'll send over some horses and a wrangler. Maybe Junior. Somebody young and nonfrightening."

Holly's heart sank at his sarcastic tone.

"Good night," she whispered, dazed but relieved.

Inside, the trailer was like an oven. By the time Holly figured out how to open the windows, her stomach had clenched itself into a ball of misery. A more sophisticated woman, she thought, would have handled him better. Leona Selby probably knew right where to draw the line—if she drew one!

Well, now she knew. She'd avoided macho men with good reason. She was lucky he stopped when she asked him. Probably he'd never have anything more to do with her, but at least she hadn't made a fool of herself, hadn't been swept away, hadn't done something she'd regret. . . .

CHAPTER SEVEN

AT THE AIRPORT the following afternoon, Holly awaited the arrival of her brother and the others with eagerness and some trepidation. Today her summer was beginning: three meals a day, seven days a week, sink or swim.

She had picked up her snapshots but had waited to look at them in peace and comfort. Holding her breath, she pulled the slightly curved stack from the yellow envelope.

The pictures of Raf were right on top—and they were good! Her fingers trembled as she riffled through them. Well, pretty good. In the first one she had caught him almost in the center of the picture—except for cutting off the top of his head. The second one was blurred—he was too close. The third must have been snapped when he'd come around again. He was looking straight at the camera. It was terrific! The hawklike nose, the high cheekbones, the flying black hair...a striking shot. Light glinted on his bronzed shoulders, highlighting bulging muscles.

Her heart swelled with joy. She had captured his likeness! However the next weeks turned out, she had this.

The other pictures were okay, nice, successful enough for her to want to take more. She slid the pictures into her bag and examined the camera she had just purchased at the recommendation of the photo-shop clerk. She would photograph Bill and fossils. Even if she never saw Raf again, she had one good picture of him looking like an Indian. Of course, he was only part Indian. He was also a rancher—an or-dinary rancher and yet so special. How wonderful he had looked that afternoon she had spotted him riding toward camp, the tall grass hiding the horses' hocks—a solitary rider, dark against a sky full of puffy white clouds, somehow symbolic of the prairie.

The plane from the east swooped onto the landing strip and taxied up to the windswept space beneath the window where Holly waited. At the entrance gate she saw Dr. Gray's shock of black hair first and then behind him, Bill's red blond head.

Laughing, she stood waiting for Bill to spot her. She had donned her Western wear: hat, boots, jeans, shirt and belt. Under the straw hat her red gold hair hung down her back like a silken waterfall. Bill's eyes swept past her, circled the straggling crowd and re-turned. His eyes widened. Grinning, he enveloped her in a brotherly hug, saying as he did so, "You look like a rodeo star!"

Dr. Gray claimed her next, shaking her hand and inquiring whether the camp was ready. He called the rest of the team and presented them: Dr. Young, a man in his thirties who would be Dr. Gray's assis-tant; the three graduate students, Marcia Steinberg, Wayne Taylor, Willie Yu. Holly and Marcia ex-changed polite smiles. They would be tentmates for the next ten weeks.

Marcia was Holly's age. She was small and unfortunately dumpy. Her straight dark hair was parted in the middle and fastened at the base of her neck with a no-nonsense metal barrette. She wore no makeup, but her dark-lashed brown eyes hardly needed intensifying. They appeared to miss nothing. Holly concluded that she must be very bright and felt somewhat intimidated. The girl was overweight. Physical labor for a summer would improve her figure.

Willie Yu was probably Chinese-American, but by now Holly had seen enough Sioux to notice the similarity of his black hair and high cheekbones to theirs.

Wayne Taylor, the last student, leered at her. He had fine even teeth that had obviously worn braces. He struck her as a self-assured young man who would be critical of everything.

A casually dressed man wearing thick glasses approached the group, saying quietly, "Dr. Gray."

"Pete!" Dr. Gray exclaimed. "So you made it. I really appreciate your taking the trouble."

The man Pete was introduced as somebody important at the School of Mines. He took the two professors, Marcia and Wayne Taylor in his car, leaving Holly, Bill and Willie Yu to lead the way in the jeep.

"I didn't know you could drive a manual shift," was Bill's first comment.

"Just learned," Holly said, her eyes hunting for the exit from the airport. Coping with traffic was not one of the things she missed about civilization.

"How was Fox Butte?" Bill asked. "Do you like it out here?"

"Oh, yes! You'll love it! Wait till you see the camp. It's in a grove of cottonwood trees, only there's no water. I mean, the water in the creek is white; the mud doesn't settle.'' She described the camp and the powwow, but made no mention of Raf Valcour, much as she longed to talk about him.

At the camp Holly realized her days of leisure were over. While the others unpacked and relaxed after their flight, she was cooking dinner. Mr. Judson had thoughtfully provided her with a large pressure cooker, and she had studied the book that came with it. She was cooking a roast in it, with potatoes, carrots and onions enough for seven, without dirtying any other pans. Its short cooking time allowed a minimum use of gas and didn't heat up the kitchen.

After the briefest of happy hours, Pete drove away. Thanks to the time difference, everyone was ready for dinner. Holly set the table and made a salad—mostly of canned vegetables. The main course was a success, and nobody turned down the chocolate cake she had bought.

By the time Holly had washed the dishes, it was dark. Not even Bill offered to help. *Not that I needed help,* she said to herself, *but I'd have been glad of company.*

Outside someone had built a fire. ''Keeping away the mosquitoes,'' Dr. Young said with a smile when she joined the group still sitting at the table.

Dr. Young might have been Dr. Gray's son, they looked so much alike. Holly wondered if gangling bony men were attracted to the science because it involved holding bones together. His hair was black, too, his eyes a pale blue behind aviator lenses.

Holly felt like the hostess of a party that had gone on too long. When she thought of everything she had to do before breakfast, she quailed, said good-night and made for her tent.

Marcia was already there, stretched on her cot and wearing striped utilitarian pajamas. She was reading a heavy tome by the light of her own battery lamp.

"Is this your first time out here?" Holly questioned.

"Yes. I wish I knew more about what I'll be doing," the other girl worried.

"I thought graduate students knew it all almost," Holly said, surprise in her voice.

"You never know it all," Marcia muttered.

Holly put her down as one of those girls who get straight A's and still study all night before finals, afraid of flunking.

The evening was warm. Holly slipped into the long T-shirt she wore to sleep in and lay on top of her sleeping bag, too tired to worry about breakfast but not too tired to look at Raf's pictures again by flashlight.

Remembering her first night in camp, she murmured before sleep claimed her, "If you hear howling, it's coyotes."

"WE'RE GOING TO NEED two jeeps," Dr. Gray said next morning. However, after breakfast they decided they could make do with one. They left the camp with Dr. Young driving, Dr. Gray beside him and the four students perched in back. They were off to take an overall look at the Badlands.

"This isn't much fun for you, Holly." Dr. Young's pale eyes peered concernedly into hers. "I don't feel right about leaving you to wash dishes while we go off for a day of pleasure.''

Being jammed into the back of a bouncing jeep didn't exactly constitute pleasure in Holly's mind, but it would be more fun than being left alone to do dishes and fix lunch. Nevertheless she said cheerfully, "That's all right. This is my job.''

"You deserve at least to know what we're doing.''

A born teacher, Holly thought. *He's compelled to impart his knowledge.*

As if echoing her thoughts, he added, "The first chance I get, I'll take you on a tour of the park. I understand you haven't seen it yet, either.''

Holly was making sandwiches for lunch when a pickup arrived from the store in Vista, bringing a barrel of water, a block of ice and three days' supply of frozen meat.

At noon the fossil hunters returned. They had located four specimens weathered out of the baked mud in a nearby ravine. Holly understood from their talk that these particular fossils were being collected for practice. After lunch they drove off again with bags of tools and preserving equipment.

Holly washed plates and glasses and made tapioca to serve over canned peaches. Then, with three free hours before it would be time to start dinner, she changed into her bikini and spread her sleeping bag in the sun. Stretched on her back, she lay listening to the hum of insects. For a while she watched the white streak of a jet stream, barely able to see the flyspeck that was the plane. Near at hand a meadowlark sang, apparently for its own pleasure. When would Raf bring the horses? She hadn't given Dr. Gray his message, partly because she hadn't had a chance and partly because she didn't want to explain how she'd met Raf.

The pressure cooker was steaming away over meatballs with tomato-soup gravy when the fossil team returned late in the afternoon, hot, tired and dusty. They quickly lined up for an improvised shower, the water for which had been warming all day in the sun. Holly no longer envied them their intellectual pursuits. Staying behind to cook had its advantages.

"Look at this, Holly!" Bill exhibited the fossil he'd found. "I spotted it right there in the clay, half weathered out, but that mud is so hard, you wouldn't believe it. That's what it is—baked mud. It's worse than stone; it's rough and crumbling. You try to walk up a slope, and it's like walking on BB shot. But look at this!" He was holding a chunk of baked mud the size of a football. Half exposed was a fragment of bone from which shiny brown stumps protruded.

"Are those teeth?" Holly asked.

Bill nodded proudly.

The chunk was the color of the fossils Holly had seen at the museum, the color of much of the earth of this queer country. She stopped grating carrots to inspect it, tapping it with her fingernail. It felt like stone.

"Do you know what it is?" she asked finally.

"Probably a jawbone from an oreodont. They're common here. I have to check it out. But this was just practice today—learning how to cut fossils out of clay. We each got one to work on. I want to get the matrix off before dark—that's the rock or clay surrounding the bone. You have to keep hardening the

exposed bone with coats of preservative as you un-
cover it. Then it gets covered with wet tissue paper so
the plaster won't stick, then covered with plaster for
shipping."

Bill's enthusiasm made Holly's heart lift. The burn
on her hand and two broken fingernails were worth
the sacrifice. She noted with concern that his neck
had turned an ominous pink.

"Looks as if you got some sun, as well."

"I sure did! It must have been a hundred and twenty degrees on that bare hillside. I probably shouldn't
have taken my shirt off, but I did."

"No, you shouldn't have," she scolded, "and you
should have used suntan lotion and a hat. Couldn't
you find a shady place?"

"Yeah, but there weren't any fossils there," he
laughed. "Today was nothing. If we find anything
big, we'll be working like convicts."

"How do they know where to dig?" Holly puzzled.

"I learned today; we don't dig till we find a fossil.
We're here to scramble up all these practically inac-
cessible gullies and hillsides, looking for fossils
weathering out of the rock. A rain or a windstorm
may reveal bones that weren't visible the previous
day. But the professors aren't gathering just any old
bone. They're looking for something special. I guess
they'll know it when they see it."

He broke off, hearing his name called. "My turn
for the shower! I'll leave this here. I have to work on
it; try to free it."

"How?"

"That's the next lesson." He ducked through the
door.

When the meal was ready, Holly emerged from the trailer's kitchen to find Dr. Gray pouring sherry to celebrate the happy hour. None of the four students was interested in celebrating. They were busily engaged at one of the worktables, freeing their fossils from the mudstone surrounding them using tools that looked like dental picks. Holly got out her camera and took pictures.

Then Dr. Young called her to join him and Dr. Gray while the students finished their homework.

"Holly deserves a tour of the park," Dr. Young announced, eyeing her warmly from behind his glasses. "I could take her for a drive after supper."

Holly waited for Dr. Gray to object to the unnecessary use of gasoline. When he didn't, she shook her head regretfully. "Could I take a rain check? It's been a long day."

She had been hoping all day that Raf would come this evening to renew his acquaintance with Dr. Gray and offer him the horses.

"Certainly. The offer's open." Dr. Young lifted his drink to her. His eyes behind his glasses gleamed with eagerness.

Given the least encouragement—or perhaps without encouragement—Dr. Young would fancy himself in love with her. She hadn't heard whether he was married. He was the kind of man she liked—gentle, thoughtful, a little humble, very intelligent. Instead she had gone and got her emotions entangled with a man as unknown to her as these windswept plains.

The evening passed, and Raf didn't appear. After the way last night had ended, he was probably through with her. Or he might be showing her she shouldn't take him seriously. Or perhaps he himself was reluctant to carry things further. He'd said he intended to offer the group the use of his pool, and he'd promised horses and a wrangler. That meant he'd come around sooner or later.

She went to bed congratulating herself that she had got through the first full day of cooking without disaster. That was what mattered.

Next day, Dr. Gray and the team went to Buffalo Table to begin hunting seriously.

"He wants to find titanothere bones," Dr. Young told Holly as he hovered about at breakfast time, offering help and getting in her way.

"Titanothere!" Happy to be a little knowledgeable on the subject, Holly said, "I saw one at the museum."

"You know, then, that they're the largest animals found here? They started out as dog-sized creatures and evolved into something like a rhinoceros. About thirty-two million years ago the climate changed, and they became extinct."

Holly thought, *Dr. Young sounds as if he's lecturing to a classroom of students, instead of stirring scrambled eggs.*

"Why is Dr. Gray particularly interested in titanotheres?" she asked, apprehensively eyeing the eggs. Dr. Young did seem capable of keeping them from sticking. He ran a pancake turner under them before he answered.

"He's made titanotheres his baby. He's probably the world authority on the subject."

Holly was impressed. "What will he do with them if he finds them?"

"If we find anything worthwhile, such as a whole skeleton, the school might sell it to a museum to help finance the expedition. Besides teaching the students how to do fieldwork, he'd like to find something out of the ordinary—like that oreodont skeleton with the unborn twins at the School of Mines, for example."

The eggs were done. Holly carried them outside. Everyone was in place; there was no need to ring the dinner bell fastened to a tree.

The day went the same as the previous one. Everybody except Holly piled into the jeep and bounced off across the grassland. Holly could only hope Dr. Young would use caution and not run the jeep over an unexpected cliff. Again they returned hot and exhausted from clambering over the steeply eroded haystacklike hills of the Chadron formation, which Bill explained was the layer containing the most fossils.

During the next couple of days Holly became accustomed to the routine. Mealtimes came around with alarming frequency, but her afternoons were free, though her choice of recreation was limited to reading or napping.

The team discovered a likely-looking jumble of fossil bones and began to work at removing them in one block. The exposed parts first had to be encased in plaster, and then the block, which Bill reported to be the size of the dining table, had to be cut out. They were using hammers, chisels and picks now, instead of dental instruments.

For Holly it meant she didn't have to serve lunch. They were taking sandwiches with them. She was therefore surprised the second morning when Dr.

Young, alone in the jeep, drove in before noon. He gave an exuberant toot on the horn.

"Get your hat!" he shouted. "I'm going to drive you through the park."

The prospect of getting away from camp to somewhere besides Vista was irresistible.

"I have to be back in time to start dinner," she reminded him as she climbed in.

"No problem," he declared. His eyes were hidden behind tinted glasses.

"Did you put them all to work and drive off?" she asked, half teasing.

"We're on a legitimate errand," he told her as the jeep bounced toward the road. "I have to drive down to headquarters at the other end of the park. We have a permit to collect, you know, but they want to know where we're working so that if someone reports people digging, they'll know it's us and not anybody illegal."

They bounced over the rutted road and continued northward through the rolling grassland. Flocks of black-and-white lark buntings flew up from the roadside. Then the ground fell away on Holly's right, and they were driving along the rim of a canyon. Holly caught her breath. It was just as Raf had said. On one side, grassland rolled to the horizon; on the other, miniature mountain ranges of bare clay stretched in a belt several miles wide, falling away to where the land lay once again flat, green, normal.

"This is it!" she exclaimed.

Dr. Young nodded as though at a particularly clever pupil.

The road continued along the rim of the canyon.

Holly was unable to keep from remarking every minute, "Look! Look at that!" as a wasteland of peaks unrolled. "Oh, why didn't I bring my camera!"

"This is the Badlands wall," Dr. Young explained. "It divides the upper grasslands from the lower ones you see way out there."

"Are you going to search all this for fossils?" Holly asked, stunned by the magnitude of the task. The fluted ridges rose steeply, looking impossible to climb, the narrow ravines impossible to walk through.

"Not these upper ridges. The Chadron layer is lower down. In some places the layers can be determined within a few inches. I could show you one place where you can put the heel of your hand on the interior layer—sediment that settled out of a sea— and the tips of your fingers on the Chadron—sediment washed down a million years later.

"But first there's something along here a little more lively." He pulled to the grassy roadside behind a small camper whose driver was hanging out of the window gazing at the prairie. Holly followed his gaze.

Out in the grass, a rodentlike animal was standing on its hind legs beside a hole in the ground. All around, the grass was dotted with bare mounds. A brown furry head and shoulders appeared at another hole.

"They must be prairie dogs!" Holly exclaimed with delight. She was familiar with their existence from stories of the West.

Scattered yips and puppylike barks sounded over

the whole area. From the corner of her eye she caught movement at another hole. Three half-grown youngsters were cavorting in the pale earth of their mound. An adult came toward them in a waddling scamper.

Dr. Young produced field glasses and handed them to Holly. She stared, fascinated, first at one fat short-legged little creature and then at another. "Oh, Dr. Young, they're darling!" she enthused.

"Dave," he corrected. "Call me Dave." He had removed his spectacles and was rubbing his eyes— gentle, considerate eyes, not like a certain person's.

"Okay, Dave," she said in a tone calculated to sound offhand. She turned back to the prairie dogs. They were such clean cuddly-looking animals, like large hamsters. The kits, as most young things, were adorable.

When they drove on, Holly gazed at the unfolding landscape, thinking. "I can't call you Dave," she said at last. "Surely you don't want your students calling you by your first name, and it will look very odd if I do and they can't."

"I suppose you're right," he agreed. "I've told them to call me Dr. Dave, but when you and I are alone...."

"I'll call you Dr. Dave, too," she said quickly, and resolved not to be alone with him any more than necessary. He was all right, but.... A vision of Raf rose before her eyes as he had looked at the pool—white trunks, strong muscular legs, copper-colored skin, his raven hair flat against his skull, his winged eyebrows rubbed into peaks.

The drive wound through formations whose shapes and color varied, yet remained essentially the same. The bare sloping sides were composed of colorful layers of different thicknesses. Overlooks all along the road provided places for tourists to stop and view the succession of hundreds of delicately colored saw-edged peaks. Imperceptibly the road descended until they were riding between the stark and fluted ridges.

"Isn't this a wonderful country!" Holly exclaimed, and a moment later, "Aren't you glad they made this a national park?"

"Doubly glad," Dr. Dave affirmed. "I'm glad for the ordinary tourist, and I'm glad the fossils are protected so that all the visitors here can see them weathering out of the clay if they're interested enough to look for them."

"Are fossils really that common?"

"In bits and pieces they are. Great numbers of animals lived here during the Oligocene Epoch, and the prairie was a vast subtropical marsh. The most common mammal throughout that time was the oreodont—something between a pig and a sheep. There were at least twenty-two species. One kind had claws. We believe great herds of them roamed these northern plains, but they have no living descendants. There were ancestors of the horse here and of camels and llamas. There was a giant pig the size of a cow and a saber-toothed tiger and three kinds of rhinoceroses. Then there was protoceras—an animal the size of a sheep, having a long narrow head with as many as five pairs of horns and knobs sticking out. Oh, and I mustn't forget hyaenodon—a wolflike beast the size of a black bear."

"And turtles crawling all over the place," Holly added, thinking of Raf's collection.

"Yes, indeed."

The road dropped until, as they neared the cluster of low buildings that housed the visitors' center and gift shop and restaurant, they were driving at the foot of towering peaks.

"I wanted to show you the buffalo herd," Dr. Dave told her, "but it's in Sage Creek Basin. We'll go there another day." He gave her a fond look that put her on guard. She wished Raf had suggested something like that.

At park headquarters, Holly joined a group of tourists watching a slide show about the Badlands. She also bought postcards.

I should have that picture of Raf at the powwow made into a postcard, she thought. But the idea of sharing him—even his picture—didn't appeal to her.

You're being totally foolish, she chided herself.

Driving back, the sun was in their eyes much of the time. The stricken land was just as awesome, but Holly had seen enough for one day; it was too much to comprehend.

"This is the same as visiting another planet," she told her companion. "I'll be glad to get back to earth."

When at last they pulled up at camp, Holly said, "Thank you, that was great! What an amazing place!"

"We'll do it again." He waved and sped off to fetch the team from their day's labor.

No wonder Raf's ancestors had been fascinated by

the Badlands, Holly thought, trying to imagine it without a paved road or tourists. Not that the people driving through made much impression on the essentially unbelievable scenery. Even if they got out and walked on it, they looked like people posed against a stage setting.

The meat Holly had left thawing was ready to go into the pressure cooker to become smothered steak. She set about peeling potatoes. A low budget, she'd learned, wouldn't support convenience food such as instant potatoes.

That evening she told her brother about her trip through the park. "Is Dr. Young married?" she asked.

"Interested?" Bill chucked her under the chin—a gesture that had annoyed her since childhood.

"No, but he seems interested in me, so I'd like to know whether he has any business playing around."

"You sound tough!" Bill's eyes looked at her with lazy amusement.

"I've learned to be."

Her brother's expression sobered. "Don't get tough! You're too sweet a kid. I hate the thought of some of the people you have to deal with in the modeling business. I wish you'd find a nice guy and marry him. Dr. Dave's a widower, I've heard."

"Thanks, but no, thanks," Holly said. *Nice guy,* she thought. Could Raf Valcour be classed as a nice guy? Somehow she didn't think so.

The following evening, spaghetti was cooking for dinner and Holly was enjoying a well-deserved glass of sherry with those of the weary team who had made themselves presentable when a flurry of hoofbeats drew everyone's attention. Two riders leading a string of five horses trotted into camp.

Raf! Holly's heart bumped against her ribs. He had come as promised. Her eyes flew to the other rider—Junior Old Elk. Was he to be the wrangler and help with the dishes? Had he actually consented to do women's work?

Raf dismounted. Removing his Stetson-style straw hat and nodding in Holly's direction, he shook hands with Dr. Gray. "How are you, sir?"

"Another year older, but happy to be here again," Dr. Gray replied cheerfully. He introduced Dr. Dave and would have introduced Holly, but Raf forestalled him.

"We've already met," he said. His expression was impassive, but his tawny eyes held a hint of mischief.

Dr. Gray shook his head, laughing. "You're a quick worker, my friend. Good to see you. Sit down. Where are you going with those horses?"

The unusual sounds had brought everyone out. Junior Old Elk dismounted on the far side of the camp and began making a rope corral around five well-placed trees.

"My contribution to science," Raf told the professors. "Same as last year. Why didn't you let me know you were coming?"

"Press of work. And I didn't want you to think I was begging." Dr. Gray handed Raf a glass of sherry. "Cheers. It's good to see you again."

Junior Old Elk came up and was introduced.

"I hope you and this young man are staying for dinner," Dr. Gray urged. "Holly, do you have enough to feed two more?"

"I'll just cook more spaghetti," she said, happy to have an excuse to disappear into the trailer and escape Dr. Dave's curious look. Why was he acting as though she belonged to him, as though he resented the intrusion of a more virile male?

The students gathered around the young Indian. They were thrilled at the idea of using horses for transportation. Besides the fun of it, the animals would save hours of plodding about on foot.

Holly added two table settings and brought out salad and meatballs. When she returned with the steaming spaghetti, Raf was seated at the far end of the table, with Dr. Dave beside him and Dr. Gray at the head. Holly took her place at the foot, where she could jump up and get anything missing.

What did Raf feel about her? His dark handsome face gave away nothing. When Dr. Gray wasn't talking, Dr. Dave and Willie Yu plied Raf with questions. Bill and Marcia directed their questions at Junior Old Elk. Holly listened and tried to keep from looking too often in Raf's direction. As far as she could tell, he never glanced at her. He did take a second helping of spaghetti and meatballs, though.

"That was delicious, Holly," Dr. Gray said, wiping his mouth with his napkin.

There was a chorus of agreement, and at last Holly caught Raf's eye. "Delicious," he echoed, his gaze fixing her with a look that melted her bones.

"And she isn't married," Dr. Gray pointed out. "What do you think of that?"

Holly didn't hear Raf's reply.

"You're blushing," Bill teased her in a low tone. "Where did you meet this guy?"

She didn't have to answer, because Dr. Gray was rapping his glass with a fork. "Mr. Valcour has not only brought us horses, he's inviting us to a Fourth of July cookout a week from Saturday. I think we'll be ready for a holiday by then, don't you?"

He received a chorus of agreement.

"He tells me there's going to be a rodeo in Vista and horse racing. After that we're all invited to a barbecue at his ranch."

During the excited questions that followed, Holly cleared the table and began washing the dishes, half grateful for the excuse to disappear. After the intimacies that had taken place between her and *Mr.* Valcour, she found herself simmering with resentment that he should treat her as a casual acquaintance. Well, now she knew. He had one thing in mind: sex, and he didn't believe in wasting time over courtesies. She sighed. Models had such crummy reputations. She was aware that people assumed models were stupid and lazy, unproductive and undependable. They seemed to think that no character or personality could lie behind a photogenic face.

By the time she emerged from the trailer, Raf and Junior had gone.

At least the Fourth of July celebration was something to look forward to, she thought, since she didn't have the others' goal of finding a titanothere bone.

CHAPTER EIGHT

JUNIOR OLD ELK TURNED UP every morning to bring the horses in from their corral and to saddle them for anyone who wanted to use them. Neither Willie Yu nor Marcia Steinberg had ridden previously, but with Junior's encouragement they learned to handle their mounts, and they put them to good use, traveling to and from the areas where they were working. Junior went with the horses. At night he returned home to the ranch, so he was never available to wash dishes or peel potatoes, but Holly didn't mind. With everybody but Dr. Gray out searching for fossils, major cooking was limited to breakfast and dinner. Between those meals she was free. She could help Dr. Gray clean a fossil or take Brown Betty on a solitary ride across the prairie or visit Buffalo Table, where Bill and the others were putting in long hours, freeing the worthwhile fossils they discovered from the baked crumbling clay.

By the end of the first week everyone was tired. Sunday was spent relaxing in the shade, talking about the work and writing letters. Holly planned the menus for the following week. She'd had no complaints so far—except at the dearth of fresh vegetables, which wasn't anything she could remedy. She had earned the team's thanks by taking the jeep to the decrepit laundromat in Vista and doing a mass laundry.

There seemed to be no chance of seeing Raf until the barbecue.

"What's your boss doing these days?" she asked the Indian youth, and received only a blank stare from obsidian eyes.

Later she heard him say to Willie Yu as they strolled past her tent, "That blond woman's no good for the boss."

"Are you kidding?" Willie's voice rose in scoffing disbelief. "That blond woman would be good for a man if he was dying."

Willie's remark soothed Holly's ego, but she puzzled over Junior's words. Why would he say a thing like that?

As the Fourth of July grew closer, the hardworking students, as well as Holly, began to look forward to the holiday.

"What if it rains?" Marcia worried.

"Never happens," Dr. Gray said. "You're in the country of long, hot, dry summers."

Sure enough, the morning of the Fourth dawned in a cloudless sky. The steady prairie wind promised to keep the day from becoming intolerably hot. Dr. Dave decided there was no reason not to spend the morning doing fieldwork as usual. The students groaned but went off to their assigned areas.

Excitement pervaded the noon meal. Even Wayne Taylor emerged from his usual bored cynicism. "What time is this shindig?" he asked.

"We can go as soon as everyone's ready," Dr. Dave said. "I think the rodeo starts about two o'clock."

"I still have to do the dishes," Holly reminded him. Whatever else happened tonight, thanks to Raf Valcour she wouldn't have to cook.

"I'll have to make two trips," Dr. Dave pointed out. "So I'll come back for you, Holly."

Holly sent a silent message to her brother, which he understood. "I'll wait for the second trip and help Holly with the dishes," Bill announced.

Dr. Dave frowned, but he could hardly object.

Dishes done, Holly put on the blue cowboy shirt and Western jeans she had bought in Rapid City. She had worn her beautiful boots often enough to feel comfortable in them. Her party dress had been hanging from the tent pole for two days to lose its wrinkles. She eyed it with anticipation. How brilliant of her to have bought it on the chance she'd be invited somewhere!

She brushed her hair until it shone. Making two small braids at her temples, she pinned them at the back of her head and let the rest of the red gold mass fall tumbling down her back. She applied more makeup than she had worn in days, noting how the wind had tanned her face and deepened the natural pink of her cheeks. All the time Raf's brown, strongly masculine face hovered in the back of her mind. How soon would she see him? Did he plan to attend the rodeo?

Hearing the jeep drive in, she put a finishing touch of mascara on her thick lashes, tilted the straw hat dashingly and left the tent, secure in the knowledge that she looked her best. On the way out she picked up her camera.

Dr. Dave unfolded himself from the driver's seat and set three cans of beer on the dining table.

"What a good-looking pair you are!" he said as Bill and Holly joined him. "Though I must say Holly's prettier."

"I hope so!" Bill laughed and pulled the tab on a beer can.

Holly said, "It's a little early for me...."

"I'll drink yours," Bill told her.

She sat up front, next to Dr. Dave, but her brother, leaning over the back of their seats, kept the conversation three-way.

Dr. Dave pulled the jeep into a field already filled with cars, pickups and horse trailers.

"Don't think I'm going to play guard dog all day," Bill muttered in Holly's ear as they made their way over dusty trampled weeds to the unpainted wooden stadium.

Holly gave him a saucy look. "I wouldn't want you to."

Of the group from New York, only the two professors had been to a rodeo previously. It began with a cowboy riding onto the field carrying the flag. He was joined by other riders as their names were announced over the loudspeaker. The spectators gave the Pledge of Allegiance, after which the riders circled the dusty trodden earth at a gallop and rode off the field.

Across the expanse of bare earth, men were milling about a row of six chutes, three on each side of the announcer's stand. The loudspeaker blared, "Event number one! Boys' cow riding!'' and the competition began. One at a time, little boys striving to keep their seats on bucking cows erupted from the chutes. Few lasted until the bell rang.

"Team roping!" the voice over the loudspeaker announced next. Holly watched, fascinated, while two cowboys burst from a gate behind a galloping calf. The first man aimed his rope for the calf's head. If he succeeded, the second cowboy tried to rope the calf's hind leg. It was a tough act; only two teams triumphed.

"You can see these people aren't star performers," Dr. Dave told Holly and Bill, "just local cowboys."

Holly had unavoidably ended up sitting beside him. They had found seats behind the rest of their group. How soon would she see Raf, she wondered.

The contestants seemed to be well known to the announcer. Shouts of encouragement were raised from time to time, but for the most part, the crowd was low-voiced and attentive. Surreptitiously Holly searched the stands, though somehow she couldn't imagine Raf as a spectator. She saw a girl selling programs and eagerly bought one. She ran her eye down the list of events and participants, noting the number of Indian names among them. Raf's name was not there.

"Who are you searching for?" Bill asked over her shoulder.

"Nobody," Holly replied airily. "Look, the next event's bareback bronc riding."

"No, it's not. They just announced a horse race."

Sure enough, a moment later horses and jockeys paraded before the stands. Bill bought a racing program. Holly almost snatched it from his hands. Three races were listed. Raf Valcour's name was on each list as owner of one of the entries. She searched the male figures coming and going about the corrals across the arena. He didn't seem to be there, either. Perhaps he was standing on the sidelines or placing a bet.

"Want to walk around a bit?" Bill asked. "We'll have a few minutes before the race."

Holly got to her feet eagerly. Maybe Raf was below. It was decent of her brother not to go off and leave her alone with Dr. Dave.

However, the people underneath the stands were teenagers, drinking soda pop and teasing one another. A line of men stood before the betting window, but Raf wasn't among them.

While Holly stood looking around, Bill disappeared. He materialized again holding two napkin-wrapped snacks.

"Here, forget your diet for once. Have one of these."

"That's what smells so good! What is it?"

"They're called Corn Dogs. I watched them being made—hot dogs dipped in cornmeal batter and deep fried."

She accepted one, holding it by the stick stuck lengthwise through the middle, and bit experimentally into the cornmeal crust. "Mmm!" She rolled her eyes. "Hot, but delicious."

They heard the loudspeaker announcing the race and moved out to stand behind a wire fence. Holly made a slow scrutiny of the stand. Raf wasn't there.

But someone else was: Leona Selby! Sitting alone.

Her heart in her throat, Holly nodded to her brother that she was going back to her seat. Had Leona come with Raf? If she was here, she must be invited to the barbecue. Holly's good spirits began to evaporate. Would Leona recognize her as one of the models she'd written up so unfairly? Holly considered pointing her out to Bill, who was following, but he wouldn't care. He didn't take her modeling career very seriously, even though her jobs paid most of the bills.

The race ended almost before it began. Holly tried to find Raf's number as the horses sped in front of the stands, but before she saw it, the jockeys were standing in their stirrups, reining in their mounts.

"Wasn't that an awfully short race?" she said brightly to Dave, determinedly turning her thoughts from Leona.

"This is quarter-horse racing," Dr. Dave replied. His pale blue eyes began to glow whenever he had a chance to give information. "These are working horses bred to make quick short dashes after cattle. At distances of up to four hundred and forty yards, they're the world's fastest. In colonial times they were called 'quarter-of-a-mile running horses.' They've had centuries of specialization for quick speed. All the horses here today in the other events are quarter horses, too, and so are the ones you've been riding."

If Holly heard the announcer correctly, Raf's horse had won.

"Look, it says Mr. Valcour owns these." She showed Bill the program for the pleasure of saying Raf's name.

Having seen Leona Selby, however, Holly was no longer much interested in finding Raf. If she found him, he'd be with Leona. Holly's anticipation of the barbecue took a sudden downturn.

Two more quarter-horse races were sandwiched between bareback bronc riding, saddle bronc riding and calf roping. Holly didn't catch the winning numbers of the horses.

But then she discovered junior barrel racing and was charmed. Little girls wheeled their ponies at breakneck speed around steel barrels. She admired their skill and determination so much that she slipped out of her seat and stood at the fence snapping pictures.

So-called ladies' barrel racing followed, though the girls were teenagers. How courageous they looked! Their hats flew from their heads as they made their wild dashes among the barrels and back to the starting point.

What a wonderful afternoon! The excitement, the pageantry.... It was a thrill to think of people all over the country gathered today to celebrate independence. The weather was perfect. A constant cooling breeze carrying aromas of horses and Corn Dogs kept the sun from being overbearing.

Suddenly she became aware of a man's bulk beside her. A voice she had heard in her night thoughts again and again said two words, "Enjoying yourself?"

She looked up, her eyes enormous and shining beneath the brim of her hat. "Raf!" Her heart was thudding so hard she feared her voice would shake. "I *am* enjoying myself! Don't those girls look wonderful?"

The sight of him was almost blinding; it was like staring into the sun. His virility or something about him stunned her, leaving her unable to think of anything but his face—the lean jaw, the firm masculine lips, the black-lashed tawny eyes like twin flames. A puff of wind brought her the sun-warmed scent of him, a scent compounded of leather, soap and masculinity. Unable to meet his eyes for more than one glance, she looked at the rest of him. He was wearing starched and ironed jeans and a golden brown cowboy shirt the color of his eyes. He was holding the black concha-banded hat in one hand, letting the breeze ruffle his shining black hair.

Holly tore her eyes away and stared straight ahead at the empty trampled arena, her heart thudding in her ears like the sound of pounding hooves.

"Are you wishing you could ride like that?" he asked.

The question brought her out of her daze. "It looks like fun," she answered wistfully, "but I wasn't thinking about myself." Her tone rang with honesty. "I was simply admiring them."

"You're dressed like one of them," he said. "But that's your business, isn't it, to look in style? You should be a rodeo queen on a palomino, leading the parade, with everyone looking at you."

She stared at him. His words rankled. Did he think she wanted to be looked at? Angrily she wondered if he were laughing at her. Did he think her nothing but a mannequin...something to be dressed up and stared at?

"I'm not wearing this outfit to show off!" she snapped. "I can ride a horse."

"I know you can." He was watching her quizzically. "Besides, bathing beauties don't have to swim. They don't have to prove they can do twenty laps of the pool. They just have to appear pretty."

She refused to look at him as tears of insulted fury sprang to her eyes. She was more than just a pretty face! For the first time in her life she wanted somebody besides her family to recognize that, and suddenly she wanted to get away from him. She was frightened by the way he could set her emotions in turmoil.

Good manners coming to her rescue, she muttered, "We'll see you this evening," and left him standing by the fence.

By the end of the last rodeo event the fossil crew was glad to stand up and stretch and walk to the jeep.

"I must say, it holds your attention," Dr. Gray commented. "I didn't realize how cramped I was getting."

Dr. Dave again made two trips to return the group to camp so they could dress for the party. As far as Holly was concerned, she no longer cared about going. She had expected too much. Leona had poisoned Raf's mind against models and was making sure it stayed poisoned.

However, as she slipped into the sheer voile dress she had bought, with its tiny print of pale blue and purple threaded with gold, she began to hope that perhaps the evening wouldn't be so bad after all. Only this morning she had said that whatever else happened, she was getting a day off from cooking. Besides, there would be other men there. If Raf didn't appreciate her, there would be others who did.

The dress had full sleeves, a full skirt and a scoop neckline. Holly undid her two braids and combed most of her red gold locks to hang in front of her shoulders, half covering the lightly tanned skin showing above the low neckline.

Even Marcia was wearing a dress—a pale blue tricot, practical but not pretty.

Holly was included in the first trip to the ranch and was pleased to learn that Dr. Gray could point out the turnoff, because she had no desire to admit she'd ever been there. They soon caught up with a shiny Cadillac taking its time over the bumpy rutted road. Ahead of it was a dusty Buick.

"I bet they won't let our jeep in the gate," Bill quipped.

"Somebody in this country has money," Wayne Taylor remarked. "They're not all cowpunchers."

When they saw the style of the cars parked in the ranch yard, the fossil party fell silent.

"Don't be nervous, children," Dr. Gray said. "These ranchers are the friendliest people on earth. You'll feel at home in no time."

Dr. Dave drove away to fetch Willie and Marcia.

Holly's high-heeled sandals clicking on the boards of the wooden footbridge started a bubble of excitement in her chest. A party—after the days of hard work! Not dressing up or wearing makeup was sort of a vacation, but it made dressing for something like this that much more pleasurable.

Behind a screen of bushes guests were scattered about the lawn, standing in little groups or sitting in chairs pulled out from a long table covered with white cloths. Holly's eyes widened at the stacks of plates set out, at the mounds of bread and bowls of potato salad. Raf must be expecting a hundred people.

On the lawn beyond was a big wooden platform that hadn't been there on her previous visit. Men were perched on the edge of it, drinking beer.

"That looks like a dance floor!" Holly said in her brother's ear.

"It does, doesn't it? Whoopee!"

"This guy does things right," Wayne agreed.

Holly's eyes were dancing with expectation when Raf came to greet them. Unlike his usual straight-lipped expression, his lips were curved in a smile. Holly smiled delightedly back, unable to suppress a thrill at the sight of him. He was wearing the tight jeans and beautifully stitched boots he'd had on at the rodeo, but he had changed his shirt to a red Western one with cuffs and yoke piped in white.

Wayne whistled between his teeth. "What movie did he play in?" he asked under his breath.

Red brought out Raf's dark good looks to an extent that was almost unfair, Holly thought. He came toward her group with his catlike stride and greeted them with relaxed friendliness.

"I'm glad you could make it. Dr. Gray, you'll find some old friends here. Bill, Wayne, don't be bashful. Everybody knows you're fossil collectors because you're the only strangers here. I hope you won't be strangers when you leave. The first stop's the bar. Right over there." He gestured with one arm, casually encircling Holly's shoulders with the other, as if to turn her in the right direction. The touch of his fingers burned through the sheer voile of her dress. "There's everything from beer to wine and mixed drinks. Just tell the bartender what you'd like."

As the others moved ahead, the arm around Holly's shoulders tightened. Black-fringed topaz eyes smiled into her blue ones. "Tell me, did you have fun this afternoon?"

"Oh, I did," she bubbled, forgetting to be angry.

He had stopped smiling, but his arm still circled her shoulders. He was looking down at her with a strange light in his eyes. One corner of his handsome mouth quirked. "I didn't mean to insult you this afternoon when I said you should be on a palomino, leading the parade."

"Oh...." If it hadn't been for that red-sleeved arm lightly holding her, making her aware of the rise and fall of her breathing, she would have shrugged. But she didn't want to shrug off that arm. Before she could find an answer, footsteps sounded on the bridge. A female voice rose in laughing comment, and a man's voice answered. Raf's hand squeezed Holly's shoulder, and he gave her a little push toward the bar.

"Get something to drink. I'll find you later."

Had she heard him right? Happiness seemed to buzz in her ears as she waited for a glass of white wine. She kept her eyes on the bar while she memorized Raf's words—*I'll find you later!* Her heart swelled. Delight must be written across her face.

By the time she was handed a glass of wine she had her expression under control. She saw Mrs. Jones crossing the terrace by the pool, carrying three heavy bowls of food. Setting her glass on a poolside table, she hurried to help.

"Mrs. Jones! Let me take one of those."

"Oh, hello, dear. That would be a help. Set it any-where on the table, and people can pass it. These are all three-bean salad. I made so much! I hope it gets eaten."

"It looks delicious," Holly commented, casting a professional eye at the mixture of green beans, pale yellow wax beans and red kidney beans, garnished with slices of onion. *Good idea,* she thought, *all out of cans. I must ask about the dressing.*

She retrieved her glass and began to look for some of her party.

The first one she saw was Bill. One could always spot his mop of red gold hair. Willie Yu had arrived and was standing beside him. Both were holding cans of beer and talking animatedly to a girl. Fast workers! The girl's back was toward Holly, and she had a moment to admire the eyelet dress, so white it seemed to sparkle. From a square neckline it hung in gathers sashed in at the waist by a strip of crimson silk cord. The girl looked delectable. Good! The boys had met someone interesting.

Then the girl's head turned. Leona Selby! By her-self again? Had she been alone at the rodeo, or had Raf been off looking to one of his entries while she waited in the stands? Holly had expected her to be here, but she'd hoped their paths wouldn't cross.

She thought, *I mustn't stand here looking forlorn.* But how could she help feeling that way when she'd just realized that Raf hadn't meant anything special by saying he'd find her later? He couldn't help finding her later if she was in his front yard.

Dr. Gray and Dave were talking to a couple of ranchers. Wayne and Marcia stood huddled together, looking faintly apprehensive. Holly joined them.

"Why aren't you mingling?" she asked with a smile.

"Why aren't you?" Wayne swirled the ice in his glass. "I don't have anything to say to these rural types."

Marcia said, "We're the strangers. They should come talk to us. Who's that girl Bill's talking to?"

"She's a reporter for some paper in Pierre. Why don't you go break it up," Holly suggested.

"Maybe I will." Marcia set off determinedly.

"Marcia's nuts if she thinks she can compete with that," Wayne muttered.

Holly tried to keep smiling and not grip her glass too tightly. Where was Raf? Still by the bridge. He was shaking hands with a burly rancher and being clapped on the shoulder.

"When's the food going to be ready?" Holly heard the man ask. "I'm about starved."

"Right away," Raf promised. "They've got it out of the pit and are cutting it up." He looked off toward the corrals. "Get your beer, Fred. Here comes the first panful now."

Holly discovered there was even a thrill about hearing him make ordinary conversation. She wished she could find a retreat and give him her whole attention. However, one of the ranch hands arrived, carrying a huge white enamel basin filled with slices of beef, and Holly and everyone else was drawn toward the side table where it was placed. A second man followed with an enormous tureen of barbecue sauce.

"All right, everybody, bring your plates." The ranch hand had tied a white apron about his waist and was preparing to serve slabs of meat, each of which looked like enough to feed several people. The combined smell of meat and sauce was making her mouth water. She was amused to realize how much she was looking forward to someone else's cooking.

She tried not to watch Raf too intently, but despite herself, her eyes kept straying in his direction. She saw him at the bar, getting himself a drink. People were already lined up with plates, on which the ranch hand placed huge portions of beef, topped with barbecue sauce for those who wanted it. The guests took seats at the table and began passing bread and salad.

Friendly glances were cast in Holly's direction, but Wayne's brooding aspect kept people from coming to talk to either of them. Bill, Marcia and Willie Yu were already in line. Where was Leona?

Raf was crossing the grass holding a glass of red wine. He seemed to be searching the crowd. For her? For Leona? Before he found the object of his search, Leona emerged from the house. Seeing Raf alone, she stepped quickly to his side. Raf's back was to Holly, so she was unable to see how warmly he welcomed the other girl. Holly all but ground her teeth. Now she'd never know whom he'd been looking for.

Wayne finished his drink and cocked his head to-

ward the people in line for the barbecued meat.
"Ready to eat?"

"Why not?" Holly said dispiritedly. She had the
very strong feeling that she was not going to see Raf
again today without Leona's company. She crossed
the lawn without looking in his direction, half hoping
that somehow he would materialize beside her. Instead she found herself in line behind a good-looking
blond cowboy whom everyone kept congratulating
on winning the calf-roping contest. The cowboy
blushed and grinned and appeared utterly speech-
less.

The ranch hand served Holly more meat than she
could possibly eat at one sitting, and then she and
Wayne carried their plates to the table, looking for
someone from their group to sit with.

"Here we are!" Marcia called.

Holly smiled hello upon finding herself across the
table from Dr. Gray and the middle-aged rancher he
had been talking to earlier. Bill was sitting next to the
rancher. The place beside him was reserved by a plate
of beef, and Bill was looking over his shoulder.

Holly followed the direction of his eyes in time to
see Leona taking laughing leave of Raf and cross the
lawn to sit at the empty place beside Bill. Raf went to
welcome some latecomers.

Bill was saying, "Leona, I'd like you to meet my
sister. . . ."

Leona glanced up from her plate, and her eyes met
Holly's. In them was instant recognition and something more—dislike.

Why, Holly wondered. *What have I ever done to
her?*

The two girls exchanged cool hellos, but Bill, Holly thought angrily, was too infatuated to notice their lack of warmth.

"So you are the expedition's cook," Leona said, faintly emphasizing "you." "Your brother's been telling me about your case."

"*My case!* What do you mean?" Holly gulped, surprise knocking her off balance.

Bill's attention was claimed by Dr. Gray.

"I should have said, 'your story,'" Leona corrected airily. "Bill mentioned you needed a holiday from your horrendous—" she emphasized the word "—work schedule and so he got you in on this." She smiled sweetly at Bill as he returned his attention to her.

"You make it sound like a picnic." Holly's smile was as false as Leona's.

"No, it's no picnic," Bill chimed in readily, as though Leona had genuinely misunderstood. "Holly gets up earlier than any of us."

Why did Leona dislike her, Holly puzzled. Had she tried to be a model and failed? Had Raf talked about Holly to her? If only that were the reason! When Raf joined his guests, he sat at the end of the table. From time to time Holly heard him laugh, because her ear was attuned. She stole quick glances in his direction, but at no time did his eyes meet hers. However, she loved seeing him chatting seriously with the man on his right and listening gravely to two women who seemed to be speaking their minds about something.

Dusk had fallen and people were still going back for seconds when the musicians began tuning up. Raf strolled to the platform. Not once did he appear aware of Holly's whereabouts as he parried the good-natured quips of his guests and received their congratulations on his winning horses. Apparently another one had taken second place.

He stepped up onto the dance floor and held up a hand. "My friends...." He spoke without raising his voice, but somehow he commanded instant attention. "Now that you've eaten all you can hold, I hope you're ready to dance it all off and go back for more." He jumped off the platform to a spatter of clapping and cheers and headed down Holly's side of the table. She pretended not to notice and turned to make a comment to Wayne. From the corner of her eye she saw Raf stop beside her chair. Almost unwillingly, she raised her eyes to his. Looking gravely down at her, he held out his hand.

"May I have the pleasure?"

Holly's heart seemed to skip several beats, but she took the hand he held out to her and stood up gracefully. Before all of his friends he was leading her to the dance floor. People began to clap, heightening the moment—if that were possible.

The three-piece band struck up a waltz as they stepped onto the platform. Raf held out his arms. Holly stepped into them, her face glowing.

"I hope you don't mind old-fashioned music," he said.

"Of course not!"

"Good! That's the kind we like out here."

Holly wished she knew how to bridge the gap that always seemed to open between them. Must they always concentrate on the differences in their backgrounds?

His next words were, "You look lovely tonight. But no doubt you know that."

How was she supposed to reply—"yes, I do know"? Her eyes misted a little, because those were words she wanted to hear him say, but without the rider tacked on. She sighed involuntarily.

"Have you heard that so often you're bored?" he gritted.

"No, it's just...." She hesitated.

"Just what?"

"Just that you never seem to understand me." She had to speak loudly in order to be heard above the music. She gazed up into his tawny eyes. They were glowing. The look in them sent a thrill to the center of her being. She realized it wasn't a time for talking.

"Hush," he said, and drew her against him.

Holly was content to float in his arms. Tall as she was, he was taller. She felt his cheek against her hair and pictured the lean brown jaw against her red gold locks.

Dreamily they swung to the music. His dancing was like the man himself—smooth, strong, graceful. Her half-closed eyes caught glimpses of darkness pinpointed by fireflies and then, as Raf swung her effortlessly, glimpses of the long white table edged by talking, laughing people—Raf's friends and neighbors.

Other couples had been quick to step onto the floor. As Raf whirled her about, her full skirt billowed delightfully. Raf's firm hand seemed to belong at her waist, and they moved as one person. She caught a glimpse of Bill's bright head bent over Leona's dark one.

She wondered briefly what Leona was thinking. Had she hoped that Raf would choose her first? Of course she had! What girl wouldn't? *She'll still be here when I've gone,* Holly thought with a pang. Resolutely she turned her mind to the present. Tonight, at least, Raf had chosen her over all others.

The dance ended. Raf walked with her to her seat at the table, introducing her on the way to more of his friends.

"Another blonde, eh, Raf?" one of the men teased.

Raf ignored him, his face a blank, and they walked on.

"'*Another* blonde?' What did he mean?" Holly dared ask when they were out of earshot.

"Just a joke." He bit off the words and looked down at her, in his eyes a hint of annoyance. "You don't object to being referred to as a blonde?"

She peeked up at him from under her lashes. "No, because he made me too curious. Are you a pushover for blondes?" she asked coquettishly.

"Do I look like a pushover?" They were standing face to face beside her seat at the table, but as far as Holly was concerned, the two of them were alone amid the noise of the party. Her breath came fast at her daring to ask such impertinent questions, but as long as he lingered, she must say something.

"No," she admitted impishly, "you look like what I've heard you are—one of South Dakota's most eligible bachelors."

He laughed out at that. "You—" he put a finger beneath her round chin to raise her face "—look like an eligible bachelor's dream. Despite which, I have to go and dance with the other ladies." He held her chin high for an instant longer, his gaze fastened on her full red lips. "Later," he whispered. As though emerging from a trance, he caught his breath and turned away.

Holly stood where he had left her, watching his retreating back, leather-belted jeans taut across his slim hips, the notched yoke of his shirt reminding her of the beautiful masculine shape of his brown back...the layered muscles on either side of his backbone. Her fingertips tingled at the thought of tracing that indentation from neck to waist.

She saw him approach a rancher's wife and lead her to the platform.

Holly loved to dance, but tonight she could have sat in a daze, watching Raf moving about the floor with his catlike grace. She saw Bill still dancing with Leona and felt a nudge of annoyance. Before she had time to think more about that, Wayne claimed her, and from then on she was seldom without a partner.

After a sprightly polka, through which her cowboy partner zestfully propelled her, she laughingly turned down the next dance to stand on the sidelines and catch her breath.

Her brother materialized beside her. "You seem to be doing all right," he commented.

Holly flashed him a challenging glance. "Did you think I wouldn't?"

"Of course not," he said, grinning. "You'll drop them all in their tracks. Including our host. He seems to be keeping an eye on you."

"Really?" Holly's dark blue eyes sparkled, and

then the delight faded. "How did you notice? You've been busy with that Leona Selby."

"Any objection?" Bill raised one eyebrow.

"She's the one who wrote that nasty piece about models. I showed it to you."

"Oh, that!" Bill laughed.

"Yes, 'oh, that!'"

"Well. . . ." He shrugged. "She was doing a job. As you were. You'd like her if—"

"Not a job like mine!" Holly interrupted. "My job doesn't involve telling half-truths—half-lies, I should say."

"Sis, you're making a mountain out of a molehill. Get that frown off your face! Here comes Dave."

Hot words rushed to Holly's lips, but she called on her model's training to control her facial muscles and produce her lovely smile. "I didn't think you'd be so disloyal," she said between her teeth.

"Here you are!" Dave exclaimed. "Will you dance this one with me?"

Holding out her hand to Dr. Dave, she ordered her brother to dance with Marcia. Dr. Dave led her to the platform, and she cast a look over her shoulder. Bill stood unmoved and grinning.

"I haven't been able to get near you all evening," Dr. Dave complained as he swung her into a fox-trot.

Across the floor, Raf led out Leona. At least the girl wasn't with Bill. But Holly didn't want her with Raf, either. She was trying to sort out this dilemma when she realized Dr. Dave was talking to her.

"I guess I haven't appreciated my luck at the camp," he was saying.

Holly's startled eyes flew to his face. "What luck?"

"Why the luck of not having so much competition."

Holly could think of no suitable reply and decided not to answer. Dr. Dave was a fair dancer, so she gave herself up to the music. Only once did her eyes stray to Raf and Leona—unfortunately at a time when Raf's tawny eyes, gazing moodily over Leona's head, were focused in Holly's direction. His look was intent, almost cold, as though she had offended him. The look stung her to her toes, and she searched her conscience. What could she have done? Had Leona said something derogatory? Was it possible he didn't like her dancing with Dr. Dave?

Many of the guests had departed by the time Raf claimed Holly for a second dance. It was a disco number, and he seemed disinclined to talk. Leona had disappeared. So had Bill. Holly found to her dismay that she'd rather think of Leona with Bill than with Raf.

When the dance ended, Raf put his arm possessively around Holly's waist. At a signal from him the musicians struck up "Dakotaland." A concerted groan rose from the younger guests. Apparently in that part of the country that tune signaled the end of the dance.

"People have to work tomorrow," Raf apologized, "and some of them have a long way to drive. Cattle don't take much notice of Sunday. Come over here." He led her to the far side of the platform away from the yard lights. "Look at that new moon. Have you seen the Badlands by starlight yet?"

"Don't you mean moonlight?"

Holly couldn't see what her companion was thinking; they were standing with their backs to the light. Anyway, his face was probably as inscrutable as ever.

"There isn't much of a moon—" his voice held faint amusement "—but the Badlands are worth seeing at night. What if I drive you back the long way around?" he asked persuasively.

A little reluctantly Holly said, "It sounds lovely."

She wanted to go, but what would it lead to? It wasn't her habit to play with fire, and now she was doing so. Yet this man stirred her as no other had ever done. She didn't want to resist his invitation.

"Good!" He helped her down from the platform. "Better tell your group to go on. I have to stay and say good-night to my last guests."

Including Leona? For an instant Holly felt sorry for her, though not sorry enough to give up Raf. She looked around for the dark-haired girl in the white dress, but she appeared to have gone—probably in her own car, the compact she'd been driving at Fox Butte.

Holly found Bill in the parking area, leaning against the jeep.

"Raf's driving me back to camp," Holly told him.

"Don't do anything I wouldn't do!" Bill laughed. "Should I ask him his intentions?"

"I'm sure I'll learn them," Holly replied recklessly, and trod back across the bridge, more anxious than she cared to admit. What were Raf's intentions?

The last of the cars pulled out of the drive. Raf gave instructions and compliments to the men who had cooked and served the barbecue, then turned to Holly.

"Let me get you a wrap. It turns cool at night out there—like the desert."

He disappeared and came back with a square shawl. Holly exclaimed at the texture.

"My mother knits those things on the finest needles you ever saw. This one she left for me—maybe hoping I'd find a woman to wear it."

"Why haven't you?" Holly caught her breath at her nerve in asking the question, but wasn't this a perfect opening?

"It's a long story," he said dismissingly, steering her to a black Mercedes. Then, as though he feared he might have spoken too sharply, he made his tone light. "Maybe I enjoy being an eligible bachelor." He cocked his head at her.

"I don't see how you have time," Holly said laughingly. "I thought eligible bachelors had to hang around resorts to get a reputation."

"Not if it's a false one. Besides," he added with an air of mock sophistication, "I have been to Jamaica and to the Bahamas. Us country folk do get away in the winter." He opened the car door for her.

Seated beside him, riding through the dark featureless countryside, Holly wondered what had possessed her to accept his invitation. She stole a look at his profile illumined by the faint light from the dashboard. In the dim glow his Indian ancestry was apparent—the hawk nose and high cheekbones, the way his hair sprang thick and vigorous from his forehead. The beautifully molded lips were his own.

Perhaps sensing her gaze, he threw her a glance. "I

get the feeling you're uncomfortable," he said.

Holly jumped. "Not at all," she lied.

"It wouldn't be surprising if you were," he suggested. "You can't have had many dates in New York City where there's no one else within miles."

"No," she agreed, a little breathless at the thought that she was very much alone with Raf and more dependent on him than when they'd gone riding. She'd had the horse then.

She said, "In New York City I wouldn't have made a date like that."

"I'm flattered. Shouldn't I be?" he pressed when Holly made no reply.

"I guess so, but there was no one else within miles the first two times you came to the camp," she said thoughtfully.

"Ah! You were aware of it, then?"

"Of course."

"I hope you've given me points for good behavior."

Holly tried to think of a witty reply but failed, so she merely said, "Yes."

Her unease increased. On the surface Raf might appear to be a rough rancher, but hadn't he just admitted he vacationed in sophisticated places? He was wealthy, mature and polished. On the other hand, Holly might be regularly pictured in designer clothing, but underneath she was a hardworking girl from a small town on Long Island. Right now she was feeling very much out of her depth. She was suddenly afraid Raf might forget she was only twenty-two. Perhaps a sophisticated South Dakota girl would know that an invitation to view the Badlands at midnight included a stop at the nearest motel.

She took a deep breath, ready to tell him that perhaps he'd better take her straight home after all.

Before she could speak, he said with another glance at her, "You're looking very serious. What is it?"

"Oh...." She raised one shoulder. Now was the time to tell him. "Nothing," she said weakly.

"Must be something." He reached for her hand.

At the touch of his warm calloused fingers, any thought of asking him to take her back to camp deserted her.

"What cold hands!" he exclaimed, and then perceptively, "Cold feet, too?" He took his eyes from the straight road and fixed them on Holly's face.

Trying to read his expression in the shadowy light was like trying to read the thoughts behind dark glasses.

"A little," she admitted, because he seemed to be looking into her brain anyway.

"You needn't have." He patted her hand reassuringly. "I'm just showing you the tourist attractions."

Contrarily Holly didn't like that, either.

They drove in silence for several miles. Holly tried furiously to think of some safe subject of conversation, turning over one thing after another in her mind. Everything she thought of sounded either simpleminded or fraught with implications. What was Raf thinking? Was he, too, having trouble finding something to say? She doubted it. She couldn't imagine him at a loss for words if he felt like talking.

As though to prove it, he brought up a subject that she should have hit on herself.

"How's the search coming?" he asked. "Has anything turned up to get excited about?"

Holly took the first really free breath she'd drawn since she'd entered the car. "I'm afraid not," she replied, enthusiastically welcoming the subject. "Everything they've brought in seems wonderful to me when I think how old it is and how miraculous that it survived at all, but Professor Gray's not thrilled so far. But, of course, we've barely begun. I help clean the fossils whenever there's something I can be trusted with," she added, smiling.

"So you like the work?" He threw her a glance.

"Oh, yes."

"And you don't mind cooking?"

"No. It's easier than I had expected."

"My hat's off to you."

"Why?" she asked sharply.

"I never thought you'd last."

"Why not?"

For answer he shrugged.

Holly's temper began to sizzle. For some reason she didn't even try to control it.

"Did you think I was just a dumb blonde who couldn't read a cookbook?" she demanded. She knew she was being childish. Sophisticated women didn't fly off the handle like this. They were cool and controlled and didn't speak hot words to men they wanted to impress. But she'd bottled up so many feelings in this one evening that now she exploded recklessly.

"Aren't you?" he asked.

She drew a furious breath before she realized he was deliberately baiting her.

"No!" She subsided grumpily.

"Don't pout," he teased. His hand left the steering wheel and grasped hers, squeezing it gently.

"It's true," he admitted. "I did think you were just another blonde—not dumb, but not much interested in anything except your looks. I felt sorry for you—dumped out there alone on the prairie for the first time in your life. Now I'm finding out that besides all the beauty you have a very interesting little personality."

"Little!"

"A very interesting *big* personality, then. Is that better?"

Holly laughed, her good humor restored. "I guess not. It makes me sound like a three-hundred-pound entertainer."

"You have to admit that a beautiful girl with brains is unexpected. Of course, beautiful girls can have brains. It's just that a man—speaking for myself—can't believe he'd be so lucky as to get both in one package."

"But given the choice he'd take looks."

"At least you see what you're getting."

Holly had to laugh. However, she was thinking, *you have both, so why shouldn't I?* "This conversation is getting ridiculous," she said with an edge of annoyance.

"Good thing we're here, then," Raf replied cheerfully, pulling into an overlook. "Out! You can't get the feel of the Badlands by sitting in a car. You have to turn your back on the road and walk on the clay."

They met in front of the car, and he reached for her hand. "What kind of shoes are you wearing? High heels! I should have thought of that. All right, this is good enough. We'll sit on this bench. No one else will be coming along this time of night."

He draped the shawl around Holly's shoulders and sat holding her hand. "Listen," he said.

Listening, she heard the sound of his breathing and sharp metallic clicks as the car's engine cooled. Far away a dog barked. Below the Badlands wall, on the horizon, she saw a sprinkle of lights—a ranch, perhaps. The nearby pinnacles gleamed palely in the starshine and seemed to shimmer.

"Hear the wind?" Raf whispered, and immediately Holly became aware of it. "Think of it, blowing for eternity, eroding these peaks, grain by grain."

"I thought the water eroded them."

"Water does it, too—snow, rain—but only now and then. The wind is unceasing. When something's really bothering me, I drive up here at night like this, and after a while no human concerns seem very important. We live; we die; we won't even turn into fossils." His hand slid around her under the shawl, the touch of his fingers warm and exciting through the sheer voile of her dress.

"Spectacular, isn't it?" His voice was reverent.

Holly agreed, wondering if his love of this wild moonscape had been inherited from his fossil-collecting French ancestors or came with his Sioux blood. Whichever it was, she silently entered into the spirit of his meditations.

The next moment he turned to her with a gentleness that was as unexpected as it was disarming.

"Let's celebrate a little life," he said, gathering her in his arms.

Holly raised her face willingly to meet his kiss. His philosophy had worked on her mind. How true it was—life lasted such a short time. To let this man, who affected her more than any man she'd ever met, send veins of fire racing through her body seemed like a thank offering to Creation. She pressed herself against him, and the shawl fell from her shoulders as she raised her arms to encircle his neck. Of its own accord, one hand went to touch his smooth black hair. As the fire swept more wildly and his arms began to feel safe and familiar, her fingers dared to plunge tingling into his thick soap-scented locks. Her lips trembled under the pressure of his.

Careful, her scattering senses screamed at her through a pleasant haze that made her want only to respond to his lovemaking.

Sensing her slight withdrawal, he ended the kiss. She was immediately sorry.

"I suppose you think lovemaking doesn't come under tourist attractions," he suggested.

With an inward sigh of relief she realized he wasn't going to get carried away.

"Do you mean you kiss all the tourists?" she countered.

"Only the prettiest," he said, nuzzling her neck. "And the smartest," he added quickly.

That made her smile.

"Did anyone ever tell you what a beautiful smile you have?" he asked, kissing the corners of her mouth and making her feel very short of breath. "Of course they have," he answered for her. "I keep forgetting that being beautiful is your business. Why do I want to think no man ever looked at you before I saw you, before you sat next to me on the plane? I daresay every man you meet thinks the same way."

Holly started to protest that if other men did think the same way, she didn't give them the opportunity to confide their feelings, but before she could say so, Raf began feathering her face with tiny kisses that tickled her skin and sent delicious thrills throughout her body.

"Forget I said that," he whispered. "Tonight... now... we're the only people alive."

And tomorrow, Holly wondered.

Nevertheless she found herself unwilling to resist his caresses. One of her arms slipped beneath his, and she was unable to control the urge to hold him tightly. She had never clasped such a hard-muscled torso before, and she thought again as she had at the pow-wow, *here is a man*.

Raf's lips strayed to the satin-smooth skin of her neck. The warm tenderness of his lips became her undoing. She bent her head to drop a kiss on his ear.

Immediately his mouth returned to seek hers with hot eagerness. In the past she had never allowed boyfriends to kiss her intimately. She had avoided high-school necking sessions and had said no more often than yes to college friends of her brother's. But Raf was a man she couldn't deny—and didn't want to.

I've been saving myself for now, she thought recklessly, and met his kiss with parted lips. His tongue slipped between her teeth. Her breath caught.

Her heart seemed to choke her, and she wondered if she might faint with sheer excited pleasure.

The kiss went on until the stars seemed to whirl overhead. He was crushing her to him until her bones seemed to give with his. With a little bubbling laugh in her throat she remembered the heavy bear-claw necklace he had worn at that first kiss. She had never really expected to see him again, and here he was! Out of all his guests he had chosen to be with her. She pressed her body closer to his.

At that his hand untangled itself from the ringlets hanging down her back and moved to cup her breast.

Holly froze, but his hand stayed firmly in possession, giving her the oddest feeling that it belonged there. Some wicked imp in her brain told her everything would be all right...he wouldn't go any farther.

But he did. Still possessively cupping her breast with his hand, one fingertip found the sensitive bud of her nipple, his touch firm and deliberate through the sheer material of her dress and bra.

Continuing to drug her senses with his kiss, he slipped her dress from one moon-whitened shoulder. Holly moved in protest, but his hold tightened. Then his hand abandoned her breast and moved to stroke the translucent skin of her neck. His work-roughened hands felt sure and masculine—the caress of a god, a lordly being from out of this otherworldly landscape. How could she deny him anything? With a moan of sheer pleasure she waited for his fingers to stroke down her neck, across her delicate collarbone, across the tender skin and back where they belonged, holding her breast as though it were something precious. He took his lips from hers, leaving her mouth desolate, and before she realized what he meant to do next, his mouth touched the now erect and throbbing nipple, and his tongue licked around and around it.

Hot waves of passion shook her body. Trembling, almost sobbing, she begged him to stop.

He raised his head at once. "Why?"

"I can't stand any more!"

"Can't you, my darling?" His face came back to hers, dark, mysterious, smiling. "Let's go, then. There's a quilt in the car, and I know a place where the grass is thick as a carpet."

"No!" she cried, passion replaced by fear.

"My God, you can't mean you want to stop now!" he exclaimed.

"I didn't want to start, remember?" Her voice broke. She reached to pull her dress over her shoulder, but his hand stopped hers. Distractedly one part of her mind noted the glow of her pale skin against his dark hand. His lips touched her flesh and seemed to brand her.

"That's right, you didn't," he said levelly.

His arms dropped from around her. He wasn't even breathing hard, she noted resentfully.

Holly stumbled to her feet, swaying but refusing to let him touch her. Somehow she walked to her side of the car and opened the door. She slid into the seat, feeling sorrowful, dazed and belligerent.

Raf slid into the driver's seat and started the motor. "I had thought we might have a pleasant summer's affair." His voice was normal, casual.

1. How do you rate _____ ?
   (Please print book TITLE)

   1.6 ☐ excellent   .4 ☐ good   .2 ☐ not so good
   .5 ☐ very good   .3 ☐ fair   .1 ☐ poor

   G 1 2 3

2. How likely are you to purchase another book in this series?
   2.1 ☐ definitely would purchase   .3 ☐ probably would not purchase
   .2 ☐ probably would purchase   .4 ☐ definitely would not purchase

3. How do you compare this book with similar books you usually read?
   3.1 ☐ far better than others   .4 ☐ not as good
   .2 ☐ better than others   .5 ☐ definitely not as good
   .3 ☐ about the same

4. Have you any additional comments about this book?
   _____ (4)
   _____ (6)

5. How did you first become aware of this book?
   8. ☐ in-store display   11. ☐ talk show
   9. ☐ radio   12. ☐ read other titles
   10. ☐ magazine _____   13. ☐ other _____
   (name)   (please specify)

6. What most prompted you to buy this book?
   14. ☐ title   17. ☐ picture on cover   20. ☐ back-cover story outline
   15. ☐ price   18. ☐ friend's recommendation   21. ☐ read a few pages
   16. ☐ author   19. ☐ product advertising   22. ☐ other _____
   (please specify)

7. What type(s) of paperback fiction have you purchased in the past
   3 months? Approximately how many?

	No. purchased		No. purchased
☐ contemporary romance	(23)____	☐ espionage	(37)____
☐ historical romance	(25)____	☐ western	(39)____
☐ gothic romance	(27)____	☐ contemporary novels	(41)____
☐ romantic suspense	(29)____	☐ historical novels	(43)____
☐ mystery	(31)____	☐ science fiction/fantasy	(45)____
☐ private eye	(33)____	☐ occult	(47)____
☐ action/adventure	(35)____	☐ other	(49)____

8. Have you purchased any books from any of these series in the past
   3 months? Approximately how many?

	No. purchased		No. purchased
☐ Harlequin Romance	(51)____	☐ Silhouette Romance	(55)____
☐ Harlequin Presents	(53)____	☐ Superromance	(57)____

9. On which date was this book purchased? (59) _____

10. Please indicate your age group and sex.
    61.1 ☐ Male   62.1 ☐ under 15   .3 ☐ 25-34   .5 ☐ 50-64
    .2 ☐ Female   .2 ☐ 15-24   .4 ☐ 35-49   .6 ☐ 65 or older

Thank you for completing and returning this questionnaire.

PRINTED IN CANADA

NAME _____
(Please Print)

ADDRESS _____

CITY _____

ZIP CODE _____

BUSINESS REPLY MAIL

FIRST CLASS   PERMIT NO. 70   TEMPE, AZ.

POSTAGE WILL BE PAID BY ADDRESSEE

NATIONAL READER SURVEYS

1440 SOUTH PRIEST DRIVE
TEMPE, AZ 85266

"Am I too late? Is something already going on between you and Young?"

"Certainly not!" Holly said indignantly.

"Not good old Gray?"

"How dare you!" she gasped.

"Are you a tease?" he demanded. "Is that it? I
can't believe it, though. To give such a hot response
and then withdraw is practically asking for force. Is
that what you want from me?" His question sounded
quite serious.

"No. Oh, no!" Holly moaned.

"A good thing," he said, backing the car out of
the parking area, "because you picked the wrong
man this time."

How cruel he was! And how ironic the situation.
All these years she'd avoided macho men. Now that
she'd met one she couldn't resist, instead of appreciating her inexperience, he was accusing her of
being kinky. What a laugh! And the joke was on her.

"Tell me something," he said bitterly, "how many
times have you been raped?"

"Never!" she cried, stung. "I'm a virgin!"

"You're what?" He brought the car almost to a
stop in order to stare at her.

"I'm a virgin," she repeated sulkily.

He faced forward, and the car shot ahead, sweeping around turns and up and over rises with speed.

Holly braced herself against the seat and hated
him. A pleasant summer affair! That's all he had in
mind. No wonder he was unattached! South Dakota
girls weren't fools. No, it took a smart model from
New York City to fall into his net. Well, she
wouldn't, no matter how passionately her body de-

sired his lovemaking. She had lowered her defenses, and what had he called her trust? A hot response! Tears filled her eyes at the death of her ideal.

They drove the whole way back in utter silence. Raf's chin jutted like one of the Badlands crags.

A lamp had been left burning for her on the dining table. Holly drew an unhappy breath. Raf swung the car around, ready for leaving, before he stopped it. He reached across her, carefully not touching her, and opened the car door.

"I'll be damned if I'm going to apologize," he growled.

"For what?" she said coldly.

"For being a pig and a boor." He laughed. "I do apologize. I didn't believe twenty-two-year-old virgins existed—not ones with your looks." He kissed her gently on the cheek. "Don't be sad, sweetheart, the man who gets you will be the luckiest guy in the world."

If ever words meant goodbye, those did. He drove away before she extinguished the light.

CHAPTER NINE

NEXT MORNING the break with Raf didn't look as final as it had the previous night.

Any girl has a right to say no, Holly told herself. Remembering some of the nice things he'd said to her, she actually began to sing while preparing breakfast.

"You sound disgustingly cheery," Dr. Dave growled when he entered the dining area. "Did your rancher propose?"

Holly flushed, despite her determination not to, and forced a laugh. "I hardly know him." It was on the tip of her tongue to tell Dr. Dave it wasn't his business, but she didn't. So far there'd been no dissension in camp, and she didn't intend to cause any.

At breakfast Willie Yu and Marcia announced that they wanted to go to Wall, home of the famous drugstore whose billboard advertising adorned the interstate out of Rapid City. The block-long drugstore's advertising had made a boom town out of a sleepy prairie village, and the proprietors employed college students during the summer season. Willie and Marcia were eager to meet some young people, and when Dr. Gray said they could take the jeep, Bill and Wayne elected to go, too.

Holly had been thinking that Raf also might be

sorry about the way the evening had ended. She wanted to see him so much she convinced herself he might come around. She couldn't bear the thought of missing him. She decided to stay in camp.

Oblivious to the heat, Dr. Gray settled himself at his desk in the trailer.

To Holly's dismay, she faced spending the day with Dr. Dave. He planned to clean fossils. Having elected to stay in camp, she could hardly avoid offering to help. She had, in fact, nothing else to do, because no one was coming back to dinner. Bill and the others intended to invade the taco and hamburger stands of Wall.

She put on jeans—perhaps Raf would invite her to go riding—and a white T-shirt. Although she wasn't aware of it, such simple costumes accented her girl-next-door beauty. She added a dash of gray eyeshadow to enhance her dark-fringed blue eyes and a trace of lipstick and left her tent.

Dr. Dave was laying out tools on the other table under the awning and grumbling about allowing all the help to take off two days in a row.

"Fossil collecting isn't a picnic," he said, scowling at Holly from behind his thick glasses, which he removed for close work such as cleaning fossils. He was tall and good-looking, but his thinning hair probably came from worry over details, Holly thought. He would never have the vision of a man like Dr. Gray, she guessed.

He gave her a jawbone to work on. For a while they picked away in silence. Holly broke the quiet, thinking she ought to try to get her mind off Raf.

"What kind of jawbone is this?" she asked.

"Titanothere."

"Isn't it awfully small?"

"No, they started out as creatures one or two feet high."

"Was Dr. Gray pleased with this one?"

"Not particularly. He wants complete skeletons."

"I see." Wouldn't it be wonderful, she thought, if Bill were to find some for Dr. Gray? Of course, it all depended on luck. She had listened to discussions about that around the camp dinner table. No matter how much a paleontologist knew, some were luckier than others at making spectacular finds. She hoped Bill would be one of the lucky ones. If not, his life would be one of frustration, as Dr. Dave's. Dave was a widower, a nice harmless man. Just not lucky.

As if he had guessed she was thinking about him, Dr. Dave laid his dental pick on the table and flexed his fingers.

"You were quite the belle of the ball last night."

"Hardly that," Holly murmured.

"Every time I saw you, you were dancing with a different man." His tone was condemnatory. "Where'd Valcour take you afterward?"

Holly kept her head bent over her work. One lock of hair fell across her forehead, veiling her face. She was glad the hair hid the pain in her eyes at the mention of Raf's name.

"Nowhere," she said quietly. "He wanted to show me the Badlands at night, that's all."

Dr. Dave snorted. "According to Dr. Gray, he has a reputation in these parts. I hope you don't let him fool you. There's something wrong with a man his age who isn't married."

Sudden fear struck Holly's heart. *Was* something wrong with Raf? Why was he free to pursue a newcomer like herself?

"*You're* not married," she pointed out to drown her fear.

"But I have been."

"He may have been, too."

"I suppose so." His tone was dissatisfied. "I, however, intend to get married again."

Holly hardly heard him. A car was passing on the road, and her head turned involuntarily. She glanced at her watch. Ten o'clock. Would Raf come this morning, or would he wait till evening? Then she reminded herself he might not come at all.

Dr. Dave's heavy eyebrows arched. "Expecting someone?"

"No." Holly tossed back her hair. "It's just that one so seldom hears a car."

"It's a damn lonely life without a woman," Dr. Dave said.

Holly looked across at him. "You must have lots of students to choose from," she suggested, hoping to inject a little humor into the conversation, but he chose to take her seriously.

"Not as many as you'd think. And most of them are like Marcia," he added gloomily.

Holly stood up. "I'm going to bake a cake before the day gets any hotter."

"Leaving me to feel sorry for myself?"

"Yes." What if Raf didn't come? What if he never paid any more attention to her? It would hurt. It would hurt a lot. But she didn't see how she could have done things differently. *All he wants,* she reminded herself, *is a summer affair.*

Except for baking the cake, she spent almost the whole day tediously picking at fossils and looking at her watch. Raf didn't come. By sundown Dr. Dave had grown positively jolly.

"What happened to your rancher?" he asked cheerily when Dr. Gray had gone for a walk to stretch his legs. "Didn't you have a date? Isn't that why you stayed in camp?"

Holly turned her back on him and went to her tent, shoulders straight. Ph.D.'s were too smart for their own good. And jealous Ph.D.'s were the pits. Raf wouldn't come now. It was almost bedtime. What had made her so hopeful he would?

THE WEEK DRAGGED BY. Each evening Holly hoped Raf would ride over, but he didn't appear. The weather turned hot. The sun burned down on the bare clay hills and turned the airless gullies to ovens. Dr. Dave and the students spent morning hours in the ravines around Buffalo Table, returning at noon to the shade of the mess tent, where they worked at cleaning and labeling the fossils they already had.

By the time Saturday arrived, everyone was eager to go to town. Holly wanted to buy fresh fruit and vegetables and a dozen other items that the store in Vista couldn't provide. Since with groceries the jeep would hold only four, the crew drew lots. Bill, Dr. Dave and Marcia won.

"Tomorrow," Dr. Dave soothed Wayne and Wil-

lie, "you can all crowd in and do the Black Hills."
His geniality surprised everyone.

Marcia spoke into a stunned silence. "How come?"

"We thought you believed in all work and no
play," Willie added.

"I do," Dr. Dave said sternly. "But Dr. Gray
thinks you ought to see the Black Hills because it was
rivers rushing down from there that deposited the
thick layers of silt that formed the Badlands, and
while you're driving around, you might as well see
the points of interest."

Holly bit her lip. That meant she'd have to spend
another day alone with him. She saw her brother
glance at her and knew he was about to protest at her
being left out, but Dr. Dave forestalled him.

"Holly, you should go, too. Dr. Gray and I can
manage to feed ourselves for one day."

Holly hesitated. What if Raf came while she was
gone? *Fat chance,* she admonished herself. She'd
hung around all last Sunday—and with what result?
A day spent in Dr. Dave's not-so-welcome company.
She couldn't do that again.

When they got to town, they dropped Dr. Dave at
the university and then didn't know what to do with
themselves.

"Let's drive around and look at civilization," Bill
suggested.

"Let's go to the shopping mall and check it out,"
Marcia urged. "We can do the grocery shopping last
before picking up Dr. Dave."

"Suits me," Holly said.

The mall was crowded with Saturday afternoon
shoppers.

"I never thought I'd enjoy watching a bunch of people," Holly said, laughing.

Marcia agreed.

Bill went off on some business of his own, leaving the two girls to stroll the length of the promenade. At the far end they came to an expensive-looking bar and restaurant.

"Let's have a drink!" Marcia proposed.

"In the middle of the afternoon?" Holly glanced at her watch. "It's only two o'clock!"

"Who cares? I want to sit and be waited on where there are rugs and it's dark...no sunshine. Come with me. Have a Coke or something."

While they stood to one side, hesitating, the double doors swung open, and a small party emerged.

"Look!" Marcia nudged Holly, drawing her attention to the group.

Holly's heart lurched. Raf—in a dark business suit, appearing so handsome she could hardly take her eyes from him. But she couldn't help seeing, on the other side of him, clinging to his arm, Leona. He was gazing down at her, listening to something she was saying, so neither of them noticed Holly and Marcia, standing like waifs outside the restaurant door.

Numb with pain, Holly stared after them. Leona was wearing white again—a billowing dress that swirled around her knees. Her slim legs looked delightfully feminine among the dark uninteresting trousers of the men. Raf's thick straight hair flipped as he nodded his head in vigorous agreement to something she was saying. The stylish cut ended half an inch above his white collar.

"Wasn't that girl at the barbecue?" Marcia was asking.

"Yes."

"And he left her for you. He plays the field, doesn't he!"

Holly shrugged. "Let's have that drink."

"That struck me as a business luncheon," Marcia said when they were seated at a black shiny-topped table in the bar.

It might have been, Holly thought, but she wasn't going to fool herself this time. Raf had taken Leona to it; he was in touch with her. *Face it,* Holly told herself, *you haven't seen him since he said the man who gets you will be the luckiest in the world.* She had feared then that he had no intention of being that man, but she'd convinced herself she was wrong. Now she knew she was right. Yet knowing was small satisfaction.

Their drinks arrived before Holly was even aware she'd ordered.

"You can't jump to conclusions just because a man walks out of a restaurant with a woman," Marcia said. "Not at two in the afternoon. Two in the morning, yes, but not two in the afternoon."

Holly forced herself to smile because Marcia was trying so hard.

She hadn't paid much attention to Marcia since her arrival, other than to conclude she had no dress sense. Holly had been too busy thinking about cooking—and about Raf. That was going to stop. Now. Today. She'd been a real fool to miss out on the trip to Wall last Sunday. Raf had probably taken Leona somewhere that day, too. It was a heart-searing thought.

"Let's go to the dime store," Marcia said. "I love shopping in dime stores! Do you?"

Holly agreed that she did, appreciating the attempt to get her mind off Raf.

The next couple of hours passed in a painful blur. At the supermarket Holly concentrated on her list, while all the time at the back of her mind was an almost intolerable ache. It was crazy! She'd only seen the man a few times. He hadn't made her any promises. He'd said himself he had only stayed at the camp because he felt sorry for her, and the next night he'd invited her for dinner. Big deal! He'd given her no cause in the world to believe he considered her special. The sooner she forgot him, the better. She tossed her head and set her pretty round jaw.

That night she made a point of not looking at his picture before going to sleep.

Next morning, wearing the thin cotton pants she'd bought during her stroll through the shopping mall and a halter top in a shade of pink that made her hair look like molten gold, Holly took her place in the jeep, determined to have a good time. Dr. Dave marked a route for them on the map.

"The Black Hills were considered sacred by the Sioux," he told them. "At one point the government signed them over by treaty. Then gold was discovered, and the treaty was broken. A few years ago the Sioux took the case to court. The government has offered them a cash settlement, but the Sioux maintain they want the land."

Holly's thought leaped to Raf. What was his opinion on the subject?

As if she had conjured him, a Scout came bouncing through the trees, and Raf climbed out of it. Bill, Willie and Wayne gathered about him.

"Another car?" Willie joked. "This is one we haven't seen previously."

"That's because my foreman likes it," Raf said. "I only get it on Sundays."

He wasn't wearing the starched faded blue jeans that were almost his trademark. Today he had on black cotton chinos and an expensive white T-shirt that fitted like a second skin, showing the bulging muscles of his chest and—no doubt, Holly thought bitterly—the graceful curves of his back.

"Dr. Gray told me you're going to the Black Hills today," he began, looking over the young men's heads at Holly, who had been about to climb into the jeep. "You can't all crowd into that thing. Why don't I go along and take the ladies with me?"

The men were unflatteringly enthusiastic. Marcia looked eagerly at Holly, who felt her face grow hot. She hadn't wanted to see him at all, and here she was, suddenly committed to spending a whole day in his company.

"Go with him, Holly," Bill urged. "You got sunburned in the jeep yesterday. You don't need any more today."

Raf's tawny eyes held Holly's, their depths unreadable.

"All right." She crossed to the Scout. "Are you going to follow us so we can all have lunch together?"

"Sure thing! Raf'll know where the buffalo are, too!" Bill opened the Scout's door and pulled the seat forward so Holly could climb into the back.

"What makes you think so?" she hissed.

"He's Indian, isn't he?" Bill laughed.

Holly took time to wonder what was making her brother so lighthearted and decided it was simply high spirits engendered by a day off.

"This is so nice of you, Mr. Valcour," Marcia purred as they drove out of camp. She turned sideways in the front seat to include Holly in the conversation.

"Call me Raf," he said, "and I shall call you Marcia."

Marcia giggled. "You really look after us, don't you, Raf." She winked at Holly.

"Do I?"

"I think you do. Barbecues and horses and outings like this. I bet if you'd seen us yesterday in the mall, you'd have bought us a drink."

Holly met Raf's unfathomable eyes in the rearview mirror and wished she had clung to the jeep.

"I take it you saw me in the mall yesterday. I wish I had been buying you a drink rather than attending a dull business lunch."

Marcia gave Holly a triumphant glance that said clearly, "You see?"

Holly didn't know whether she saw. Plainly Raf hadn't been finding Leona dull. She still ought to pursue the course she'd decided on—which was to put him out of her mind. But today that would be a little hard.

The drive to the Black Hills was short. The road left the rolling green plain and began to climb and wind. Suddenly they were driving among pines and boulders.

"It's like a miniature mountain range," Holly exclaimed.

"That's what it is according to this folder," Marcia said, looking at the other side of the marked map—which she had forgotten to give to the boys in the jeep. "It says they're called the Black Hills because the pines make them look black from a distance."

"That's right," Raf agreed.

Hanging on to the seat as Raf swung the Scout around the curves, Holly felt her spirits rise. "This is like a roller coaster," she laughed. "And what views!"

She had brought her camera. When they came to the Needles—gray black rocks rising above the pines—Raf stopped, and the jeep pulled up beside the Scout. The smooth weathered rocks begged to be clambered over and photographed against the thunderheads spawning in the deep blue sky.

Holly's heart beat faster when she realized that here she had another chance to snap Raf's picture—which was a crazy thing to do if she was going to forget him. He had left the car to stand with his back against the guardrail of the overlook, watching Bill and Willie walk up a sloping pinnacle.

"Don't they get enough climbing during the week?" he asked, sounding amused.

Holly pretended to be busy taking pictures.

"They like having something solid underfoot instead of crumbling clay, I guess," Marcia answered.

"Aren't you going to take our picture?" she said to Holly. "Do we have to go climbing to get photographed?"

So, to be polite, Holly had no choice but to take Raf's picture along with Marcia's. His expression was taciturn and his behavior so aloof that Holly wondered what had prompted him to come. He didn't appear to be having a good time.

"Next stop Mount Rushmore." Marcia consulted the map when everyone had returned to the cars, ready to continue their trip.

"Listen, why should you have both ladies?" Willie playfully demanded of Raf. "We'll trade you Wayne for Marcia. Okay, Wayne?"

"Why not?" Wayne shrugged.

Holly threw Marcia a regretful glance but knew she mustn't be unfair. Marcia would have more fun with Bill and Willie.

"We'll keep following you," Marcia informed Raf before she took Wayne's place in the jeep.

"Don't forget to watch for buffalo," Willie reminded everyone.

Raf shook his head. "Not here. Custer State Park is where the buffalo roam—in the wildlife loop marked on your map."

"Then watch for deer, goats, anything," Willie amended.

The views were beautiful and unspoiled; the valleys small, almost cozy. The few log cabins they passed lent interest to the pine-forest scenery. Wayne forgot to be bored and exclaimed at the sight of deer grazing in a picture-book meadow.

"When Wayne says, 'Look at that!' you know it's worth turning your head for," Holly told Raf with a smile in her voice. She had decided it would be awkward not to talk to him at all, and he certainly must not think she was miffed because of that Saturday night.

"Everything's so *pretty*!" she exclaimed a little later. "You wouldn't believe the stark bare Badlands could be so nearby."

A dead porcupine lay beside the road. The Black Hills were not perfect after all.

Mount Rushmore turned out to be more impressive than Holly had expected.

"When the federal government does something, it spares no expense," Raf remarked after they were directed to the appropriate parking area.

Holly dropped back to photograph the rest of her group following the flag-decorated path to the terrace and visitor's building. Flags of every state snapped in the breeze, colorful against the somber pines.

As she took the camera from her eye and advanced the film, she saw Raf standing to one side, waiting for her. She felt tongue-tied. She feared he wasn't going to say anything, either, and she thought she'd die if she had to walk the whole length of this approach with him in total silence.

"I hope you aren't finding this tour too boring," she finally uttered.

"No," he said easily. "Every time I come here, I'm impressed all over again. Besides, the company's stimulating—these bright young minds being trained by Dr. Dave and Dr. Gray," he added, just as Holly thought he was alluding to her.

It was on the tip of her tongue to say, "I'm sorry you're stuck with me," when he grasped her arm. Her heart missed a beat.

"Slow down a minute. I didn't come on this trip to play games." He glanced over his shoulder. People from a tourist bus were straggling up the walk.

"Damnation!" he muttered. "I wanted to say I'm sorry about last weekend. I behaved like a boor. If you're a virgin, you're a virgin. I had no business getting angry over that."

Before Holly could catch her breath, his hand was moving her along. He said, "Let's forget it and have a good time. Okay?"

"Okay," she agreed warily. Did he really think she could forget what he'd done to her emotions, alone with her in that raw scenery? He'd roused her in a way she had never allowed anyone else to do, and now he was treating her as if virginity was some kind of disease—a disease he wasn't offering to cure. Not that she'd let him!

Despite the danger that being in his company might break her determination to put him out of her mind, Holly couldn't help being aware of the admiring glances he received from female tourists. She stole an objective look. His strong profile was as sharply cut as though it had been molded and baked in red clay. The handsome nose with its flaring nostrils, the proud carriage of his head, proclaimed his descent from chieftains.

Holly was unaware that her own golden beauty served as a foil to Raf's dark masculinity. She stepped onto the broad terrace, proudly conscious of the man at her side, until she turned her eyes to the sculptures and for a time forgot her personal affairs.

The four heads sculpted from the living stone were breathtakingly alive, brooding between dark pines and sky. They dominated everything—the blue sky, the sunlight, the crisp clear air. They looked no different from all the pictures Holly had seen, but the immensity of those four symbolic faces was more stirring than any photograph could convey.

Holly couldn't resist taking pictures nevertheless. Then her group watched the slide show that summarized the lives of the four men and explained why the sculptor had chosen those presidents to commemorate.

"I was more impressed than I thought I'd be," Wayne admitted on the way back to the parking lot.

"I think we all were," Bill agreed.

Again they drove through lovely scenery to where a monument to Chief Crazy Horse was being cut out of another mountain.

"Do you think the sculptor will ever get it done?" Holly asked Raf when they drove away. "Carving out a mountain is such an enormous project."

"His sons will finish it," Raf replied. "They've grown up with the work, and one or two are helping now."

"The buffalo herd is next," Wayne said, consulting the map. "What do you bet we won't see any?"

"Don't be such a cynic!" Holly exclaimed. "Why won't we?"

"Because they advertise jeep rides to the buffalo. That means you have to go someplace out of the way, not just on this so-called nature loop."

"Raf will find them," Holly said securely.

Again he met her eyes in the rearview mirror. Amusement sparked his own eyes. "Your faith is touching, but first, I think, we'll have lunch. We're coming to the town of Custer.''

However, he drove right through it.

"Where are we going?" Holly asked sharply. Her stomach was beginning to demand food.

"Here." Raf pulled into the parking lot of a road-side eatery.

Holly read the sign and began to laugh. It said, CUSTER'S LAST HAMBURGER STAND. The jeep parked beside the Scout and its three grinning occupants climbed out.

"Too much!" Willie commented, shaking his head.

"I don't know how their food is, but I thought you'd enjoy the sign," Raf commented, taking Holly's arm possessively.

Her heart sang at his touch, but her appetite deserted her. All she could think of was that Raf seemed to have forgiven her for disappointing him the other night. She couldn't imagine where it would lead and didn't want to try. For now she was thrilled simply to be at his side.

She ordered a hamburger with the others. The six of them sat around two tables pulled together. Holly toyed with her food when it came, expecting everyone to be too busy talking to notice. Raf, instead of joining in the conversation, which probably sounded sophomoric and immature to a man of his age, took note of Holly's failure to eat.

"Isn't the cooking up to your standard?" he asked humorously under cover of the others' discussion.

"It's fine!" Holly told him.

"Then why aren't you eating?"

"I am!"

He shrugged and turned his attention to Willie, who wanted to know what Raf thought of the Sioux's chances of regaining the Black Hills.

"It's no subject to go into over lunch," Raf said, "unless you want to stay here till breakfast."

When it came time to pay, Raf picked up the check. The protest from the impecunious students was not very forceful, but they were loud in their thanks. Holly would have liked to pay for her uneaten hamburger. She wasn't a schoolgirl, after all. The incident left her feeling out of place. Was she, in Raf's eyes, just one of the children?

"Would you like to sit up front?" Wayne asked in the parking lot.

Overhearing him, Willie said, "Of course she would, you chump!" so Holly had no choice but to take the seat beside Raf, where she was immediately, insanely, conscious of his hard-muscled arm reaching out to change gears, the shapely brown hands holding the steering wheel.

His hawklike glance missed nothing on either side of the road. If there were buffalo, he would see them.

The wildlife loop ran through a valley of rolling meadows between pine-clad hills. Raf stopped once to point out to those in the jeep the bright white-and-brown of antelope on a hillside and again to show them, through binoculars, a porcupine perched in a tree nibbling succulent twigs. The sunlight on its bristles made it look like a small furry bear.

"But where are the buffalo?" Marcia demanded while she waited for her turn with the field glasses.

"How about over there?" Raf asked, his voice tinged with amusement.

Sure enough, in the tall grass of a distant meadow, Holly and the others made out four or five great brown lumps that were buffalo, lying down chewing cud. The thrill Holly had expected did not happen.

"Five!" Willie exclaimed disparagingly. "That's a herd?"

"Those will be the bulls," Raf told them. "They separate from the cows and calves this time of year."

They drove on through a vast open stretch that should have contained buffalo but didn't. Holly began to think Wayne was right—that those five faraway specimens were all they would see.

The road wound through a hilly stretch and curved around one last hill to enter a little pine-studded valley. At last came the thrill Holly had expected. There, on both sides of the road, were buffalo—several hundred. Calves cavorted among the adults, whose hides were patchy with shedding hair. One shaggy beast stood posed in the classic side view. These living symbols, a link with the West's colorful past, excited Holly's imagination far more than the thought of discovering a titanothere bone. She glanced at Raf. He met her look with a raised eyebrow.

"Are you wondering if they make my blood run faster?" His reading of her mind was so accurate that her delightful laugh bubbled forth even as her cheeks reddened.

"They do," he admitted, "but no more than yours, I daresay. We're all raised on Western lore, aren't we?"

As though the admission embarrassed him, he turned in his seat to speak to Wayne. "Satisfied?" he asked.

"Yeah," Wayne said, without removing his eyes from the herd.

Holly produced her camera and, between exclamations, snapped picture after picture as Raf drove at five miles an hour. One burly creature disputed the road while Raf ran the Scout alongside the patchy brown hide and Holly stared through the lens into one great brown eye.

She was saddened that these animals had come to this—to be gawked at from automobiles when once they had thundered over the plains in mighty herds. The titanotheres had come and gone, too, and the oreodonts and the wandering tribes of Indians. Nothing lasted.

A strong warm finger touched her chin, making her start. Raf turned her face to him. "Have you seen enough buffalo?"

Holly realized that despite her philosophical thoughts she was immensely thrilled.

"I'll never forget it!" she promised. "When I was a little girl, I wanted to see a buffalo more than anything else."

"You're still a little girl," he said softly.

Holly bit her lip to keep from looking too pleased. She mustn't start expecting attention from him again. She mustn't!

They returned to the park restaurant for cold drinks and bought postcards and souvenirs as any group of tourists would. When it was time to leave, Willie was at the wheel of the jeep. Holly looked about for her brother. "Where's Bill?" she inquired casually.

"He hitched a ride to Rapid City," Willie told her.

"Rapid City!"

"Yeah. Said he had a date." Willie laughed disbelievingly, and Holly laughed with him. Still, it was strange of Bill to go off like that.

"How's he going to get back to camp?" she worried.

"Hitchhike, he said. Personally I think he's gonna have a long walk." ·

"Me, too," Holly agreed.

Raf stopped at a tourist resort several miles outside of Rapid City and treated everyone to pizza. He insisted on sending slices to the professors, too.

It was dark by the time they reached camp. The day hadn't been a restful one, after all. Holly undressed and fell onto her cot. She wasn't so much tired, she realized, as let down. Raf had shaken her hand and said good-night just as he had Wayne's and the others'. She had nothing to look forward to but a week of hard work.

CHAPTER TEN

THE WEEK PASSED at the steady pace of three meals a day.

"All people do is eat," Holly grumbled to Willie Yu one evening while he was drying the dishes.

"You need a break," Willie told her. "Why don't you go riding when we get through here. That horse you like is still here. Junior Old Elk went off with the others before I got back. I unsaddled, but I can saddle her for you."

"Maybe that is what I need," Holly said.

"Sure. Break the monotony."

She switched shorts and sandals for jeans and boots but didn't change her pink halter. The sun was on its way down. However, sunset made little difference in the heat this time of year.

"Don't get lost," Willie cautioned offhandedly a quarter of an hour later, when Holly bestrode Brown Betty.

"I have a good sense of direction," Holly assured him.

The trail to Buffalo Table led along the bare banks of the creek with its ugly white water. Brown Betty struck an easy pace. Holly wished she were riding the other way—toward the ranch and Raf. She hadn't seen him since Sunday, but she had continued to think about him, despite her determination not to.

The trail crossed the shallow creek and led out over the prairie. Holly rode contentedly, her thoughts on nothing more than the sensations of the moment— the sensuous movement of Brown Betty, the creak of leather, the horsey smell. Grasshoppers sprang up buzzing from beneath the plodding hooves. The wind carried the scent of drying grass, and a meadowlark sang from a clump of pinkish lavender flowers.

Suddenly the wind brought different sounds— high-pitched shouts overriding the bawling of cattle. But the whole vast expanse of plain appeared empty. At last Holly's searching eyes found a rising cloud of dust.

"That's where they are!" She spoke aloud to Brown Betty. "They're driving cattle down some draw. Let's go take a look!" A touch of the reins guided the mare toward the dust cloud.

The gully took longer to reach than Holly had expected. The face of the prairie looked perfectly level, but it was veined everywhere by draws and washouts, forerunners of erosion to come sometime in the future.

By the time she reached the valley's rim, the herd and cowboys had moved on, leaving only trodden earth and settling dust to mark their passage. Holly sat looking at the parklike setting. The sun's last rays gilded the tops of two cottonwood trees. The rest of the valley lay in shadow.

Suddenly she saw movement beneath one of the trees—a man...throwing his leg over a saddled horse. Raf!

Holly's heart jumped. At the same moment Brown

Betty whinnied. Raf looked up and stared for an instant before he raised a gloved hand in recognition.
The steep cliff prevented him from riding up to her.
He pointed in the direction the herd had taken and
shouted, indicating he'd meet her farther along the
rim. Then a growth of wild plum bushes immediately
hid him from sight.

Holly rode the way he'd pointed, wondering if she
had understood his signal correctly. She heard a
scrambling of hooves and then saw him, urging his
buckskin mount up the last steep incline. He swung
the horse to meet her, poker-faced as ever.

Her breath caught as she took in his appearance.
He was powdered from hat to boots with white dust,
and the sweat running down from his hatband had
made trails along his brown cheeks. Dust had grayed
his blue shirt and jeans. Despite all that he was as attractive as ever.

Removing his hat, he wiped his forehead with his
sleeve. Holly searched his features for some indica-
tion that he was glad to see her and found twin
flames glowing in his eyes.

"This is an unexpected sight at the end of a hot
day's work. Are you real?" he said quietly.

Holly's lovely smile lighted her face at his welcome. "I didn't expect to see you, either," she told
him.

"How long have you been standing here?"

"Not long. I saw the dust and heard the noise. I
wanted to see a herd on the move, but I was too
late."

"I'd much rather see you," Raf said. "We've been
rounding up all day to switch them to new pasture.

You'd have missed me, too, if this horse hadn't picked up a stone."

He dismounted in one fluid motion. Gripping Brown Betty's bridle, he offered his other hand to help Holly from the saddle. "Get down and stretch your legs."

"Shouldn't you—I mean, I'm keeping you from your work."

He shook his head. "They can get along, but if I'm too slow, they're liable to come looking for me."

Holly had been studying the buckskin. "This horse looks like the one that won the Fourth of July race," she said. "Is he related?"

"Very closely." Raf's eyes twinkled. "He's the one."

"And you ride him?" Holly exclaimed. "I mean, you make him work?"

"He's one of the best workers. Aren't you, old boy?" Raf stroked the buckskin's nose. The horse tossed his head as if he understood. "He's a cow pony, like the other two I entered. At a guess I'd say none of the horses you saw were strictly racehorses. They earn their keep on the range."

Walking their mounts, Raf and Holly scuffed through the grass. She was oblivious to everything but his presence. His musky male odor, heightened by sun and sweat, sent the blood racing through her veins. Every pore of her skin felt open and receptive to his virility. Nothing was real but that she was here with him.

He seemed to sense her vulnerability, seemed to want to make an effort to show her the reality.

"Now you see the real Raf Valcour." His voice

was without humor. "A dirty, sweaty, half-Indian cowpuncher."

Holly choked on the denial rising to her lips. He was rejecting her again, telling her their lives could have no parallel course.

I see a man, she wanted to tell him. But it would have no effect. He didn't want her—he'd made that clear.

Tears gathered in her open sky-blue eyes as though she had no control over them—which indeed she hadn't. Before she could turn her head, two rolled down her cheeks. She whipped her head around to stare over her shoulder, but Raf's sharp gaze saw them fall.

"Holly! My God!" He caught her chin in one lean calloused hand and made her face him. "Holly? Oh, sweetheart, what's wrong?" he groaned.

"Nothing." His face was so close to hers she had not one thought in her head. Her tear-washed eyes centered on the sensuous masculine lips hovering inches away.

With another groan he pulled her against him, and his lips tasted the salty wetness of her sweeping lashes.

"Don't tell me you were crying because I'm a dirty cowboy," he teased, putting up a finger to tilt her head and nibbling her lips as she answered.

"No." She sighed. "You made us sound so far apart."

"We're not far apart now, are we?" He held her more closely.

She shook her head, unable to speak. He was joking her into good humor, as one would a child.

I'll show him I'm not a child, she thought angrily, and did something she'd never done to any man previously. Fastening her fingers in his dusty hair, she pulled his face down to hers and began kissing him as seductively as she knew how.

Evidently it was seductive enough. She heard his hat and gloves plop in the dust as he caught her against his chest but continued to let her be the temptress, letting himself be seduced.

"Whew!" he said when she paused to catch her breath. "So that's the way it is!"

Leaving the horses with reins trailing, he half led, half carried her to a sandy spot between clumps of wheatgrass. Sitting on the ground, he pulled her across his legs to face him.

"You are the loveliest thing a man could see after a day's work," he told her again, lazily pulling her to him and holding her by the shoulders while he rained kisses on her face and neck.

She whispered his name—the only word in her head. Mingled with his male scent, dust powdered her nostrils. She felt the scrape of his day's beard when his face dipped between her breasts. Her hands slid over his back, caressing the hard curves of taut muscles. One hand slipped under his collar to feel the corded neck that held his proud head. His lips returned to hers, drugging her while he deftly untied both sets of halter straps. The next instant Holly's breasts were bared to the caressing prairie wind and Raf's work-roughened hands. She could only think crazily that she wanted two things at once—to feel her breasts crushed against the male-smelling cotton of his shirt and to feel his lips tasting her nipples.

Instead Raf coolly set her back a bit and feasted his tawny eyes upon her nakedness.

"Beautiful...beautiful," he whispered, before his lips went to the round pale globes.

Holly thought her blush must be turning her pink to the navel.

As if he knew how her lips yearned to touch him, his hand groped for her face. She caught it to her, dropping kisses into the palm and on the soft skin of his inner wrist.

He raised his head and appeared to become conscious of their surroundings.

"Look what you started, you little witch!" he exclaimed. "Let's get you dressed. One of my riders might be along any minute."

He picked the pink halter out of the grass clump where he'd flung it and began to tie the straps behind Holly's neck, asking, "How do you know how tight to make it?"

She raised her hands to take the ends and tie it herself. At sight of her upraised arms, Raf's tawny eyes turned to yellow flame.

"Once more," he breathed. Running his hands beneath the cloth, he cupped her breasts. His lips sought her mouth.

With a gasp Holly dropped the knotted cloth and dug her fingers into his thick black hair, burning his lips closer to hers.

It was Raf again who broke away, leaving her shaking. In one lithe motion he was on his feet.

"Get up," he said heartlessly. "Get dressed." He turned away and walked to Brown Betty to pick up the trailing lines.

"It'll be dark now before you get back to camp," he called over his shoulder.

Holly knotted the pink ties behind her back. What was to stop him from riding back with her? Would he have behaved this way if she had been willing to go all the way that Saturday night—*"get up; get dressed"*?

"I can take care of myself," she said angrily.

His reply was a derisive look as he handed her into the saddle. She had trouble believing those firm brown lips had been locked on hers, had been soft when he had devoured her with his eyes. She tried desperately to think of something to say to alter the shuttered expression with which he was regarding her, but no words came.

He mounted his weary horse and turned it toward the creek bottom.

"You know the way back?" he asked.

"Oh, yes."

"Good night, then." He settled his hat and rode off without a backward glance. The silver conchas on his hatband glittered in the setting sun.

If that doesn't tell you where you're at, nothing will, Holly thought bitterly.

Crossing the quiet prairie, she kept seeing Raf's figure floating before her—dusty and hot, with tired lines about his eyes. She heard him say again, "the real Raf Valcour... a dirty, sweaty, half-Indian cowpuncher." Did he think she cared about that? She realized with a sinking thud that every guise she had seen him in—businessman, brave, rancher, host and now cowboy—had imprinted him more deeply on her heart. She could no longer avoid the truth: she was in love—a sentiment Raf Valcour had never mentioned.

NEXT DAY AT NOON Dr. Dave awoke the heat-dulled interest of everyone around the table by announcing, "I met Valcour this morning. He wants to take us all to Deadwood Saturday night. To dinner," Dr. Dave said pointedly to Holly.

She kept her face from betraying the pleasure she felt.

"We can't all get in his car!" Marcia objected.

"He'll drive the Mercedes, and he said I can drive the Scout if we all want to go."

Holly's spirits soared. She would see Raf sooner than she had hoped.

Before she could be swept away on a tide of happiness, she heard Willie Yu say, "I thought you didn't like Raf, Dr. Dave."

The professor cocked his head judiciously. "He's not a bad fellow. Certainly he's generous."

Holly took due note of Dr. Dave's change of attitude. Raf had only to exert his charm, extend an invitation with an offer of the Scout and Dr. Dave began to like him. Raf probably knew he had simply to bend his tawny glance on women to have them fall at his feet. As she had done.

Nevertheless her thoughts turned happily to what she would wear. The slinky black dress she'd brought from New York would be suitable for a night on the town—any town.

WILLIE AND WAYNE BOTH WHISTLED when the girls emerged from their tent on Saturday night, Holly stepping carefully over the rough ground in her high-heeled black sandals. She had wound her golden hair into a knot on the crown of her head. Escaping tendrils dangled fetchingly at her temples.

"You're riding with me, aren't you, Holly?" Dr. Dave hailed her from Raf's Scout. "I trust you'll spurn the comfort of a Mercedes for our intellectual company." He and Bill had already driven to the ranch in the jeep and picked up the other car.

"If she wants intellectual company, she'd be better off in the Mercedes with Dr. Gray," Willie needled, "but if it's charm, ride with us!" He waved her into the Scout.

Holly began to fear the evening wouldn't be so wonderful after all.

At the ranch Raf came out wearing a dark Western-cut suit. His white shirt emphasized the clear bronze of his skin. Those in the jeep transferred to the Mercedes. Regretfully Holly kept her seat. Raf merely glanced in her direction before they set off. If she'd been in the Mercedes, she realized, she'd have had to sit in back because Dr. Gray was naturally offered the place beside their host.

Bill and Willie were in high spirits and looking forward to a night out. They enlivened the trip with joking commentary that kept Holly's thoughts from dwelling on Raf.

Squeezed into a sharp valley, Deadwood appeared to have only one street. The two cars were parked, and the party set out on foot. Raf guided them past the Number Eleven Saloon, where Wild Bill Hickok had been shot in the back while playing poker, to another quieter bar that was not such a tourist attraction. Sawdust covered the floor, and men were sitting at round tables, drinking and playing cards. Holly's eyes popped. Without thinking, she turned to Raf.

"Are they real?" she murmured when he bent his ear to catch her voice.

"Oh, yes. You notice there's no television set? I've lost a few dollars here myself. Won some, too," he added reflectively.

They sat at a round table in the back near a stuffed buffalo. Raf managed to reserve a chair for himself next to Holly.

"I recommend the steak here," he told his guests. "That's about all they know how to cook."

Everyone was hungry for steak. Holly's food budget hadn't run to that kind of meat.

"Did you get home all right the other night?" Raf asked her under cover of the general conversation.

Holly felt the blood rise to her cheeks as she recalled her wanton behavior. From under her eyelashes she saw Dave watching her across the table.

"Yes, thank you," she answered quietly.

"But you didn't want to ride with me tonight?"

She hesitated. How could she explain? "I couldn't refuse to go in the Scout," she said low voiced, hoping that Dave couldn't hear.

"I suppose he didn't approve of your horseback ride the other evening, either," Raf queried in an undertone while facing her squarely and taking her hand, making his interest obvious to everyone.

Holly hid her hot face behind the cardboard square of the menu and refused to look at him.

"All right, I'll stop teasing you," Raf conceded. "But your Dr. Dave mustn't think to have it all his way. Not that I blame him for trying." His eyes swept over her, ending at the curls at her temples. "You look totally beautiful."

"He doesn't have it his way!" Holly contradicted hotly. Did Raf think it was her habit to kiss men the way she'd kissed him?

The steaks were as delicious as Raf had promised. They were accompanied by baked potatoes with sour cream and the kind of tossed salad everyone in the group was hungry for.

Holly forced herself to eat. The party was small enough that the conversation was general. From time to time she glanced covertly at Raf. Was he more handsome in that suit or in a plaid shirt, boots and jeans? She couldn't decide, but rather than eat steak she would have preferred to feast her eyes on him—his face, his deft fingers cutting the meat. She thought of those hands on her breasts and shivered.

"Cold?" he asked, apparently more aware of her than she had realized.

"No, I just thought of something," she denied.

His eyes slid sideways. "Was it what I'm thinking?" His gaze rested on her breasts.

Holly drew a sharp breath and choked. Desperate to change the subject, she said sweetly, "You're free tonight. Leona's vacation must have ended."

The look he gave her was derisive, but all he said was, "Yes."

A moment later he was telling the incredulous students, "Yes, there is a black market in fossils. As you know, it's against the law to take fossils from the park without a permit. One of my more unsavory neighbors has been arrested and sent to jail three times, but the business pays so well he takes up right where he left off. Park rangers aren't hired to do guard duty and night patrols. There aren't enough of them, for one thing."

"Who'd buy fossils on the black market?" Wayne asked disparagingly.

"Yeah, who'd want a bunch of oreodont bones scattered around the living room?" Bill chimed in.

"Museums," Raf said, and Dr. Gray nodded in agreement. "Not in this country, I hope, but around the world...emerging nations. Turtles are our most common fossil. Everybody can recognize a turtle, and it makes a conversation piece. A huge turtle fossil looks impressive in the foyer of a modern office or home with a background of carpeting and glass."

Bill shook his head. "Everything's being ripped off."

"On the other hand—" Raf nodded deferentially to Dr. Gray "—American museums have all the huge turtle fossils they want. Is it better to let the fossil fall apart and wash away when someone might enjoy its preservation and the local people can earn some badly needed cash?" He shrugged. "There are two sides to the question."

Everyone had an opinion. At last Marcia said, "When are we going to see one of these much touted rainstorms?"

"Maybe tomorrow, maybe next month." Raf shrugged again. "I suppose Dr. Gray or Dr. Dave have warned you about them?"

"Nobody warned me," Bill said. Other eyebrows were raised.

Looking a little guilty, Dr. Gray shook his head.

"Time enough when we see some clouds," Dr. Dave said carelessly.

Raf disagreed. "That could be too late. It takes only a little water for those hills to become slippery. If you're on top of a pinnacle and want to get down, you could slip and break a leg. If you're caught in a gully, it's difficult to get out. A trickle can become a torrent in minutes."

Holly was glad to see the students looking suitably impressed. How careless of Dave not to mention the danger. The physical part of recovering fossils was his business.

"You have to see it to understand how slippery that clay can get," Raf went on. "The dirt roads, too. The rangers warn visitors not to go off on back roads if it looks like rain. I guess they figure paleontologists can take care of themselves."

"I'd like to see a good rain," Bill said.

"So you can lie in the sack all day!" Willie hooted.

"I doubt that." Bill eyed Dr. Dave, who ruthlessly shook his head.

"The work goes on."

They were discussing dessert when faraway shouts and the sound of shooting brought some of the patrons to their feet.

"What's happening out there?" Marcia demanded, looking a little pale.

Raf clucked and bit his lip. "I shouldn't have brought you here on a Saturday night!" He sounded perturbed, but Holly read the sparkle in his golden gaze.

"Deadwood's roaring past comes to life on Saturday night," Dr. Gray said, smiling. "I imagine that's what Raf has brought us here to see."

Raf pushed back his chair. "Coming?" The rest of the party rose hastily to their feet.

Holly felt Raf's hand on the small of her back. Scuffing through the sawdust, she resented the familiar way he touched her, yet didn't want her....

A crowd had collected along the narrow sidewalk. A stagecoach, looking unexpectedly small among the parked automobiles, came rattling down the street, drawn by galloping horses. It pulled up in front of the Number Eleven Saloon, and a woman wearing an 1880s dress was helped down.

"Belle Starr," Raf said at Holly's shoulder. His hand on her hip was making her self-conscious. Did the way he was acting tonight mean he was still interested in her?

A trio of stagey-looking cowboys rode down the street from the opposite direction and dismounted, tying their horses to a hitching rail. They stalked into the saloon. Seconds later more shots rang out. Men erupted from the saloon, and a woman screamed. The three cowboys came running out, shooting their pistols into the air. With wild yippees they leaped on their horses and galloped back the way they had come. Belle Starr helped the wounded Wild Bill Hickok into the stagecoach, and they rode away, waving to onlookers, after which people drifted back inside the various bars and cafés that lined the street.

"That was it?" Wayne scoffed, coloring when he realized his remark was hardly polite.

"That was it," Raf agreed cheerfully, guiding Holly back to their table.

Much as the younger members of the party had

looked forward to a Saturday night in town, by the time they had lingered over dessert, yawns were beginning to be hidden.

Raf settled the check and stood up. "I'd like to invite you all to stop in for coffee and liqueur when we get back to the ranch." His eyes went round the circle and rested on Holly.

She seemed to read a special message in his darkened pupils. Was he trying to tell her not to let Dr. Dave dissuade her?

"Well, was it worth driving all this way?" Dr. Dave criticized when the Scout was headed back toward Rapid City.

"The steak alone was worth the trip," Willie exclaimed.

"And we've seen Deadwood," Bill added.

"*I* enjoyed it," Holly stated.

Dr. Dave looked grumpy. "If all Valcour wanted was to talk to you, Holly, why'd he drag all of us along?"

Holly was too annoyed to reply. In the back Bill and Willie were talking baseball.

After a few miles Dr. Dave reached over and squeezed Holly's hand. "Don't be angry," he murmured.

She could think of no excuse to snatch her hand back. Luckily he soon needed both hands for the wheel. Holly folded her arms, but Dr. Dave determinedly recaptured her hand. She suspected that Bill and Willie had fallen asleep and did her best to do likewise.

As they approached the ranch, Dr. Dave said, "I suppose you want to stop?"

"I think it would be rude not to," Holly said

sharply. She had been promising herself she would
ride absolutely no farther with Dr. Dave than the
ranch. She'd make Marcia trade cars with her.

The occupants of the Mercedes were already in the
living room, sipping liqueur or coffee, according to
their choice, and admiring Raf's collection of turtle
fossils.

"We thought you'd fallen by the wayside," Dr.
Gray greeted them when they entered.

Holly's eyes flew to Raf, coming to welcome them.
He couldn't think they'd deliberately lingered, with
Bill and Willie in the car. Nevertheless she felt in need
of something to perk up her spirits. Dr. Dave was
hovering at her side like a determined bodyguard.
But liqueurs were so sweet....

"Could I have a little white wine?" she asked hesitantly.

"Certainly." Despite Dr. Dave's grunt of annoyance, Raf looked down into her eyes as though he
would willingly give her his ranch. Holly suspected he
was getting a kick out of Dr. Dave's bristling behavior.

When he returned with a glass of wine, Dr. Dave
was still guarding her.

"Come over here, doctor, I'd like to ask you something about this particular fossil," Raf purred, neatly
detaching the professor from Holly. Leading him
away, Raf glanced over his shoulder. His eyes glis-
tened with mischief.

Seconds later, while she was studying an old por-
trait of Indians in buckskin costumes, Raf materialized before her.

"That's called cutting out," he said darkly.

Holly had been determined to treat him with no more than ordinary civility, but she couldn't help laughing, especially since his successful maneuver relieved her of Dr. Dave's unwanted company.

Perhaps Raf, too, had decided his own attentions to Holly had been too particular. At any rate, he made it a point to chat individually with each of his guests.

However, when it came time to leave, he threw another spoke in Dr. Dave's wheel. "I'll drive you over in the Scout," he said, "and then I can bring it back."

Dr. Dave looked chagrined, but he could hardly object.

Holly slid into the back seat beside her brother. Willie drove the jeep.

When they reached the camp, Dr. Dave bade Raf a formal good-night and stalked to his tent. When Holly attempted to do the same, Raf said, "Wait a minute," and gravely accepted the others' thanks.

"Come for a walk with me, Holly," he ordered when they were alone. "Oh, you're wearing heels again? Get your sandals. I'll wait."

As though she had no mind of her own, Holly did as she was told. Marcia was undressing when Holly entered their tent and explained she had only come to change her shoes.

"He's crazy about you!" Marcia hissed. "I could see it in his eyes every time he looked at you. My goodness he's handsome!"

"He's looking for a summer affair," Holly muttered.

"So?"

"I don't think I could deal with that," Holly said, grateful for the slang phrase, which said exactly what she felt.

"Have fun anyway," Marcia recommended when Holly slipped out.

Raf was standing beside a cottonwood. She joined him, her heart racing.

"How you've shrunk," he said. When she wasn't wearing heels, his lips were on a level with her forehead. He leaned forward to drop a kiss on her brow.

"Let's take the path along the creek." Taking her hand, he led the way through the trees.

I must be out of my mind, Holly thought, *to let him lead me off like this after what happened last time.* Yet nothing could have kept her from going. The knowledge that she loved him was still new. It had to make a difference, she thought. Perhaps he had guessed and wanted to discuss the situation. He must have arrived at some compromise. She didn't ask herself what compromise could exist for a virile masculine man.

The moon had been full the past two nights. Its light was still bright enough to make the pale earth almost brilliant. Raf's catlike tread slowed. His arm encircled her, and they proceeded side by side.

"Did you have a good time?" he asked.

"Yes, did you?"

"If you did."

Holly's eyes sparkled. "It was a real touch of the West—people playing cards in the saloon—and the steak was so good! The stagecoach and the shooting were fun, too."

"Not too corny for a sophisticated model?"

"Don't call me that, please."

"But you are."

Holly was silent and suddenly uneasy.

Raf said, "There's not much excitement here—that's a fact. Most of the year it's just cattle and weather. The women around here get pretty bored, even when they've lived here all their lives. Some, of course, simply move heaven and earth to get away— like Leona. She's heading for Denver or Chicago."

Holly's heart thumped. Had he asked Leona to marry him and been turned down? Surely it wasn't possible.... Yet what but loneliness could drive a man of Raf's charm—yes, and sophistication—to spend a Sunday driving a bunch of college students around to look at buffalo or make him spend Saturday night playing host to these same strangers?

Her whole body felt leaden. He had brought her out here because he wanted to talk—not about his feelings or Holly's feelings, but about his disappointment. And yet she couldn't believe it. No woman would turn down an offer of marriage from Raf. Maybe not even the offer of an affair—if he asked twice. If she truly loved him, would she willingly listen to his problems with other women, she asked herself. Her honest answer was no. Over a drink, maybe, in a bar, but not when she was being taken for a moonlight stroll.

At last, feeling she had a right to bring herself into the conversation, she said humorously, "Are you warning me away from South Dakota?"

"Sounds like it, doesn't it?" She was surprised to see a smile cross his moonlight-etched features.

Suddenly, then, she ached with despair. He wasn't

going to kiss her. This was another rejection scene. Some game of torture.

She whirled in the pathway, sliding out of the circle of his arm. "It's late. You forget I have to cook breakfast."

"So you do. Not tired of it yet?"

"I won't deny it's a day's work. But so is modeling, though you don't think so."

"You taught me the hard way, remember?" He was referring to the way she had slapped him.

"I never expected to see you again," she recalled.

Surprisingly, for a man who didn't show his feelings, he sighed. "Come on," he said, "I'd better get you back."

Holly walked quickly, because she longed for her cot and the darkness of the tent where she could give way to her misery. It still came down to the basic fact: in his mind they were poles apart. An affair wouldn't make them any closer. Now, apparently, he wasn't even interested in that.

Before her tent he kissed her on the forehead and walked away to climb into the Scout. She was choking back angry tears when she heard it roar off.

CHAPTER ELEVEN

ANOTHER WEEK PASSED—hot July days that made fossil collecting in the afternoon impossible. Instead the crew began work at daybreak and knocked off each afternoon to clean and pack fossils already collected. Saturday and Sunday mornings were no exception. On Sunday afternoon they stopped work and went for a swim in Raf's pool. His Mercedes was not in the garage, and he did not appear.

Holly ached to see him, and though she swam and joked and drank the cold drinks provided by Mrs. Jones, the ache did not go away.

"I have to forget him," she told Marcia calmly that night—as though love were a grocery list you could walk off and leave. Her work, whether it was cooking or cleaning fossils, allowed too much time to think. What if.... What if....

Another monotonous week passed—the last in July. Holly could be thankful for one thing—it brought the time of leaving closer. For a second Sunday afternoon the crew swam in Raf's pool, and again the garage was empty. A fire of jealousy burned in Holly's chest, unquenched by the number of laps she swam.

"Where do you suppose he goes?" Marcia asked curiously when Holly dropped panting beside her.

"He wouldn't take the Mercedes if he were working, would he?"

"He goes to a resort in the Black Hills, where the temperature is ten—no, fifteen—degrees cooler and the pool is surrounded by girls in bikinis. He can have his choice." Holly spoke her worst fears.

"Nonsense!" Marcia snapped. "He goes to church, and then the preacher's wife or one of the church ladies drags him off to dinner to meet her frumpy niece, and he's too polite to get away."

The picture of Raf being roped in by a matchmaking matron made Holly smile despite her misery. But her own answer to his whereabouts was far more likely to be true.

I love him, she thought. *He knows it, but he doesn't care. A virgin's too inconvenient to his conscience.*

The weather changed slightly. The days of burning blue skies were followed by days in which enormous towering thunderheads built up in the west and sailed overhead, bringing relief when they blocked the fierce sun, but only brief violent downpours over a few square miles. Day after day prairie and Badlands baked under the unyielding sun.

In the middle of the first week in August Marcia made the discovery they were all hoping for. The heat was forgotten. She had been standing on Buffalo Table, surveying the walls of the deep canyons and spires along the table's edge through binoculars, when the right light conditions, combined with her sharp eyes, enabled her to spot a group of bleached bones weathering out of the clay. Dr. Dave was called to look at them. They appeared to be in the

Chadron formation of the early Oligocene and could be titanothere fossils. Some looked big enough. The problem was how to reach them.

Next morning, Bill and Dr. Dave took the horses and rode the several miles around the base of the table to what they judged was the mouth of the right canyon. It took two days of threading the mazelike gullies to find the right ones, but when they did, it was worthwhile. They picked up a fair sampling of titanothere bones that had already eroded out, broken apart and washed down. When they reached a place where they could look up at the embedded fossils, they decided the wall was impossible to climb from below.

Back at camp, Dr. Gray looked at one of the fossils they had picked up and grew very excited.

"A juvenile!" he exclaimed. "See, this bone isn't developed yet—here...and here! I've always wanted to find a young titanothere. Do you realize how rare a good specimen is? This could be a major find. Where did you say it's located?"

"In the most impossible place you ever saw."

"Then we must build a scaffold," came the implacable answer. "I'll drive up with you and have a look. We'd all better go. Who's here?"

The other students were at the site, scrambling about in the canyon, Bill told him.

"Good, then there'll be room in the jeep for Holly. Come, girl," he called. "This may be the raison d'être for all your cooking...indeed, for the whole summer."

They drove up the winding track—one could hardly call it a road—paying no attention to the afternoon sun, which popped in and out of the thunderheads like a bowling ball through a flock of sheep.

Holly walked through the clumps of crackling dried grass to the vantage point from which Marcia had first glimpsed the fossils, admiring Marcia's ability to distinguish them from the surrounding mudstone. Then they all tramped across the level tableland to a spot directly above the fossils and peered over the brink.

"See that level place down there?" Dr. Dave pointed. "We could probably lower a scaffold from there. We have better access from here than from down in the canyon."

"I think you're right," Dr. Gray agreed. "Bill, as soon as we get back, I want you to take a message to Valcour.

"We'll see what he suggests," he told Dr. Dave. "Whatever it is, we must work fast. One hard rainstorm could destroy the whole thing."

"Or it could wash it out for us," Dr. Dave cheerfully reminded him.

"Hmf! I'd rather not take that chance."

So Bill was dispatched to the ranch to deliver a message to Raf. The rest of the day passed with Holly in a tizzy, but Raf did not appear.

"He has to come!" Marcia moaned that evening. She could think of nothing but the safety of her find.

By nine o'clock next morning Raf still had not put in an appearance.

"He has a ranch to run, after all," Dr. Gray said. "He'll be moving stock or something," he added vaguely. "Dave, I think you and I had better go into town and confer with my friends at the museum.

They'll help me locate a scaffold. We'll need that in any case. Let's not waste any more time. Tomorrow's Sunday.''

Holly was surprised—she had often suspected that Dr. Gray had no idea what day it was. But the thought of Raf overrode her amusement. Why hadn't he come? Her fears told her it was because he had something more exciting to do, something involving a woman. The thought made her heartsick. She had tried unswervingly for days to believe, as he did, that their worlds opposed each other, but love continued to defy reason. Forget him she couldn't. Not from the first time she had met him.

He won't come today, either, she told herself, and bent her mind to writing out a quick grocery list to send with Dr. Dave.

"If Valcour shows up while we're gone, Holly can show him up there, can't she?" Dr. Gray asked when the two men were setting off.

"I suppose so," Dr. Dave agreed reluctantly. The students had taken sandwiches and planned to remain in the field if it stayed cloudy.

"We'll be back as soon as we can," Dr. Dave told Holly, obviously hoping Raf wouldn't turn up before they returned.

Holly spent the morning looking over her shoulder. The cloud cover continued. Rain seemed to threaten at any time, but none fell. She took advantage of the fact that Dr. Gray was out of the trailer to bake a cake. If Raf came while it was in the oven, he'd have to wait.

The cake baked and cooled, and Raf didn't appear. Holly ate a lonely lunch and was in her tent collecting some underthings to wash when she heard the car. Assuming it was the professors returning, she did not hurry out. The impatient toot of a horn brought her up short.

Popping her head out of the tent, she saw the battered pickup, with Raf at the wheel. Her stomach did a flip-flop, and the blood left her face. Dreading the encounter, she emerged from the tent.

"You the only one home?" Raf called, getting out of the car. "I got a message I was wanted."

How businesslike he sounded, she thought wretchedly while her eyes tried to memorize every detail of his appearance. His expression was as impassive as ever. Nevertheless Holly received the distinct impression he wasn't happy. Maybe he didn't like being summoned without being told what was wanted of him. He certainly hadn't bothered to change his clothes. His boots and blue jeans were dusty, his shirt old and faded, but as he approached, she caught a whiff of men's cologne and realized he had shaved before he'd come.

"Where's Dr. Gray?" he asked.

Holly blinked, stricken by the horrible feeling she had been staring mindlessly at him for a long time.

She swallowed. "They went to town."

"Oh." He seemed as ill at ease as she was. "Well, tell them I was here." He turned to leave.

"I know what it's about. . . ." Why was her mouth so dry?

He was quick to swing around.

She said, "They've spotted some good fossils, only they don't know how to get at them. They wanted your advice."

"Where?"

"Up on Buffalo Table. I mean, you can see them from there."

"Oh? Too bad I missed the professors. I didn't get back to the ranch until late last night, and we were out early again this morning. Mrs. Jones didn't catch up with me till I came in for a late lunch. I shaved and came right over."

His explanation melted Holly's reserve.

"They wanted your advice," she repeated. "They expect to use a scaffold in any case, so they've gone to arrange for one. They told me if you came in the meantime to show you the place...if you don't mind driving up there," she added on a questioning note.

"Are you ready to go?"

She had, she realized, been ready all morning, though she wouldn't have admitted it to herself till now. She was wearing cuffed shorts of a suntan color only a tone deeper than the smooth tan of her lovely long legs. She certainly wasn't wearing a halter but had donned a fresh white T-shirt that could in no way be accused of outlining her figure. It hung loosely from her shoulders, effectively disguising her trim waist. Leather-soled fisherman's sandals protected her toes. She had pinned her red gold hair into a topknot of curls.

"I'll just get my sunglasses," she told him, and walked self-consciously to her tent. Out of sight inside, she took a moment to compose herself. Emerging, she knew that no matter how her knees quaked, her eyes—and any expression of love or hurt—would be hidden behind dark glasses. She looked as cool and collected as he did.

"I'm glad you folks have been using the pool," he said after they had driven a while in silence. "This is the weather for it."

"Yes, it is," she agreed. Must they meet as strangers, she wondered.

"Tell me about this find," he prompted.

Holly told him how Marcia had first seen the fossils through binoculars.

"Open that glove compartment," Raf requested. "See if I have a pair in there."

She did as she was told and produced expensive gray field glasses wrapped in a plastic bag.

He travels with everything, she thought, conscious of the rifle and lassos on the rack behind her head.

She continued the story of how Dr. Dave and Bill had searched at the foot of the table for the canyon opening and had threaded their way up through it after several tries.

"Dr. Gray is quite excited," she ended. "Some bones washed out seem to be from a young titanothere—a juvenile, he calls it."

"That *would* be a find," Raf agreed, and Holly was impressed again at his knowledge. Why should he want to pass himself off to her as an ignorant cowboy? The difference in their backgrounds didn't matter a whit. He was a man and she was a woman, and as far as she was concerned, they belonged together. She wasn't going to agonize any longer, trying to make herself believe differently.

I'd be glad to stay out here the rest of my life, she thought, letting her gaze roam over the cloud formations above the flat landscape. *I'd like to see it in winter.*

The silence between them grew long, but Holly found it comfortable. Bouncing over the rough track with Raf was totally satisfying; as far as she was concerned, it was a treat just to be with him. She felt she could look at his face for the rest of her life and never be bored, never count herself anything but inexpressibly lucky. In fact, it would be too lucky ever to happen. Without meaning, to, she sighed.

"Too rough for you?"

"No...." Forgetting his cool behavior and following up her feelings, she flashed her beautiful smile.

"Then what was the sigh for?"

"Contentment, I guess. It's fun bucketing across the prairie like this."

"Being bounced about in a pickup? Most girls wouldn't think so." He shook his head as though she were mad, but a moment later his hand groped for hers, clasping it firmly until a series of ruts demanded both hands on the steering wheel. How different from Dr. Dave's possessive grasp! Raf's handhold seemed like a promise. Of what?

"How's your brother doing?" he asked suddenly.

"Bill? All right, I guess."

"I meant, is he getting what he hoped out of the summer? Has it been worth your time?"

"My time?" she echoed stupidly.

"All the work you've been putting in was so he could be here, wasn't it?"

"I suppose so." She shrugged. She'd forgotten her original reason for coming with the crew. She seemed so much a part of it now. Why must Raf keep reminding her she didn't belong? She wasn't studying paleontology. They didn't need her. Anybody could cook. Raf had made it abundantly clear he didn't need her, either. She sat beside him glumly while the pickup made the ascent to Buffalo Table, her pleasure in the trip turned to ashes by his unfeeling reminder.

"I'm surprised you aren't afraid to drive up here on a day like this," she said waspishly.

He turned his head, black lashes drooping over yellow brown eyes. "Why?"

"You warned us about going up here if it looks like rain."

"That's for people who don't know this country. It's not going to rain today."

Evilly Holly wished the heavens would open up and pour a deluge over the pickup, even if it meant being stuck with him. It would be worth it to watch him brought down a peg.

The track that zigzagged to the grass-covered top was no more than a path made by four-wheel-drive vehicles. The table itself was what remained of the higher plain—several acres of grassland that had not yet eroded along with the land on either side. It was in the process of doing so, as evidenced by the fluted walls and pinnacles that edged it. Junipers grew artistically along the rim and in the shallow draws, making the table look like a cultivated park, but from the south and west sides one looked down into contorted rocky depths that were dizzying.

She directed Raf to the place from which Marcia had seen the fossils. While he studied their situation, Holly's gaze followed the fluted peaks growing smaller and smaller until they diminished into the plain. She strained for a glimpse of Bill or one of the others, but if they were down there, the deep gullies effectively hid them.

Raf put down the binoculars and pointed. "See that flat shelf above the fossils? If a scaffold could be hung from there. . . ."

"*Flat?*" Holly exclaimed.

"Well, sloping. Flat enough to stand on anyhow. Let's drive on around there. I'm going to climb down and have a better look."

When they reached the spot and Holly understood what he intended, she drew a deep breath.

Raf gave her a sidelong look.

"I don't think Dr. Gray wanted you to risk your life," she said mildly, not wanting him to guess how madly her heart was beating. The spot looked so dangerous! It was so high up. She mustn't make a fuss, she knew that, but oh, she wished he wouldn't take such a chance!

"Be careful," she whispered as he disappeared over the edge. She could hear him slipping and sliding as he made the descent. At least he had changed his cowboy boots for canvas-sided hiking boots like those the fossil hunters wore. His pickup truck came equipped with everything, it appeared.

She stood cautiously back from the brink, her heart pounding while her good sense told her the confident way he moved meant he had clambered over these weird formations hundreds of times. Probably he knew exactly what he was doing.

Looking down at the uncompromisingly stark drop made her uneasy. Against her will she imagined herself—or Raf—falling, striking one of the bulging sides and sliding, helpless, down and down. She stepped backward and looked hard at the grass and trees on her level. *Silly thoughts! Stop them,* she scolded herself.

"Holly!" Raf was calling. "Holly, where are you?"

Obeying his voice instead of her quite pointless imaginings, she moved forward to where she could see him.

He was standing with his legs braced wide and his head thrown back, exposing the strong brown column of his neck. "There's a bunch of fossils here, too," he called. "Might be something good. Anyhow, I'm going to gather them up before they get trampled on. I think we can brace something in this deep crack well enough to hang the scaffold. There's a blanket behind the seat in the pickup. Toss it down, will you? I'll gather up the fossils in it."

Holly found the blanket—an old army one, by its color—and carried it to the edge. Raf had made a little pile of objects, which, from overhead, looked like oddly shaped stones.

"Here it is!" she called.

"Stand back!" he shouted at the same moment.

His command came too late. Holly's leather-soled sandals slipped on a tuft of dried grass. Off balance from tossing the blanket, she began to slide, tumbling downward behind the folded square of wool. With a cry of terror she flung out her arms to stop herself and felt them scrape cruelly against the rough baked cliff. She threw herself back against the crumbling wall to slow the speed of her descent, bruising her backbone against rock-hard protuberances, knocking the air out of her lungs. The gravelly surface of the mudstone rolled with her, making her helpless to break her slithering fall. Unable to stop herself, she could already imagine the rolling gravelly bits carrying her right across the slope and over the precipice.

That didn't happen. Raf's hands caught her, and she sprawled on the sloping ledge. How wonderful to find herself safe in his arms! Hard muscular arms padded with flesh. She had come near to saying goodbye to all that. She shivered and laughed and felt herself close to hysteria.

"I told you to throw down the blanket. I didn't mean for you to come with it," he drawled, and the world stopped spinning. She was in his arms, and he was carefully lowering her to the rock. As her breath began coming back, the numbness left her. Scraped flesh began to burn.

Raf had caught the blanket and then dropped it to catch her. Now he spread it with one hand and lowered her gently onto it. He crouched beside her.

"You're all right," he soothed, reaching up to brush dust from her face. "Just winded. And darned near skinned," he added tenderly, examining her bare arms. Blood was beginning to seep through the scrapes.

"How could I have been so clumsy?" she whispered shakily.

"Don't blame yourself," Raf said. "Blame me. I knew you were wearing leather-soled shoes. I should have warned you to stand back instead of asking you to drop something down."

Holly noticed that her anklebones had not escaped the effects of her abrasive slide.

"I've got Merthiolate in the truck," Raf said, "but I'm afraid you're going to have some mean-looking scabs." His black-fringed tawny eyes were gazing at her so intently that Holly began to feel cheered. Of course, nobody's attention was worth falling down cliffs for, but since she *had* fallen, having Raf look at her like that seemed a just reward. She still felt weak and fragile.

"How's your back?" he was asking. Before she could answer he pulled up her T-shirt to make his own examination.

"No skin broken, but you're also going to have some mean-looking bruises. I don't know whether I dare take you back to camp in this condition."

She managed a wavery smile, becoming aware at the same time that her palms and the backs of her thighs seemed to be on fire.

"I scraped my legs, too," she said plaintively.

"Poor little chickie." Before she knew what to expect, he again cradled her in his arms.

"I'm not a chickie!" she exclaimed, feebly seeking to escape his hold.

"And you're not little, either," he agreed dryly. "But you've been knocked about, and I thought a hug might be welcome. Last time we were together—alone—you seemed to want it."

In addition to the other discomforts the ledge offered, it had become unbearably warm. Holly held her scraped palms to her burning cheeks.

"Never mind, sweetheart." Raf's eyes were tender. "As soon as you feel able, I'll help you back up to the top, and then I'll make it feel better." As a promise he dropped a kiss in her palm.

"Look at all the fossils here," he urged, using a common tactic to take her mind off her hurts. He moved over to the little pile in a crouch.

Despite her shaken condition, Holly noticed the way the cloth of his jeans stretched tight across his hard thighs. He must be in great physical condition to be able to move around in a crouch like that. Something about a body in tip-top form suggested sensuality. His vitality was compelling enough to take her mind off her discomfort.

"Look," he was saying, "this jaw might be a titanothere, except I think it's in the wrong layer of rock. Titanotheres were extinct by the time this level was laid down. But here's a nice skull of something." He held it up. "Probably an oreodont."

Unnoticed by either of them, the sky had darkened. Without warning a crack of thunder rolled across the heavens, and as though the thunder had released it, rain pelted the ledge, sending up little puffs of dust. As they looked skyward in astonishment, rain poured down in earnest.

Holly struggled to her feet, smothering a cry. Raf snatched up the thick wool blanket and flung it over their heads and shoulders. He huddled Holly against him, holding the blanket with his free hand. The wool smelled of straw and disuse, but its protection against the fierce onslaught of nature made it very welcome. The cold rain brought a chill that raised goose flesh on Holly's arms. She shivered, partly from the sensation of coziness—the strong desirable shelter of Raf's arm and shoulder and ribs and the heavy, tightly woven wool, which would soon be wet through. *Enjoy the comfort while you have it,* her senses told her...and she shivered again.

His arm tightened. She twisted her head to peer up into his face. His eyes when he looked down at her were unreadable.

"I thought you said it wouldn't rain," she couldn't resist commenting.

His lips twitched. "I was wondering how long you could go without reminding me of that."

"Does it mean we're stuck up here?" she asked, more to needle him than anything else, not really believing that the pickup wouldn't be able—with a determined driver—to run down the not very steep track.

"It means we're stuck *down* here," Raf said grimly.

"No!"

"I'm afraid so. When I said this clay turns to soap when it rains, I meant it."

The thunder rumbling overhead grew fainter. It seemed to control the rain, for the downpour stopped as suddenly as it began. Overhead the sky grew much lighter.

"Just a local shower," Raf said, removing the soaked blanket from their shoulders, "but it puts us in a heck of a fix.

"Don't move," he cautioned. "This ledge is dangerously slippery now. One step and you could slide right over. I'm going to spread the blanket. Thank God, we have it. Wet as it is, you'll have to sit on it. At least we know it won't slide under us."

"How...long?" Holly asked, frightened.

"Till the sun comes out and dries this place up," Raf replied harshly. "Till tomorrow, probably, the way the sky looks. Holly...." He turned to her, his face showing more emotion than she'd ever seen him exhibit. "I'm sorry. I did a danged fool thing in coming up here, but I knew the professors must be anxious about their fossils, and I was careless."

"I hope the rain hasn't hurt the fossils!" Holly interrupted. "Dislodged them or something. If they fall to the bottom of the canyon, they could get all broken up."

"Possibly," Raf said wryly. "Right now I'm more concerned about us." He stared stonily into the distance.

Holly lowered herself carefully, mindful of her many bruises. She sat with her arms clasping her bent knees, her back erect. Then Raf settled himself comfortably against the muddy wall, legs stretched in front of him, and pulled her into the hollow of his arm.

It was ridiculous, but her mind refused to worry. She knew she should, but she couldn't bring herself to be anything but excited by their situation. *This is a lot of trouble to go to to be alone with a man,* she thought, stifling a mad desire to giggle.

The ledge appeared safe as long as they didn't move around. By nightfall it might get pretty uncomfortable, but as of now, alone with Raf on a blanket...it wasn't all that bad! She tried to think of a subject that would lighten his mood.

After turning over several comments in her mind, she said lightly, "I don't suppose they'll miss me till they get hungry."

Raf brought his angry gaze back from the distance, and his eyes softened. "You're a scout."

Holly wasn't sure if that was a big compliment or a small one.

"They'll miss you as soon as they get back," he affirmed, "but even when they realize where you've gone, they won't be able to do anything."

"Why not?"

"Because the jeep won't climb the track!"

She had wished it would rain, to take Raf down a peg, and now it had, and, ironically, she was sorry. She didn't like seeing him mistaken, though it didn't make him less a hero, only a little more human.

"We just have to be patient and wait, then," she said resignedly. "Does it get cold at night up here?"

"Cold enough," he growled.

"We have the blanket." And each other, she added to herself. "They say wool stays warm even when it's wet."

"Let's hope so. How do you feel now?" he suddenly asked. He gently took one of her arms in both hands and examined the scraped skin. "It didn't bleed too much, but it must hurt like hell." He stared into her eyes, as though to draw the admission from her.

"No, it doesn't," she disclaimed. "Nothing hurts as long as I sit still."

We can talk the rest of the day, she was thinking happily. *Really get to know each other. He'll see I'm no different from South Dakota women*—although apparently South Dakota women hadn't suited him.

For a time they sat in silence.

"Have you never wanted to live anywhere else?" Holly asked, her eyes roving the plain beyond the diminished clay spires.

"No." The single syllable was uncompromising. "But then my dad died about the time I was old enough to go anywhere on my own, and I was in charge of the ranch. My mother and sister depended on me to run it. I had Joe Old Elk's help and advice, but I had to make my own decisions. Today the ranch is making more money than my dad ever dreamed of, and I can afford to see any part of the world I take a notion to."

Holly's heart sank. That meant he could look all over the world for a wife, too, if he wanted one. And whatever made her keep thinking he did? He wanted a summer affair—he'd said so—and all the talking and getting to know one another wasn't going to change his mind. Why did she think it was?

"I wonder what they'll do when they miss me," she said broodingly. "How long will it take them to realize something's wrong?" She twisted around to give him an impish smile. "I don't care what you say, I bet they don't begin to wonder until dinnertime. They'll just think we're a long time getting back."

"Your boyfriend won't like that."

"You mean Dr. Dave? He's not my boyfriend." She watched for his reaction.

Raf's look was like a spark of yellow flame. "He certainly wants to be."

"It takes two to polka," she quipped.

"I thought it was 'tango.'"

"Whatever," she answered, but the thought of Dr. Dave trying to tango made her smile. "He's not much of a dancer in any case."

"If you married him, you'd be in the same university crowd as your brother," Raf suggested.

Nettled, Holly sat up straight and turned to face him. "That's the most ridiculous reason for marrying I've ever heard!"

"You know that's not the way I meant it." He pulled her back against his shoulder. "I meant you'd have that in addition to everything else."

"What else?" she demanded.

"He's obviously in love with you, for one thing. He earns a good living as a professor, and I think you want someone older, don't you?" Taking her by the shoulders, he shifted her to face him. Her eyes fell before his searching glance.

Not just anyone older—you! she thought, shielding her eyes with her thick lashes. "I don't love him," she said. "Or does that matter?"

He shrugged. "I guess if you think it does, it does."

Make the most of this predicament, Holly's inner self told her, *because this is the closest you'll come to sharing Raf's thoughts.* His words were a dash of cold water. *He's good at that,* she thought.

"Look—" she sat up straight again "—when I need brotherly advice, I'll ask my brother. I was talking about how soon they might miss us," she reminded him.

Neither of them was wearing a watch.

"Can you tell time by the sun?" Holly challenged.

"What sun?"

He was so right she giggled.

He said, "I guess about as well as the next person. What time do you think it is now?"

"About four, maybe?"

Raf agreed.

Holly strained her eyes, trying to find a road out there on the shimmering plain. There seemed to be nothing but a vast expanse of green. She mentioned it to Raf.

"That's right, it's all grazing land," he said. "Most of what we're looking at is mine."

"As far as we can see?"

"Just about."

"It's beautiful," Holly commented. "I'm not just saying that. It really is."

"I think so," Raf agreed again. "But not exciting."

"A person makes his own excitement."

"You certainly make yours." She felt his lips touch the back of her neck. His brown hands were holding her shoulders.

"I do?" she asked in a small voice.

"You do—falling down cliffs, letting it rain on us.... You make my excitement, too, don't think you don't."

She bit her lip to keep from showing how his words pleased her.

"Holly," he said thickly. "I've done my darnedest to stay away from you. You know that, don't you? You haven't helped any, either. Wearing halters, falling down here on top of me, making me jealous...." He nipped her ear, and she gave a little shriek.

"Jealous?" She eyed him provocatively over her shoulder.

"Your possessive Dr. Dave. You don't know how often I've longed to haul off and punch that guy! He's such an absolute zero."

"You just said I ought to marry him!" Holly

swung around so she could look straight into Raf's golden eyes. She read amusement in his black-lashed squint.

"That would be one way to get you out of my hair," he remarked.

"Thanks a lot!" She tried to sound annoyed, but she was too delighted. His previous words echoed in her head—he'd had to work at staying away these past two weeks. That meant—well, at least it meant she was special. But it also meant she'd better go carefully. If he was drawn to her against his better judgment, his better judgment might take over at any time. She couldn't do what she most wanted to do— capitulate; cry, "Oh, Raf!" and fall into his arms.

He began kissing the underside of her arm in a way that sent little tremors tickling up her shoulder and across her chest.

"Maybe you'd prefer to have me sit with my back to you and not talk," she suggested, pushing forward her underlip in a pretended pout.

"Talk all you want," he said thickly, gathering her to him. She could feel the strength of his arms. It amazed her how arms so strong could be so gentle and loving.

His lips tasted her neck lightly, teasingly, but with a suggestion of leashed passion.

"I must have been crazy to want to stay away from you," he muttered.

"Why did you?" she asked, reveling in awareness of their situation. The whole evening, the whole night stretched before them. They could talk and kiss and keep warm with the blanket and, at morning, watch the sun rise.

"I can't for the life of me remember why," he replied, peppering her face with tiny fiery kisses that sent her blood leaping.

Her hands came up to hold his face; her palms against his lean jawline demanded that his lips find hers. Even with her eyes closed, she could see his face in her mind—brown forehead, flying black brows, the straight black lashes shut over tawny eyes, the high cheekbones and proud flaring nostrils. What a man! That he couldn't stop thinking of her was heaven.

She gave herself to the ecstasy of his kiss. It began to make up for all the time they had been separated, as if that time hadn't really existed.

Fire coursed through her veins. No time existed now, only Raf and this place where they were suspended above an empty world. Raf's lips were warm and masculine. The musky male scent that was peculiarly his had her mind reeling. Her lips opened; his tongue slid into her mouth, pulsing a thrill to her nerve ends.

When at last he ended the kiss, she clutched him with a soft moan.

"Easy, honey," he said, disengaging himself from her arms. "We've got all night. Let's get a little more comfortable."

Putting her from him, he laid her back upon the blanket. She felt limp.

For what seemed a very long time, during which her arms ached for him, he sat upright, letting his eyes rove over her body—the high full breasts; the waistband of her shorts fitting around her smooth skin between hipbone and rib cage; the brown shorts themselves curving over delicious hips, then revealing long, brown, smooth-skinned thighs. Pretty knees led to slim scraped calves and ankles. The betraying sandals were plastered with pale mud.

Holly longed for him to acknowledge a wish to possess what he saw—by putting a ring on her finger, of course!

As if in answer he shook his head. "I can't bear the thought of letting someone else have you," he growled.

"You certainly make me sound like an object," she said. "A bone!"

"Meaning I'm a dog in the manger?"

"You said it. I didn't." Her tone sounded surly in her own ears. After the hot-blooded way he'd kissed her, how could he turn cool so fast?

With a lithe movement he stretched beside her, amusement in the tawny eyes. "You're an impatient little thing, aren't you. You can't wait for what I'm going to do to you."

At his words her body tensed with such a wickedly sensual spasm that it frightened her, and she struggled to sit up, gasping, "No!" Her blue eyes darkened with fear.

A shaft of westering sun broke through the clouds, striking the ledge and gleaming across Raf's face. For a moment his features appeared cast in bronze. Then he spoke—and became human again.

"You want to be kissed, but nothing more, is that it?"

"Yes." She set her jaw.

"Then what were you saying no to? Do you really think I'm some kind of savage? Do you think this is some ancient Indian ritual—bringing maidens to Badlands ledges and deflowering them?''

She shook her head and had the sense to feel foolish and very unsophisticated. ''I didn't know what you meant,'' she said breathlessly. ''All I know is I want to be with you.''

She saw his jaw relax, and the grim expression left his face.

''That's fair,'' he responded, adding, ''lucky, too, since at the moment you don't have much choice.''

She laughed at that, and the tension between them eased, to be entirely swept away when he pulled her against him for another long delicious kiss. Boldly her fingers tore at buttons, opening his shirt to the waist for her hands to slip inside and explore his muscle-rippled chest. His smooth warm skin smelled intoxicating.

Too late she realized she'd given him the same privilege. With practiced ease, calloused fingers slid under her loose T-shirt, rasped up her rib cage and undid her bra. His thumbs played with the weight of her breasts for a moment before his strong hands gripped her sides, holding her captive while his tongue probed her very soul.

She gasped for breath and slid her hands around his back, eager to pull him against her, to feel his heart beat against her breasts, but he held her off.

''Wait,'' he whispered. ''Relax. We've got all night.''

This is some kind of torture, she thought.

With maddening slowness he exposed her breasts to the sky and to his gaze until her nipples throbbed with eagerness. When at last he touched one with the tip of his tongue, she didn't try to suppress a cry of pleasure. She lay back on the blanket, completely abandoned to the touch of his hands and lips and tongue.

Again and again he kissed her, long throbbing kisses that left her trembling because there seemed to be no end, no satiation. Again and again, with fingertips and tongue, he titillated the pink buds of her breasts until she felt ready to explode, until she knew she would have done anything he'd asked—only he didn't ask. Until, heaven help her, she hated the fact that she was a virgin, that she'd told him she wanted no more than kisses.

Still, she thought wildly, when he allowed her a moment in which she *could* think, there was a long night ahead of them. Maybe he'd change his mind . . . or not be able to control himself. Time and again she clamped her teeth shut to keep from crying, "Raf, I love you!"

In the west the clouds cleared, and the sun went down in a blaze of glory. The air began to grow cool. Raf shook the heavy black hair out of his eyes and leaned back on one elbow.

"Had enough 'just kissing'?" he asked coolly, but a pulse at the base of his bronze throat belied his offhand attitude.

"Enough for how long?" Holly's lovely smile and simple honesty melted any wall he had been in the process of erecting, and he actually laughed.

"What a girl!"

Suddenly he held up one hand. "Listen!"

No sound above her own breathing came to Holly's ear.

"There it is again!"

She cocked her head.

"Sounds like a truck," Raf muttered.

"You must have very good hearing," she commented.

"It's a vehicle of some kind," he said. "They must be down at the bottom of that last hill. I can't imagine how they got that far!" He glanced at Holly. "Perhaps you'd better fix your clothes." He began buttoning his shirt.

"Do you think it's someone coming to rescue us?" Her voice was shrill.

"Probably your professor," Raf said dryly.

How could he talk like that? Holly's throat constricted with fear. This was just a game to him!

She had no chance to accuse him of mistreating her or to discuss anything. While the jeep—she finally heard it, too—was still growling at the bottom of the last steep incline, Bill and Dr. Young appeared at the top of the cliff, against the sky. Ropes were slung over their shoulders. Holly felt ridiculously disappointed.

Following Raf's instructions, they hitched the ropes to the pickup, and Holly, seated in a loop of the rope, was hoisted up, using her feet to keep from scraping the still slippery rock. They pulled up the blanket filled with fossils then Raf.

"What in hell made him take you down there?" Dr. Dave asked, exploding as soon as Holly had been helped to Raf's car.

"I slipped when I threw him the blanket and landed down there," she said, too weary and disappointed to take offense at his manner.

"How did you fellows make it up here?" Raf wanted to know when he, too, stood on the grassy summit, catching his breath.

"It was dry every place but this last bit," Bill told him. "We left Willie trying to make it with the jeep and walked on up, leaping from tuft to tuft. That's why we couldn't figure out sooner where you were. It didn't rain anyplace west of the table. You must have been right on the edge of the rain. But I knew if Holly wasn't back in time to cook, there must be a reason. Then Marcia remembered the thundershower. We were down below. When the rain started, we quit and went back to camp."

The track was still slippery enough that Raf didn't try to move his pickup. The five of them rode back to camp in the jeep.

"What did you and Dr. Gray find out about scaffolds?" Holly asked.

Dr. Dave snorted. "The people at the museum recommended we work from the bottom. So your ordeal wasn't necessary. Aluminum extension ladders will be relatively easy to carry in because they come apart in sections. Sorry to have troubled you, Valcour," he added ungraciously.

"No trouble," Raf said impassively. Bill winked at Holly.

He drove Raf on to the ranch. Holly had no chance to say goodbye. Raf did give her a significant look, and with that she had to be content.

CHAPTER TWELVE

NEXT DAY the ravine was still too slippery to walk through. Willie and Dr. Dave drove up onto Buffalo Table to see what the downpour had accomplished toward freeing the fossils, and Willie reported that the pickup was still parked atop the table.

"It seemed to me the fossil area looked quite different," Dr. Dave hurriedly reported to Dr. Gray when he returned. "I'm afraid a lot of them may have washed out and fallen to the bottom of the ravine. We'll know when the clay dries out and we can get in there."

At the other end of the trailer, Holly was peeling boiled potatoes for salad and couldn't help overhearing.

"I've been cleaning up some of the first ones you brought from this site," Dr. Gray said. "They look more and more promising. What are the students doing this morning?"

"I sent them off with the horses to scout Rabbit Basin, which got no rain at all."

"Good. That'll keep them out of mischief until the ravine dries up. If the ladders arrive today, we should be able to set them up tomorrow, wouldn't you think?"

"Hope so," Dr. Dave said. With a wounded look

at Holly, he left the trailer. He was behaving as though she had purposely got herself marooned with Raf.

She bit her lip. Why should she feel responsible for Dr. Dave's unhappiness? She had tried to make it clear she wasn't interested in him. She sighed with annoyed frustration.

The afternoon was miserably hot. The ceaseless wind felt as though it came off a blast furnace.

"I'm sure we'll be able to get into that ravine tomorrow," Marcia remarked when she returned to camp. "Even in the shade the heat is enough to bake anything."

The truck delivering the ladders had come and gone.

"We're all set," Dr. Gray agreed. "Tomorrow morning at sunup we'll start the assault."

Holly laughed. Dr. Gray made everything adventurous.

NEXT MORNING AFTER BREAKFAST the ladders were tied to the jeep, and as soon as Junior Old Elk arrived with the horses, everyone set off in high excitement, leaving Holly to her dishwashing.

That done, she began to feel left out and lonesome. All these weeks she had seldom been alone in camp. Dr. Gray only occasionally went into the field. Usually he was at his desk, documenting the finds, writing pages of records. Holly began to wish Raf would come and keep her company, the way he'd done before the crew arrived. Her lips curved in a fond memory of the two nights he had prevented her from being lonely and frightened. Then she wondered if he and Leona had ever gone camping, and her mood darkened. She wanted to see him, find out how he felt about their wild lovemaking on the cliff shelf. Did he regret the things he'd said? Had his caresses been merely a way of passing the time, taking advantage of a good thing? How could she know until she saw him again?

For once her thoughts conjured him. He came riding up from the creek through the cottonwoods a little before ten. He was wearing cowboy clothes—dusty boots, jeans, plaid shirt, straw hat.

Holly was writing another grocery list. She had won the menu battle and become proficient at estimating the amount of food needed each week. She was wearing a thin cotton playsuit of pastel green that made her hair, piled high on her head for comfort, look like a bright flower.

Her heart pounded madly when he rode up. He greeted her pleasantly enough, but his face, as usual, masked his mood.

"Dr. Gray around?" he asked, dismounting.

"They all went to Buffalo Table a couple of hours ago. Or to the ravine, I should say."

Raf fastened the horse's reins to one of the poles supporting the awning and sat down across the table. Suddenly shy, she jumped up.

Avoiding his eye, she said, "Let me get you some iced tea. I just made it."

"All right." He laid his hat on the table.

She returned with a rapidly frosting glass of cold tea and feeling suddenly bold, said daringly, "What if your horse pulls the awning down?"

"He won't." Raf sounded amused.

"How do you know?" she pursued, conscious that the conversation resembled the opening moves in a game of chess. She was waiting to learn what was on his mind. Her guess was that he was doing the same, though his self-assured manner made it hard to believe he had doubts about anything, even the trend of her thoughts.

He drank the iced tea slowly, as though he had nothing on his mind but to sit and rest.

Finally Holly could stand it no longer. "Are you sorry about the other night?" she burst out.

The thin black line of his brows raised, the tawny eyes widened. "Should I be sorry?"

All right, so she'd lost that ploy. "You blamed me for falling down on top of you," she reminded him.

"No, I didn't. I blamed myself."

He won't admit he was glad, she thought. *He'd rather pretend nothing happened.*

She was wrong. He was looking her over critically, and his next question was, "How are all your bruises and scrapes?"

"Oh, okay."

He studied her through half-closed eyes, his look both flattering and sensual. "You certainly appear okay. But then you always do." He drained his glass and set it on the red-checked plastic. "I've got to go up to Buffalo Table and retrieve the pickup. I was afraid I'd be too late to catch anybody going that way. How would you feel about riding up with me?" He looked off through the trees. "Did Junior bring Brown Betty this morning? I told him to."

So he'd planned ahead to ask her to ride with him! She drew a suddenly carefree breath.

"I think he did."

Raf got up from the table, his movements lazy and graceful.

Like a mountain lion at home in his lair, Holly thought dementedly. She caught her breath. The way she responded to his masculinity was frightening. She forced herself to speak rationally.

"I have to be back by eleven-thirty or thereabouts."

"No problem. We'll ride up and drive back—fasten the horses to the car."

He came around the table to where Holly was standing. Her heartbeats quickened at his approach. She stood rooted to the ground, knees trembling.

"Go and change," he ordered, his tawny eyes drinking in her features. How could she ever have thought his face expressionless? His mouth—so masculinely beautiful, so firmly possessive.... Trancelike, her eyes dwelled on the finely chiseled lips, remembering how she had kissed the corners.

His face came closer. "Surely a good morning kiss is in order," he was saying lightly, but his hands gripped her shoulders with a fierceness that belied the casual words. Blood was coursing hotly through his veins, too. She saw the pulse throbbing in his brown throat.

Her hand rose involuntarily to stroke the brown column of his neck. The other lay lightly on his shoulder.

His kiss grew passionate almost as soon as their lips touched. Holly could feel him swept away by the same desire that was firing her blood.

She would have drawn back, frightened by the hot

plunge of his tongue, but his arms wrapped her too closely for that. Her pulses were leaping in response.

He cared, her heart sang. He still cared!

She slipped her arms around his hard lean back and gloried in the way he crushed her against him.

At last, reluctantly, he let her go. She drew a shaky breath and managed a trembling smile.

"This is a fine way to be carrying on at ten o'clock in the morning," Raf said, making a move away from her. "Who'd believe I have a ranch to run?"

"I'll put on some jeans," Holly said demurely, her heart singing. He'd left his work to see her!

He said, "Go ahead. I'll saddle your horse."

She was starting for her tent when she saw him stand tense and listening. He reminded her of a cat pricking its ears at a mouse in the wall, every muscle alert.

"They're coming back," he said. "I hear the jeep."

She felt instant disappointment. Maybe he wouldn't go with her now. Straining her ears, she couldn't hear a thing but the gentle patter of cottonwood leaves and, out on the prairie, a meadowlark singing.

The next breeze brought the unmistakable sound of the jeep, and soon it came roaring over the dusty track among the cottonwoods and drew up near where Raf and Holly stood.

Dr. Dave was driving. Dr. Gray sat beside him, his arm in an improvised sling, his face pale and twisted with pain. His black hair was falling across his forehead, and the side of his face was scraped and smeared with dried blood.

"What happened?" Holly cried as she and Raf sprang to help him from the vehicle.

"Don't panic," Dr. Gray said testily. "I've broken my arm. Nothing to get excited about. And twisted my back a little," he added, moving with difficulty. Sweat dripped from his forehead. It was easy to see he was making light of his difficulties.

"He fell coming down the ladder," Dr. Dave said, frowning at the sight of Raf and Holly together. "He insisted on going up before anyone else to take a close look, and the ladder slipped.

"You should have let me go first." He addressed Dr. Gray. "I told you I didn't trust it."

"I shouldn't have been so eager," the older man growled. "However—" his mouth quirked "—I got my look. It's what we thought. Holly, in the lower left-hand drawer of my desk there's a bottle. Will you fetch it, please—and four glasses—and then I'll let you cart me off to the hospital."

"I'll drive you in the Mercedes, sir," Raf said quietly.

Holly heard Dr. Gray answer, "I'd appreciate that."

She found the bottle—a fifth of Scotch, half full— and collected four glasses, along with a washcloth for Dr. Gray's face.

When she returned, the men were seated at the dinner table. Raf took the bottle from her and splashed neat whiskey into the glasses.

Wincing with pain, Dr. Gray raised his glass to make a toast.

"To one of the best juvenile titanothere fossils ever found!"

They drank solemnly.

"Worth breaking a bone for," Dr. Gray cried valiantly. "Dave, you better get back to work. These folks can look after me."

Raf said, "Dave, you can run me over to get the car first, if you will. Just give me a moment to unsaddle." He led his horse off to join Brown Betty in the rope corral.

"What was he doing here?" Dr. Dave demanded as soon as Raf was out of earshot.

"We were going up to get the pickup," Holly said, nettled by the question. She turned to Dr. Gray. "I'm going along with you." She spoke firmly, half expecting him to say, "No, you're not," but he didn't.

He said, "Better pack what you think I'll need for a few days. I have a feeling that once I'm in their clutches, they'll try to keep me. This back's given me trouble previously."

Dr. Dave got up when he saw Raf returning. "I'll drop him and go back to Buffalo Table," he said.

"Good!" Dr. Gray agreed. "Those kids shouldn't be left alone with a find like this. And don't come visiting me at the hospital. I want everybody to use his energy getting those fossils out of there. Carefully!"

"What a time to break an arm!" he complained to Holly as the men drove off. "But it's a great find, Holly, really it is. One in a lifetime."

Holly packed what she considered the professor would need and thought about Raf. How disappointing not to get to ride to Buffalo Table with him, but coming back from Rapid City they'd be alone in the car. They would have a chance to talk then.

The drive into Rapid City was anything but exciting. In the front seat Dr. Gray seemed to fall asleep. Holly sat behind him, where her view of the back of Raf's head, his ear and jaw palled after a while. He didn't speak, perhaps because he didn't want to disturb the professor. Her fingers itched to reach up and smooth Raf's thick black hair, but he wouldn't welcome it.

She watched the flat landscape roll by and regretted the missed horseback ride. She hoped it was only postponed.

At the hospital an attendant wheeled Dr. Gray away. Holly and Raf sat in the waiting room. Hospitals depressed Holly, and she could see this one was doing the same for Raf. The memory of that never-to-be-forgotten night she had waited with Bill while doctors fought for the lives of the victims of the stadium collapse came back with all its horror.

At last, her voice hushed in response to the surroundings, she said, "After the night my parents died, I promised myself I'd never go to a hospital again if I could help it."

"You were brave to come today, then." The approving look he gave her was worth the mental discomfort she was undergoing.

"I thought Dr. Gray needed a little extra attention. He's not a young man, despite his black hair," she said with a hint of amusement in her voice.

"Is that what you think of me, too?" The topaz eyes glinted.

"That you dye it? Of course not!"

"That I'm not a young man."

She stared at him, astonished. "But you are!"

"I'm thirty-six," he said broodingly. "A doctor calls that middle-aged."

She laughed, letting the ardor she felt for him shine in her eyes. "You're letting this place get you down."

"I suppose I am," he agreed with a self-conscious shrug. "It reminds me of the brevity of life. So do the Badlands, but in a more graceful way. They make me feel I'm part of a great plan."

He stood up and began to pace the floor like a caged healthy mountain lion, his boot heels clicking on the institutional tan floors. She admired his silhouette against the bright light coming through the frosted glass windows. Her eyes rested on him lovingly, while her thoughts warned her she was in for trouble. *The difference,* she thought sadly, *is that I'm content even here because I'm with him, whereas for him my presence isn't enough.* She sighed.

He paused in his pacing. "Want some coffee?"

Before she could answer, he strode off. His behavior was proof of how impatient he was at any kind of restraint. She understood now why he wasn't married. That kind of restraint would gall him, too.

The coffee, bitter and in Styrofoam cups, helped pass the time. At last a doctor came to report. He talked directly of putting the patient in traction for several days because of his strained back. They were not allowed to see Dr. Gray.

There being nothing more they could do, they left the hospital.

"How are we going to know when he's ready to leave?" Holly asked.

"I plan to phone the hospital every day. He didn't order us not to do that."

"He can't order you anyway," Holly pointed out with a tinge of humor.

"Nobody can order me," Raf said arrogantly.

Holly made no attempt to answer such a pointed remark. What was he talking about? She hadn't given him any orders.

They talked about the accident and Dr. Gray and the meaning of the discovery—about everything but themselves. Holly decided she hated bucket seats that wouldn't let a person sit sideways comfortably and look at the driver. She would have liked that, even if he had to keep his eyes on the road. Actually, the road to Vista was so empty of traffic he could have paid her a lot of attention had he wanted to.

The scattered buildings of the tiny town were rising out of the distance when Holly made herself say, "Can we still ride up and get the pickup?"

"Not today." And he still didn't take his eyes from the road.

Holly wanted to kick him. What had put him in such a bad mood?

"Would you mind stopping as long as we're here?" she asked coldly as they drove down the main street. "I have a list of things I need."

He parked the car in front of the general store.

"Hungry?" he asked. "Shall we have a hamburger in the bar?"

Holly had hoped he might invite her to lunch at the ranch, but perhaps Mrs. Jones wasn't expecting him.

"Fine with me," she agreed.

"Come into the bar when you're finished, then." He stalked off.

Holly entered the store feeling awful. *This is how it would be if you were married to him,* she told herself angrily. *He's right; it would be boring to live out here.* But she was kidding herself. Marriage to Raf would never be boring. Besides the time his wife shared with him, she would have a ranch house to run. In addition, Holly knew well from her own background that people in small communities have a deep involvement in local affairs.

That life's not for you; it's not for you! she chided herself, while Henry Brightwing assembled the groceries on her list. *You've a good career. It's going places fast. You'd be a fool to give it up...and it's perfectly plain he's not going to ask you to do so.*

"Holly!"

As if reaffirming her statement, she heard her name spoken by an unfamiliar but elated voice. She turned to find herself facing a grinning young man with a mustache. He looked familiar, but it took her a moment to recall where she'd met him. Oh, yes, the TV photographer Charles and Buddy had made friends with.

"Gary," he reminded her. "At Fox Butte, remember?"

"Gary. Of course, I do!" She became suddenly conscious of her windblown hair and her sunburned nose.

Gary turned to the older man standing behind him. "Scoop, this is the girl I was telling you about."

Holly smilingly acknowledged the introduction.

Scoop was a mouselike man with receding gray hair, wearing a gray short-sleeved shirt and gray trousers.

"Scoop works for the wire service. We're here to make you famous."

"Me?" Holly looked startled.

"Well, the fossil hunters, actually." Gary grinned engagingly. "We asked at park headquarters, and they sent us to inquire here, and here you are! Remember, I told you I'd do a story on you. I couldn't get the station interested. They've done a lot on the Badlands through the years. But they hadn't seen Holly, had they, Scoop?"

Scoop, involved in lighting a cigarette, shook his head.

Dr. Gray's words of that morning leaped to Holly's mind, but it certainly wasn't her business to make statements to the press.

"Don't forget, I'm just the cook," she warned Gary. "But I can show you the way to the camp as soon as I get these groceries."

"Don't tell me that's your Mercedes out front!" Gary exclaimed.

Holly twinkled. "No, that belongs to a local rancher—well, you know him—Raf Valcour. We're camping near his ranch. He's waiting for me in the bar next door."

"You're kidding!" Gary whooped. "Didn't I tell you he's one of the richest ranchers in the state?"

"You did," Holly agreed distastefully. "But I think you're exaggerating. He works right along with his wranglers." *Wranglers—there's a word I've never used previously,* she thought.

"Oh, sure, he's not snooty." Gary nodded. "So

how come he's waiting for you? Have you made a conquest?''

Holly had seen the question coming and answered casually without blushing. "We drove Dr. Gray to the hospital. He climbed up to look at a fossil and fell and broke his arm.''

Gary was looking out the window. Scoop's eyes were everywhere.

Gary said, "That's some car to ride the range in.''

"He rides the range in an old pickup...or on a horse," Holly said shortly. "When I'm through here, I'll introduce you.''

Henry Brightwing signed for her to go ahead. She took him to mean he'd have the groceries sacked by the time she was ready to leave.

They trailed into the bar, and Holly introduced the two men to Raf. She watched him carefully. He didn't look the least put out at having to share her attention with Gary and Scoop.

The two men went to the counter to fetch beer for themselves. Holly was pleased to see that Raf had obtained white wine for her.

He said quietly, "I hope you didn't mention the titanothere fossils.''

"Certainly not," Holly said reproachfully. How could he think she'd take it upon herself to do that?

"How'd they get on the scent so fast?" he puzzled.

"They didn't," she said with satisfaction. "Gary planned to do a story on the project when I told him about it at Fox Butte.''

"On you, you mean." The tawny eyes raked her. Something had made him angry. Could he really be jealous of Gary? Then it dawned on her—he wanted the story for Leona! Well, she wasn't going to get it! Blood beat in Holly's ears, and her anger rose with alarming swiftness. Before she could think of controlling it, she was seething with fury. She began to flirt outrageously with Gary to see if it would have any effect on Raf at all. It didn't.

Even when they were alone together in the car, the groceries stowed in the trunk and the reporters' car following, he didn't comment.

For several miles no word passed between them.

"I suppose you're mad because you were saving the story for Leona Selby," Holly said at last.

He actually turned his head to look at her, his face a bronze mask. "What gave you that idea?"

"It's pretty obvious."

"*Is* it?" There was, of course, no response in his expression.

"Yes, it is!" She longed for him to tell her she was mistaken, but. . .she wasn't.

As they approached his ranch, she said coldly, "I can put the groceries in Gary's car and ride the rest of the way with them."

"As you wish."

She knew she was being a perfect bitch, but she couldn't seem to stop.

"Don't forget to call Leona," she said nastily when he handed her the last sack.

On the drive to the camp Holly responded to Gary's good-natured chatter and Scoop's intelligent questions with part of her mind. She felt devastated by her behavior to Raf. What could have come over her? The answer to that was embarrassingly simple. She had been consumed by a burning jealousy such as she had never dreamed she was capable of. No man had ever aroused such emotional turmoil in her previously, so how could she have learned to curb it? What she had done shocked her. The way she had talked—maybe even given him the idea to call Leona! Heartsick, she told herself it was the end. Raf wasn't the man to put up with temper tantrums. At last she managed a mental shrug and told herself she didn't care.

None of the crew was back from the site, despite the afternoon heat. Holly showed the two men a few recent fossils that had been cleaned but not yet packed for shipment. They were interested in every aspect of the work. Gary behind a camera became as intense and businesslike as Charles. The two men were equipped to stay a day or two if the story warranted, with a tent, canned food, tiny cooking stove and an ice chest full of cold beer.

"I'm sure Dr. Dave will invite you to share our meals," Holly told them. "New faces around the table will be welcome."

She busied herself unpacking groceries and cutting up the chickens she had bought, readying them for baking with bread crumbs and lemon juice. Instead of flaring up at Raf, she should have invited him to dinner as thanks for delivering Dr. Gray to the hospital. What if he did phone Leona about the latest find? He could call Leona anytime; he didn't have to wait for a special occasion.

The field crew came dragging in later than usual, ready to celebrate a productive day. More than a dozen fossils washed out by the downpour had been retrieved, treated against exposure to air and packed for transportation to camp. One by one they were unwrapped for display on one of the worktables. In addition, a good start had been made toward undermining the bones still in the sediment.

Dr. Dave welcomed the newsmen and indicated he would be particularly pleased to have record shots of the whole proceeding, in return for which he would gladly share with them the camp chow if Holly didn't mind cooking an extra potato or two.

Holly willingly agreed.

"I'll wash dishes," Gary offered.

The cold beer was set out on the table for everyone to help himself and the battery radio turned up at full blast. Dr. Dave explained to the reporters what had been discovered. Suddenly they were in the midst of a full-scale celebration.

If only Raf would come riding in, Holly thought achingly. How quickly she would apologize for her behavior that morning. She would say Dr. Gray's accident had upset her—which was true.

Dr. Dave was explaining the fossils' location.

"They're up on a cliff face, and it was obvious from the ones already washed out that the find is worth spending all our time on. We've carried ladders in there, and we're starting to work. The first thing we do is cover the exposed parts with wet tissue paper so the plaster won't stick. Then we cover it with strips of burlap soaked in plaster of paris. That means carrying water and plaster a mile or more up a winding ravine to the place where we're working and then up the ladder. After the plaster sets so the piece has a hard protective shell, we start undermining. We have to be careful not to ruin any other pieces embedded in the mud beneath it.

"Hunting fossils sounds exciting," Dr. Dave ended, "but it's mostly tedious hard work—and often under a blistering sun. Look at my co-workers if you don't believe it." The crew groaned in agreement.

Observing Bill with the eye of a stranger, Holly realized that even her fair-skinned brother had turned brown, his freckles melting together. She hadn't looked at herself lately except in the small mirror in the trailer. She hadn't taken time to notice whether the lines of strain around her mouth had disappeared.

GARY SPENT THE NEXT TWO DAYS taking photographs all over the place, including the ravine. Scoop stayed only one day, and the second morning Gary drove him to Rapid City's airport. Gary returned while Dr. Dave and Bill were unloading two massive chunks they had cut out of the cliff face and carried down the ravine in slings.

Gary photographed them carrying the slings from the jeep and watched them place the chunks of clay on the table.

"Aren't you going to unwrap it?" he asked, disappointed.

"Not till we get it back to the laboratory," Dr. Dave explained. "It's safer in the matrix till we can deal with it under proper conditions."

"Then how do you know for sure what it is?"

"As I told your friend, Scoop, Dr. Gray saw

enough of the pieces already weathered out to be fairly certain we have the world's first juvenile titanothere. The young of all the prehistoric animals are conspicuously missing. For instance, no one has ever found a baby dinosaur."

"Why not?"

"We can only guess. One supposition is that young animals got eaten by predators and their bones broken and scattered, or they lived to grow up. I'll talk to you more about it tonight. For now, we're going back out there. Do you want to come?" Dr. Dave glanced jealously at Holly.

"No, thanks," Gary said absently. "I'm going to photograph these while the light's right."

Bill waved, and he and Dr. Dave roared away.

"These plaster casts aren't going to look like much in black-and-white photos," Gary complained. "How about you sitting beside them, Holly, so people will have some idea of the size, at least, of these chunks of mud?

"You're dressed okay," he said when she protested. "Shorts are good—as though you've been out in the field. Take the pins out of your hair." He lowered his camera to arrange her golden locks to hang in front of her shoulders.

That morning she had decided to wear the cuffed khaki shorts since they were fresh from the laundromat, and because the weather was so hot, she topped them with the pink halter. A person who had to work in a hundred-degree kitchen in August had a right to wear something cool.

Gary took a number of serious shots and then, as photographing chunks of plaster-covered mudstone grew dull, his natural high spirits got the better of him.

"Sit on the table behind the rock, Holly," he ordered blithely. "Sideways. Pull your knees up so I can see your legs. . . that's it. Beautiful! Now the other way. . . . Great! Great!"

And Holly, her burning heart slightly assuaged by Gary's attentions, let him take picture after picture.

CHAPTER THIRTEEN

GARY LEFT THAT EVENING. Holly spent the next days alone in camp, hoping every moment that Raf would show up, if only to bring a message from Dr. Gray. They heard nothing from the hospital. Every evening they discussed over the dinner table whether they should disobey instructions and visit him.

"You know darned well we'd get no thanks," Willie said. "Most likely we'd get a black mark for disobeying orders. Holly, how about you going?"

"I don't want to get a black mark, either," she said with a smile. Besides, if she went into town, Raf would have no message to bring to camp.

Dr. Dave trusted her with cleaning some unimportant fossils discovered earlier in the month, and she began going to greater efforts over the cooking, baking cakes and making tasty sandwiches to give them something to look forward to when they paused for lunch in the hot ravine.

Sunday came—another working day—and still they had heard nothing.

"Raf said he'd call the hospital every day," Holly told the assembled crew at noon. "There must be some news."

"But did Raf say he'd report to us?" Wayne asked.

Scientists, Holly thought disgustedly. They took things so literally. "He didn't actually say he would," she admitted, "but I took it for granted...." *Before I blew up at him,* she added in her mind.

"If we don't hear tomorrow, I'll drive in Tuesday morning," Dr. Dave stated. "It looks as if Valcour isn't to be depended on." He flashed Holly a triumphant glance. "The work at Buffalo Table is coming along fine. I know you people can deal with it."

MONDAY AFTERNOON when the crew came in from the field, hot, dusty and tired, there was still no word from Dr. Gray or from Raf.

Holly was in the trailer preparing dinner when she heard a commotion outside. She wiped her hands hastily, glanced in the mirror and hurried to the door.

Dr. Gray was emerging from the Mercedes, already surrounded by his eager students. Raf was opening the rear door for someone.

That should have been me, Holly thought with a pang. *If I hadn't quarreled with him, he might have asked me to ride into town.* Instead the person stepping out was Leona Selby.

Jealousy seared through Holly's blood, inflaming her cheeks.

"I'm all right; I'm all right!" Dr. Gray was exclaiming testily. "That's what eight days in the hospital are for. At least I was all right—until I saw the Sunday paper." The cast on his left arm was cradled in a sling.

Raf was taking Dr. Gray's suitcase out of the

trunk. His topaz eyes met Holly's for an instant before he looked away.

If Leona hadn't been present, Holly would have rushed to him and apologized while the rest of the group were gathered around Dr. Gray. But she couldn't bring herself to hurry to Raf with the other girl looking superciliously on. What if Raf repulsed her? Bill was talking to Leona at the moment, but Holly didn't think for a minute that Bill would distract Leona's awareness from Raf.

"Come over to the table," Dr. Gray said. He sounded angry. "You, too, Holly." She was still standing in the doorway of the trailer.

He waited till everyone had gathered around the table. Holly was conscious of Raf behind her, putting the professor's suitcase and briefcase in the trailer. She was planning to speak to him when he came out, but Dr. Gray distracted her attention by slamming a newspaper on the table.

"I would like to know the meaning of this disgusting and repugnant display of idiocy," he said coldly. His eyes were as cold as his voice, his face stony.

The crew gaped at him in astonishment or twisted their heads to peer at the newspaper. No one dared pick it up.

"I can only conclude that you have all taken leave of your senses." Dr. Gray spoke into dead silence. "Dr. Young, I would never have believed you would jump at the chance to make a fool of me the minute my back was turned. Were you prompted by professional jealousy or simply by an irresistible urge to make trouble?"

Dr. Dave's face went white and then red. "I have no idea what you mean," he stammered.

"This—" the professor picked the paper from the table and shook it "—this cheesecake! This farrago of nonsense!" Again he dropped the paper on the table.

Willie broke the suspense by snatching it up.

"It's Holly! With the fossils!" he exclaimed for the enlightenment of those across the table.

Holly glimpsed the photograph over his shoulder. One glimpse told her all she needed to know. Gary had let Scoop use one of the pictures he had taken when they were acting silly.

"This is not just something run in the local paper," Dr. Gray was saying through gritted teeth. "It's a wire-service story. No doubt papers all over the country are using it. My only satisfaction is that it makes you look like a fool, too, Young."

"But I gave you credit for everything!" Dr. Dave expostulated, reaching for the paper.

Willie gave it to him as though it were contaminated and looked at Holly, his eyes round.

Dr. Gray was glaring at her, too. "In this picture Miss Cameron appears to be taking all the credit."

Holly's face burned anew.

"I didn't know!" Dr. Dave agonized. "They were around, those newsmen, asking questions, taking pictures. I may have been overenthusiastic when I talked to them, sir, but I never dreamed...Holly....We brought those specimens in completely encased in plaster and returned to the site. That young man offered to make record shots for us, and he did. They arrived in Saturday's mail. Really fine photos. You'll be pleased. I had no idea...." His voice faded. Dr. Gray was no longer listening.

"Well, miss, what do you have to say for yourself?" he demanded.

Holly's throat tightened with misery. Why did Raf have to witness this?

"We were just fooling around," she choked.

"Is that your opinion of this project—that we're fooling around?"

"No! Gary took some serious pictures first. I never dreamed he'd use this." Her face burned. Her eyes blurred with embarrassed tears, but she kept her chin up. How would this affect her brother's standing? She looked to him for reassurance and support, but he was whispering to Leona.

She gave a swift glance around the circle. Everyone looked ashamed. Yet they weren't to blame, only she and Dr. Dave. Bitter regret welled in her throat. If she had realized.... Posing for Gary had seemed harmless—an amusement for a hot afternoon. She couldn't find it in her heart to be angry with him. He was a professional photographer. Interesting pictures were his business. No, she was to blame for being so stupid.

Nobody moved. At last Raf touched Dr. Gray's sleeve.

"We're going now," he said.

Leona was standing between Raf and Bill, looking inexpressibly smug. She said, "I'll do what I can, Dr. Gray, to repudiate the story."

"You'll be sure to say the announcement was premature?"

"I will. Do you want me to deny the importance of the find?" Why did she sound so triumphant?

"I'm not ready to say yet whether it's important. That's the way I want it handled."

"Let me tell you again how very, very sorry I am." Leona looked at Holly with dislike. "Please don't tar all the press with the same brush, doctor."

Raf had already walked away and was getting into the Mercedes. He didn't glance in Holly's direction. She could guess what he was probably thinking—that her true colors had come out at last, that she loved displaying herself and had seized the first opportunity to do so.

"I'm glad to meet a serious journalist, young lady, and I will appreciate whatever you can do," Dr. Gray told Leona, "but I'm afraid this is beyond correcting."

Leona patted his arm consolingly before she strode off to the car. She was wearing black—full cotton pants gathered at her bare ankles and a full shirt open at the neck. A wisp of pink silk tied around her throat relieved the somberness of the costume. She got in beside Raf, and the car rolled quietly away.

Holly was serving oven-fried chicken again. She returned to the trailer kitchen and began mashing the potatoes, her tears in danger of falling into the pot. On top of the regrettable mischance of the photograph, her mind was occupied with the idea of two people cavorting in Raf's swimming pool—Leona, in a black suit, of course, displaying her slim brown body, and Raf, browner yet, in black trunks, the water running from his bronze skin, dripping from his black hair. She could envision his wet eyelashes, his perfect muscular body—broad-shouldered, narrow-hipped—and after their swim.... Jealousy gnawed at her stomach, making her physically ill.

"Holly?" Marcia's voice, sounding cautious.

Holly blinked away her tears as the other girl stepped into the trailer.

"Listen," Marcia began, "I don't care what Dr. Gray says, that's a great picture of you."

Holly managed a watery smile.

"If I looked like that in a photograph," Marcia muttered, "I wouldn't care how much anybody griped. Besides, that picture will attract a lot more attention to our discovery than any old picture of fossils by themselves."

Holly sniffed. "I gather Dr. Gray doesn't want to attract attention."

"Baloney!" Marcia responded cynically. "The more attention he attracts, the more funding he'll get for the next expedition. My dad, for one, will cough up a pretty penny when he sees the publicity. I'll set the table, shall I?"

"Thanks," Holly managed with heartfelt appreciation.

Conversation over the fried chicken was minimal, but by the time dinner was finished, the crew was talking animatedly, if in subdued tones.

Like at a wake, Holly thought unhappily. *Mine.*

However, when Wayne rose to leave the table, he said pleasantly, "That was good chicken, Holly."

"Yes, it was," the other three chorused.

Holly dared not look at Dr. Gray. How was she going to work with him in the trailer after this? If he didn't forgive her, it would be impossible to share such confined quarters.

Without a word to anyone, Dr. Dave climbed into

the jeep and roared off. Dr. Gray went into the trailer bedroom and closed the door.

"If Dr. Dave's gone off to get drunk, he might have given us a chance to go, too," Willie said aggrievedly while Holly cleared the table. "I'll bet the bar in Vista is really jumping."

"On Monday night?" Marcia scoffed.

In a mood of deep depression, Holly washed and dried the dishes. It would have been balm to her wounded spirit if Bill had come to help her and at least to discuss her terrible blunder.

She finished the dishes and went to look for him, but he was nowhere in camp.

"I still don't understand why Dr. Gray was so furious," Holly told Marcia when they were undressing. "I can see why he wouldn't like the photo, but why is he mad at Dave?"

"Because he wanted to make the announcement himself! University professors have their games and power trips same as anybody else." She shrugged. "He may want to make absolutely sure it is a titanothere."

"But the article doesn't say anything definite. It doesn't give any details." Holly had at last read it. She had found the newspaper lying on the work-table—shoved, ironically, between two plaster-covered chunks of titanothere. The picture of her wasn't bad from a professional standpoint. In fact, for a black-and-white newspaper photo, it was quite good. And in all honesty Gary was right. Those plaster-covered chunks would have looked like nothing by themselves.

She wondered what Raf had thought of the picture. Had he looked at it with scorn? Had he been the least little jealous she had posed for Gary?

Eaten by her own jealousy of Leona, she lay sleepless for hours, going over and over her actions on the day of Dr. Gray's accident. She had been right about one thing: Raf *had* contacted Leona about the titanothere discovery. His attention to Holly had been no more than he would pay to any pretty girl who came so willingly within his orbit.

DURING THE DAYS THAT FOLLOWED, everyone worked with quiet intensity. To the relief of all, Dr. Gray calmed down and became his cheerful distracted self. But they knew now he was capable of anger, and they still treated him like a basket of eggs.

He accepted Holly's carefully memorized but still stammered apology with good grace, even telling her he could understand how a photographer and a model with nothing to do might easily wind up making frisky photographs. In this instance, however, their irresponsbility had had serious consequences.

"But," Dr. Gray shrugged, "we'll see whether the young lady Valcour brought can get us out of the mess. I doubt it." He shrugged again and gave Holly a wintry smile over his glasses. "We can but hope."

The last fossil-containing rocks were hewn out of the precipice and brought to camp. Dr. Gray decreed certain of the fossils were to be freed from their matrices without delay, instead of being shipped, rock and all, to the university lab.

"Since you've already spilled the beans," Dr. Gray told Dr. Dave in front of everyone, "we'd better find out whether we've got what you claimed." His dour face made his students stifle their groans at the thought of picking away morning and afternoon at rocklike clay when they could be scrambling about the wild formations, hunting more "treasure." That was the exciting work, despite the broiling sun.

After the first morning, when everyone stayed in camp and worked at freeing the bones from the very sediment that had turned them into fossils, Dr. Gray relented and sent a team of two back into the field— Bill and Wayne one morning, Marcia and Willie the next.

As bone after bone emerged, Dr. Gray pronounced them to be indeed parts of the skeleton of a half-grown titanothere.

Holly helped, hopeful that her industry would restore her to Dr. Gray's good graces.

While the group worked, they talked—joking, teasing, sometimes even discussing paleontology. A pleasant camaraderie pervaded the scene. Inevitably Raf's name came up.

"What's happened to Valcour?" Wayne said one afternoon. "He seems to have dropped us."

Looking up, Holly met his mocking gaze. "He has a ranch to run," she snapped, and was then sorry she'd risen to the bait. Her stomach tightened with annoyance.

"He also has company," Willie commented with a look at Bill.

"No, he hasn't," Bill said curtly. "Not who you mean, anyhow."

"How do you know?"

"She's gone back to Pierre." Bill's tone was clipped.

Holly had no idea how Bill was so well informed, but it was disgusting the way the information raised her spirits.

"Gone back to write us up proper, eh?" Marcia suggested.

"Let's hope to God she has," Dr. Dave rasped.

THURSDAY EVENING AFTER SUPPER, Willie, Marcia and Holly were voluntarily working away on fossil cleaning while the light lasted when Holly saw Raf riding through the cottonwoods. She bent over her work and pretended to be unaware of his arrival until he rode into the camp clearing.

At first sight of him her heart had given a great mindless leap of joy. Then had come the memory of the last time she'd seen him—with Leona. She reminded herself that he had no regard for her. She had been a momentary diversion, nothing more.

As the others called greetings, he dismounted and came to join them at the table. He was wearing cowboy garb and carrying a rolled newspaper. His glance flicked over Holly, but she avoided his eye. His, "Good evening," was general.

Anyhow, I'm not frivolously clothed, Holly told herself encouragingly. She was wearing a simple cotton shirt and shorts.

"I see you've brought the paper," Willie said.

Dr. Dave looked up from his portable typewriter.

"Yes." Raf's golden eyes looked grave. Holly had the distinct sensation of the bottom dropping out of her stomach.

"Dr. Gray here?" Raf asked.

"He's inside," Willie said. "I'll get him." He

jumped up and strode to the open door of the trailer.

Raf's eyes slid to Holly. No matter what, she was glad to see him. Her blue eyes brightened, and her lovely smile spread across her face.

Raf's expression softened. "Bad news, I'm afraid," he said quietly.

Dr. Gray joined them at the table, and Raf handed him the paper.

"Leona filed her story with the other wire service and the *Rapid City Gazette* picked it up."

"Bet her story won't get national coverage," Willie said in an aside to Holly. "Without your picture, nobody except a handful of crazy paleos would care about fossils of an animal they've never heard of."

Holly shushed him, her eyes never leaving Dr. Gray's face.

Dr. Gray was reading the story through, with Dr. Dave peering unembarrassedly over his shoulder.

Holly's breath caught as she watched an angry red begin at Dr. Gray's open collar and slowly suffuse his face.

"My Lord! Is this supposed to rectify matters?" he shouted, slamming the newspaper on the table.

Dr. Dave picked it up to finish reading.

"She said she'd do what she could to repudiate the story! Instead of that she's repudiated the whole expedition!" Dr. Gray exploded.

"Easy, my friend," Raf said. "It can't be as bad as that."

"The hell it isn't! She's twisted my words! She's made Dave's announcement sound like a publicity stunt. Originally it merely sounded stupid and ill-prepared. Now it sounds phony! She's made it all Holly's fault—as though the poor girl had to look for chances to model.''

Holly felt the blood drain from her face. What had Leona written? She tried to look at Raf, but her sight was curiously blurred.

Dr. Dave was still peering at the article through his spectacles. Marcia and Willie were attempting to read over his shoulders.

"She quotes an undisclosed source," Dr. Dave read aloud, "as saying Miss Cameron is a New York model who has gone from exploiting Indians to exploiting prehistoric animals in order to get her picture taken. She says that Miss Cameron, although a successful model, came to South Dakota for a 'rest.'" Dr. Dave snorted. "She makes Holly sound like an aging actress."

Holly's gaze fastened on his angrily twitching hand.

Dr. Gray was sitting at the table, shaking his head. "What have we done to merit this?" he asked, no longer angry, merely bewildered.

"And thanks to Holly we all look phony," Dr. Dave added.

All eyes were directed at her, all accusing her of wrongdoing. "Why me," she wanted to cry out. "I didn't tell Scoop anything. Or Leona. Why am I to blame?"

One thought thrust itself uppermost. She had to escape those eyes—Raf's most of all.

Wordlessly she turned and stumbled toward her tent, but when she reached it, she veered and kept going, moving through the sparse undergrowth like

someone in a trance, her main thought to get away
from that ring of accusers. Angry faces made her
shrivel inside. She wasn't desperate for approval, but
disapproval when she hadn't meant any harm. . . .
How quickly one's spirit faded! She couldn't cope
with such heartless misunderstanding.

Where was Bill, she asked herself. Resting in his
tent probably. But she couldn't go running to him
like a kid sister.

Her footsteps carried her to the bare creek bank,
where the pale earth still reflected the lingering
daylight. Feeling painfully exposed, she stepped back
into the shelter of the trees and leaned her back
against one of the giant cottonwoods. She tossed an
unwilling glance over her shoulder, but her path was
hidden by a stand of saplings. She was safe from ran-
cor and accusations for the time being.

Let them exclaim and blame and get it over with.
She didn't intend to hang around and be railed at all
over again. She'd already apologized.

Good, she told herself, *I'm angry now, instead of
hurt.*

She smoothed away the twigs beneath the mon-
strous tree and sat down, leaning her back against the
rough bark. The sounds of the camp were almost indistinguishable.

She was finding a measure of peace in the silence
when she raised her eyes to see Raf coming light-
footed along the creek bank. He'd seen her of course.

Before she could scramble to her feet, he squatted
nearby, balancing on his toes. She settled back
against the tree and glowered at him. In the gathering dusk his topaz eyes were shadowed. His mouth
looked grim.

At last she goaded him. "I see you're still creeping about like an Indian."

"I see you've come out here to sulk," he returned.

"I came to be alone."

"Have you?" Instead of taking the hint, he continued to crouch beside her.

Her mind shot off at a crazy tangent, and she thought, *the men out here must practice that position from the time they're boys.* She couldn't help noticing the hard lean thighs, the taut buttocks, the way men's knees looked different from women's. Well-fitting boots were flattering to a man, too, and so was Raf's balancing act. It was poised, controlled, masculine. She felt a sharp desire to shove him off balance, but he was too practiced. She had seen him shift about previously, using his knee for a third point of contact. If she pushed him, he would brace himself with one hand on the ground, and she'd be the one to look silly.

He said, "I didn't think you were the kind to cut and run in the face of trouble. Unless, of course, you knew you had it coming."

"I don't have it coming!" she cried, her blue eyes blazing. "I've been all through this once! I apologized to Dr. Gray for letting Gary photograph such silly poses, and he said he understood. Now he's mad all over again. Why did you have to bring that paper?"

"I don't think he's angry at you."

Holly's eyes filled with tears, but she blinked them away. "It's your fault for upsetting everything a second time. Why did you do it?" she asked reproachfully.

"I sure as hell didn't mean to!" His eyes met hers.

"You must have known what would happen."

"No, I didn't!" he disclaimed. "Dr. Gray wanted to see the other article repudiated, and it was. I had no idea they'd get all worked up again." His voice was rueful.

"Well, you know now!" Holly said unforgivingly. "So please go away and leave me alone." She stared into the distance, biting her lip.

"Are you going to stay out here? You'll get cold." His voice held a trace of amusement.

"No, I'm going to creep back after dark...like a rat. I suppose you'd like to see me go back now and be scolded and yelled at some more," she said bitterly. "Well, too bad! You'll have to miss the second show!"

"You've got to face them sometime."

Holly turned over his words in her mind. It was true she'd have to face Dr. Gray, but by morning maybe he'd have a change of heart. He'd have cooled off. How many times must she apologize for the same mistake? Her bosom rose and fell at the injustice of her treatment.

"Why are they still blaming me?" she demanded. "I didn't tell Scoop or Gary what we'd found. They wouldn't have *had* any story to illustrate if Dr. Young had kept his mouth shut."

"Ever heard of a scapegoat?" Raf's raised brows curved like narrow wings. A reflection of the last light on the white water of the creek glinted in his eyes. "Both professors know Young is at fault. As I see it, so is Gray. He should have told all of you the discovery was to be hush-hush. My advice is, don't let him make you feel guilty."

Holly brooded over his words. His advice seemed sound—until she remembered his part in her present difficulties. She had relented toward him because he'd come after her. He had made her forget Leona's contribution.

"You're the one who should feel guilty!" Holly said fiercely. "You're the one who gave Leona all the ammunition."

"Me?" He sounded taken aback.

"Yes, you! How else did she know so much about me?"

Raf's silence lasted while a bat swooped twice over the creek. At last he said, "You'd better ask your brother that."

"My brother! What do you mean?"

"Ask him," Raf said, and stood up.

"My brother doesn't know Leona!"

"I think you'll find he does."

Raf was leaving. He hadn't tried to kiss her. He hadn't touched her. He took two steps away and stopped. Reluctantly, it appeared, he returned.

"Holly, stop acting like a child and come back to camp. I guarantee nobody will say any more to you. They've had a chance to realize—"

"I'm to get the silent treatment, is that it?" she interrupted. "No, thank you."

He reached out his hand. "Come on, get up."

Unwillingly she let him grasp her arm. In one smooth movement he drew her to her feet and into his arms. His embrace was like an oasis after a long trip through the desert.

"Oh, Raf...." Her arms went around his waist, and she laid her head on his shoulder. His shirt

smelled of sun and himself. How easy it was to forget
how long he'd stayed away, to believe his absences
had been unavoidable.

"I'm not going to start kissing you now," he
began, pulling at her single thick braid to raise her
head and look into her face, "or we'll never get anything else...." His voice stopped as his lips brushed
hers.

She stood stiff and unrelenting, her hands lightly
clasping his waist. She didn't want him to twist her
emotions around. She was angry and hurt, and Raf
Valcour had done his share to cause these feelings by
bringing in Leona. Holly was determined not to
capitulate easily to his lovemaking—no matter how
much she wanted to.

"You've hardly been out of my mind since they
rescued us from Buffalo Table," he muttered, pulling her against him. She felt her bones give as his
arms tightened.

"I've been here all the time," she said with a gasp,
her voice slightly reproachful. "I guess you'd rather
think about me than see me."

"You were busy with your buddy Gary. I had the
distinct impression you preferred younger men who
would admire you at a distance. But now he's done
you wrong...."

"He wasn't the only one!" Holly said bitterly.
"But I do owe you an apology. When I realized you
wanted Leona to get the story, I—I guess I didn't behave very well."

Raf shook his head. "It still beats me how you
came up with that idea."

"You did call her."

"Not I! She saw the story when it came over the wire and called me. The next thing I knew she met me at the hospital when I went to pick up the professor."

"Really?" Holly said coldly, her mind clicking furiously, trying to reconcile this information with her previously held beliefs.

Raf shook his head. "I thought I was a pretty slick businessman, but modeling and reporting are two fields I know nothing about. You girls' wheeling and dealing make me feel like an ignorant cowpoke."

She didn't believe him for a minute. Gary had reminded her how rich Raf was, and she recalled the men she'd seen lounging on the beaches of Jamaica and Barbados. Raf was one of them when he chose to be. Very sophisticated.

Perhaps he caught her disbelieving look and wished to change the subject, for he said, "Kiss me," and took command of her lips with a practiced skill that swept her mind clear of everything but his lips and his arms. His ragged breathing stirred her profoundly.

I must mean something to him, she thought. He admitted she'd been on his mind. Perhaps he didn't think of her as just a summer flirtation. Nevertheless his kisses were controlled. He didn't say, "Come home with me." Would she have gone? It would be a relief to get away from this camp for a few hours. She wanted to respond with abandon to the promise his mouth seemed to be making, but her mind, skipping off in another direction, presented her with a picture of her return at daylight, no longer a virgin, sneaking into camp like a gray cat on the prowl. She turned from the picture with distaste.

As though Raf, too, could see into her mind, he turned her from him. With a swat on her bottom he said, "If we stay out here any longer, your brother will think I'm seducing you. I want you to go back there with your head up, and stop taking all the blame for this very tiny tempest."

Tonight, she realized, was not the right time for making love—for either of them. She had too much on her mind. Bill, for one thing. She felt a coldness in the pit of her stomach. Bill couldn't know Leona. Yet why would Raf lie when she could so easily check up. *Ask him,* he'd said. Her mind whirled dizzily. What opportunity had Bill had? Leona hadn't been in town much. Funny she should be thinking that way. When she had pictured Leona with Raf, the girl seemed to be present constantly.

Okay, so Bill had met her at the Fourth of July party. The following Sunday he'd slipped off to Rapid City on his own after the trip to see the buffalo, and then he'd dragged off to the bar in Vista a couple of nights. But surely.... There might have been other times she didn't know about. She wasn't her brother's keeper.

She said, "I want to talk to Bill first—alone. Do me a favor, ask him to come out here, will you? I'll go back when I've had it out with him."

Raf studied her. It was too dark now to see his eyes.

"All right, sweetheart," he said finally. "I'll send him out. Don't let them get you down. Remember, you've got the upper hand. You can always poison them." He cupped her chin in his fingers and kissed her firmly.

By the time she opened her eyes, he was cat-footing it along the creek bank as silently as he had come.

She sat in the deepening twilight, knowing she had to go back to camp but reluctant to face everyone. Had she made more of a fool of herself by running...or would they be sorry?

She was about to get up when she heard Bill calling her name. He, too, was coming along the creek bank, but he was making a lot of noise about it. Clumsy, she thought, unconsciously comparing him with Raf.

"Here I am!" she called.

"Holly...." He dropped down beside her and leaned his back against the tree. "Raf said you were out here. Come on back. It'll blow over."

"Oh, Bill...." She was close to tears. "You're not mad at me? I haven't ruined your whole future?"

"Don't be silly. You're a little fool, but you haven't done anything as bad as that."

"But I haven't done you any good, have I? Is that why you've been avoiding me?"

"You have to admit you haven't been too smart—cavorting all over the place for that hick kid to photograph. What will your agency say when they see that photograph?"

"Cavorting!"

"What would you call it?" Bill's voice had grown censorious.

Holly drew a deep breath. "Bill, have you been dating Leona Selby?"

"What business is that of yours?"

"I told you what a nasty write-up she gave us at Fox Butte."

"She was just doing her job."

"Is that what she told you?" Holly heard her voice rise, and suddenly she didn't care. It was a pleasure to take her anger out on someone. She didn't care if Bill was her brother. She was justified. It was downright satisfying to raise her voice, with no neighbors downstairs or upstairs or next door.

Bill glared back at her without answering.

"She made it sound as if we never did a hand's turn."

"Well, you don't work very hard, do you?"

"Don't I?" she asked, her voice dangerously soft.

"Anyone seeing your pictures would find it hard to believe."

"It keeps you in college," she said bitingly. "Have you forgotten that? That must take *some* work. I work hard enough that you thought I needed a rest. You've changed, Bill...." Her voice broke. "I wouldn't have believed you could be so disloyal."

Bill hung his head, but after a moment he looked away and shrugged. "Okay, so I've been dating Leona. She's a really terrific girl. You two just didn't hit it off right. I didn't tell her anything she didn't already know."

"Are you going to keep seeing her now? After this?" Holly demanded.

"How can I? She's in Pierre."

"Oh, too bad! You would if you could. Too bad she can't hang around here and write more spiteful things about your sister."

"Damn right I'd see her! I like her. If you don't want people to write about you, you shouldn't do things to give them ammunition. You shouldn't have been so publicity crazy, Holly. If you hadn't been so eager to pose for Gary, you wouldn't have got into trouble. Of course Dave Young shouldn't have talked. Everyone knows that. But it was your picture that put everything in the limelight." He gave her a brotherly pat. "Come on back to camp. You'll be forgiven."

Publicity crazy! The words rang across the dark prairie. Publicity crazy. That's what they thought!

Silently she followed him back to camp. On the way her brother stopped to admonish her once more. "Even your great admirer, Dr. Dave, is down on you. Face it, Holly, you've made us all look like amateurs. You can't expect everyone to love you and admire you and think you're the sweetest little thing on earth after a blunder like that."

It's not fair...it's not fair, a voice inside Holly complained when she lay sleepless in her tent. But perhaps Bill was right. Perhaps she had done wrong and it was fair that everyone should be angry with her. Even Raf was angry.

CHAPTER FOURTEEN

"HOLLY'S DECIDED to poison us," Willie joked next morning when Wayne and Dr. Dave joined him at the breakfast table. "The biscuits are burned, and the coffee's strong enough to dissolve your insides."

"You're welcome to eat out," Holly replied sweetly, setting out boxes of dry cereal and a pitcher of milk mixed from powder. She took orders for eggs and began frying them. She had slept poorly and had wakened often to total sick awareness of her unhappy situation. Despite what Raf maintained, she had caused trouble for the professors, and she had quarreled with her brother.

The calendar in the trailer had escaped her attention because she hadn't wanted to know how the time was flying, how the time was drawing nearer when she must leave South Dakota. She had been unable to believe that her love for Raf could come to naught. Such a strong emotion must set up its own vibrations, have some result. But when she thought of the only possible result, she faced a blank wall. She would not cheapen her love by a tawdry affair that Raf would forget as soon as she was gone—or that he might brag about if he ever saw her photograph.

No one mentioned the newspaper report at breakfast, though from the scowls and grunts and grouchy replies, some of the others apparently hadn't slept well, either.

The weather had turned cool during the night— one of the many small signs that autumn was approaching.

Dr. Dave was the only one who spoke directly to Holly. He asked her to make sandwiches. His manner was grave, as though she had let him down and he was deeply disappointed. Junior Old Elk arrived with the horses, and the professors took the jeep. They left to go out scouting, not remembering to provide Holly with any fossils to work on. Perhaps they weren't going to trust her for that, either.

She dealt with the breakfast dishes and stirred up and baked a big coffee cake made with prunes and raisins. If Raf should stop by.... And if he didn't, her regular crew would demolish it quickly enough and perhaps forgive her for burning this morning's biscuits. She was aware she wanted to be forgiven for more than burning biscuits. She had felt left out at other times when they'd all gone off prospecting for fossils, but today was different. Today she felt left alone as punishment. Ridiculous, of course, but she couldn't rid herself of the impression.

She roamed disconsolately about the camp and walked to the creek, which was as white and dead-looking as ever. No animals lived in its murky waters, although Raf had shown her where cliff swallows nested under the bridge on the way to Vista.

The thought of Vista made her realize she would need supplies before tomorrow. She had laundry to be done, too. Probably everyone else had some, as well.

It occurred to her she could very well drive into town after dinner. Henry Brightwing stayed open late. She could do her laundry, and she wouldn't have to spend the evening in camp, feeling like an outcast.

I'll offer to do everyone else's clothes, too, she thought magnanimously, *so it won't look as if I'm avoiding them,* though in fact that was her purpose.

The day dragged. Raf did not appear.

If he were strongly attracted, she thought, he wouldn't be able to stay away.

She washed her hair and rewrote her shopping list, then made a gelatin dessert. She even got out her camera and took photographs of the camp, though the pictures were going to look lifeless with no people in them. That reminded her of what she was trying to forget.

They don't understand, she agonized. *They're not in the business. Pictures of things without people are a dead bore. If Gary's editor had only used the pictures he was supposed to....*

"No use crying over spilled milk," she said aloud.

The sound of her voice made the camp seem emptier than ever. She looked at her watch. Thank heaven—it was time to start supper.

The crew straggled in, full of the day's doings. Bill had found a large fossil jaw that might be worth excavating after Dr. Gray checked the records. It appeared to be in a rock formation in which that type had never been found previously. Over a happy hour sherry they decided to excavate.

Everyone treated Holly as though nothing had happened. In fact, they almost overdid it, complimenting her excessively on the cheese-and-onion appetizers made with biscuit mix.

"I'll need the jeep this evening," she announced, trying not to sound belligerent. "We need bread for tomorrow and quite a few other groceries."

Dr. Dave pulled the keys from his pocket. A shade reluctantly, Holly thought. He couldn't refuse to trust her with the jeep!

"You don't mind going alone?" he asked, sounding still more reluctant.

"Certainly not." She heard the frostiness in her voice and tried to soften it by saying, "I'll be glad to do any laundry. My first stop's the laundromat."

Her offer was quickly taken up by the boys and Marcia.

Dr. Dave said, "I have an admission to make. Dr. Gray and I did ours there this afternoon."

The chorus of hoots from the students followed Holly as she went to her tent to change. Sick of wearing pants and shorts, she hauled out the full skirt of the two-piece dress she had worn to the barbecue and paired it with a simple white T-shirt that gathered in soft folds at the scoop neck. Bare-legged and wearing her fisherman's sandals, she considered herself well dressed for Vista.

She loaded the bundles into the back of the jeep and set off. Bumping down the dusty road with nothing in sight but some black cattle, Holly felt remarkably light, as though in leaving camp she had shed a great burden.

"I'll be glad when it's over," she told herself fiercely. "Back in New York I'll forget Raf in no time."

She passed his ranch in a burst of speed and a cloud of dust, but she couldn't resist seeking a glimpse of him. In one of the corrals surrounding the barns, three riders were driving a small bunch of animals through a gate—whitefaces, as she had learned to call the cattle with curly red hides and cream-colored heads.

In Vista she commandeered all five washing machines in the dilapidated laundromat and dumped in muddy and sweat-stained clothes, glad to have a separate machine for her own. Crossing her fingers that none of the machines would break down, she left them to their work and took her list to the general store.

By the time Henry Brightwing had assembled and bagged her purchases, the washing was done. She tossed the clothes into two dryers and went to stand in the doorway, looking across at the Shorthorn Saloon, recalling the day she'd met Raf in front of it. How surprised he'd looked, and how delighted she'd been.

She could hear the saloon jukebox playing a cowboy song. Three pickups were parked in front. A corrugated tin awning formed a porch roof over the front. Determined weeds grew full and tall at either end of the wooden bench beside the entrance. Along the edge of the roof a row of deer antlers had bleached white. The bar looked as authentically Old West as a movie set. Was it authentic?

She looked over her shoulder at the clothes in the dryers. The music and a burst of male laughter from the Shorthorn Saloon sounded infinitely appealing.

Dared she go in there and have a drink while the

clothes were drying? She'd been there twice with Raf. How much different could it be on Friday night? Only three cars besides her own were parked in the street.

While she hesitated, another pickup bowled into town and pulled up before the saloon with a screech. Two men in boots and straw hats got out. They lounged to the front door and pushed it open. So they did open it at night!

Why shouldn't I go over there, she challenged herself. *Are women liberated or not? I'll sit quietly in a booth, drink a soda and listen to the music.*

Crossing the street, she thought wryly, *my friends in New York should see me now—going to Vista for a taste of civilization.*

The minute she entered the door she knew she'd done the wrong thing. The room seemed full of men, all wearing their hats. There wasn't a woman in the place. She was too embarrassed to turn on her heel and scuttle out. Her face felt stiff as she dragged her feet through the sawdust to the nearest empty booth. Most of the drinkers were at the bar, with their backs to her, except for four beefy males in a rear booth. She heard a low appreciative whistle.

She sat in the bare wooden booth feeling foolish, remembering that the other times she'd been here, someone had gone to the bar to get the drinks. She would not, could not, bring herself to elbow up there and ask for a Coke. How long could she sit here confronting an empty table?

One of the two bartenders solved her dilemma by coming to ask her what she wanted to drink, his voice friendly.

"A Coke," she said gratefully, bestowing on him her lovely smile.

He brought it in a glass with clinking ice, and for all anyone knew, there was rum in it. With something in front of her and something to do with her hands, she began to feel less frozen. She became aware of the music again and the good-natured joshing going on at the bar.

They'll think I'm waiting for someone, she told herself, studying the floating ice. A date! In Vista? She was scoffing at that idea when a man from the end of the bar lounged across the room, carrying his drink, and slid into the seat across the table from her.

"Hello, sweetheart. Waiting for someone?" His dirty felt hat was tipped back on his head, showing a lot of black hair badly cut. He had several days' growth of whiskers and a leer. He sat with his elbows on the table, his arms brown and muscular. His work had to do with horses; there was no mistaking the smell, even over stale beer. Her first thought was to get up and leave. But no! Why let him drive her away?

"Yes, I am!" she snapped.

"You're too pretty a gal to have to wait all by yourself."

"I prefer it that way." Holly's blue eyes were icy. His too friendly tone made her acutely uncomfortable. At least he was on the other side of the table.

"Where is this fellow? Maybe he stood you up?"

"I—I'm a little early," she stammered, knowing she ought to get up and leave. But what if he followed her across the street into the empty laundromat and the clothes weren't dry? If she took them back to camp to hang out, they'd get drenched with dew.

She was weighing alternatives when her escape was blocked by a second man, dressed like the first in blue jeans and faded shirt, holding a beer bottle in one hand and a glass in the other.

"Scoot over, honey!"

Before Holly could refuse, he slid in beside her.

"You can't keep this little lady all to yourself, Clarence," he admonished his friend.

Holly had no choice but to accommodate the newcomer, unless she wanted to sit thigh to thigh with him. Oddly enough, with two of them she felt a little safer, though the second man was more pushy.

"What's your name, little lady?" he demanded.

"Juanita," Holly said tartly.

"Well, now, Juanita, I'm Tom and that ornery cuss is Clarence. What are you drinking?"

"A Coke." Holly bit her lip. It looked as if these two were sitting down for the evening. She gulped nervously at her drink.

Tom threw money on the table. "Clarence, go get us another round," he directed, perhaps guessing that if he himself went for the drinks, Holly would be gone like a shot.

"I really don't want another Coke," she protested as Clarence rose.

"Have something else, then," Tom urged. "Have a rum and Coke. You're a big girl." His eyes rested on her bosom.

"No! I don't want another drink."

"Get her a rum and Coke," Tom told Clarence.

Clarence went obediently to the bar, and Tom grinned at her.

"What's a pretty girl like you doing in Vista?"

"The laundry," she said shortly, abandoning her story of waiting for someone. She made up her mind that as soon as Clarence came back, she would excuse herself and head for the ladies' room. From there she'd slip out the back door, grab the clothes and drive off.

Clarence returned with the drinks, and Holly executed her plan. It meant running the gauntlet of all the eyes in the room, which was not the same as parading down the runway at a style show. But she endured it, thanking heaven she knew about the open back door and the path through the weeds.

Minutes later she left the ladies' room, her heart thudding. A few steps away the open rectangle showed darkness and a glint of fireflies. Before she could step toward it, the door to the men's room opened, and Tom emerged, standing between her and freedom. She turned away, shivering at the thought of his following her onto the weedy path.

With him behind her she marched back to the booth. There, however, she dug in her heels and refused to be intimidated.

"I really must go," she told the two men instead of sliding into the booth.

"What about the fellow you're waiting for?" Clarence asked with exaggerated concern. "You gonna walk out on him?"

"What fellow?" Tom demanded. "She never said anything about no fellow to me."

"There isn't one," she confessed urgently. "My

laundry's done, and I want to go home." She took a quick glance around the bar. Nobody was paying any attention to their corner of the room.

"You can't go now. You gotta finish your drink." Grabbing her arm, Tom tried to push her into the booth.

"No!" She struggled to break away, but his arm had the power of a piece of construction machinery, inexorably putting her where it wanted her to go.

"The lady doesn't want to sit with you, cowboy." The quiet words were authoritative. That voice! Holly had never been so glad to hear that voice. Her head snapped around to see Raf standing inside the front door.

He didn't move forward. He merely said calmly, "Ready to go, Holly?"

"Yes!" Her voice was vibrant with relief.

"She just told us she wasn't waiting for anyone!" Clarence sounded aggrieved.

"You know you can't believe a woman." Raf jerked his head. "Come on, Holly."

"Sorry, Mr. Valcour, we didn't know she was waiting for you," Tom mumbled.

"How could you, if the lady didn't tell you?" Raf said affably. His firm hand on Holly's back propelling her out the door told her he was not pleased.

"I was never so glad to see anybody in my life!" Holly exclaimed as they crossed the wide street.

"What the hell made you go in there alone?" Raf exploded.

"I was waiting for the clothes to dry." Holly's teeth set as she realized he was going to bawl her out.

"And you couldn't have waited in the laundromat?"

"I could have," she drawled, beginning a slow burn, "but I didn't." Why should she admit she'd been a fool—again.

"Were you trying to get picked up? Did I interrupt your evening's entertainment?" His eyes raked her. "I see you're dressed for a night on the town."

Furiously she denied it.

"I suppose you came to get groceries."

"Yes, I did."

"Henry Brightwing's been closed for an hour!"

"So what? I'm not on any schedule that I know of."

That shut him up. He stood under the flickering fluorescent lights of the laundromat, dressed in a black shirt and pants, wearing his black hat with the silver conchas, waiting while she pulled the clothes out of the dryer and folded them. He made no move to help.

"Thank you for rescuing me," she said unwillingly.

"You were making it pretty obvious you wanted to leave," he admitted.

"You mean if I'd just been sitting there with those two fellows, you'd have left me to my fate?"

"That's what you were looking for, wasn't it— some excitement?"

"No, it was not! I told you—I was waiting for the clothes to dry. I've been in that bar with you—twice. How was I to know it wasn't the same at night? I suppose you're mad because I spoiled your evening."

His snort was a denial.

"You're dressed up as much as I am," she accused. "As a matter of fact, you look like the bad guy in a western."

She thought the way his eyelids flickered over the tawny eyes meant that her intended insult pleased him. He leaned against the nearest washing machine.

"Maybe I am the bad guy."

"I wouldn't be surprised." She went on with her folding.

"Except just now I rescued the damsel in distress. I'm surprised they allowed you a night in town. They should know you'd get in trouble."

Her face flushed. Did he have to remind her?

"They didn't allow it. I took it. What are you doing here if you weren't planning a night off? Why are you dressed up?"

"I saw you zoom past."

The answer pleased her. "How did you know I was coming here?"

"I took a chance."

"I'm glad you did," she admitted, smiling at him. She put the last of the clothes into the plastic garbage bags they used for laundry.

"So ends the big night in town," she said on the way to the cars. His battered pickup was parked beside the jeep.

Raf said, "I'm afraid we'd both get in trouble if I took you back to the saloon...."

"Why?" She was startled.

"The boys have had a few more beers by now. Someone might say something, and I'd have to defend your honor."

"Oh." He didn't sound very gallant.

He helped her into the jeep and stood with one arm hanging on the windshield, his face very near hers. "My dad taught me something a long time ago: don't kick a skunk."

He looked at her from under thick lashes, and she giggled. Tom and Clarence were potential skunks, all right.

"Want to stop at the ranch? We can have a drink there, and you can go for a swim if you like."

Her heart leaped at his invitation, but she said primly, "I don't have a suit."

"You don't need a suit. No one will see you."

"Where will you be?" She felt a little disappointed.

"I'll turn my back." He reached into the car and turned the key. Before removing his hand, he squeezed her knee. "Get going. I'll follow."

She couldn't drive fast over the gravel road. The stones thudding up to hit the bottom of the jeep sounded like boulders, and she'd been told to look out for deer and straying cattle. The night wind blew through her hair. She thought that if Raf insisted, she would go swimming. He would have to promise, though, to stay out of sight.

So he had really wanted to see her. Perhaps he had even rushed to finish with the cattle and change his clothes...and eat. Or perhaps he had already finished with the cattle when he saw her, had eaten a leisurely dinner nicely served by Mrs. Jones and then, at loose ends, had taken a drive to Vista—on the off chance she was still there. Possibly he'd only driven to Vista to have a few drinks at the saloon, and his rescue of her had been purely chance.

The balmy night wind blew gloomy reflections away. Raf was behind her; he had come to Vista to find her, and he had invited her home for a drink.

She recognized the turnoff and caught flashes of the hollyhocks lining the drive. Raf stopped the pickup by one of the barns. Taking her arm, he guided her across the white wooden bridge to the patio.

"Drink first?" he asked.

"Before what?"

Her question hung in the air until he replied smoothly, "While we decide what to do next. White wine?"

Not wanting him to be so sure of her, she said, "I'd like—oh, a vodka and tonic."

His nod and the sideways slant of his eyes told her she had amused him again.

"Come with me while I fix it," he invited. "We can also make sure Mrs. Jones has gone to her quarters on the other side of the house."

Holly sniffed. "If she works for South Dakota's most eligible bachelor, I suppose she's had to learn not to be shocked."

"Quite right."

His answer annoyed her. He might have had the grace to deny it, to say he'd never had naked women swimming in his pool.

"I've never had naked beauties swimming in the pool.... Is that what you want me to say?"

Holly burst into laughter. "I think you're a wizard the way you read my mind."

"Should I tell you my secret?" He came to stand close to her. Her heart began to race. Tawny eyes scanned her features. "It's not your mind, sweet thing. It's your beautiful expressive face that tells me what you're thinking.''

Holly's breath caught. If he understood her so well, did he know she loved him? Had that shown on her face, too? Did he know now how happy she was to be here?

His arms closed lightly about her. She slipped her arms around his waist and rested her head on his shoulder, thinking, *I must not be possessive,* though she longed to pull his face down to hers and give him the kind of passionate kiss he had taught her she was capable of.

Gently he disengaged her. ''Let's have that drink.''

How could he be so cool? Something told her it came from wide experience and not caring much.

He brought ice cubes from the kitchen and mixed identical drinks at the bar trolley in the living room. They sat in a glider on the patio and watched bats swoop over the pool.

''Where do they go in the daytime?'' Holly asked.

''Barns, mostly. There aren't as many as there used to be. It's a pity; they eat a lot of insects.''

''Are you going to swim with me?'' he asked finally. ''Or are you going to be a prude?''

After a moment's hesitation she laughed. ''I'm going to be a prude. But don't let me stop you.''

''I don't intend to. I've been looking forward to this all day.'' He stood up, then bent and kissed her lips. ''Don't go 'way.''

He opened another of the sliding glass doors and disappeared into a darkened room. His bedroom? A lamp came on, and sheer curtains were pulled across the glass doors, leaving a luminous glow. What would it be like simply to open a door from your bedroom and step out into a swimming pool? If only she had a suit....

Raf came out wearing tan trunks that fit like a second skin. At first glance, in fact, she thought he wasn't wearing anything.

He made a running dive into the end of the pool and surfaced in front of her. Gripping the side with one brown hand, he flung wet hair back from his face. Holly heard a splash. A shower of drops flashed in the light before they sprinkled her.

"The water's great! Come on in," he coaxed.

"You're wearing trunks, and you want me to come in naked?" she cried. Her resistance was lessening. Seeing him swimming made her think how good the water would feel on her warm skin.

"Have you ever been swimming at night?" he asked, still holding the side.

She shook her head.

"Scaredy-cat! Come on in! I'll take my trunks off if that'll make you feel better."

"No! I mean, don't do that!"

His hand disappeared from the tiled rim. She watched him cut through the water with a swift strong stroke that took him from one end to the other in seconds, though the pool was no mean size.

What if she stripped and went in? It didn't mean he was going to rape her there in the swimming pool or outside it, either. Maybe by today's standards she was being a prude. How much did her bikini cover, for that matter? Darned little!

"I'll come in if you'll promise to behave," she called.

"I won't do anything you don't want me to."

An old line, but if he said it, he meant it. "Look the other way till I get in the water," she demanded. "No, wait! I have to braid my hair."

"How long is that going to take?"

"Seconds," she said, laughing at his resigned tone.

The wind touched the bare skin of her breasts, her flat tummy, the silken insides of her thighs, with caressing fingertips, making her feel bold and open. The pale light from the half-moon blurred her limbs, blending her with the rest of the universe. Without the shell of clothing it was hard to tell where her body left off and the universe began.

"Ready or not, here I come!" Raf called.

"Wait!" she screeched, giving her hair a final twist and fastening it with a clasp dug from her purse. She was keeping her eyes on the back of his head, ready to cover herself with her skirt should he cheat and turn around. She realized they were playing the kind of delicious game that little girls only dream about.

The water looked too enticing for her to remain out of it for another second.

"Whee!" she cried, and took a running jump. The freedom of totally bare skin was a revelation as the water closed over her. She came up laughing with pure joy. She swam in Raf's direction, but when she reached the side, he wasn't there. She clung to the tiles, searching the empty water, feeling the air bubbles rising along her sides.

"Where are you?" she cried, laughter lilting her voice. She stiffened in sudden playful fear. "Raf?"

She screamed when a calloused hand scraped her leg. Then remembering how late it was, she clapped a hand over her mouth. Hands went around her ankles, and she was pulled backward, away from the edge.

She struggled, laughing, keeping her grip on the side of the pool. Raf burst gasping from the water beside her.

He reached a dripping hand to cup her head and bring her face to his. "Brave girl," he commended, and covered her lips with a watery kiss.

As though swimming were but a preliminary leading to this, their bodies fused together, the lean length of him all bone and muscle. Holly's toes touched the bottom of the pool. One of Raf's hard thighs slid between her legs, and she pressed the satin skin of her inner thighs against him. He held her tight, tight. Their kiss was long and breathless, accompanied by the slap-slap of the water and, out in the grass, a chorus of crickets.

At last he let her go. Slipping his hands under her armpits with a splash, he lifted her high out of the water, looking up at the dripping length of her.

"Oh, my beautiful girl!" He sank his teeth in the soft wet skin of her belly.

Laughing, Holly shrieked and struggled. Her knee made contact with his chest, and she shoved him off balance just as he let go of her. She fell backward with a satisfactory splash.

"Oh, you!" she cried, finding her equilibrium on the bottom of the pool and dashing the water out of her eyes. "You said you wouldn't do anything!"

"I didn't say I wouldn't look!" With that he sank into the water and disappeared. She knew he meant to attack like a submarine and duck her again.

She swam wildly for the ladder at the end of the pool, remembered her total nudity and struck off at a right angle. His hands clutched her sides. She squeaked and lost her stroke. The two of them bobbed laughing in water over their heads. Raf was grinning! She hugged the knowledge close.

"How can you find me when it's so dark?" she gurgled seconds later as they were clinging to the side.

"Pale face, pale bottom."

She shook her head at him. Cavorting about in the water was too suggestive, too dangerous to her determination. "Race you to the other end," she challenged.

Raf swam like a seal. When she joined him, panting, at the far end, she gasped, "Where did you learn to swim like this? Not out here on the prairie."

Raf shrugged. "Lakes . . . rivers. My father was a great fisherman. He fished. I swam. Had enough?"

Before she could answer, he slid one strong hand between her thighs, and balancing her with the other at her waist, he lifted till her breasts were clear of the water, gleaming white in the glow from his bedroom. She would have allowed his eyes to feast their fill, but his hand at her crotch was giving frightening sensations to nerves she didn't even know she possessed. She wanted his hand to stay there. In another minute she'd lose what sense she had.

Her toes found the bones of his hips, tingling at the touch. His hipbones were so different from hers. She pushed against him, and he lost his hold. She toppled and came up spluttering but in command of her senses.

"Stay there," Raf ordered. "I'll bring you a robe."

He sprang out of the pool with easy grace and paced catlike across the terrace. Watching him was like watching moving perfection. No wonder sculptors were inspired to do naked figures!

Holly did a leisurely sidestroke to the side of the pool nearest the house. Raf returned with a brown towel thrown over his shoulders and draped the robe over the ladder.

"Put that on and come dry off properly in my bathroom." He went back through the sliding doors.

Holly put her arms into the terry robe, loving its soft rough dryness on her wet skin. A sigh of relief escaped her lips when the robe hung from her shoulders and the sleeves dangled over her hands, proving to her that it was a man's robe—his.

She gathered up her clothes and stepped barefoot through the open door. The half-opened drapes threw a shaft of light across the patio. She heard water running in the bathroom and looked around her. The room seemed cool. Air conditioning! How heavenly! She closed the glass door and pulled the curtains together.

The room sent a faint prickle of discomfort down her backbone—it looked so totally masculine, decorated in tones of brown and black. The big brass bed—undoubtedly an heirloom—was covered with a brown bedspread of heavy silk embroidered with peacocks. The wall-to-wall carpeting was the same color as the bedspread. The walls were lighter, textured. The furniture was marvelous—rattan chests with brass corners. A black ceiling fan turned lazily overhead. A glass shelf, lighted from beneath, ran around the room a little above eye level. It held a collection of fossil jaws.

Raf emerged from the bathroom, drying his face. Holly smelled shaving lotion and cringed. Shaving now? What did that portend?

Nevertheless she spoke with enthusiasm. "I love your room. It looks...." She laughed. "It looks as if you've returned from trading voyages to far Cathay."

Raf grinned a bit self-consciously. "My sister did the place up before she moved to California."

He came toward Holly, the brown trunks exchanged for a brown towel twisted about his hips.

Her eyes widened with premonition.

"You're wearing my robe," he pointed out, and for an instant she thought he was going to claim it. She took a step backward. His eyes were slits of gold between black lashes as his hands removed the little pile of clothing from her unresisting arms. He laid her things on one of the chests and turned back to her.

"Oh, no!" she exclaimed, backing away and pulling the terry-cloth belt tighter around her middle.

"Your hair's still dripping. Let me get another bath towel and dry it," he offered.

"I can dry it," she told him. "Where's that dryer I used previously?"

"Still out in the cabana."

"I should have gone there to dress," she muttered.

"We'll be more comfortable here."

He emerged from the bathroom with another huge fluffy towel. Holly removed the clip from her hair and shook out the braid. She sat sideways on the edge of the bed and let him towel her head roughly and efficiently.

"That'll do," he said after a time, and flung the damp towel to land on the bathroom floor.

"Who picks up after you?" Holly asked, feeling dazed from the brisk rub but doing her best to keep the atmosphere casual.

"Want to apply for the job?" He sat on the bed behind her, one knee drawn up, so that she was sitting between his legs.

Apply for the job! She turned to face him. "You never mentioned you had an opening!"

"I didn't know I did till now."

Was he kidding her? His face gave away nothing. His eyes were liquid gold in the lamp's glow. So, no doubt, were a mountain lion's in certain lights.

A hundred delicate nerves and muscles were tingling in Holly's body in a way that had nothing to do with their bantering conversation. With maddening slowness he pulled her against him. His face came down to hers. Her eyes were on his lips—mobile, strong, masculine. She curled into his embrace with a sigh of gratification.

"Little witch," he murmured. "I had no more intention of following you into Vista tonight than I did of flying to the moon. And I have to get up at dawn."

"I do, too," she recalled.

With a groan he cradled her head in his arms and kissed her with hard forceful passion. Her hands spread possessively over his shoulder blades; reached to touch the column of his neck, to run fingertips through his hair.

His cool rough hand slipped inside the terry-cloth robe to cup her breast, as she had wanted it to do.

She gasped with pleasure.

Gently he laid her back on the bedspread, taking his lips from hers long enough to say, "This is a bit better than Buffalo Table."

She loved the rough scrape of his fingers as he spread the robe open. Leaning above her on one elbow, he feathered her lips, her face, her neck with kisses, while he made a game of trying to capture both of her breasts at once in his long-fingered hand.

"Can't be done," he said lightly, kissing first one nipple and then the other while Holly lay gasping with pleasure and with something more—the buildup to. . . to what?

To anything he wanted to do, she decided.

Peeping from under lowered lids, she ran a fore-finger along the dear line of silky hairs that made a feathery valley between his breasts and down his rib cage to disappear beneath the wrapped towel. With a little moan she pulled herself against his body, eager to feel his hard-muscled chest against her throbbing breasts.

Beneath the robe his hands ran down her back to clutch her round plump bottom. His mouth captured hers in a deep kiss. With a groan he rolled onto his back, pulling her on top of him. Between her legs she felt the hard male shape of his desire.

But not for long. His groan became a grunt as, with a snakelike twist of legs and torso, he rolled her off him. Giving her bottom a spank, he broke the embrace and sat up.

"Enough of this fun," he said, smoothing back his

hair. "You make me feel eighteen again—which is all very well, but I wasn't running a ranch then."

"What do you mean?" Holly pulled the robe about her, wishing she could do the same with the shreds of her pride.

"I mean I've got work to do tomorrow and so have you. This is no time to initiate you into the joys of sex."

"What about you?" she asked in a small embarrassed voice. "I thought it wasn't good for men to get all excited and then—I thought men hated girls who did that."

"It's what I deserve tonight," he said roughly. "I knew what I was up against."

"I don't understand!" She was fighting back tears of disappointment...or letdown. "I'd made up my mind...."

"You did, did you?" He chucked her under the chin. "Didn't you tell me once it takes two to tango?"

"Are you getting even with me for something?"

"Certainly not. Get dressed before I change my mind." Taking her by the shoulders, he looked into her eyes. "The first time you don't want it to happen like this—hurried, careless, the aftermath of an evening horsing about in a swimming pool."

Suddenly his eyes narrowed. "Is that why you were hanging about the Shorthorn Saloon? You'd made up your mind?"

Her face went white with anger. "I hate you!" she screamed, beating at him with her fists.

He captured both her wrists in one hand.

"No, you don't." He stood up and hauled her to

her feet. "One of these days before you leave, if you still want me to make love to you, we'll make a night of it."

"I'd like to kill you!" she said between clenched teeth.

"You'll feel better in the morning," he replied tolerantly. "Go on, get dressed."

She scooped up her clothes and stomped into the bathroom.

I hate him! I hate him! she repeated to herself over and over while she dressed.

Stiff with fury, she suffered him to accompany her to the jeep. Once there he wrapped his arms about her. To her further indignation, all her anger melted. What was wrong with her? This man could play on her emotions as though she had no mind of her own. Perhaps she didn't. Perhaps with her love she'd given him her will, too.

He kissed her tenderly. "You'll see," he said provocatively.

Driving the dusty graveled road to the camp, teeth clenched, she thought, *what I want to see is Raf Valcour dying of desire.*

Whether she would gratify him or not was something she didn't try to decide.

CHAPTER FIFTEEN

When Holly steered the jeep into the camp, her pain at Raf's behavior switched to guilt. The half-moon had advanced to the western sky, and quiet pervaded the grove. She turned off the headlights, hoping the sounds of her arrival wouldn't wake anybody.

Undressing in the dark tent, she was overcome by the way Raf had rejected her. Numb with misery, she lay staring into the darkness, wondering where she had gone wrong. He had seemed to want her, had followed her all the way to Vista. He had coaxed her into the swimming pool and into his bedroom—and then turned her out. If he loved her the least little bit, he would have made love to her, and damn the ranch.

Someone was jiggling the bed. Holly rolled over, grumbling. Marcia was calling her name.

Holly opened her eyes to see the other girl fully dressed. The clear light in the tent indicated the sun was well up.

"Holly, are you sick? Everybody's ready for breakfast, and Dr. Gray looks like a thundercloud."

Holly swung long shapely legs from under the sheet. She sat up groggily and looked at the alarm clock.

"I forgot to set it! Oh, my gosh! I'll be out in a minute. Could you put on the coffee?"

"Willie's already done that. Don't worry, everybody's capable of getting themselves some cold cereal and mixing milk powder. I was concerned about you. Where did you go last night? Dr. Gray wasn't too happy when you weren't back by ten o'clock."

Holly stopped her hurried dressing to give Marcia a hard look. "What is this—a children's camp?"

"We're supposed to work hard enough to be too tired for gallivanting," Marcia said wryly.

"I wasn't 'gallivanting.'" Holly pronounced the word with distaste.

"Too bad. I'd hoped you were! I hoped you'd met some marvelous cowboy in Vista. Or Raf."

"I did," Holly said shortly. "He invited me to his place for a drink." She gave her hair a final brush. "Thanks for waking me."

Everyone around the table had finished eating and was drinking second cups of coffee.

"Here she is," Wayne said. "We'll forgive you for not getting breakfast, Holly, if you got our laundry done."

"It's in the jeep," Holly snapped. "Did you want it delivered to your door?"

"What time did you get back?" her brother asked.

"I didn't know there was a curfew." With effort Holly kept her voice pleasant.

"We were afraid something happened to you," Dr. Dave said reproachfully.

"Well, nothing did," Holly replied levelly, and began gathering up dirty dishes.

All day she felt tired and disgruntled. Dr. Gray

took the jeep and went off on some business of his own, probably to Rapid City. His arm was much better, and the cast did not hamper his driving.

He might have invited me to go along, Holly thought angrily. She still considered she had been unfairly treated over the business of the photos. A gesture of friendliness on Dr. Gray's part would have gone a long way to help her forgive him. *His students may like him,* she thought, *but they don't bruise his tender ego the way I did.*

At four o'clock she put a pot roast and potatoes into the pressure cooker, adjusted the burner beneath it and stretched out in the camp's hammock to wait until it was nearly done before slicing the cucumbers she planned to serve for salad. Gelatin with canned fruit salad was stiffening in the refrigerator—not an inspired dessert. But it was something that could be prepared ahead of time, and everyone seemed to like it.

The slight breeze and the deep quiet soothed her troubled thoughts.

The next thing she knew, Dr. Gray was running past her shouting, "What's burning?"

The acrid smell of scorching meat filled the air. Holly tumbled out of the hammock and dived into the trailer while Dr. Gray waited outside. The pressure gauge stood where it should, at fifteen pounds, but the cooker had run out of water. Holly switched off the flame.

"I guess it didn't have enough water," she told Dr. Gray, feeling—and sounding—like a schoolgirl. The truth was, she couldn't remember putting in any water at all.

"This isn't my day," she muttered.

Dr. Gray looked as if he agreed, but he didn't say anything. Not then.

She salvaged the roast and most of the potatoes, but there was no denying they tasted slightly burned.

When Junior Old Elk rode in with the students, Holly sought him out and requested him to leave Brown Betty or one of the other horses so she could take a ride after dinner. She wasn't going to hang about waiting for Raf!

Dr. Gray had stopped in Vista and picked up the mail. He handed it out at the happy hour. Holly noted Bill looked pleased as he tore open a lavender envelope. He glanced over the letter and came to sit beside her.

"Listen to this! Leona said she wanted to come to New York. I told her she could stay with me—us—and she's accepted!"

"*What?* When?"

"In a month or so." Bill tried to sound nonchalant.

"You invited Leona Selby to stay in our apartment? Without even asking me?"

Bill looked a little shamefaced. "The truth is, I never thought she'd come."

"Now you can tell her she can't."

Bill scowled. "Are you crazy? I want her to come!"

Holly felt her temper slipping and strove to control it. "What about me?" she asked icily, "or doesn't my opinion matter?"

Bill cocked his head with a half smile. "It's my apartment," he reminded her.

"And who pays the rent?" She was seething with suppressed fury.

"If Leona gets a job, she'll pay her share," Bill said loudly.

"Over my dead body!" Holly shouted. "You might as well know now: if she comes, I go!" She stalked into the trailer to slice the cucumbers. Before the job was done, she had sliced her finger—not deep but bloodily.

The meal was a disaster. The roast was dry; the potatoes tasted burned, and the gravy turned out lumpy. While she was putting it through a sieve to get out the lumps, the peas boiled over and made a new smell.

As a final blow, when she brought dessert to the table, two people groaned.

"Gelatin again," Willie said disparagingly.

Holly cleared the table and washed the dishes in sullen silence. She hadn't wanted this job. She was doing it for Bill, and this was how he repaid her. Where did he expect Leona to sleep, for Pete's sake? With him? With her?

Dr. Gray came into the trailer and sat down at his desk.

"Holly, when you're through, I'd like to speak to you," he said ominously.

She hung the wet dish towels outside to dry and re-entered the trailer.

"Sit down." Dr. Gray indicated the extra chair. "Holly, I'm sorry to say this, but I don't feel your heart's in this work anymore."

"How could it be," she wanted to explode, "when

I got all the blame for that stupid newspaper story!"
Instead she remained rebelliously silent.

"I'm sure you don't want to give your brother a
bad mark," Dr. Gray pursued unfairly.

"No, I don't want to do that," Holly was forced
to say.

"We have less than a week left," Dr. Gray pointed
out. "I hope the situation won't continue to deteri-
orate."

"Most cooks burn something sooner or later,"
Holly said lightly, with no idea whether the statement
was true or not.

"It's not just tonight's dinner. It's your attitude
recently. Going off and giving us no idea when you
planned to return, sleeping through breakfast. I'm
afraid your mind is more on.... Well, that's not my
business."

Darn right, it's not, Holly thought belligerently, if
he meant what she thought.

"What is my business," he went on, "is that we
have breakfast on time, and I'd appreciate it if you'd
keep your mind on your work. I know the people out
here may be more interesting than the food...but
not to me," he finished jocularly.

Holly stalked out of the trailer, eyes blurred with
angry tears, and headed toward the horse patiently
awaiting her. If only she could take her embarrassed
face and tear-filled eyes away from camp before she
met somebody! She hoisted herself into the saddle
and blindly pointed the horse in the direction of the
trail to Buffalo Table.

The wind dried her hot tears, but her mind remained in turmoil. Less than a week remained. What

if she simply packed up and left them to get along as best they could? The temptation was great. They'd have a chance to find out that raspberry gelatin with fruit in it was better than no dessert at all! What was more, she'd get back to New York in time to find a new apartment. Bill could have Leona all to himself.

But if she left now, she knew who'd get stuck with the cooking—Marcia—and that wouldn't be fair; Marcia had always taken Holly's side.

Or Bill might get stuck with it. She gave a little choke of laughter. Serve him right! Still, she'd agreed to do it. Her quarrel with her brother had nothing to do with the expedition. She brooded over Leona Selby's behavior and about the things Dr. Gray had said. Perhaps he had some cause to object. She should not have stayed away from camp so long. Raf had probably done right to send her home.

But how could he have made himself be so practical if he had really been swept away, as she had?

Brown Betty was following a trail, and the camp was on the up side of the Badlands wall. She couldn't lose it.

For a while she mulled over Raf's actions, but there weren't really any answers, and she began to enjoy her present surroundings. The peace of the open countryside stole over her.

Bit by bit the land descended. Stretches of grass known as sod tables gave way to eroded gullies two or three feet deep, like dry riverbeds. It was easy going for the mare. The way led gently down and down. She saw evidence of other horses, and Brown Betty seemed to know the way. This was probably the route the crew took.

Away to the right and left the terrain rose more
steeply, forming intricately eroded pinnacles. The
mare stepped delicately. Overhead the sky was laced
with high feathery clouds. Nothing else moved in the
entire expanse of sky and earth. Even the turkey
vultures had gone to roost somewhere.

Holly rode along the edge of the nearly perpendicular formations, straining her eyes to spot a fossil—
not anything earthshaking.... Sliding out of the
saddle, she walked awhile, holding fast to the reins
and bending close to observe the rough bare mudstone that rose straight out of the level grassland.

She found a bit of jawbone with four teeth, held it
in her hand a moment and gave it back to the earth.
It was against park rules for ordinary people to remove fossils.

She used a convenient chunk of mudstone as a
mounting block and rode back along the jutting formations toward the place where she had come down
through the wall by easy stages.

But where was that? Nothing marked it. All she
could see was unbroken grassland on her left and
steeply slanting grayish colored cliffs on her right.

"Now you know we came through here somewhere!" She spoke aloud to Brown Betty. "But
where?" She rode with a slack rein, scanning the
distance ahead. Each time she rounded one of the out-
juttings of the escarpment, she expected to see the pass
down through which she had ridden so easily. But it
didn't appear. Ravines led into the gray white mass,
but their slanting sides grew narrower and narrower.

"The way has *got* to be around this next corner,"
Holly muttered.

Around the jutting ridge the scene was exactly the same: clifflike formations rose tier upon tier like the maddening landscape of a nightmare. Moreover, the light was fading. The sun had gone down.

Then, to her relief, she spotted a pickup truck. People! Her breath escaped in a whoosh of relief. Someone local could probably direct her out of this stupid predicament.

She urged Brown Betty across the dried grass flat, but no one was to be seen.

Now what? Where could the driver be? Halting the mare some distance away, Holly studied the scene. The pickup's look of abandonment began to appear sinister. From the vantage point of the sod table Holly looked down into the pickup's bed. A coil of rope lay there, a pick and a large round brown object. A turtle shell. A fossil! Like the ones Raf's grandfather had collected. But this one was being collected now, almost certainly illegally. No wonder the unoccupied truck had a sinister aura. Someone was hunting fossils to sell on the black market, as Raf had talked about.

Holly was turning away when a man appeared out of the ravine. With a shock of recognition she saw he was one of the overfriendly ranch hands from the Shorthorn Saloon.

He started at the sight of her and thrust some object behind his back. Sharp black eyes under his Stetson-style straw hat swept the surroundings before he spoke.

"Say," he began, squinting up at her, "you're the little lady that was in the Shorthorn."

"Yes." Holly smiled, feeling more confident.

"You all alone out here?"

She decided to play dumb. "Yes, I'm lost," she said forlornly. "I took this horse for a little ride, and now I can't find my way back." She waved a hand at the sharp ravines and peaks.

"Come on over to the pickup," the man directed.

As he passed her, she said, "You're Tom, aren't you?"

"That's right." He brought his hand from behind his back. The fossil was too big to conceal—about the size of a flattened grapefruit. Brown Betty followed him at a walk. He was wearing the usual blue jeans and high-heeled boots. Like Raf, he didn't appear to have an ounce of fat—which must mean he did hard work for a living. He didn't spend all his time in thievery. She felt a bit more comfortable with that deduction.

Reaching the car, he pulled two burlap sacks from behind the seat. Seeing Holly still in the saddle, he said, "Come on down, honey. I ain't gonna bite you. Want a hand?"

"No, thank you." She climbed stiffly down.

Tom was wrapping the fossils in burlap.

"Know what these are?" he asked.

"Rocks?" said Holly brightly.

"They're turtle fossils. I collect them for a man at the college."

Like fun you do! Holly thought. "I guess that's what you do in your spare time," she said.

Tom chuckled. "Yeah, it keeps me in spending money. So you want to get back to where you came from? Where's that?"

Holly had her answer ready. "I'm camping with

some people in a little grove south of the Valcour ranch. If you could just tell me how to find my way through here...." Her voice faltered to a stop. He was grinning at her in a way she didn't like.

"Why's a pretty girl like you riding on her own?" he asked chattily.

"I found the people at camp kind of dull."

"So you took a ride and found me!"

"I really have to get back, or they'll worry," she said primly.

"Don't you fret, Juanita. I'll drive you back. We'll stop on the way and get a couple of six-packs."

"What about my horse?"

"We'll tie her to the tailgate."

"I'd rather go back the way I came," Holly protested. "If you could just tell me where—?"

"I don't know nothing about horse trails through here," Tom said. She was sure he was lying, but he opened the passenger door and took the reins from her hand. She felt she had no choice but to go with him—at least till they got back to civilization and a telephone. At this point she wouldn't hesitate to call Raf. She'd gladly call Dr. Gray if the camp had a phone! Poor Betty would have a long trot, but it couldn't be helped.

Tom slid behind the wheel and turned the key. The starter whirred, and nothing happened. Tom squinted at the gas gauge.

"Son of a gun!" He slammed the steering wheel with his hat.

With relief Holly realized she wasn't going anywhere with Tom, but the sensation was short-lived.

"You'll have to lend me the mare," he told her.

"I'll have to ride out and get gas." He was out of the truck before she could reply.

"Wait!" She jumped out on her side.

Tom was hauling a red gas can from its brackets. He looked at her angrily. "You got any better idea?"

"No."

"I won't be gone long. Look, you can see the station from here." He pointed to a flickering light on the horizon. Between the light and where she stood, the land was totally black. It was impossible to guess how far away the light was.

"Sit in the cab like a good girl till I come back, honey."

He swung into the saddle and rode off through the gathering darkness.

Holly listened to the forlorn sound of Brown Betty's retreating hooves. Oh, if only she'd paid attention to where she was going earlier this evening!

For a while she stood beside the pickup, her face raised to the sky. Wind whistled through the gully. The stars were perfectly remote. So was Raf and the camp. What a scrape she was in now! She opened the pickup door and climbed in. If she knew the way back, she would set out and walk. Anything would be better than hanging around waiting for this creep to return.

The wind moaned lonesomely. Despite the discomfort of her thoughts, she dozed.

She woke with a start when the tailgate rattled. The noise came again, and she realized it was the wind. She was growing stiff and cramped and very cold. She decided to get out and walk around. According to Raf, there was nothing to harm her. Only cow-hands like Tom, she amended.

It occurred to her to turn on the headlights. How else was Tom going to find the truck? Maybe, by some miraculous chance, Raf was already searching for her. He might get to the pickup first, and then everything would be all right.

But when at last a horseman appeared, it was Tom. Holly glimpsed his green plaid shirt in the headlights. Now at least they could get out of here.

"That was smart to turn the lights on," he greeted her. "Of course, you could have run down the bat-tery."

"I decided that if you couldn't find your way back, a dead battery wouldn't matter."

"I'd have found my way back, honey," he bragged. "I know this country like the back of my hand."

She could tell by his breath that he'd stopped for beer, too. He poured the gas into the tank and started the truck. The engine roared into life. Holly heaved a deep sigh. Then he turned the key, and the engine died.

"Why'd you do that?" she demanded sharply.

"Have to hitch up the horse."

But he made no move to leave the cab. Instead he slid closer to Holly. "How about a little thanks first for all the miles I rode?" he coaxed.

"That wasn't for me!" Holly argued laughingly. "You were out of gas before I came along. You were lucky I had a horse."

Tom grinned. One of his teeth was broken. "It

don't make me no mind! I got some big thanks for you, baby." He slid closer on the seat and locked her in a viselike grip. His arm was lean and sinewy, and she hated it. He smelled of sweat, and the beer on his breath made her choke. Before she could fend him off, his mouth covered hers fiercely, bruising her lips against her teeth. Her cry of protest was locked in her throat. She tried desperately to fight him off, but he was far too strong. However, he did break off the kiss to say, "Come on, baby, a pretty thing like you shouldn't get lost if you don't want to be found. I knew what you was wanting when I saw you hanging around the Shorthorn. Honey, I'm going to give it to you tonight, sure as God made little green apples!"

He clamped his mouth over hers, painfully pressing her lips back. Holly kept her jaw clenched, and his teeth clicked against hers. She hoped he bruised his lip! She managed to raise her arms to where she could exert some pressure against his shoulders, at least enough to push herself away and end the objectionable kiss. She shuddered with disgust.

"Relax, honey," he muttered. "This isn't going to hurt!"

"Let me go!" she begged. "Please let me go!"

Instead of answering, he renewed his assault upon her lips. One harsh hand grasped her breast, squeezing cruelly.

She whimpered with muffled pain and fury. Then she twisted like an eel, with no thought in her mind but to get away. Slipping one hand behind her, she found the door handle and pulled.

With his weight against the door as well as hers, it swung open. Before Tom realized what she intended,

she tore herself from his hold and threw herself down
from the seat, dimly aware of the sound of tearing
cloth.

She landed on the ground in a tumbled heap. Driv-
en by fear and insensible to the thump with which she
had landed, she scrambled to her feet and backed
into the darkness. She saw Tom sliding out after her
and ran, terrified that at every step she would miss
her footing and plunge headlong.

He shouted, but her mind was closed to any offers
he might make. He wasn't to be trusted! She'd rather
spend the night in the desert. He shouted something
more. From the sound of his voice he wasn't trying to
follow her, so she slowed her progress, stepping more
warily.

The pickup's headlights flared, not aimed in her
direction—thank heaven! Still, the lights might show
her retreating form and make him decide to come
after her. Black shadows to one side of the gully offered a hiding place. She flung herself into them and
crouched.

With surprise she heard the engine start. The light
in the gully dimmed. He was driving away! Her only
feeling was one of thankfulness.

With a gasp of relief she shifted from her crouched
position to a sitting one while she caught her breath
and assured herself he really had gone. The sound of
the pickup was truly growing fainter. He must be taking Raf's horse! That made him a horse thief!

Ugh! His sweaty odor still clung to her nostrils.
She vigorously scrubbed her soft lips with her sleeve
and discovered that the sound of tearing had been
from her shirt. The sleeve was nearly ripped from the

armhole. She felt bruised and defiled. *Oh, Raf,* her heart cried. *Why aren't you here to look after me?*

She listened gratefully to the sounds of the pickup fading in the distance. There were worse things than spending the night alone out here, though the breeze was growing distinctly cool.

She was about to stand up and see if she could find a spot more sheltered from the wind when she heard footsteps. Every muscle froze, and her skin rose in goose bumps. Who was walking out there? What menace this time?

The footsteps were slow but noisy, as though someone were taking an evening stroll. Cautiously she raised her head and caught sight of a silhouette. She dropped back against the dirt bank with a shriek of laughter that carried a hint of hysteria. Brown Betty! That was right; he hadn't tied the mare to the tailgate. Instead he'd tried to force himself on Holly.

She got up painfully, stiff from too much riding and falling out of cars but suddenly determined not to add losing Raf's horse to the rest of her mistakes.

In her ignorance she made another error: she startled the mare. With a snort of fright at the two-legged creature rearing up in front of her, Brown Betty whirled and galloped back down the gully. She scrambled up onto the broad sod table and trotted to a standstill.

"Brown Betty!" Holly called, "it's only me!" Tiredly she followed the moving black shape, almost indistinguishable against the flat-appearing background. She climbed to the higher elevation and trudged painfully across the rough ground.

"I don't know what I'm going to do with you

when I get you." She spoke her thoughts aloud, hoping the mare would recognize the sound of her voice and let her approach.

She got within a stone's throw before Brown Betty threw up her head with another snort, ran a few paces and halted.

"Here, girl," Holly coaxed. "Let's take off that saddle." She wanted the saddle blanket. No matter how smelly and covered with horsehair, it would be a warmer covering than a torn shirt. She renewed her efforts to catch the mare, hoping by persistence to bend the animal to her will. Time and again Brown Betty almost allowed herself to be caught.

"This is one way to pass the night, you wicked creature," Holly said, keeping her tone lighthearted and coaxing, despite an urgent desire to pelt the perverse animal with stones.

"This is the last time," she stated, moving stealthily forward. "You wretched beast!" Holly's knees were shaking with fatigue.

She approached from behind, at an angle, talking softly. "Hey, sweetheart...hey, honey...please, please stand still." The mare was only a few feet away. She threw up her head and Holly leaped to grasp the bridle. The blackness underfoot looked no different from the rest of the terrain, but when Holly bounded forward, the ground gave way to nothingness. Her hands flew out to block her fall and encountered empty space.

She was tumbling headfirst! For a breathtaking instant she thought she had fallen over a cliff. Then her head and shoulder crashed against a wall. She was sliding and rolling into a bottomless pit.

She came to a cramped halt lying headfirst at the

narrow bottom of what must be a crack in the eroded mudstone. Her weight was all on her shoulders, her legs above. Her only feeling was that this shouldn't be happening to her...she'd been a good girl, and daddy should have looked after her better. Her brain whirled. She had a sickening memory of having gone through this once. But this time Raf wasn't here to comfort her. If she could...somehow...get straightened around, she could surely think better. She wriggled painfully until her feet were underneath her and pushed herself up. Her head seemed to have nothing to do with the rest of her. Her knees crumpled. She slid down against the rough wall. The darkness beyond her eyes merged with the darkness in her head. With a sigh she fainted.

Up on the sod table Brown Betty heard the noise of Holly's fall. Though she had no wish to be ridden anymore, she began to miss the girl's company. She walked to the edge of the hole and sniffed and listened. The girl was down there, all right. Brown Betty decided to stay nearby; perhaps the girl would come up. After a while the mare slept.

Near midnight Holly stirred, wondering why she was sleeping in such a cramped position. The truth filtered into the swirling blackness when she tried to move her benumbed legs. She was at the bottom of a long narrow hole. It was dark; she couldn't see to climb out. Tipping back her head, she focused on a sprinkling of stars. There was an edge on either side, not far away. When her head felt better and stopped aching so fiercely, or maybe when daylight came, she would climb out, but not now.... In a mist of pain she lost consciousness again.

CHAPTER SIXTEEN

WHEN HOLLY NEXT BECAME AWARE of pain and discomfort, she opened blurred eyes to discover that the sky at the top of the hole had turned gray. She was trapped in a narrow pit, her back against a slope of accumulated dust and gravel, her legs straight in front of her. The walls of her prison rose close on either side. There was barely room to sit. Her body was a bundle of aches, and it hurt to make the slightest movement. Nevertheless she tried, hoping to ease her misery. Her head still throbbed. She raised a trembling arm and explored her scalp with cautious fingers. Above her brow she discovered a lump the size of an egg. No wonder her head ached!

Slowly, carefully, she assessed the extent of her other damages. She could move her legs, though painfully, and her arms were all right except for scrapes and bruises. Her right shoulder was stiff and sore, but apparently, thank God, she hadn't broken anything.

The walls of the crack looked rough—but not rough enough to provide footholds. She decided not to try to climb out until the light improved. She knew she was reluctant to put the attempt to the test. She didn't want to face the possibility of failure and the sure knowledge that she was trapped.

She closed her eyes and lay quiescent, dozing. As long as she didn't move, she felt very little pain. Even her head almost stopped hurting.

Some time later she roused herself. Daylight had come. The walls of her prison were shown to be nearly perpendicular. Her heart fell. But she mustn't give up hope until she tried to climb them. It was essential to try and to succeed, because how would anyone ever find her down here? If they hunted for her at all, she thought dispiritedly.

Of course, they'll hunt, she told herself sternly. Raf will want his horse back! The feeble attempt at humor raised her spirits.

With groans and exclamations she raised herself to her feet, leaning against the side for support. Her head was spinning. She felt sick to her stomach and dreadfully frightened. She hesitated to try scaling the rough sides; she could see the attempt would be hopeless. Nevertheless she did her best, and of course it wasn't enough. The muscles of her bruised shoulder were painfully weak. She succeeded in hoisting her body no more than two feet up the side before her fingers slipped and she was forced to drop back. Breathing hard and groaning, she glared at the edge not more than four feet above her head. It ought to be possible to climb that little way!

The walls at one end of the crack were so close together that under normal circumstances she might have made her way up between them, using first one and then the other as steps of opposing ladders. But the way she felt now, with every muscle trembling just from her attempt to stand and her head banging away, such a climb was impossible. Later, when she felt better, she would try it.

Meanwhile, if rescuers came looking for her, they might pass through the gully and not even know she was nearby if she didn't hear them. Even if they hunted by helicopter, they might not be able to see her.

On a rising tide of panic she began to scream. Someone *must* hear! She thought she heard footsteps, and the panic turned to wild sudden hope.

"Help!" she cried. "Here I am! Help!"

She tried for a while to believe the footsteps were approaching, but at last she faced the fact she could no longer hear them at all. She recalled the footsteps she had heard last night. These sounded similar. Would Brown Betty still be walking around out there? She had counted on the mare finding her way back to her barn. Didn't horses do that? Probably not Brown Betty. If it hadn't been for that perverse beast, she wouldn't have fallen into this hole!

For a while Holly went on croaking, "Help," until it occurred to her to save her voice. Perhaps she could use it at intervals, like a foghorn. Her mind pictured a foggy New York morning and the deep intermittent blasts of tugboats. If only she were there now!

The thought made her realize that before long the sun would be blazing on this barren flat, running the temperature up above a hundred degrees. Her prison would become an oven.

She'd surely be rescued soon! There couldn't be that many miles of open country to search if that rot-ten cowboy had been able to point out the light of the gas station. Damn him! She hoped he got what he deserved—and soon!

How soon would someone miss her? If that fool horse had gone back to its stable, Raf would already know, but the mare was probably still out there somewhere. Would the people at camp shrug and get their own breakfast, like yesterday? No, mustn't think like that. Marcia would have to notice that Holly's bed hadn't been slept in, and they knew she'd gone off riding.

She forced her mind back to a more immediate problem. When they did come to look for her, how could they possibly discover this hole? Perhaps she should throw her shirt up over the side. Someone finding that would look around for the rest of her.

Could a shirt be seen from a helicopter? Did they use helicopters to hunt for people in the Badlands? Did other people get lost out here? Probably not. *If I weren't trapped in this hole, I could certainly walk to a road and hitch a ride to a telephone,* she thought. A helicopter probably wasn't available closer than Rapid City. Holly hoped they wouldn't go to the bother and expense of getting one. A helicopter couldn't find her.

Perhaps Tom would have an attack of conscience and come back to get her...or maybe he'd hear about her disappearance on the radio. That might take twenty-four hours! She couldn't hold out that long. She'd be baked.

Before she could panic again, she forced herself to pray. Miraculously calm returned. She put her mind to puzzling how she could toss up a signal. Should she try to throw up her shirt? She really needed it to prevent sunburn. Nor could she face the thought of being rescued in her bra. What could she spare? A boot. She wasn't going anywhere, and it would be fairly easy to toss up. Would anyone searching for her—her mind pictured Raf in the saddle—pick a brown boot out of brown surroundings? Admittedly Raf had the eyesight of an Indian, but her boot would be so much more visible if it had something attached that would flutter.

The struggle with Tom had nearly ripped off her shirt sleeve. She could spare that. With a brisk tug she tore it the rest of the way around the armhole and slipped it off her arm. Getting her boot off wasn't easy, what with confined space and sore muscles, but she accomplished it after a time. Using her teeth, she ripped the shirt sleeve down its length to give more cloth to flutter. She knotted the cloth through the leather loops designed for pulling the boot on and climbed painfully to her feet.

Throwing something straight up in such confined space turned out to be next to impossible. At every attempt pain shot agonizingly through her right shoulder and her head throbbed, but at last she managed to hurl the boot so it landed on the edge of the hole. The cloth began to flap in a breeze. Certainly anyone seeing the cloth blowing would investigate.

"Well done," she said aloud. She slid back down to a sitting position and, for the first time, looked closely at the lumpy walls before her eyes. Light streamed down now, making visibility perfect. She was surrounded by fossils!

She gave an ironic unladylike snort.

They were embedded on both sides of the crack. No wonder she hadn't noticed them sooner—they were such huge pieces she had taken them for stones. The more she looked, the more she saw. But how could anyone get them out?

How would they get her out? That was more to the point! Raf would know how. But what if nobody told him she was missing?

She closed her eyes and tried to relax, ordering her mind to stop presenting her with frightening thoughts. For a while she kept herself under strict control. She sat with her eyes closed and listened for sounds of vehicles or approaching footsteps. She heard only the wind and the irate screams of a prairie falcon. Presently, though her ears were still on the alert, her mind wandered. She began to think about the way Dr. Gray had scolded her for letting Gary take her picture with the fossils. How angry they'd been! Bill, too. He didn't appreciate what she'd done for him. He'd changed, it seemed to her. And Leona! What had Holly ever done to turn that girl against her? Not only had Leona pooh-poohed Holly's career, now Leona was doing her best to turn Bill against his own sister.

The sun climbed higher. Holly watched its progress down the west wall of the crack. Sooner or later it would glare directly down, heating the walls, baking her. The heat was becoming unbearable already. Holly began to think about water. Her closed eyes brought her a series of pictures: a brook splashing over black rocks... water splashing from the camp's hundred-gallon drum...then half a glass of water sitting on the camp table. She reached for it—and woke with a start.

She licked dry lips, but her mouth was dry, too. She didn't seem to be sweating, though her armpits pricked. The heat drew the moisture from her pores. Her mind wandered crazily. Those fossils...those bones. What animal had walked the earth, living, procreating, dying trapped in mud and slime? If she wasn't found, she could die here! Sooner or later her bones would be added to the collection, but first her clothes would have to rot away...and her flesh. The vultures wouldn't be able to get at her down here. They might circle overhead and alert Raf or some other rancher. Would Raf be sorry he hadn't loved her when he'd had the chance? Sorry he'd treated her so badly? She puzzled awhile, trying to remember how he'd mistreated her, but it was all very vague.

The heat was coming from an oven. She told herself to wake up and turn it off, but when she brought her wandering mind back to brief reality, her situation seemed quite hopeless. The chances of being found before she died of dehydration were probably, she reasoned muzzily, a hundred to one.

She focused her mind on dying and made a strong effort to forgive the people who had put her down here: Leona Selby, Dr. Gray, Dr. Dave, Bill, Raf, that man at the saloon...what was his name? She realized her mind was wandering. Soon she would call it back....

Her next dream was that the sun had gone under a

cloud, a very noisy cloud that rained pebbles on her head, and Raf was shouting, "Toss me that canteen!" so loud she winced.

She became conscious of him standing over her, his booted feet straddling her legs in the narrow space. He poured water onto a red bandanna and mopped her face with it. Indignantly she ordered him not to step on the fossils. He was frowning when he bent down to observe her more closely. She focused on his face. The bright anxious gleam in his eyes changed to satisfaction.

"How did you get here?" she croaked, beginning to shake with dry sobs.

"I'm going to put this rope around you, and Junior Old Elk will pull you out." His voice was tight with an emotion she couldn't define.

"Oh!" Her words came through cracked lips. "I thought you'd fallen in, too."

"Holly?" He splashed more water on her face. "Holly, listen to me. You're safe now. It's hot as Hades down here, and you're a bit off your head, but you're all right. Understand?"

She nodded dumbly, feeling him put the rope under her arms.

"Holly, when I give Junior the signal to pull, can you fend yourself off from the sides?"

"I'll try," she mumbled.

It was ecstasy to be hauled out of the hole. She had never felt such gratitude, such thankfulness—to Raf, to Junior Old Elk, to Providence. It was like being presented with a whole new life. Junior helped her over the edge.

Out of breath from the tightness of the rope

around her chest, she collapsed on the ground, managing to roll into a sitting position.

"Thank you," she panted. "Oh, thank you!" She raised her arms so Junior could remove the rope.

Junior grinned, a flash of white teeth in his brown face. "The world looks good, eh?"

"Oh, it does!" Her eyes moved beyond him to sweep the deep blue sky, the brown country, the towering tan pinnacles. This landscape might not be beautiful by everyone's standards, but just now it looked like paradise.

Junior dropped the rope back into the hole. Raf's head soon appeared as he came walking up the side, hand over hand, the way he had done at Buffalo Table. He was still wearing his black hat with the silver conchas. Holly began to laugh weakly.

"She's taken a heck of a bump on the head," Holly heard Raf tell Junior. "We're going to need the jeep. Take my rifle and climb up the rock over there as high as you can. Be careful, though. Don't *you* fall. Fire three shots, and if you see anybody, start waving your bandanna.

"You'd better stay there till you see the jeep," he added. "I hope to heck they won't be long."

Holly was still sitting by the edge of the hole. Junior scurried away, and Raf came to squat beside her.

"How do you feel?" he inquired. The look of anxiety was back in his eyes.

"Pretty awful," she admitted.

"I wish I could get you in the shade, but there isn't any. Would my hat help?"

"I don't think so." The black felt looked heavy,

and she thought she couldn't bear anything pressing on the pain. She watched him dampen his bandanna and fold it. He laid it gently against her forehead. She felt momentarily better at the touch of his hands.

"Don't you want to know what happened?" she croaked.

"Later, when you feel better."

She closed her eyes. She felt him beside her, and the next thing she knew, he pulled her gently against him. Holding her with one arm, he began to fan her with his hat. "You're going home, my darling," he muttered against her hair. Evidently he didn't think she was a complete fool for getting lost and falling in a hole.

She heard him talking to her, asking some question and urging her to answer. She must have answered properly because he kissed her. She tried to respond, but she felt so weird. He told her to keep her eyes closed and rest.

Some time later she became aware that other people had arrived. The mist in front of her eyes cleared, and she recognized Dr. Gray and Dr. Dave, both looking concerned and talking over her head to Raf.

"There are fossils down there," she announced. "Big ones."

Her words were met by sudden silence, as though she had startled them.

A moment later she heard Dr. Gray exclaim, "By Jove, there are! It looks promising." He came swimming into focus. "Holly, if they turn out to be something special, I'm personally going to insist that your picture be taken with them."

The next voice was Raf's. She felt the rumble of his chest as he spoke, and his breath stirred her hair. "Sorry to contradict you, sir, but she's retiring as a photographer's model. The next pictures of Holly are going to be taken at our wedding. Let's get her into that jeep! I'm afraid she's unconscious."

I must be, Holly thought. But she wasn't afraid; she was in Raf's arms.

SHE CAME TO HER SENSES to find herself in a strange bedroom beautifully decorated in cool sea-green and white. Her first sensation was disappointment. She had thought Raf was taking her to the ranch. Then, with a rush of hope, she realized this might be the ranch; she hadn't seen all the bedrooms. All the furniture in this room was white rattan, giving it a summery air that was further enhanced by frothing ruffled curtains in a delicate green-and-white pattern. The sheets and pillowcases matched the wallpaper's green calico print. The room was as feminine as Raf's was masculine. To whom did it belong?

The name that popped into Holly's mind was Leona Selby, but her reaction was one of great peace. She had forgiven everyone. She was grateful to be alive. The vain strivings that had driven her previously were no longer in control. Did that mean she no longer desired Raf, she asked herself. The question made her smile when she realized she had not gone that far from human desire. She hadn't died and become an angel!

Dimly she remembered being put to bed. She had listened to a woman clucking; she had heard Raf swear once—quite violently—and the same voice telling him to hush. Raf had made her drink something. Someone—not Raf—had bathed her, but she'd been too drowsy to care. Strange, she also seemed to remember that Raf had said she was getting married. Whom was she marrying? She puzzled for a while but at last gave up, deciding to wait and ask him. She wondered vaguely what time it was; the house was so quiet.

When she woke again, the light outside the windows told her it was late afternoon. She knew deep quiet joy at the thought that Raf would come soon. It must be time for him to quit work. She felt a hazy sense of well-being, almost light-headedness. Slowly she realized it was because her head no longer hurt. She was wearing something different—a white satin nightgown with lace insets! Perhaps this wasn't Raf's ranch house after all.

Her spirits sagged, and she became aware of all the aches and twinges the sleek satin covered. Nevertheless she felt wrapped in a cocoon of care, whosever house this was. She supposed someone would eventually come and bring her up to date. She recalled Raf's arms about her on the ride back and his shoulder convenient for her head. She had felt his indrawn breath of satisfaction when she nestled against him. When she thought of his strength, contentment enfolded her. She stilled her mind from worrying about other people—Leona, Bill, Dr. Gray—and drifted. Before she knew it, she was back in the hole, surrounded by fossils.

She woke with a cry of terror when the door opened. Her dark lashes fluttered. She sat up, wide-eyed.

Raf crossed the floor in quick strides to stand

beside the bed, his tawny eyes dark with anxiety. He had changed from working clothes to light brown pants and a beige cowboy shirt that brought his deeply tanned skin into dark contrast. He had showered and shaved. His thick hair was still wet, and he smelled of soap and shaving lotion.

"I'm all right." Holly blinked up at him and managed a smile. "For a moment I thought I was back in the hole." She shuddered.

"You're in my house," he said. His eyes between their dark-fringed lashes sent her a loving message. Her bosom rose as she took an exultant breath, and his gaze dropped to the cleavage between her breasts, where white lace and satin frothed across the swell of sun-browned skin.

In a burst of modesty Holly pulled the sheet up to her neck.

"Don't do that," Raf said. Springs creaked as he perched on the side of the bed and one brown hand took the sheet from her fingers and folded it back to her waist. "Mrs. Jones didn't lend you that nightgown so you could hide it under a sheet."

"Mrs. Jones!"

"That's right." His eyes laughed into hers. "A present from her nieces. Not her style, she says. How are you feeling?" He sat with his hands resting on his knees.

"Dismal," Holly admitted, but followed her one-word report with her lovely smile. "I haven't thanked you for finding me."

"Did you think I wouldn't?" His eyes blazed, suddenly intense, as though he drew deeper meaning from her words than she intended.

"I—I was afraid it might be a long time." Her hand crept across the sheet to cover the back of his. His hand turned, clutching hers. The fingers of his other hand circled her wrist, sending a tingling message the length of her arm.

His golden eyes flashed. "It should have been sooner! If those fools at your camp kept as good track of people as they do fossils...." He shook his head unbelievingly. "They didn't miss you till you didn't appear to cook breakfast," he said angrily. "Then they didn't know what to do. You can thank Junior Old Elk. When he heard you and Brown Betty were missing, he didn't waste time talking. He came tearing back to get me."

"You mean the professors and Bill didn't do anything? But they were there when you found me. I remembering seeing Dr. Gray...."

"They ran in circles." Raf dismissed them with a shrug. "Actually, there wasn't much they could do. They couldn't track Brown Betty."

"You mean you could? You literally tracked us down? It wasn't just luck that you found me?"

"No, it wasn't luck," Raf said impressively. "The way you doubled back and forth along the wall didn't help, but Junior's turning into a pretty smart tracker, too."

"I didn't think he liked me," Holly murmured.

"Whyever not?"

"I overheard him say once that blondes were no good for the boss."

Raf's face assumed the blank expression that Holly had learned meant he was taken aback.

"Why he must have been referring to Annie!" he

exclaimed. "He was a little kid then, too young to remember, I'd have thought. But I suppose he's heard gossip. She was blond, all right, silvery blond." It seemed to Holly his voice held reminiscent sadness.

"Who was she?" Holly asked gently.

His eyes focused again on her, and he returned to the present. "The girl next door," he said with a cynical shrug. "We were in love with each other from the time we were kids...I thought. The womenfolk had the wedding all planned, but she met an engineer. He took her off to San Francisco. I suppose that's what Junior meant."

"And you've never seen her since?"

"Sure, I've seen her. She was at the barbecue. I thought you met her. She's divorced, got two kids and can't wait to get away from South Dakota again."

He sounded as though he didn't care, but pain seared Holly's heart, worse than any of her physical hurts. She suspected he was still in love with this woman, but he was too proud to go begging to her.

"And you've been a woman hater ever since," she said to ease her hurt.

Raf's narrowed eyes didn't hide the satirical gleam. "I don't think you could call me that," he offered.

Was he deliberately referring to the passes he'd made at her? Wounded, she turned her face away, aware that he was eyeing her sharply.

Mrs. Jones appeared in the doorway with a tray and saved Holly from having to reply.

"Oh, my dear, it's good to see you looking better," Mrs. Jones said. "Do you feel able to eat something?"

"I'm starving," Holly told her. Her blue eyes brightened as the laden tray was set on the night table beside the bed. Mrs. Jones bustled about, fluffing pillows so Holly could sit up.

"Raf, I brought your usual bourbon and water," she told him, indicating the tray.

He picked up the glass and retreated out of Mrs. Jones's way. "Maybe I'd better come back later."

"No, you don't!" Mrs. Jones said sharply. "We need you. She can't eat lying down! Lift her up in the bed so she can sit against the pillows."

"I can do it," Holly protested. But when she tried to move herself, her weary muscles refused to respond.

"Let him do it," Mrs. Jones directed. "What's the point of having a man around if you don't put him to work?"

So Holly submitted to letting Raf slide his arms under her back and knees and hoist her up to sit against stacked pillows.

"That's better!" Mrs. Jones set the tray across Holly's lap. The tray was white wicker, like the other furnishings, and had legs like a little table. The pretty dishes were green-and-white, matching the room. Under them a hand-embroidered tray cloth added its elegance. Raf pulled a chair to the bedside and seated himself in it.

"See that she eats everything," Mrs. Jones directed. "She's too thin."

"I'll do that." Raf winked at Holly.

She felt suddenly bursting with happiness. His

staying while she ate was such a little thing, but it was like frosting atop a cake. Here she was, with food, comfort and loving care—all the things she'd thought she might never have again.

"Did you find Brown Betty?" she asked.

"We had her with us when we found you, don't you remember?"

"Oh, yes, of course I remember," she lied, for the simple reason she didn't want him worrying about the bump on her head. She felt all right now. Her head didn't ache, and she was hungry. Mrs. Jones had fixed scrambled eggs from the ranch's own chickens, fluffy white biscuits with butter and honey and—in case that wasn't enough—a small thick steak, cooked medium rare.

"Have you had your supper?" Holly bethought herself to ask.

"Do you think I'd sit down to a meal before I checked on you?"

"I thought you might be furious with me," Holly said, eyeing him over a forkful of egg.

"Why, for Pete's sake?"

"For being so stupid as to get lost."

"I'm furious with myself for not looking after you better," Raf told her. "I know this country. I should have warned you not to ride around the Badlands alone. Unexpected things can happen easier than folks who see the country from a car window think. I don't have to tell you that now. What did happen?"

Between bites Holly told him how she'd been unable to find the pass back through the wall and how she'd come upon the ranch hand called Tom, stealing turtle fossils. At her description of Tom's behavior, Raf's eyes began to blaze like angry flames.

"Wait till I find that bucko!" he gritted.

"Raf! You won't fight him, will you?" Holly was appalled. For all she knew, men still went after one another with guns out here. "It wasn't his fault I fell into the hole!" she pressed.

"It sure as hell was! He had no business to go off and leave a woman alone out there."

"Please don't fight him!"

"Believe me, I'd take great pleasure in punishing the bastard. But I'd just as soon not give the neighborhood something to gossip about. No telling what kind of story people would cook up."

In her relief she didn't ask what he meant. She hurried to change the subject. "Speaking of cooking, you must be starving. Must I stay in bed? Can't I come out and keep you company while you eat?"

He frowned. "The doctor's supposed to call. Tell you what, I'll bring a tray in here."

He returned in a short time with the wicker tray laden with a steak that almost hid the dinner plate that held it. Side dishes were filled with fried potatoes and creamed peas.

"I suppose that's from one of your own cows, too," Holly said when he set the tray on the night table.

"Our own beef, our own potatoes, our own peas, which Mrs. Jones freezes." He kissed the tip of her nose. "Where am I going to sit? You look so comfortable. How about if I join you on the bed?"

Holly laughed delightedly, loving the suggestion of

wicked intimacy, and fire began to run along her veins. Perhaps...tonight...he'd stay here, too.

He brought more pillows from the room's spacious closets and piled them beside Holly. Slipping his feet out of casual leather shoes, he stretched his lean length beside her. She studied his dark stockinged toes. There was something sensuous about men's feet, about his.

"This feels good!" He let his head fall back on the pillows and closed his eyes. His hand searched for hers and squeezed it. He turned his face to look at her on the neighboring pillow.

"Soon...." His look held a promise that made her loins melt.

"When?" She wanted to know, yet shrank from the event.

Sensing her hesitation, he cupped her face in one brown hand. "When you kiss me the way you did that evening I met you out riding."

"I'm ready anytime," she murmured, unconsciously running the tip of her tongue over her lips.

His mouth covered hers with a sureness of ownership and filled her with eagerness. He turned to her, his hand sliding over the satin nightdress, over the curve of her breast, her waist, across her belly. Then it was withdrawn.

"That damn doctor is liable to be here any minute."

"And your steak's getting cold," Holly reminded him teasingly.

She took absurd pleasure in watching him dine. She loved seeing the movements of his hard masculine jaw, the deft way he handled knife and fork.

Following that line of thought, she was struck by a new worry. "Who's cooking at the camp?" she exclaimed.

"I made a deal with Junior Old Elk."

"Junior? Nothing would get him near a cookstove!"

"It was a matter of making the bribe high enough."

"Why should you have to pay him?" she expostulated.

"Because I'm taking their cook."

"But—"

A knock interrupted. Raf gestured for Holly to answer.

"Come in!" she called, and the door was flung wide.

"Bill!" she cried joyously.

"Holly! Thank God nothing terrible happened to you!" He looked from Holly, holding the sheet to her neck, to Raf, propped on the bedspread, eating his dinner in his stocking feet, and grinned. "How are you feeling?"

"Fine." She smiled at him forgivingly. "Just fine, Bill."

"What did the doctor say?"

"Damn his hide, he hasn't arrived," Raf growled. "But she says her head doesn't hurt. She's wanting to get up. That's why you see me here. I'm trying to keep her in bed."

Bill grinned again. "I heard the news. Marcia and I arrived as you people were driving off. Junior Old Elk told us while we were waiting for Wayne and Willie. Congratulations!"

Before Holly could ask, "What news?" Raf said, "Thank you. I'll take this tray to the kitchen and bring you a drink, Bill. What'll it be?"

"Just beer, please. No. Great heavens, make it something strong!" He was still grinning.

Raf's tawny eyes laughed across the room into Holly's blue ones.

As soon as Raf had gone away, thoughtfully closing the door, Bill said, "I knew he had his eye on you, but—*marriage*! I didn't think he was the marrying kind."

"What are you talking about?" Holly's heart began to pound.

Bill stared, his grin fading. "Did I get it wrong? Didn't Raf say the next pictures of you were going to be at your wedding? Junior said that's what Raf told the profs."

Holly stared back at her brother while her mind raced. Had Raf asked her to marry him? Had she forgotten? Why that was impossible! With a sinking sensation she realized she could recall nothing that had happened while they'd waited for the jeep. A blow on the head could do that. Had he proposed? Had she accepted? How could she forget?

"Holly!" she heard Bill exclaim. "Are you all right? You look pale."

She put her hand to her head but tried to smile reassuringly. "Just a little dizzy."

"I suppose it's all been too much," Bill said.

"Yes, it has. A little," she stalled.

To her relief the door opened, and Raf came in holding two glasses clinking with ice cubes.

"Scotch okay?" he asked Bill.

"Fine. Are you joining us?"

"This one's for me—bourbon. I don't think Holly should celebrate till the doctor's checked her out. Meantime we can drink to her health."

"Here's to both of you," Bill said hesitantly. He looked uncomfortable. Holly's replies must have made him wonder if he'd got things wrong. As usual, Raf's impassive face was no help at all. Despite her bewilderment, a warm glow in Holly's breast began to expand. It couldn't be true!

Could it be true?

If he'd proposed, she must have said yes. She might have been out of her head, but she wasn't crazy. She stole a wondering look at Raf from the corners of her eyes. He caught her at it and saluted her with his glass.

"What are your plans?" Bill asked, looking pleased with himself for coming up with a noncommittal question.

"It depends on what the doctor says and how Holly feels," Raf replied, which left both Camerons no wiser than earlier.

Raf seemed to sense something was putting a damper on conversation. He said, "You'll want to talk to your brother, Holly, so if you'll both excuse me, I have ranch business to attend to."

Holly threw him a look that was a mixture of gratitude and frustration.

As soon as the door closed, she said, "He's arranged for Junior Old Elk to do the cooking."

"That's a relief! I was afraid I'd get stuck with it. Not that I'd have minded," Bill added quickly, "but they'd be disappointed after the meals you've given us."

"You mean they've missed me already?"

"Sure we have. Dr. Gray and Dr. Dave are feeling pretty guilty, I can tell you."

"Guilty! Why?"

Bill looked shamefaced. "Well, when you turned up missing, we all had some time to think. We had some pretty uneasy consciences, too. Look, sis, I'm sorry for the way I behaved about Leona. I should have asked you before I invited her, but...well... I knew you'd object. Good God, that's not why you're marrying *him*, is it?" He nodded toward the door.

"Of course not!" Holly bit her lip.

"Do you think you'll enjoy living out here? Leona doesn't."

"You better make sure Leona likes the idea of being a professor's wife before you get too involved," she said sharply.

Bill shrugged. "It's nothing serious. She's using me to get to New York."

"I'm glad you realize that."

"She's not a bad kid, really, Holly," he said. "You two just hit it off wrong."

"I suppose that's possible," Holly conceded, remembering her decision to forgive Leona. "We got off to a bad start."

It was seeing Leona with Raf that turned me against her, she admitted to herself. And maybe Raf was the reason Leona hadn't liked her.

"She's a pretty good reporter," Bill was saying. "Her news stories are slanted because that's the orders she gets. That's one reason she wants to move on."

Raf tapped on the door. "The doctor's here," he announced, showing him in.

"Okay," Bill said. "I'm leaving. Good night, sis." He kissed her cheek. "I'm really happy about your news. Dr. Dave was livid," he chortled on his way out.

Raf waved to Holly before he, too, shut himself out.

Holly submitted to the doctor's examination. He inspected the lump on her head and, pulling up a chair, asked a great many questions. At last he said, "Raf tells me you're going to marry him."

"He did?" Holly's heart surged with happiness.

The doctor's eyes twinkled. "We'd about given up on him. I'll say this, though. He waited till he got a pretty one!" He stood up. "It's a mild concussion. About all you can do is rest and let nature heal it. If you feel dizzy or have any fainting spells, call me, of course, but I don't think you'll suffer anything more than a headache for a few days. And let me wish you the best of luck, young lady." He shook her hand and departed.

She heard his car leave and lay contemplating his words—"Raf tells me you're going to marry him." Raf must have asked her; she must have said yes! She could hardly wait for him to return.

At length he quietly opened the door. When he saw she was awake, he came to sit beside her on the bed and take her into his arms. He ran a strand of golden hair through his fingers.

"Did they call you Goldilocks when you were little?"

Holly smiled. "They called me Hollyhocks," she confessed.

"Then this is where you belong." Raf's tawny eyes, half-hidden by black lashes, made her short of breath.

She leaned back against the pillows, gazing at him. The conviction began to grow in her mind that he truly wanted to marry her. She felt as if she'd been running a wild race, a marathon that had gone on for days, weeks, all the time she'd been in South Dakota, and suddenly someone had said, "Stop!" She didn't know where to look.

"I love you, you know," he said conversationally. "I think I've loved you from the moment I saw you on that plane."

"But—but when I left at Pierre, for all you knew, you'd never see me again!"

"For half an hour, yes. Before the plane landed in Rapid City, I'd decided to attend the powwow."

Holly gasped. "You all but ignored me there!"

"Did I?"

The room's deepening shadows made it difficult for her to see his face. As if he wished to see her better, too, he switched on a lamp and came back to sit on the bed.

"By the way, how did the pictures of me turn out?" His eyes twinkled.

But Holly was recalling the way he had kissed her there at Fox Butte, the way his bear-claw necklace had been a small sharp barrier between them.

"You took everything Leona Selby said about models as the gospel truth," she accused.

Raf nodded. "I didn't like being snagged by a blond filly who thought only about her looks, no matter how beautiful she was. I tried to believe everything Leona said against you. It worked, too, as long as you were around to dislike." He shook his head reminiscently. "You may not believe this, but before we met in Vista, I was seriously trying to figure out how to locate you if I went to New York. You could've knocked me over with a feather, as they say, when I saw you on the sidewalk there." His handsome lips twitched. "From then on it was easy to fight my feelings. You were right there on my range. I took great satisfaction in ignoring you, knowing all the time that you weren't going anywhere."

Holly couldn't keep from smiling triumphantly.

"But this morning," he said, "when I thought I might have lost you forever, I faced the truth. Different backgrounds be damned! I love you, Holly. I can make you happy here if you'll give me the chance."

"I love you," she whispered, her heart in her eyes. "You must have known that."

"How could I know it? I watched you turn the same beautiful smile on Dave Young and your friend Gary." He gathered her into his arms. "All I could think was how easily I could be roped and hog-tied if I wasn't careful. And all the time it was too late. I was already corralled."

"You wanted to keep on being South Dakota's most eligible bachelor," she twinkled.

He shook his head. "Not after I met New York's most beautiful model."

"Are you sure you won't be sorry?" she asked

seriously. "You held out for so long." In her mind's eye she saw him as he sometimes stood, arms folded across his chest, looking out over the prairie, arrogance in his stance and pride in his lifted chin, as though he were the natural heir of the land from horizon to horizon.

But it was the fallible human being who answered her. "I didn't want to fall head over heels for some female who would marry me and then take off. It can be a boring life out here for the wrong woman. It happened to a friend I went to agricultural college with. He has a fine place in Wyoming, two kids and no wife. She pranced off to Chicago two years ago."

"Well, you won't have to worry about me going to Chicago," Holly laughed. "Or New York, for that matter. I know what's there, and it isn't much."

"You really like it here, don't you." He made it a statement.

"I love it. I can't wait to see it in winter."

"You won't miss being a glamorous model?"

Holly shook her head. "It *is* hard work, you know. Remember when you first saw me? Bill told me I'd been working too hard, and then you guessed I was twenty-six! I was furious."

"Remember?" Raf's eyes crinkled. "You clammed up and wouldn't speak to me for half of the flight. Speaking of Bill, we came to a financial understanding before he left. He was reluctant, but I finally convinced him. Oh, my love!" He gathered her more tightly in his arms, and she recalled the offer he had made to her. She wanted him with all the strength of her healthy young body. Taking his face in her hands, she kissed him with a passion she hadn't known herself capable of. His handsome masculine lips parted. Daringly she thrust her tongue into his mouth. She heard him gasp and knew that at last she had touched his emotions on the raw. She gloried in the instant response of his quickened breathing. She could feel his pounding heart against her breast.

For an instant longer he remained submissive, then his muscles tensed with catlike speed, and he became the aggressor. Crushing her against him, his tongue thrust to drink the pleasure of her mouth. Holding her with one sinewy arm across her back, he used his free hand to fling back the offending sheet and bedspread before he laid her gently across the bed, one arm under her shoulders, and lowered himself upon her. His free hand followed the satin-covered curves of her body, and her skin tingled with the desire to be touched with that hand with nothing between, for him to claim all her body as his, touch all the places where no man yet had touched her. She ran her hand inside his collar, feeling the contours of his proud neck, up to the secret hollow behind his ear, from the baby softness of his earlobe to the crisp curve at the top. He bent his head to kiss the hollow of her neck, and she ran the tip of her tongue into his ear, making him jump.

"Oh, you!" he murmured. "Hollyhocks. Pretend I'm a bee." He made a buzzing sound with his lips. Slipping the flimsy straps of the gown from her shoulders, he buzzed across her sun-browned chest to the rounded white mounds of her breasts, to her nipples, until she shrieked with the tickling sensation.

He was playing with her again, and she wanted to belong to him utterly! Fiercely she sought his mouth with her lips, and her fingers tore frantically at the snaps of the pearl-studded shirt.

"Darling," he murmured, ending the kiss. He sat up on the bed, and then, as though loath to let her go long enough to remove his shirt, he took her by the upper arms and pulled her against him.

Pain shot through her bruised shoulder, and she flinched, unable to suppress a gasp.

He loosed her instantly and looked searchingly into her dark blue eyes. "I hurt you, didn't I?"

"No," she moaned. "Hold me."

He drew a deep breath. "I completely forgot what you've been through. What a savage you must think me!" His tone told her he was thinking of leaving her. She sighed with angry frustration.

"I don't think you're a savage!" she cried.

"And I don't intend to be, either. A man has to be able to say no, too." He stood up. Unselfconsciously he unzipped his trousers and tucked in his shirt. Then he smoothed his hair.

Holly watched silently, regret making her feel hollow. Her blood was still pounding, but she knew he was right.

"You'll be fit as a fiddle in a couple of days," he promised her. "Wouldn't you like to get married before your friends leave? If you're going to stay here, the sooner we make it legal, the better, don't you think?"

Holly managed to smile through her disappointment.

"Or would you rather do it big—church wedding and all?" Raf asked.

Holly shook her head emphatically. "I've modeled

so many wedding gowns I don't care if I ever wear another.''

"Good, then we'll get married the day before your friends leave, and we'll have our honeymoon here on the ranch. This winter we'll take a wedding trip to any place you say. But for now—'' he kissed her lightly "—I'm going to take a cold shower.''

He left her with such mixed emotions she thought she could never sleep. But some time later, when Raf looked in, she was breathing regularly, her hair a gold halo about her face. He stood a moment gazing at her.

"My love," he whispered, before he switched off the lamp and tiptoed out.

The bestselling epic saga of the Irish. An intriguing and passionate story that spans 400 years.

FIRST...

The Defiant

Lady Elizabeth Hatton, highborn Englishwoman, was not above using her position to get what she wanted ...and more than anything in the world she wanted Rory O'Donnell, the fiery Irish rebel. But it was an alliance that promised only ruin....

THEN...

The Survivors

Against a turbulent background of political intrigue and royal corruption, the determined, passionate Shanna O'Hara searched for peace in her beloved but troubled Ireland. Meanwhile in England, hot-tempered Brenna Coke fought against a loveless marriage.